The Boy Who Loves Horses

Pegasus Equestrian Center Series: Book 2

Diana Vincent

This is a work of fiction. Names, characters, places, and incidents are the product of the author's imagination. Any resemblance to real events or persons is purely coincidental.

Cover design: Kimberly Killion
www.hotdamndesigns.com

ISBN-13: 978-1478385448
ISBN-10: 1478385448

DEDICATION

Dedicated to my three sons; Jeff, Michael, and Matt, who never complained about all the time their mom spent with horses.

Life is a short course
Let me spend what days I have
Astride a fine horse

Also by Diana Vincent
The Girl Who Loves Horses, Pegasus Equestrian Center Series: Book 1

CONTENTS

1 AUTUMN

No hour of life is lost that is spent in the saddle. – Winston Churchill

Heart attack; what a stupid phrase. Sierra Landsing visualized a heart pulsing within a chest, bubbling into fists and punching out at the surrounding ribs. That shouldn't happen to a man in his early fifties; there is medicine, surgery, all kinds of treatments. Her mother had told her so, and her mother was in training to be a registered nurse, so she should know.

Yet João Mateus, her riding instructor, mentor, but most of all, a very dear friend; died of a massive heart attack just a few weeks ago.

Sierra rolled over in bed and thumped her damp pillow. Sometimes she felt so angry at him for dying, and then she felt ashamed and guilty, and then tears came.

João had told his friends not to mourn him, but to celebrate his memory. And he had bequeathed Sierra his horse Fiel, a beautiful dapple-gray Lusitano gelding. Sierra had won the Pacific Regional Combined Training Championship at junior novice level on his wonderful horse.

"I miss you, João," Sierra whispered into the darkness of the middle of the night. *I love Fiel with all my heart, but I would give anything for him to belong to you again; just to have you alive.*

"Ready to gallop?" River, the rider on WinSome Gold (nicknamed Moose), a tall, rangy, bay thoroughbred; glanced over his shoulder. Beneath the shadow of his riding helmet, River's dark eyes shone in anticipation of picking up the pace. The unruly ends of his black hair sticking out from the back of his helmet matched the high gloss of his horse's black mane and tail, gleaming in the late afternoon light. The creamy brown of his complexion caught in a spot of sunlight, reflected the golden tones of the turning autumn leaves. His slender frame melded with that of his mount; boy and horse one harmonious body and spirit. River Girard was always at his best on the back of a horse.

Sierra smiled, her own brown eyes shining in exhilaration, and answered, "Let's go!"

The bay jumped from walk to canter. Fiel snorted and flicked his ears back; clearly letting his rider know he did not want to be left behind.

"Okay, Fiel," she spoke softly to him and gave with the reins. She felt his powerful hind end muscles bunch underneath her as he sprang forward into an energetic gallop to keep pace with the long-legged thoroughbred.

Early October has to be one of the best times of year to gallop a horse out in the open. The crisp scent of fallen leaves and the last cutting of hay filled the air. Flickers and jays scolded at the two riders from tree branches, in chorus with geese honking overhead on their southward flight. A flash of black darted through the trees as Storm, River's dog, chased after squirrels, crunching leaves and branches as she ran. The cool temperature prevented the horses from working up much of a sweat in spite of their coats growing in thick for the upcoming winter.

Fiel's mood matched that of the young girl on his back. He galloped with easy energy, his strong legs propelling him forward with his shoulders uplifted and light on his front end. The dapple-gray of his neck gleamed in flashes of sunlight that poured in through the trees. He kept his ears pricked forward or flicking towards his rider, intensely interested in everything around him; but not fearful. His luxuriously thick, dark gray mane that hung past his neck, filled out like a sail with the speed of his gallop, and his tail flowed like a triumphant banner.

Sierra imagined the crinkling blue eyes of their friend João watching her and River, and in her mind she distinctly heard his voice, as he so often said during her lessons, "Ahh, this is good." She felt his spirit joining them as they rode, and she suddenly realized, *I am happy today*!

Most of the trail wended through woods except for one stretch through an open field where a side path branched off and led to a log jump. The riders emerged from the woods into the field and River turned Moose onto the side path with Sierra following two lengths behind. Moose cleared the log.

Fiel, his ears forward, snorted in rhythm with his galloping stride, and gathered his muscles. Sierra felt his body arch underneath her as he sailed over the log. She let his motion push her weight forward over his withers, her hands moving to keep a feel of the bit in his mouth. "Good boy," Sierra called out to him as he landed and her weight shifted back in the saddle. She reached forward to pat his neck as they galloped on.

At the final bend of the trail, River brought Moose back down to walk.

Sierra spoke words to help slow Fiel, "Easy, whoa up now," and sat deep in her saddle, engaging her stomach muscles as she held her legs steady against his sides and squeezed her fingers on the reins. Fiel obediently transitioned down to trot and then to a walk behind Moose for the last stretch of trail.

They stepped off the trail and onto an open field of rolling hills and cross country jumps, all part of Pegasus Equestrian Center, where both River and Sierra worked and Sierra boarded Fiel. Storm bounded out from the woods to follow behind at a respectful distance from the horses' back hooves.

"What a perfect ride!" Sierra exclaimed as she brought Fiel alongside Moose.

River looked at her, and his eyes crinkled with warmth that spread over his face, twisting his mouth upward in a genuine smile; the first she had seen on his face since…before João's death?

His smile triggered a rush of warmth to erupt from deep within Sierra to diffuse outward into her limbs and up into her face, causing her to blush. It surprised her how happy it made her feel to see him smile; for he had been morose and withdrawn since her return to working at Pegasus a week ago; his moodiness enhancing her own sense of loss.

She looked away and between Fiel's ears to hide the flush of her face, and distractedly weaving her fingers throughout his thick mane, she prattled on to hide her embarrassment. "I have missed this trail more than I realized. It really is good to be back to work here. Thanks again for talking to Tess."

"I think Tess was relieved when I told her you wanted your job back."

They both laughed. Tess Holmes, half owner of Pegasus and its resident trainer and riding instructor, had fired Sierra last summer after Sierra had confronted her about an abusive training technique. Tess had hired a series of girls to replace her, but none had worked out, and no one had been willing to work in exchange for lessons the way Sierra had. Sierra never wanted to take lessons from Tess again, so now she worked in exchange for Fiel's board.

"She still hasn't said one word to me since I've come back," Sierra stated.

"Yeah, well, she might have to say something like 'sorry', and I don't think she knows that word." They both laughed again.

The laughter died away, and they rode on in silence, both with loose reins to allow the horses to stretch their necks forward and down. When they reached the upper edge of the field, they dismounted to lead the horses back to the stable.

"River, what do you think I should do with Fiel now that show season is over. How much riding should I do?" Sierra asked.

He thought for a minute before answering. "You trained pretty hard right up to the championship. I think trail riding him three days a week is good. He likes it out on the trail and it keeps him fresh. Then maybe thirty to forty minutes of flat work two to three days a week, and give him one or two days off. Just pay attention to his attitude. He'll let you know if he's getting overworked.

"What about jumping?"

"I'd back off on the jumping. You can do low jumps like the log we did today and maybe one or two of the field jumps when you go out on the trails. But I wouldn't stress him anymore than that for a few months."

"Okay. It sounds like a good plan for him."

"Are you going to want to compete again next year?"

"Yes, I would like to."

"On Fiel?"

"Sure. Well, he is my horse now."

"Do you want to move up to training level?"

"I hadn't really thought that far ahead. I guess I would like to try."

"It's just that I don't know if Fiel can handle training level."

That was a surprise to Sierra. "I thought you said all horses can jump. João said so too." She had come to believe her horse could do anything.

"Up to certain heights. In training level, the jumps go up to three foot, three, and the combinations are more difficult. I'm sure Fiel can jump that height but it could strain him. He's an Iberian horse. He's not really bred for jumping you know. He's bred for bullfighting and dressage."

"Oh, yeah; João did tell me stories about the horses on his father's farm." João had grown up in Portugal and had talked a lot about Iberian horses; the Lusitano of Portugal and the Andalusian of Spain.

They were bred so that their conformation allowed them to easily learn and perform upper level dressage movements, which happened to suit in the bull ring as well.

"You don't think I should go training level with Fiel?"

"He's your horse. It's up to you. It's just something to think about."

"What would you do if he were your horse?"

"Fiel is twelve years old and he's already trained to grand prix level in dressage, and he does it well. I would stick to dressage with him. He likes jumping and it won't hurt to do low jumps once in awhile. But if you want to compete, do it in dressage."

Sierra thought that over. She had really looked forward to eventing again next season. But she also didn't want to take chances with her horse. She wanted Fiel to stay sound and live a long and happy life. She had already seen too many bad outcomes with horses that had been pushed too hard and at too young an age.

Sierra sighed deeply. "Okay, good advice…dressage it is then. But I don't know how to ride the upper level movements."

"You can learn them," he assured her. "You know, you might be able to compete on one of the horses Tess has in training."

Sierra snorted a laugh. "Not very likely."

"No, really; she's pretty sly when it comes to working things to her advantage. To have last year's junior novice champion on the Pegasus team can only help her reputation."

"Thanks for that little bit of hope," Sierra stated, somewhat bitterly. "She'd actually have to acknowledge that I exist."

"She knows you exist. Just wait; I'll bet she'll say something when it's time to start conditioning for next season."

"Hmm, I'll believe it when it happens." She personally doubted it, but she appreciated the encouragement from River. Without thinking she suddenly blurted out, "River, you actually seem happy today. Are you feeling a little better?" Then she held her breath. River didn't like these kinds of questions.

He reached over to Moose and stroked his neck intently. Sierra knew he was thinking and she waited, unconsciously reaching up to stroke Fiel's neck.

Finally River answered, "I guess I am. This was a good day." A few minutes later he added, "I miss him a lot. Him dying…it was almost like losing my mother all over again. But you know what he said about not wanting anyone to mourn for him, but to think of him with good memories. I have a lot of good memories of João." He looked over at Sierra. "I thought it would be hard to have Fiel at Pegasus, but you know, I actually feel good when I see him. He's happy and has an owner who loves him and takes great care of him. That's what João would have wanted."

Sierra felt such relief to hear those words. Maybe they were both starting to heal. It brought tears to her eyes that she quickly brushed away. There had been far too many tears between them lately. She looked up to meet his dark eyes studying her and she smiled.

"River, come to dinner tonight…please," she pleaded. "My mother would like to see you." Over the summer Sierra had started inviting River to join her and her mother after he finished his work at the stable. They both believed he did not get regular meals at his own home. But since João's death, River had declined all her invitations.

River still had his hand softly stroking his horse's neck, and perhaps the contact with a warm, living creature unconsciously convinced him that being around other living beings was a good thing...comforting. "Okay," he accepted.

"Can you help me change the bandage on Morris's leg?" River asked after they had finished untacking and grooming their horses.

"Of course," Sierra replied. Morris, one of the school horses owned by Pegasus, had been kicked by another horse, resulting in a deep gash on his hind leg that required Dr. Patterson, the stable's veterinarian, to attend to the wound and place stitches. Dr. Patterson had shown River how to change the dressing every few days. It helped during the process to have someone stand at Morris's head to distract him. "Do you want me to bring him to the wash stall?"

"Yeah, thanks; I'll get the stuff."

Morris stood sulkily in his stall, his head facing a corner. The vet had advised stall rest, and poor Morris demonstrated to everyone around that he was not happy about his confinement; in no way agreeing that it was for his own good.

"Hey, guy," Sierra called to him. He lifted his head at her voice and with a low whicker, turned slowly to amble toward her. He knew Sierra always had pocketfuls of treats. Sierra had a special attachment to this little bay horse. He was the first horse she rode at Pegasus, and she had spent many hours on his broad, comfortable back in riding lessons. She gave him a piece of carrot and slipped on his halter.

Sierra led Morris into the wash stall where River waited with the stable's veterinary kit. Standing at his head, she petted him and fed him small bits of carrots to keep him distracted while River undid the vet wrap and removed the dressing covering the wound on his back leg. He spoke to Morris in soothing Spanish words while he worked, "*está bien, es facil.*"

"It looks good," he commented. Sierra stepped around to see and agreed that it looked like the swelling had gone way down from the last time she had seen the wound. "I think the stitches can come out the next time Dr. Patterson comes." River applied an antibiotic ointment and redressed the leg. He stood and gave Morris a pat on the rump.

"River, get Galaxy," a sharp voice called. Both kids turned their heads as Crystal Douglas, daughter of the other half owner of Pegasus marched toward them. Dressed in a navy and red tank top, short denim skirt, and bright blue patterned cowboy boots that obviously had been designed for a dance floor rather than the saddle; it did not appear she had come to ride.

River ignored her, repacking the veterinary kit.

"I'll take Morris back to his stall," Sierra said, happy to have an excuse to escape a potentially unpleasant scene. Even though Crystal was the same age as Sierra and both freshmen at Firwood High School, they were not friends. She led Morris out and past Crystal, who never even once glanced at her.

River finished packing up and stepped past Crystal, still not acknowledging her presence.

"River, I gave you an order," Crystal barked at his retreating back.

"I heard you," he stated without turning around.

Crystal spun away, her professionally styled blonde hair undulating in waves as she strode haughtily back down the aisle where her best friend Gloria Sanders, and Kate Ogilvie, another girl from school, both waited, giggling together.

After returning Morris to his stall, Sierra met River leading Crystal's latest horse, Galaxy, in from one of the paddocks. "What's up with Crystal?" she asked.

River shrugged, his face dark with displeasure.

At the crossties a man waited, his arms loaded with various pieces of horse shipping equipment. Crystal stood in the stable doorway talking on her cell phone, her two friends flanking her. An unfamiliar truck and horse trailer waited in the stable yard, the name of a stable with its logo printed on both truck and trailer.

"Yeah, they sent some idiot who can't even speak English." They overheard Crystal complain into her phone. "We ended up having to drive to the stupid barn to show him the way…I know…I know… we'll be there soon….don't order onions on the pizza."

As he led Galaxy into the crosstie bay, River spoke to the man in Spanish.

Relief flooded over the man's face as he responded to River's greeting in an animated explanation. River nodded in understanding. He picked up a brush from a grooming box and gave Galaxy a quick brush over his coat as the man dropped his armload and picked out a halter.

"What's going on?" Sierra asked, stepping up to stroke Galaxy's neck.

"This is one of the stable hands that works for Galaxy's new owner. He was given directions to Crystal's house rather than here."

"Galaxy's leaving?" Sierra said, surprised. She knew Crystal had immediately put him up for sale when he disappointed her at the championship, but didn't realize he had already sold.

"Yeah." River finished with the brush, picked out Galaxy's feet, and then helped the man change the halter, put on shipping boots and a stable sheet.

"I'm glad I get to say goodbye to you," Sierra murmured to the lovely black and white paint horse, stroking his nose. "I'll miss you." And that was true. Galaxy was a sweet-natured but un-ambitious, lazy-tempered horse. River believed he had been pushed too hard in competitions at too early an age, and was soured on work. Where some horses would become nervous or stressed, Galaxy's temperament responded in loss of spirit. But Sierra, who was often assigned to trail ride him, enjoyed his placid nature. When she was in a mood to just ride out without having to concentrate on her horse's manners, he was the perfect mount.

River led Galaxy from the crossties and past Crystal, still talking on her phone.

"At least you didn't kill this one," River said without looking at Crystal but loud enough to be sure she heard.

"Shut up," Crystal retorted, glaring with murderous hatred at River. "Not you," she snarled into the phone.

Her friends giggled until Crystal's murderous look shifted to them.

Sierra watched the scene with detached amusement, putting the pieces together. Crystal's friends were dressed in outfits almost identical to that which Crystal wore; and very much like an outfit Sierra recalled seeing on a contestant in a recent star search television episode. It was Friday night and the girls were obviously on their way to a party. Sitting behind the wheel of a car parked next to the truck and trailer, Sierra recognized Kate's older brother. Kate had not been a part of Crystal's crowd last year. But having an older brother, a junior with his driver's license, and one willing to hang out with freshmen girls and drive them around, had given Kate her entrance into the elite group.

Gloria was busy texting with frantic speed on her own phone. She boarded her horse, Silver Knight, at Pegasus, but hadn't even looked around for him. Sierra could not imagine coming to the stable and not at least checking on one's own horse.

River led Galaxy around in a circle while the stable hand opened up the trailer doors and dropped the ramp. Sierra came up to him one last time to give him a piece of carrot from her pocket and one last pat on the neck. "I hope you're going to a good home."

"Me too," River echoed. He led Galaxy into the trailer and hooked the trailer tie to his halter. "*Buena suerte, hombre.*" He gave him a goodbye pat and then stepped out to help the stable hand close up the ramp and latch the doors.

"Let's go," Crystal spoke to her friends, having finished her conversation and leading the way to the car. She never once glanced over at Galaxy.

"Hey, River," Kate called out. "Want to come to a party?" She laughed as Crystal punched her shoulder. The girls piled into the car and the driver immediately backed out and away. The truck pulling the horse trailer followed at a much slower speed.

Sierra watched them disappear out the driveway, wondering again why Crystal rode at all. She had owned three horses in the year that Sierra had worked at Pegasus, and had not shown any attachment or the slightest affection for any of them. Magic, the horse she had owned prior to Galaxy, had been seriously injured at a competition. Crystal had ordered him euthanized, rather than giving him a chance with surgery and a long recovery.

River had loved Magic and Sierra believed he still mourned his loss and harbored a deep resentment against Crystal and even Tess.

Manuel, the stable manager, emerged from the lane between rows of paddocks, whistling a tune in his usual cheerful manner as he led two horses into the stable.

“Time to bring horses in,” River said, and he and Sierra joined Manuel in the evening chores.

2 COBBLER, DUMPLINGS, AND BASIL

Moderation of the aids: the legs will never be used strongly and the reins only used for the shortest possible duration. - Jean-Claude Racinet, *Another Horsemanship, A Manual of Riding in the French Classical Tradition*

Sierra and River crossed behind a large farmhouse to an intersecting driveway that led to a small cottage where Sierra and her mother Pam lived. Charlie, a lively Border Collie, jumped up from where he had been snoozing under a cherry tree, and ran up to greet them with a welcoming bark. He had belonged to João, and Sierra and Pam had adopted him. Storm burst forth between the kids to meet the collie nose to nose, both their tails wagging. Then the two ran off together on important dog business. They were old friends.

"Something smells good," River said as they entered the back door and into the kitchen through the utility room.

"It does, doesn't it?" Sierra agreed. "And it doesn't smell like my chicken stew."

"Hi River," Pam greeted from in front of the sink as the kids stepped into the kitchen. "It's good to see you; I've missed you here." Sierra went over to her mother's open arms and they hugged hello.

"Thank you," River responded. "It's nice to see you too." He added, "It smells really good in here."

Pam smiled at him warmly. "It's the cobbler…for your birthday, Kitten," she said to Sierra as she smoothed some of the light brown straggles of hair that had escaped Sierra's braids and kissed the top of her head. "Since I didn't get a chance to bake a cake for your birthday, I thought this might atone a little for that."

"Mom, you know I didn't even want you to bake me a cake," Sierra assured her, hugging her again. "Cobbler is much better."

"It's your birthday?" River asked.

"It was two weeks ago but I wasn't in the mood to celebrate. It was right after the memorial service."

"Oh…how old are you now?"

"Fourteen."

"Can you believe that?" Pam asked, laughing and holding Sierra by the shoulders.

"No." He shook his head. "I can't."

"Stop it," Sierra complained. She had always been small for her age and probably looked two years younger, but she didn't need to be reminded of that. "When's your birthday?" she asked River.

"January."

"What day in January?" Sierra persisted. Getting information from River often involved bit-by-bit extraction.

"Thirty-first."

"And that's when you turn sixteen?"

"Umhm; I'm going to wash my hands." He turned and walked away to the bathroom.

"So much for that conversation," Sierra said as she moved to the sink to wash her own hands. Last summer, River had told her he planned to quit school when he turned sixteen. João had left him money in a college fund so she hoped that might change River's mind and he would stick it out in school.

"Hmm," Pam mused. "Well, I'm done with my part. The timer's on for the cobbler. Can you take it out of the oven when it goes off?"

"Sure."

Pam left the kitchen as River returned. "What do you want me to do?" he asked.

"Can you start a salad?"

"Okay." River pulled down the salad bowl from the cupboard and then opened the refrigerator to pick out vegetables. He had started helping Sierra after the second invitation to dinner, and always helped clean up afterwards. One thing for sure about River, he didn't shirk doing any kind of chores.

After washing her hands, Sierra pulled the bowl of dumpling batter from the refrigerator. She had mixed the dumplings up right after school, along with getting the chicken stew simmering in a crock pot.

"How does that work?" River asked curiously, watching Sierra remove the lid from the crock pot and spoon in clumps of batter.

"It's like biscuit batter," Sierra explained. "Only they get steamed in the crock pot rather than baked in the oven."

He came closer and watched over her shoulder. They both ogled the clumps of dough as Sierra plopped spoonfuls into the simmering broth. She grinned over her shoulder at River and he smiled back. "That's it," she said, spooning in the last bit of batter and settling the lid back on top.

"Cool," River commented and then stepped away to resume making the salad.

Sierra carried the empty batter bowl to the sink and glanced back to ask a question. "Riv…" She stopped in shock.

River was pulling his sweatshirt over his head and it had pulled his tee-shirt part way up exposing his bare midriff; and a large, yellowing bruise that spread from his side to his back. "What?" He slung his sweatshirt over the back of a chair and looking over at Sierra, frowned at the startled look on her face.

"What happened?" she gasped out.

"What do you mean?"

Sierra's eyes dropped to his side and he reflexively put his hand over his bruise but dropped it quickly.

"I fell." He stepped over to the counter where the vegetables waited, turning away from her.

"Off a horse?" River never fell off.

"Yeah," he lied. If he had answered immediately Sierra might have believed him, but he hesitated long enough that she knew it wasn't the truth.

"You never fall off!"

"Everybody falls off once in awhile."

"How did it happen? When did it happen?"

"It was just a stupid accident, okay?" He looked up from the salad bowl, where he was tearing lettuce somewhat violently, and glared at her with his 'I don't want to talk about it' look.

"Okay." Sierra finished washing the bowl. "I was going to ask if you want some fresh basil for the salad."

"Yes, I'll go get some." River tossed the last lettuce leaf into the bowl and without looking at her, went outside to Pam's herb garden. Sierra hoped a few minutes by himself would refresh his mood. She picked up a cucumber and began to peel it for the salad.

River returned about ten minutes later with a handful of fresh basil which he kept bringing up to his nose to sniff.

"I can smell it from here," Sierra commented. *Nothing like the smell of fresh basil to mellow one's attitude.*

"Your mom sure knows how to grow stuff," he said as he rinsed the basil and patted it dry, still sniffing a leaf every once in awhile.

"Yeah, she always has." The timer went off and Sierra pulled the cobbler out of the oven. The two kids finished the salad together, set the table, and called Pam.

The stew and dumplings turned out excellent. River ate three bowlfuls plus two helpings of cobbler. It always amazed Sierra how much he could eat and remain so skinny.

"I didn't get you anything for your birthday," River said, scraping up the remains of cobbler in his bowl.

"There's one thing you could give me," Sierra responded in a hopeful tone.

"What?"

"Could you give me riding lessons again?"

"Sure, no problem." He smiled in a way that Sierra believed he meant it.

"Great!" She jumped up and gave him a hug; it just seemed the right thing to do.

River left after helping clean up the supper dishes, and Sierra and her mother settled onto the sofa in the living room; both with homework.

"River seemed in a good mood tonight," Pam commented, flipping through pages of her textbook.

Sierra snuggled into the sofa cushions, folding her legs up. Socrates, her scruffy black cat, curled up in the hollow created by her bent legs, purring. Charlie snored; sound asleep on the rug in front of the sofa. "Yeah, I think he's doing better. We even talked a little about João today."

"Good, that's a good sign. You should have seen his face when you hugged him. He liked it."

"Oh yeah?" Sierra smiled at the thought.

"Be careful with him," Pam said in a gentle tone. "He doesn't need any more hurt. Don't give him the impression that you feel things you might not actually feel for him."

"Mom, what are you talking about? We're friends; friends hug friends."

"Yes, sometimes. I don't imagine River has very many friends that hug him."

"You don't think I should hug him?"

"Do you think he feels only friendship for you?"

"Well, I think we've become much closer since João died…maybe more like brother and sister."

Pam smiled at her daughter. "Maybe," she said.

"Mom?" Sierra asked hesitantly.

"Yes, Kitten?"

"I think his father beat him again. I accidentally got a look at a huge bruise on his side today. He didn't like it when I asked what happened."

Pam's face clouded in concern. "I wonder if we should report it."

"No, I know he would get mad. And I don't know for sure how it happened."

"What did he tell you?"

"I asked if he had fallen off a horse and he said yes, but I don't believe it."

"Maybe I'll talk to my pediatrics nursing instructor and get her advice."

"Mom, don't do anything, please."

"Honey, I'll talk to you before I do anything. I just worry about him getting seriously hurt."

Sierra's cell phone rang and her heart sped up as she recognized the caller. "Hello," she answered, trying to sound calm.

"Sierra, hi," greeted the friendly voice of her friend, Luke Abrams. Sierra's crush on Luke began a year ago when they were both in eighth grade. He had always been friendly to her, and had been especially sympathetic since hearing about the death of João. It had been quite a pleasant surprise when he had asked her to the homecoming dance coming up in two weeks. And ever since inviting her, he sought her out at school and called her a few times a week.

"Hi," she answered, feeling tongue-tied as usual.

"Guess what; we won our game this afternoon."

"Awesome! Congratulations," she responded enthusiastically, knowing how proud he was to have made the junior varsity football team.

"Are you done with your homework?" he asked. Pam had a rule that Sierra couldn't talk on the phone for more than ten minutes unless all her homework was finished, and Luke knew the rules.

"Not quite."

"I won't keep you. Some of the guys are going to Justin's house for a victory party and I guess I'm going. I just wanted to tell you that we won."

"That is so cool, Luke. Well, have fun at the party. Think of me sitting here doing homework."

"Hey, do you want to come? I could probably find someone to pick you up later on when you're done with your homework."

"No, that's okay. I'm pretty tired and I need to get up early to clean stalls tomorrow. But thanks."

"You sure?"

"Yeah, really." Sierra didn't want to explain that first of all, her mother wouldn't allow her to ride in a car unless an adult drove, and secondly, wouldn't let her go to a party unless the parents were home and would probably embarrass her by insisting on talking to the parents. But the biggest reason was that she did not want to go to a party at Justin's house. Justin was Crystal's boyfriend, and she guessed this was probably the party Crystal and her friends had been dressed up to attend. "But I do appreciate the offer," she lied.

"Okay, guess I'll talk to you on Monday."

"See you then, and congratulations on winning. Did you get to play?"

"Yeah, every quarter."

"Great! Tell me about it on Monday."

They said goodbye and hung up.

3 ROGUE HORSE

When the knowledge of riding comes to an end, abuse begins. - Lt. Col. A. L. d'Endrödy, *Give Your Horse A Chance*

Sunday morning, with the horses fed and turned out into either the pasture or paddocks for the day, Sierra and River worked together mucking out the stalls, and then filled each with fresh shavings. All they had left to do was sweep up and then they had the rest of the day to ride.

A car pulled into the stable yard; Sierra assumed one of the boarders arriving to ride. It was another beautiful fall day with patchy clouds and a slight breeze. It had showered last night, leaving everything crisp and clean-smelling.

"River," Tess Holmes called out sharply as she appeared in the aisle and walked toward them. "Where is your phone?"

River looked up, frowning. He reached in his pocket and pulled out a cell phone as Tess came up to him.

She scowled as she took the phone from his hand, turned it on, and handed it back. "I didn't get this for you to leave in your pocket turned off. I want to be able to get in touch with you when I need to," she reprimanded.

Still frowning, River stuffed the phone back in his pocket.

"Understand?" she persisted.

"Yeah," he answered.

"I'm going to look at a horse for Crystal and since you seem to have so many opinions about a suitable horse for her, I suggest you come along." Tess continued to speak directly to River, not acknowledging Sierra's presence. To Sierra, it was almost funny the way Tess ignored her.

River sighed in annoyed resignation.

"I can finish sweeping," Sierra offered.

"Why don't you come too?" he asked.

Sierra wanted to answer, *are you crazy*? Tess certainly would not want her coming along.

But to her amazement, Tess glanced at Sierra and in a neutral tone said, "Come if you want."

Sierra certainly did not want. She didn't like being around Tess, but River looked at her with a pleading look so she said, "Okay."

"We just need to sweep up," River said to Tess.

"I'll be in the office. Come get me when you're done." Tess left.

"She got you a cell phone?" Sierra asked as they took down the brooms from the tool rack.

"Yeah." He pulled it out again and handed it to her.

"That's generous of her," Sierra mused, examining the phone. "This is a pretty nice model."

"Oh yeah? I haven't figured out how to use it other than to answer calls."

"You even have a camera." It was a later model with a lot more features than her own cell phone. They took a few minutes to play with it. Sierra showed River how to make calls, check for messages, use the camera function, and how to enter contacts into a directory. Then she entered her own phone number into his contacts, and let him use it to call her. They laughed as she answered and they talked on their phones while looking at each other. Then she showed him how she could easily enter his number into her own contacts since he had called her. He seemed fascinated by everything the phone could do, and Sierra was surprised at how little he seemed to know about electronic devices.

They finished sweeping and then just for fun, River used his phone to call Tess to let her know they were ready. They left the barn and met Tess exiting a side building that contained her office and a lounge. They all piled into her Lexus, River in the front passenger seat and Sierra in the back.

"What kind of horse is it?" River asked as they pulled onto the main highway.

"Hanoverian; twelve years old. The owner rode preliminary last season. I think she qualified for the championship but I don't think she placed. She has left for college and the horse is now for sale. Walt called me this morning. He knows the girl's father and they are anxious to sell."

River mumbled a response and then stared out the window.

The rest of the drive was spent in silence.

Sierra had started to doze off, but awoke when the car slowed and made a right hand turn onto a poorly maintained dirt road. It led up to a group of ramshackle buildings; an older single wide mobile home, an unpainted, tumbling barn, and electric-wire pens with a few horses standing in mud and covered in flies. Tess parked the car and they all got out.

"This place is despicable," Tess stated, looking around.

A door creaked and a man stepped out of the mobile home preceded by a short-haired, very overweight, bull-faced dog that waddled over to the arrivals and sniffed around their legs. The man was equally overweight, with a large belly stretching a stained sweatshirt hanging over a pair of baggy jeans.

"Jocko, git away," the man yelled at the dog. "Mornin'," he greeted. "You the lady who called about the horse?" He lumbered awkwardly down the steps.

"Yes, you have a warmblood for sale?" Tess asked with the distaste apparent on her face.

"Yup." He yelled over his shoulder in a nerve grating, loud voice, "Frank!" He turned back to Tess. "Tom Gunnerson's the name." He held out his hand.

Tess quickly looked away, pretending not to notice the proffered hand. "How do you happen to have the horse?" There were five horses in the electric-wire pens, all with their heads hanging low and swarms of flies mottling their hides and especially their faces. None looked like a potential eventing prospect. The place did not appear to be an operation that would have a horse of the quality Crystal would demand.

A bow-legged man in dirty coveralls stepped out of the tumbled barn, carrying a shovel.

"Git that bay horse out here," Tom ordered. He turned back to Tess. "Well you see, the owner went off to college and the horse didn't sell quickly enough. Her parents didn't want to pay the board and they heard about me. I offered to keep the horse to save them the board, and sell it on commission."

Even Sierra thought this all sounded rather shady.

The bow-legged man had stepped back into the barn and now returned, leading an attractive bay horse. He actually did look like a warmblood.

"He's lame," River said, watching the horse walk at the end of the lead rope.

"I don't see it," Tess remarked.

"It's the way he blinks and flicks his tail when he steps on the off hind," River explained.

Tom narrowed his eyes at River but chose to ignore the comment. "They paid fifteen thousand for this horse three years ago," Tom started on his sales pitch. "He's won or placed in almost every show the girl entered. He's doubled his value."

Tess watched the man lead the horse in a circle in front of them, then requested, "Trot him."

"Well, ma'am, Frank here, his knees won't hold up to trot a horse. Best have your boy do that." Sierra got the feeling the man didn't want River in a position where he could see the horse trot.

River stepped up to the horse and stroked his neck, then ran his hand along his back and down each leg. He looked into the horse's eye, gave him a final pat and turned back to Tess. "He's drugged."

Tom scowled and said in an admonishing tone, "Now look here, that horse is getting vitamin supplements, that's all. You just go ahead and trot him. You got to see his action to appreciate him."

River shook his head and walked away from the horse. He said to Tess, "We should go."

Suddenly they heard a horse squeal, a loud thunk, and then a dog yelping. All of them turned toward the direction of the noise.

"Jocko!" Tom yelled out in horror.

In the last pen, the fat dog lay on his side where it looked like he had landed after a kick from a tall black horse, who stood with his ears pinned flat and his back toward the dog. As they watched, the horse kicked out again and then whirled to face the dog that scrabbled away, having got to his feet but obviously in pain. With his ears menacingly tight, the horse lowered his head with teeth bared, snaking his neck toward the dog.

"You, Demon!" Tom yelled, and with amazing speed for his bulk, raced toward the pen waving his arms. "Git back!"

The black horse raised his head to face this new menace; and with his ears still flat and teeth bared, he lunged forward, half-reared, and struck out with his forelegs.

That's when Sierra noticed the deplorable condition of the horse's hooves, grown out so that the toes actually curled upward; and her eyes then took in the rest of the neglected animal. He was a skeleton; every single rib and his hip bones protruding. His dull black hide had bare patches and he had open sores on several parts of his body. Flies swarmed in thick clouds, especially in the sores and around the corners of his runny eyes. He wore a rope halter with a dangling lead, and there were abrasions across his nose under the halter.

Tom picked up a metal pipe, about three feet long, stashed on the ground in front of the horse's pen, and brandished it at the charging horse. At the sight of the raised pipe, the horse backed away, but he remained facing the man and pawing with one foreleg. Tom held the horse at bay with the raised pipe until Jocko managed to limp out of the enclosure.

"Oh my God," Tess stated in utter disgust and horror. She turned away and strode off toward the car. "We're finished here."

Sierra felt sick. She turned to follow Tess.

"River?" Tess called from the driver's side of the car.

River remained where they had stood watching the scene, his eyes on the black horse. Hearing his name, he turned away and walked back to the car. "I want that horse," he said in a low voice.

"What?" Tess frowned in confusion.

"I want that horse," he repeated.

"Get in the car," Tess ordered, opening her door.

"Tess," River said again, "I want you to buy that horse."

Tess and Sierra both looked at him in disbelief. "What are you talking about?" Tess demanded. "Get in the car."

He shook his head. "You can buy that horse. They can't want very much for him."

Tess studied River with a tight frown. Then she walked around the car to confront him. Sierra just then realized how much River had grown over the summer, for he and Tess were now of equal height, standing eye to eye.

"You expect me to buy that mangy animal that just kicked the dog and almost attacked a man?"

"Yes."

"What's this about, River?" she demanded.

"I want that horse and you owe me."

"What? I don't owe you anything," Tess hissed through tight teeth, but there was a certain lack of conviction in her tone.

"You do."

"I don't know what you're talking about. Now get in the car and let's get out of this miserable place."

"You could have saved Magic." River glared back at her, unmoving.

Tess actually took a step backward, her expression shifting from annoyance to shock. "I could not! It was not my decision to make."

"You could have convinced Crystal," he persisted.

"River, if you want your own horse I will help you find a decent one. Why this horse?" Tess's tone had reverted to pleading.

"He has potential."

"You can't possibly see that."

"I do."

They glared at each other in silence. Tom, just getting up from where he had bent over his dog checking him for damage, watched them. Frank also stared, still holding onto the lead rope of the bay horse. Sierra stood frozen.

"How would we ever get him home? The barn is full right now. Where would you keep him?" Tess finally asked.

"Manuel and I can come back with the trailer. I'll get him loaded. He can stay in the lower paddock."

"But your…"

"My father won't be bringing the stallion in for another month," he interrupted, anticipating her response.

Tess sighed deeply and reverted to another tactic. "All right, River, I'll talk to the man. But I'll buy that horse for you on one condition."

River waited silently.

"You compete next season."

Sierra's eyes opened wide, and she waited hopefully for River's answer. He had once told her he didn't ever want to compete because he feared it would change his relationship with horses. She personally didn't feel that would be true, and she liked the idea of him as a teammate.

River's face tightened into a frown as he considered. Finally he nodded and said, "Okay."

"And it's not because I owe you anything over Magic," Tess insisted. "I'm grateful that you rode Gunsmoke for the demo ride at the championship. If anything, I owe you for that." She stepped around him. "Wait here."

Tom strolled to meet her, greed lighting up his face as he sensed a sale.

"How much do you want to take that beast off your hands?" Tess asked.

"He's going to auction next week," Tom answered. "I'll probably get eight hundred dollars for him."

Tess snorted in disgust. "That horse doesn't have enough meat on him to even make hauling him away worthwhile. And he looks diseased. No meat buyers are going to bid on him. I'll give you two hundred dollars right now and we'll take him off your hands today."

Tom narrowed his eyes, mulling over what profit he might be able to make from this unexpected interest in the black horse. "Eight hundred dollars," he stated.

Tess turned away.

"Okay, I can see your boy wants the horse. I can be generous. Five hundred dollars."

Tess kept walking to the car.

"Come on, lady, I've spent more than what you're offering just feeding this animal. I need to make a little profit."

Tess froze and turned back around. "It looks to me like you have spent nothing on this horse or any of these others, and I imagine the humane society would agree with me."

"Don't threaten me, lady," Tom growled back.

Tess turned away again.

"All right, three hundred," Tom called out.

Tess took two more steps and stopped. She looked over her shoulder at Tom and countered, "Two hundred and fifty."

Tom considered and as Tess started walking again, he gave in. "Okay, two hundred and fifty, but I want cash."

Tess reached the car and had her hand on the driver's side door handle. "Draw up a bill of sale. We'll be back with a trailer and I will have your cash." She slipped into the car and slammed the door. Sierra and River quickly got in. Tess already had the engine started and as soon as their doors closed, she accelerated away. "Once you have that horse away from there, I'm making a phone call," she declared.

For once, Sierra was in full agreement with Tess.

Back at Pegasus, River immediately went to find Manuel. Sierra headed off to the paddocks to get Fala, a black Arabian mare she had been assigned to trail ride that day.

"Sierra," Tess called her name.

Surprised, Sierra stopped and turned.

"Are you planning on showing your horse next season?" she asked.

"Just in dressage," Sierra replied.

"That's probably a good decision," Tess said. "Would you like to compete on the Pegasus team in eventing?"

"Um, well sure," Sierra answered hesitantly.

"Good, we'll decide which horse over the winter. Is River going to give you lessons?"

"Yes," Sierra confirmed.

And that was that; River had been right. *Awesome*! she thought to herself; very pleased she would get to continue competing in combined training, and also imagining how great it would be to have River as a teammate.

Sierra had finished riding both Fala and Fiel and was leading Fiel back to his paddock when the truck and trailer pulled into the stable yard. She gave Fiel his carrot and a pat before leaving, and hurried back to watch the unloading of the black horse.

Manuel had lowered the ramp and stood watching with wide eyes as River slowly backed the black down the ramp. The horse's head hung low and his body swayed as he took each tentative step.

"How'd it go?" Sierra asked, coming up to Manuel.

He smiled as he greeted her but then frowned, shaking his head. "I do not know why Reever, 'ee want dees 'orse; very dangerous."

The black had all four feet on the ground now and stood awkwardly, trying to figure out what was happening to him.

"Dey drug 'eem," Manuel explained.

River led the horse slowly down a side path that led to a small barn and paddock near a mobile home where Manuel and his wife Rosa lived. Sierra and Manuel followed and watched as River carefully led the horse into the paddock and removed the halter. The black flattened his ears and tried to raise his head, but apparently was still too tranquilized to do more than stagger on his feet. River left the paddock and joined Sierra and Manuel at the rail. The three of them watched the horse swaying with his nose to the ground, looking perfectly miserable.

"Did you have much trouble getting him loaded?" Sierra asked.

"No, when we got there that man had two other guys with him. They drove him into a corner with a wire stretched between them and using a cattle prod, and then they shot him with a tranquilizer gun. We just waited for the drug to take effect. I would have liked to take more time with him, but I also just wanted to get him out of there." River narrated his story in a grim tone.

"So, really, why do you want this horse?" Sierra asked.

"I don't know for sure," River answered. "There's just something about him…I just couldn't leave him at that place and let them sell him for slaughter."

"But Tess was going to call the humane society."

"Yeah, but…"

"You really do think he has potential?"

"Yes."

Sierra studied the black horse, trying to see what River saw in him. He was tall, close to seventeen hands she guessed; solid black except for a white patch, almost heart-shaped in the center of his forehead. He had wide-set eyes that looked dull with the drug and disease. But she did remember a fire in them when he had faced Tom. She tried to imagine filled out flesh and muscle on his emaciated frame. Somehow, the image she conjured in her mind matched that of an imaginary horse she had amused herself with for years; True Heart.

"How are you going to take care of him?" Sierra wondered out loud. "He doesn't let anyone near him."

"Time," River answered. Sierra glanced at him and noted a faraway look in his eye as he stared at the black. She wondered what images he saw beyond the pathetic animal.

"*Peligroso*," Manuel stated his opinion, shaking his head. "Dangerous."

They watched the horse for a while until he could lift his head and take a few steps without staggering. He looked around, blew once hard through his nose and then moved off to the far side of the paddock, away from the humans.

River went into the barn's storage area and brought out an armload of hay which he tossed into the feed crib, then rejoined Sierra and Manuel.

The black watched them warily. When no one moved, he began to sidle toward the hay. He reached the crib and shot his head down to grab a bite, then brought it up quickly to keep an eye on the humans as he chewed.

"Let's leave him in peace," River said and they slowly backed away and left the black to eat his hay without an audience.

4 ALLISON

To practice equestrian art is to establish a conversation on a higher level with the horse; a dialogue of courtesy and finesse. - Nuno Oliveira

"What are you going to wear to homecoming?" Allison Ferguise, Sierra's best friend, asked on Monday as they wove through the tables in the cafeteria.

"Wear?" Sierra responded in sudden horror. "I haven't thought about it." She worried about being out on an actual date with Luke; wondering what she would say and how to act. It was one thing to be around him at school or talk to him on the telephone; but quite another when she visualized him picking her up at her house and being alone with him in the back seat of a car. She hadn't thought about what to wear. She didn't even own a dress. Her entire wardrobe consisted of jeans, tee-shirts, sweatshirts, riding breeches, a show shirt, and a hunt coat.

"Sierra, you've only got two weeks," Allison stated. When she saw the look of dismay on Sierra's face, she took charge. "Okay, we're going shopping this week. I hope there'll be dresses left. I'll text my mom and see if she can pick us up after school." They reached an empty table and Allison dropped her backpack, already searching its contents for her phone.

"Allison, you know I go to the stable every afternoon."

"Then after supper. The mall is open until ten. What night do you want to go?" Allison waited with phone poised.

"But I don't have money to buy a dress."

Allison shrugged her shoulders with an 'oh well' look and said, "I guess you'll just have to wear your best jeans and most formal tee-shirt."

Sierra sighed deeply as she shrugged off her own backpack and took her seat. "I think accepting this date with Luke is a big mistake." She had been so excited and happy when Luke had asked her to the dance. But as the days passed, her apprehension mounted. She had almost as much fear and dread of the event as she had excited anticipation. And now this clothes thing!

"What do you mean?" Allison frowned and set her phone down carefully.

"It's just...well...okay; you've gone out with three different guys since school started, and now you're pretty much going out with Peter Eisenberg. Do you have fun?" Sometimes Sierra harbored a bit of envy toward her best friend; in her opinion one of the most attractive girls in the school with her mixed race heritage of white, black, and Asian. But more than her beauty, Sierra envied whatever it was Allison possessed that gave her the ability to think of quick and clever retorts whenever guys flirted with her (and they flirted with her a lot), to never blush, and that aura of comfort within her own skin. She could not imagine Allison ever tongue-tied.

Allison studied her friend, sensing the insecurity and worry in the question. "Yeah, I have fun; but Peter and I mostly just talk," she answered in a serious tone. "If you want to know about normal dates you'll probably have to ask someone like Katrina."

"Do you kiss him?" Just asking the question caused Sierra's face to heat up.

"Who...Peter?"

"Yeah, or any of those other guys you went out with." Sierra wondered about Allison and her relationship with boys. Other girls gossiped easily and loudly about their experiences in details that caused Sierra to blush just overhearing the conversations. She knew many of her classmates were no longer virgins and seemed proud of the fact. But Allison so far had never revealed to Sierra details of her dates.

Allison smiled and said, "I have kissed Peter, but kissing is not Peter's best quality…yet." Her eyes twinkled. "He's brilliant; that's what I like most about him and he's much better at talking than kissing."

"Do you like kissing him?" Sierra asked just above a whisper. It embarrassed her to ask these questions, but she really wanted to know from someone she respected.

This time Allison laughed. "I do, and I like kissing him better than other guys who might be better looking and more experienced but have nothing between their ears." In a more serious tone she advised, "Sierra, don't worry so much. Just let Luke do all the talking. He's good at that. You'll be fine. Now, what about a dress?"

"Okay, you're right," Sierra agreed. "And with what João has given my mother and me, I guess I can afford a dress. We can go any night this week." She added a weak smile. "It will be fun."

"Of course it will be fun," Allison laughed. "You are so funny."

They finished their lunch and then wove again through the cafeteria tables toward the exit. Back in eighth grade, they had started going to the library during the lunch recess to work on homework together, and continued the practice now. With her time taken up at the stable, Sierra needed to get as much homework done at school as she could, and working together, the two girls could work through the assignments much faster.

At the back of the cafeteria near the exit, Sierra suddenly spotted a boy sitting at a table by himself. "That's River!" Sierra exclaimed.

"Who?" Allison asked and then noticed where Sierra stared. "That's River?"

"Yeah, this is the first time I've seen him at school. I wonder if he has a new schedule."

"Introduce me," Allison suggested. Sierra had often talked to Allison about River; how well he rode, how difficult he could be to work with sometimes, that she suspected his father abused him, and that he planned to quit school.

"No, I don't think…"

"Come on." Allison grabbed Sierra's wrist and pulled her along to River's table.

"Hi, River," Sierra greeted as she and Allison approached.

He looked up at the girls and mumbled, "Hi." Sierra couldn't tell if he was glad to see her here away from the stable or not.

"This is my friend Allison. She wants to meet you."

Without waiting for an invitation Allison had already pulled out a chair and sat down. Sierra sat down next to her, feeling uncomfortable.

River took a bite of food, chewed and swallowed, before he looked up at Allison and asked bluntly, "Why?"

"You're a legend. Sierra has told me all about you; how beautifully you ride. When she talks about you, you sound like a masterpiece…a work of art. I love art."

River stared at Allison, frowning and with an expression as if he wondered if she was making fun of him. Then he flashed a disturbed look at Sierra.

Sierra felt the hot rush of color from her neck to her forehead and she dropped her head, embarrassed. She had no idea Allison would say that to him.

"Is it true?" Allison asked.

"What?"

"Are you a work of art?"

"I don't know. Ask Sierra."

Allison burst out laughing. "You're exactly how she described you."

River sat back with arms folded and studied Allison through narrowed eyes. "What do you want?"

"I want to get to know you," Allison flashed her most disarming smile.

"I don't think so," he answered.

"I'd like to watch you ride sometime."

He hunched forward, shoveled in the last bite of food and then abruptly stood up, gathering up the tray.

Sierra somehow felt like she should apologize. "River..."

"I have to go get ready to flunk a test," he stated, cutting her off.

"What test?" Allison asked.

"American History."

"With Mr. Kennedy?"

"Yeah."

"I can help you pass that test."

"I doubt it."

"No, really; I just took the test. I have him second period." She brightly rattled off a series of questions and answers. When she finished, she grinned impishly at him.

River watched her, looking bewildered during her recitation. His expression shifted to a frown and he turned and walked away. He didn't even say goodbye to Sierra.

Allison watched him go with a look of amusement on her face. "Sierra, he is absolutely gorgeous."

"What?" Sierra almost choked.

"Totally…in that sort of James Dean melancholy angst sort of way."

"Who?"

"Never mind," Allison laughed. "Just a dead actor my mother likes."

"Allison, you can't be serious about River. You like intellectual types."

"I'm not interested in him like that. He intrigues me. And I think he is not as dumb as he'd like you to think."

Well, Sierra had always thought that about River. "Didn't you just cheat? Giving him test answers?"

"Perhaps," Allison answered sheepishly. "I guess I didn't think. But if giving him answers can help him pass a test, it just might provide him with a little motivation. Sierra!" She turned to her friend with her eyes bright with excitement. "We can help him."

"How do you mean?"

"We can help him get through school, help him study…sort of like a project."

"He will never agree to that. He wouldn't even let João help him."

"We'll see," Allison persisted with a wicked grin.

"Besides, River is a person, not a project," Sierra insisted.

"Hi guys," Katrina Lund, a girl who boarded her horse at Pegasus and had become friends with Sierra, joined them at the table. "Sierra, was that River?"

"Yes," Sierra answered. "It's the first time I've seen him here."

"Oh, his tutor probably quit. She was working with him at lunch time," Katrina stated.

"He has a tutor?" That was news to Sierra.

"Yeah, my brother's girlfriend's best friend works as a tutor and I overhead her complaining about River. He didn't pass most of his classes since he missed so much school last year when he ran away, and she got assigned to him. She says he's rude and he doesn't try and she wanted to quit," Katrina related.

It was all news to Sierra, but then River never talked to her about anything except horses.

"What are you wearing to homecoming?" Katrina changed the subject.

5 DEMON

By nature, horses are very sensitive – consider, for example, how strongly they react to a fly! You should endeavour to retain and make positive use of this sensitivity in your communication with the horse. - Kyra Kyrklund, *Dressage With Kyra*

After school, Sierra rode her bicycle into the stable yard and parked it in its usual spot. She stopped to pet Storm, basking in a spot of sunlight, and then headed for the stable to say hi to River before she brought in her assigned horse to ride today. She found River at the crossties getting Silver ready for Gloria's lesson.

"Hi, River," Sierra greeted, stepping up to stroke Silver's nose and feed him a piece of carrot from the supply she always carried in her pockets.

River was bent over, snugging up the Velcro flaps on a splint boot he had placed on Silver's front leg. When he finished, he stood and turned to look at Sierra with a cold expression. "Why are you talking about me to other people?" he asked in a low voice, tight with anger.

"What?" Sierra physically stepped back from him, shocked at the intensity of his mood, almost as if he had slapped her. *What did I do?*

"I thought you were my friend."

Sierra had often seen River angry at Tess and some of the boarders, usually over treatment of a horse, but never had his anger been directed at her. Her stomach cramped into a knot and radiated uncomfortable heat throughout her body. Her face flushed. “We are friends,” she responded defensively.

Gloria came up to the crossties, dressed in her riding clothes. “Is Silver ready?” she asked.

River shifted his gaze to Gloria, his expression unchanged. Gloria stopped in her tracks, taken aback by his demeanor, and both she and Sierra stood frozen as he turned back to Silver, the animosity palpable in the air. He tightened the saddle girth, and then slipped off Silver’s halter, replacing it with a bridle. He tossed the reins to Gloria and wordlessly walked away.

“What a jerk,” Gloria grumbled, leading Silver out of the crossties.

Sierra stood indecisively a few moments, still confused by what had caused River’s anger. Then she set off at a jog to catch up to him halfway down the lane between the paddocks. “River,” she called to his back. “What is wrong?”

He stopped and waited for her to catch up to him. “I don’t like that girl and I don’t like people talking about me.”

“Who, Gloria?” Sierra already knew he didn’t like either Crystal or Gloria, so that didn’t make sense.

“Your friend at school.”

“Allison?” Sierra was beginning to feel this argument was ridiculously unnecessary.

“How can you be friends with her?”

“She’s my best friend at school,” Sierra replied in bewilderment.

“What did you say to her about me?”

“River,” Sierra replied, exasperated. “You heard what she said. I’ve told her a lot about you, especially what a great rider you are. Friends talk about things that are interesting and that they care about. I care about you. That’s not a bad thing.”

“She cheats.” He spoke through tight lips.

“Okay, that was a mistake, but she wanted to help you.”

"I don't cheat."

"Good…I'm glad. Allison doesn't cheat either. She just thought if she could help you pass your test it might encourage you." Sierra sensed immediately that was the wrong thing to say as River's eyes narrowed and his jaw clenched tighter.

"You think the only way I can pass a test is by cheating?" He spoke barely above a whisper which was almost more menacing than if he had shouted. But he didn't just sound angry; he also sounded hurt.

"No…, River…" He turned away but Sierra stepped up to his side and grabbed his arm. "Please, I'm sorry," she pleaded. But she wasn't sure what she was apologizing about; that Allison was her friend, or that she stood by while her friend gave him test answers even though she had no idea what Allison was going to do, or that she had talked about River to Allison. She didn't know exactly how she was at fault, but she knew River was mad at her and that was unbearable.

He pulled his arm away from her. "What was I supposed to do on my test? She gave me the answers. Should I have put down wrong ones? Well, I didn't, so now I'm a cheater too."

"I'm so sorry. I honestly didn't know she was going to do what she did. Please don't be mad at me."

"I am mad at you." He spun away and strode off, but called back over his shoulder, "Don't talk about me."

She stood watching his back as iciness seeped from the middle of her spine into her heart. It was bad enough that he was mad at her, but to be mad at her for talking about him; well that was just stupid and unfair.

River's phone must have vibrated for he pulled it out of his pocket and answered gruffly, "What…okay." Without looking back at Sierra he said loud enough for her to hear, "The vet's here."

She took that as an invitation and followed him back to the stable.

Dr. Patterson and Tess stood talking by the open hatch of his van, parked in the stable yard. As River and Sierra came into view, the vet waved and greeted, "Hi, kids."

"Hi, Dr. Patterson," Sierra returned the greeting as they came up to the van.

"Tess tells me River's got himself a horse," Dr. Patterson said, sounding amused.

River nodded. "He's down in the lower paddock."

"From what Tess has told me, I think we better take a look at Morris first." He chuckled with a twinkle in his eye.

"I'll get him," Sierra offered and left to bring Morris to the wash stall where River and Dr. Patterson waited. Tess left for the arena to start Gloria's riding lesson.

"He doesn't look like he's favoring the leg at all," Dr. Patterson commented. He bent down and undid the bandages. "Nice, it's healing well; I think we can remove the sutures and leave the bandage off." He pulled an instrument from his pocket and set to work.

Sierra remained at Morris's head but River bent over the vet, watching.

"See what I'm doing?" Dr. Patterson said to River. "You try." He handed the instrument to River and talked him through the process of removing the sutures.

"Very good," the vet said when River finished and they both stood up. "Keep him on stall rest for a couple more days and as long as there isn't a return of swelling or any drainage, you can start turning him out in one of the smaller paddocks. You've done a good job caring for him."

"Sierra helps me," River said, giving her credit.

"I always feel confident leaving the care of an injured animal in both your hands. You're quite the team," Dr. Patterson complimented.

A lump rose in Sierra's throat at his words; for she and River might not be a team anymore. "Shall I take Morris back to his stall?" she asked, feeling uncomfortable.

"Yes, and then we'll go have a look at this wild horse," Dr. Patterson replied.

Sierra led Morris back to his stall and gave him the usual bit of carrot before returning to where Dr. Patterson waited at his van. River had sprinted on ahead to the lower paddock.

"Hop in." Dr. Patterson indicated the passenger seat. Sierra climbed in and the vet drove the short distance, explaining that he might need supplies from the van.

At the paddock, they joined River at the rail. The black had backed into a corner and eyed them warily, his ears laid flat.

"Oh my, oh dear," Dr. Patterson said softly to himself, as he noted the black's pathetic condition.

"He doesn't let anyone near him," River stated.

"Not even you?" The vet smiled at River.

"Not yet."

"Hmm, tranquilizers it is then." He stepped back to his van and returned with a stainless steel device that looked like a gun with a syringe barrel. "Tess warned me I might need this."

River stepped into the paddock to keep the black's attention focused on him as the vet circled behind to where he could move in closer to the back fence, and then shot him in the neck. "Shouldn't take more than ten to fifteen minutes," he said as he came back around.

They waited, watching the horse gradually lower his head as the drug took effect. Dr. Patterson asked a few questions as to where they had found the horse and why River even wanted him.

"It's just the way he stands and faces off. Even as run down as he is, he has a spark to him. I think he has a lot of heart," River explained, speaking hesitantly as he tried to put his feelings about the horse into words.

"Umm," Dr. Patterson said noncommittally. "You know there's a good possibility he's stolen."

"Yeah, I've thought that," River answered. "I want to give him a chance though, even if his owner turns up. They were going to take him to the auction and I'm sure the only bidders would have been meat buyers."

"I see. Does he have a name?"

"They called him Demon."

Dr. Patterson laughed. "Looks like we might be able to get close to the demon now." The black horse with his nose almost to the ground, swayed on his feet.

River and the vet entered the paddock. Demon halfway raised his head and tried to turn his back end towards the approaching humans, but only managed to wobble a few steps to the side. River carried a halter, and talking in a low, soothing tone, moved up to Demon's head and gently put it on. He stayed by his head as Dr. Patterson began his exam. The vet listened with his stethoscope, took his temperature, ran his hands along his body and legs, pushing and probing; and inspected the sores. As River held Demon's head up, Dr. Patterson lifted his lips and inspected his mouth.

"There's no lip tattoo or any brands. He's not that old," the vet said as he squinted at and then palpated inside the mouth. "See here," he pointed out to River. "His permanent corner incisors are just in…feel here…that's a canine pushing through. Notice how all his teeth have these indentures; we call them cusps."

River nodded. "How old do you think he is?"

"I'd say between four and six years old."

"That young," River said incredulously.

"These sores appear to be rain rot," Dr. Patterson said, studying the scabs and bare patches on the horse's hide.

"I thought it might be ringworm," River said.

"No, I don't think we're dealing with ringworm. But the treatment is pretty much the same. Probably would be best to keep him isolated until the sores heal. Try to keep him in a dry environment. He may not like it, but it would be best to confine him in the stall when it rains."

"Okay," River agreed. "What else can I do?"

"The best treatment is bathing him with an antimicrobial shampoo several times, and removing this crustiness as you're able. I'll leave you some shampoo but of course you're going to need to be able to handle him. In his case, I think a shot of penicillin might also benefit." The vet continued around the horse, palpating joints and inspecting sores. "Well, I really don't find anything seriously wrong other than malnutrition and his neglected feet. Without being able to watch him move I can't tell about lameness. I don't see any point in the expense of x-rays until you get his feet into shape. Then if you notice persistent lameness we can get films." He stepped back from the horse. "Do you want to try to trim his hooves a little now?"

"Will he be able to stand?" River asked.

"I think so. Let's give it a try. Sierra," he called to her. "Can you bring those tools over here?"

Sierra picked up the hoof knife and trimmers that River had set down at the edge of the paddock and brought them over to the black. She handed off the tools and took the lead rope from River. Dr. Patterson helped steady the black's shoulder as River lifted each hoof and trimmed away the overgrowth as the vet directed.

"Okay, good enough for now. I'll take a blood sample for analysis and then give him his vaccinations, the penicillin, and a vitamin booster. We might as well worm him now, too." Dr. Patterson walked back to his van to get the medicines, which left Sierra awkwardly alone with River, still holding onto Demon's lead rope. Ignoring her, River absorbed his attention in inspecting Demon's sores.

Dr. Patterson returned with syringes protruding from his pocket and a small rectangular device. After drawing blood samples and injecting the medicines, he said, "Let's check for a microchip just in case." He used the rectangular device to scan along the left side of Demon's neck. "Nope, nothing," he said and replaced the device in his pocket. "Well, I think that's all we can do today."

River removed the halter and they left the paddock.

"If you want, we can take a few pictures and I can pass the word around through my connections to see if anyone has reported a stolen horse that might match. Most people who lose a horse tell their vet about it, so there's quite a network of unofficial stolen horse reports I can search through."

"Okay," River agreed.

"River, you can take pictures with your phone," Sierra reminded him.

"Oh, yeah," he said, still not looking at her. He took out his phone and Dr. Patterson brought a small camera from his van and they both took pictures.

"I recommend these supplements and feeding routine," Dr. Patterson said, writing out a list. "Give him as much grass hay as he'll eat and supplement with alfalfa three times a day, but introduce the alfalfa gradually. Here's the shampoo; of course you'll need to be able to get close enough to bathe him." Dr. Patterson laughed. "I suspect you'll eventually work that out."

"I hope so," River said with his eyes on Demon, standing forlornly where they had left him.

The vet packed up his van, said goodbye and drove away.

"River…" Sierra started.

Without looking at her, he walked away.

Sierra sighed and followed him back up the hill, feeling hurt but also very irritated. *Why does he have to be so difficult?*

6 LAILA

Courage, wisdom born of insight and humility, empathy born of compassion and love, all can be bequeathed by a horse to his rider. - Charles de Kunffy

Sierra and River spent the rest of the afternoon in avoidance; stepping out of each other's way or averting their eyes if they happened to pass. A mixture of anger and guilt roiled within River. Deep inside he knew his anger towards Sierra was not justified, but even so, it was how he felt. *How dare she talk about me to other people!* He could imagine the conversation; telling her friend how stupid he was and what a loser. The only thing River believed he had going for him was his ability to work with horses, and he didn't believe telling someone about that could take more than a few words.

He did not like her friend and he blamed Sierra for introducing them.

Sierra usually helped Manuel and him bring the horses in for the night and feed, even though it was not part of her job. Today he noticed her leave on her bicycle right after she had finished cleaning her tack. Well, he guessed she was mad at him in return.

After the horses had all been brought in and fed, he said goodnight to Manuel. Then he walked down to the lower paddock to check on the black. The tranquilizer had worn off and as usual, the horse threw his head high as River approached, watching him warily with ears back. River tossed in an armload of hay and sat on the ground next to the paddock fence near the feed crib. He waited silently, his eyes averted from looking directly at the black. He heard the horse snort and paw, but eventually he approached the hay. From the corner of his eye, River saw the black grab a mouthful and then fling his head up to keep his eye on the human.

I know how you feel. River sensed the mixture of fear, anger, hurt, and confusion as the abused animal defiantly faced survival. It was the defiance that attracted him; his unbroken spirit which he had not surrendered to abuse.

Plus, the horse came from good stock. In spite of the neglect, River recognized a well-bred conformation.

"*Hermano*," he whispered out loud. "*Que pasa*? What happened to you?"

At the sound of his voice, the black backed up a few steps, flung his head high and shook it with his ears flat, daring the human to approach his hay. River continued to talk to him in a whisper until the horse returned to grabbing mouthfuls. Finally, the black ate without flinging his head up after each bite. *Progress.*

When the starving horse had eaten most of the hay, River slowly stood up. The black backed away and spun around; clearly indicating his readiness to kick.

River went inside the barn and filled a bucket with grain and supplements. *Now the dangerous part.* A stall inside the barn connected to the paddock, and River went through the stall with the bucket. He spoke out loud but in soft tones as he approached the feed crib. The horse backed quickly away, then suddenly lunged toward the boy with flattened ears and snaking head. River stopped and raised one arm with palm forward. "No," he stated firmly. The black halted with a loud snort. River lowered his arm and they stared at each other. The black flicked his ears forward, smelling the grain, and snorted again. He whirled and River flinched involuntarily as he visualized the hooves kicking out at him. But the horse trotted away and turned again to face the intruder. River continued on to the feed crib and dumped in the grain and then sidled away and back out through the stall door.

The horse stepped back to the feed crib and thrusting his muzzle deep into the pile of grain, ate greedily, still bringing his head up between bites, aware of River watching.

"*Buenas noches*," River said softly, and left the horse in peace.

The sun had long set and it began to drizzle as River walked home from the stable. He hunched his shoulders within his sweatshirt, put up the hood, and stepped up into a jog. Storm raced ahead; eager for her supper and a dry place.

If he was lucky, no one would be around and he could shower, find something to eat, and escape to his room before he had to face any of his family. His father was away at the track for another month so no worries there. But he never knew when his Aunt Hazel would emerge from her bedroom where she spent most of her days in a drunken stupor watching television; especially towards the end of the month when the welfare check and food stamps were used up. Or his cousin Steve might be hanging out with his friends. With no adult supervision, his was a favorite party house.

River's stomach rumbled noisily and pangs of remorse churned with his hunger as he thought of his stupid fight with Sierra. He was already very sorry. *She won't be inviting me for dinner and I can't blame her.* Heaviness weighted his chest and sank into his stomach as he thought about working next to Sierra in her bright, cheerful kitchen that always smelled good, the welcoming warmth radiating from her mother toward him, and eating good food until his belly could hold no more. The cottage with Sierra and her mother felt like a family, or what he imagined a family that loved one another was like. A surge of loneliness waved throughout him, aching more than the emptiness of his stomach.

He jogged into the yard of a large two-story house that bore only remote traces of a past grandeur. A pillared front verandah and railed porches off two upper-story rooms sagged with warped flooring, and most of the railings fractured. The few remaining shutters hung askew held up by one or two remaining nails, and only vestiges of peeling paint hinted the house might once have been white rather than the current weathered gray. Three wide, splintered and bowed wooden steps led up to a double-door entryway flanked by boarded up windows. Thick moss covered the sagging roof that leaked constantly after prolonged rains. The yard consisted of patches of weeds and mud amid fir trees and junk.

The house had been in his father's family for two generations, and now belonged to his father's sister. Here his father brought him to live after River's mother had been killed in a horse racing accident.

A dim light escaped between cracks in the window boards and music poured forth from the living room stereo, drowning out any hope of finding no one home. River walked past the house to the backyard and into an old barn.

"Here you go," he spoke to Storm as he retrieved a bag of dog kibble from a corner of the barn and filled her bowl. She wagged her tail and hind end enthusiastically as she dove into her dinner. He filled her water bowl from an outside faucet, and then retreated back toward the house. Storm did not like it inside and would wait for him in the barn.

River entered the house through a back door that led into a smoke-hazed, cluttered, dirty kitchen. A girl sat cross-legged on the kitchen counter, leaning back against a cupboard and smoking a cigarette. She stared at him as he crossed the kitchen and into a hall that led to the living room.

A corner lamp and two candles on a stand by the sofa provided dim light. An emaciated appearing boy lay sprawled on his back on the sofa, one arm and leg hanging over the side. He snored through his open mouth and River smelled the alcohol as well as a strong body odor as he approached. An ashtray with cigarette butts and the end of a joint sat on the floor near his dangling fingers. River went over to the stereo and shut it off. "Steve?" he addressed his cousin on the sofa, but received no response. He blew out the candles and went back into the kitchen.

The girl sitting on the counter finished her cigarette and dropped it into the sink overflowing with dirty dishes, staring all the while at River. "Why did you turn off the music?" she asked in a tone that sounded like she doubted his right to be there in the kitchen.

He shot her a discouraging glance without answering…*who is she*?..and then stepped over to the refrigerator to peer inside with a sense of pointless hope. The interior was well stocked with beer, both in cans and bottles; the only other occupants a few cans of soda, a bottle of catsup, something unidentifiable covered in green mold in a package, and a pizza box. River lifted the lid enough to expose the contents in the box, and dropped it quickly, screwing up his nose at the smell. *Looks like coke and crackers for supper.* He grabbed a cola can and the catsup, pushed the door closed with his shoulder and hooked a kitchen chair with his foot. He set his armload on the table in front of the chair and stepped back two paces to open a lower cupboard and grab a box of saltine crackers. He plopped into the chair, setting the crackers down.

"You must be the gay cousin," the girl said.

He ignored her and popped open the top of his coke and took a long swig. Then he pulled a wax paper-wrapped column of crackers from the box and laid several squares out in front of him. He squirted a dollop of catsup in the center of each cracker and popped them one at a time in his mouth, washing them down with the soda.

The girl jumped off the counter and sauntered over to the table, staring at him with a tangible intensity that drew him to look up and watch her approach.

She wore a cropped black spandex top with a deep neckline, and tight, black hip-hugger jeans. The edges of a tattoo wriggled with the movement of a thin line of bare skin between her top and jeans, and a red jewel glinted from her navel. Thick heeled black boots came up to her knees. On her hands she wore some sort of lacey black stuff twined around her fingers and up to her forearms, meeting the sleeves of her top. Spiky black hair with one section dyed blood red and another turquoise blue, and an array of earrings framed a pale face that appeared even whiter in contrast with black lipstick.

She pulled out the chair across from him and kneeling on one knee, leaned forward on her elbows, her hands supporting her chin.

He stared into deep jade green eyes enhanced by thick black eye-liner and mascara, with two tiny silver rings pierced through her right eyebrow. Her complexion was sallow and bumpy in spots where thick make-up camouflaged acne; her cheeks hollow with deep shadows under her eyes. *Gothic girl.* He recognized her from school; a senior, probably a year or two older than him.

Her mouth smirked at him mockingly. He dropped his eyes and inadvertently found himself staring into the deep cleavage revealed as she leaned over. His face heated and deepened in color and he quickly brought his eyes down to gaze at his pile of crackers. She didn't move and he could not help looking back up at her chest.

She laughed. "I don't think you're all that gay."

From her chest he looked up to meet her eyes. She smiled triumphantly, exposing a stud in her tongue, and leaned back, dropping her knee to sit in the chair.

"Are you?" she persisted.

Embarrassed, River focused on more crackers, applying catsup.

She laughed again. "Whether you are or not, you're cute." Her laugh, though mocking, was friendly.

He looked up and half-smiled. "Cracker?" He shoved the package toward her.

"Thanks." She pulled a saltine from the proffered wax paper column and nibbled at it, as if it were a rare treat.

He pushed the catsup toward her.

"That's actually disgusting." She made a face that River thought was rather cute as it softened her features into more of the look of a little girl.

"Are you Steve's girlfriend?" he asked.

"I'm nobody's girlfriend and I never will be." She said the word girlfriend, making it sound distasteful.

"But you're here with him?"

"He said there was a party so I let him bring me here. Some party. I can't wake him up so now I'm stuck here."

"What did he take?"

"I don't know. Some pills and he smoked a lot. I have no idea how much he drank. I might take a hit or two, but I'm not really into that kind of stuff."

"Umm," River nodded.

"Do you drive?" she asked.

"I don't have a license."

"But could you drive his car and take me back to town? I've called everyone I know and can't get a hold of anyone who can pick me up."

"Can't you call your parents?"

She snorted. "Could you call your parents if you needed a ride?"

"Oh…why don't you just take his car?"

"It's a stick. I can't drive a stick. Can you?"

"Yeah, but I've only driven in the fields. I've never driven on the highway."

"But you could drive me." She smiled and leaned toward him again. He could smell smoke on her breath, but also a musky scent emanating from her skin; a nice scent.

"I don't know." He felt bad she was stuck here, but it really wasn't his problem.

"Please," she said in a low, husky voice.

River shoved the column of saltines back into the box, rose from the table, and tossed the box on the counter. He put the catsup back in the refrigerator and then leaned back against the door, giving himself time to think.

"What's your name, gay cousin?" she asked in a lighter tone.

"River. What's yours?"

"I'm Laila."

"Like the girl in the song?"

"No." She scowled and he realized she must hear that all the time. "I spell it different. Are you River like the one in the song?"

"What song?"

"I don't know. There must be hundreds of songs about a river."

He laughed. "Maybe, but only one Laila that I know of."

"Well, what about it?"

"What?"

"Can you drive me back to town?"

He frowned, thinking. Strange, but he kind of liked this girl and wanted to help her; but he wasn't sure if he dared. He had driven his father's truck many times around the fields and back roads, but never in any kind of traffic. He was a little afraid but he didn't want to admit that to her. "I have to take a shower before I do anything," he said.

Laila came around to stand directly in front of him, inches away. "Sure; want me to help, gay cousin?" She glanced down at her chest which drew his eyes helplessly to follow where she led. Then she placed her hands on his shoulders and brought her body against his.

River pushed his palms flat against the refrigerator, and met her eyes. His face flushed again with heat as he felt himself responding to her closeness.

"Hmm, I don't think you're gay at all, cousin." She kept her eyes open, gazing into his, and then kissed him softly on his lips.

River could not turn away from her eyes, ensnared by their intensity and the feel of her mouth on his. He felt confused and embarrassed. *Who is she? What would Steve do if he walked in right now?*

"Are you?" she whispered, pressing tighter against him and moving her hips.

"No," he whispered back and he brought his arms up to place around her. When she moved her face in, this time he started the kiss. Her lips parted; they were pliant and warm, and he liked the smoky and salty taste of her. He dared to touch her with his tongue and it was almost a shock when her tongue met his. It sent a surge of electricity from his mouth down his spine and resulted in a throbbing hardness.

The noise of a car driving into the yard shattered the silence. The engine cut and car doors opened and slammed amid loud voices and laughter. Many footsteps crossed the yard and pounded up the front steps of the house.

Laila gave a little squeal and the kiss ended. River dropped his arms. Laila smiled and touched the tip of his nose with her black nail-polished index finger.

"You're nice, gay boy," she whispered, and then skipped off to greet the new arrivals.

River heard the front door open and her voice greeting the others as they stepped inside. He shivered with cold, his clothes still damp, and especially with the sudden loss of her body's warmth against him. Disconsolately, he left the kitchen and went back out to the barn. Storm stood up from where she had laid down next to her food dish, wagging her tail. The thumping of loud bass vibrated through the air as someone in the house turned the stereo back on.

River climbed up an open wooden staircase to the barn's loft where he had constructed a room out of plywood panels and scrap lumber. He didn't like it in the house any more than Storm, and he had long ago created this space for himself. He had furnished his room with a mattress on the floor made up with old sheets, a sleeping bag for a blanket, and one pillow. He had two large plastic tubs for his clothes; a wide board on two cement blocks for a shelf; an electric heater, a boom box, and an old lamp on a block of wood next to his mattress. A heavy duty orange extension cord threaded up through a crack in the floor provided power from an outlet below.

River pulled off his damp clothes, put on a pair of baggy dark gray sweatpants and a thermal shirt, and threw himself face down on his bed. Storm jumped up to lay down beside him and he absently stroked her fur, finding comfort in her warm presence and the softness of her coat beneath his fingers.

He had really liked that kiss…and the feel of the girl in his arms!

Loneliness seeped into him, and Sierra's face appeared behind his closed eyes. Her image triggered a knot in his stomach and emptiness worse than that from hunger. Storm emitted a soft whine and nudged against his neck with her cold wet nose, tickling him.

River laughed and sat up, allowing Storm to scrabble part way onto his lap. "What have I done?" he asked, looking into her sympathetic eyes. Storm gazed back at him, and River imagined it a reproachful look. "Okay, I'm the stupid one," he admitted. "She's the sweetest person in the world and she doesn't deserve someone like me making her sad."

Storm licked his hand, as if agreeing with him.

He laughed again and reached for his jeans, dragging them close enough to fumble in the pocket for his cell phone. He scrolled through the photos for a picture of Sierra; one he had taken the day she had shown him how to use the camera. He had caught her by surprise and she gazed back from the phone's screen, her large brown eyes opened wide and a hint of a smile on her lips. The camera had caught the flush of her cheeks and the freckles across her nose that he had always thought so cute. "I'm sorry," he whispered. He flicked her image away and instead looked at the one of the black horse and turned his thoughts to the pitiful condition of the neglected animal. He wondered again about the history of this horse and where he came from. The one bright spot of his day had been when the horse had finally relaxed enough to eat in his presence without bringing his head up between bites. It was going to take a long time, but River felt sure he could win the black's confidence.

He shut off the phone and set it aside. Then resolutely he rolled off his mattress to grab his school backpack and bring it to his lap.

Schoolwork had always been hard for him. Many times João had offered to help him and River had stubbornly refused. It resulted in a contentious rift in their friendship every school year since João pushed and pushed, not letting the subject rest until River avoided visiting him. Ironically, now with João gone, the shame of his past behavior motivated him to at least try to do homework, for his friend's sake. Why had he always refused help? João had called him a coward, and perhaps it was true. Perhaps he had been afraid that even with help, he would still fail. And failure would prove what a teacher had once said to him, "River, some people are only meant to shovel manure." He did not want proof of his stupidity.

He pulled out his history book to start reading the assigned chapter. He knew he would have failed the last exam without the answers Allison had given him. But now he probably had passed, so maybe he should try to keep up in this class. Leaning back on his pillow, he started to read.

But the light was poor and it strained his eyes. The growling of his empty stomach distracted his ability to focus. He closed his eyes to rest them and almost immediately fell asleep.

7 PROBLEMS, PROMISES, AND A PROM

A true horseman does not look at the horse with his eyes, he looks at his horse with his heart. – Author Unknown

Throughout the afternoon, as Sierra and River moved around each other in avoidance, the lump of hurt that began as an icy point of pain in the middle of Sierra's chest, melted into a smoldering pit of resentment and anger. *I've done nothing wrong.* She determined she had quite enough of his foul moods and rudeness. She had even apologized when he should have been the one to apologize to her. Well, two could play at the avoidance game and she was not going to chase after him and beg him to forgive her so they could be friends again. She was more than happy to restore their friendship, but he was the one who was going to have to patch things up…if he ever wanted to.

Instead of helping with the evening chores, Sierra left the stable as soon as she finished cleaning her tack. She passed by Fiel's stall one last time to give him a carrot and hug him around the neck, always finding comfort in his solid, warm presence.

Tonight, Allison and her mother were picking Sierra up to go shopping, and as she pedaled home, she switched her thoughts to Luke; wondering what he would think of her in a dress.

"Sierra, I am so sorry," Allison moaned after Sierra related to her River's reaction to their meeting. They sat at a table in the food pavilion at the mall, eating wraps from the Mediterranean booth. "I really didn't think when I gave him the answers, but I guess it was cheating."

"Of course it was cheating," Allison's mother said. "Just what were you thinking?"

"Like I said, I didn't think," Allison admitted. "I just wanted to help him pass his test. I thought it might encourage him. I can see now how dumb that was."

Allison's mother emitted a short laugh and said, "We are all smarter looking backwards."

"What should I do?" Allison asked.

"What do you think you should do?" her mother countered, raising her eyebrows.

"I guess I can start by apologizing and letting him know Sierra had nothing to do with my stupid blunder."

"Yes," her mother agreed. "What do you think, Sierra?"

"That might help," Sierra said. "I never know with River."

"I will apologize at the first opportunity," Allison stated definitively.

"Girls, we better start shopping," Allison's mother stated as she looked at her watch, and then began to gather the trash.

It took two and a half hours and trying on at least thirty dresses before Allison surrendered to Sierra's declarations that she was not a 'frilly, formal dress kind of girl'.

"Sophisticatedly simple and elegant," Allison described the dress they finally agreed on, which Sierra thought was a fancy way of saying plain. But Sierra did like the dress and it was the only one she really felt comfortable in; a navy blue knit with a scooped neckline, capped sleeves, and knee-length flared skirt. It pulled on over the head without a zipper or other fastenings, so retained very sleek and simple lines.

They found a pair of navy blue pumps with a short heel that Sierra was willing to wear. She had never in her life worn anything but sneakers and riding boots.

"Now for accessories," Allison said as they took a break at a juice stand where they ordered fruit smoothies. "Sierra, why don't we get your ears pierced while we're here?"

"No way," Sierra stated emphatically. "Allison, I am not a jewelry kind of girl either. It's going to be a big enough change for me just to wear a dress!"

Allison pleaded, but Sierra stubbornly would not give in. "Okay then," Allison said with a sigh of resignation. "I guess no accessories will be your signature style. Is Luke going to get you a corsage?"

"I don't know."

"I'm sure he will. Mums are traditional for homecoming and Peter showed me the order form so I could pick one to go with my dress. They're all in our school colors; blue and gold, and will go very nice with your dress," she relented, and then added more graciously, "flowers will suit you."

Throughout the week they kept a look out for River so that Allison could apologize, but they never saw him at school. At the stable, Sierra purposefully stayed out of his way.

Saturday, when they had finished cleaning stalls in poignant silence and were sweeping the aisles, River suddenly spoke up, "I'll give you a lesson today."

Startled, Sierra looked up from her broom. "What did you say?"

"Do you want a lesson today?" He answered without looking at her, still sweeping.

"I thought you hated me."

"No, I don't. I promised you lessons. I keep my promises."

Sierra stopped sweeping to study him. He refused to look at her but at least he admitted he didn't hate her. *Is this his way of apologizing?* It didn't feel like an apology and she didn't feel like making it easy for him. "Oh, well that's very nice," she said in a sarcastic tone.

He glanced at her with a dark frown on his face.

"You are so very honest. You don't cheat. You keep your promises. But what about lying, River? Do you tell lies?"

He stopped his sweeping to look at her again, his frown deepening into suspicion.

"Do you?" Sierra persisted.

"No," he retorted and returned to sweeping.

"Good. Tell me about how you fell off the horse."

He froze. Sierra heard Storm emit a brief whine, sensitive to his mood. "That's none of your business," he said so low she almost didn't hear.

Sierra went back to sweeping, her anger churning in her stomach along with her bitter feelings over his rudeness. They finished the aisles, moving in opposite directions from each other, but met again at the equipment bay to hang up the brooms.

"Okay, I didn't fall off," River snapped out.

"I knew that," Sierra said, speaking calmly. She stood with arms folded, facing him.

"What difference does it make? I don't even remember how I fell." He turned from hanging up his broom to glare at her.

"Liar."

"Why do you even care?"

"Because I do; because we were friends." She met his glaring eyes and kept her own expression soft and her voice low.

"Friends don't talk about each other to other people," he retorted back.

"Wrong; that's exactly what friends do. They talk about people who matter to them." She forced herself to keep her voice soft and neutral, although she wanted to yell at him.

She watched him struggle to find a response. Finally he managed, "Do you want a lesson or not?"

Sierra's pride wanted to refuse. But she had been having difficulties riding Fiel in dressage movements. She couldn't seem to keep him on a straight arc when trotting circles to the left and their transitions from canter to trot were not as smooth and fluid as they used to be. She had not had instruction since her last lesson with João. When she had him to constantly tell her what to do with her hands, her seat, her legs, from moment to moment; then riding Fiel was easy. Things had deteriorated since then. Until she was old enough to drive so she could haul Fiel in the trailer to some other instructor, she was limited to either River or Tess to teach her, and she would never take lessons from Tess again. She swallowed her pride. "Yes," she answered. "I'll go get him ready." She added, "Thanks."

"No problem," he responded in a tight voice. "I'm doing it for Fiel's sake."

That really stung! Sierra froze in her tracks and almost changed her mind. *Is my riding that bad? Does he think I'm ruining my horse?* Instead, she flung back over her shoulder, "Right, for Fiel," and hurried away. She would take the lessons; for Fiel and also for João. She didn't want his wonderful horse ruined by her inexperience. But at that moment, River's unkind remark ended their friendship. He deserved all his problems.

The lesson actually went very well. River, like João, could see exactly what Sierra needed to do to keep Fiel in correct, energetic movements. The improved responses from Fiel confirmed for her how much she needed River's coaching.

"That's good," River complimented their last figure eight and transition from trot to walk. "Cool him out now. We can do this next Saturday if you want."

"Fine," Sierra agreed. "Thanks," she said to his retreating back, not hiding the sarcasm in her voice. *Tess didn't like me either when I took lessons from her*, Sierra reminded herself. *I suppose I can take the same from River. At least he doesn't yell at me the way Tess used to.*

Still, an aching sense of loss wafted up from a vague empty space deep inside; a mourning for the way things used to be. Instead of working and riding together, she and River avoided each other. When she went out on the trail, he worked a horse in the arena, and when she rode in the arena, he went out on the trail. She no longer stuck around to help with the evening chores.

"You okay?" Manuel asked Sierra one afternoon as she retrieved her bicycle.

"I'm fine, thanks, Manuel," she smiled at him.

"You and Reever?"

Sierra just shook her head and for some reason with Manuel asking, she had to fight back tears.

"Reever, 'ee sometime need a knock in 'ees 'ead," Manuel said, shaking his own head.

Sierra laughed, feeling a little comforted by his sympathy.

Homecoming week! The atmosphere at school radiated excitement as pep rallies, skits performed during lunch, a costume day, and voting for the homecoming king and queen and their royal court, all led up to the football game on Friday night and the homecoming prom on Saturday night. Sierra's mood vacillated between eager anticipation of her date with Luke, and stomach-wrenching dread that he would not like her dress, she would not be able to think of anything to say, and he would be bored and disappointed with her.

"Are you going to watch our JV game Friday afternoon?" Luke asked, stopping by the girls' lunch table early in the week.

"Um, yes…I guess I could," Sierra answered, even though she hadn't actually planned on going.

"Great, we can meet after our game and watch the varsity game together if you want."

Allison smirked as Sierra blushed.

"What am I going to do now?" Sierra moaned after Luke left. "My mom has swing shift clinicals this Friday and she won't be able to pick me up. I know Luke rides around with Justin's older brother and my mom will only let me ride with an adult driver."

"Don't worry," Allison soothed. "My dad loves football and he never misses a home game, so my parents are coming. You can get a ride home with me. I'll ask Peter if he wants to watch the JV game and then you can sit with us."

"Thanks, if you don't mind me tagging along."

"Don't be silly. And, this will give you practice for the prom; sort of a dress rehearsal."

With Luke and homecoming absorbing all her thoughts, it became easy for Sierra to ignore River. He had really hurt her feelings last Saturday, and quite frankly, she felt as if she no longer cared about him. He was simply a blight in her vision that she had to move around and avoid while at the stable.

Friday morning, Sierra woke feeling the same queasiness in her stomach that she experienced on horse show mornings. She spent extra time getting ready for school; glad now that Allison had made her stop at the make-up counter in one of the large department stores and undergo a professional make-up demonstration. She had bought all the recommended products but so far they had remained in a drawer, still in the packages. This morning, she carefully applied make-up, following the instructions the professional had written out for her; and then donned her favorite jeans and a dark green sweater that Allison always told her was 'her color'. She tossed the make-up bag into her backpack, thinking she might want to touch up after school.

Concentrating on lectures and class work proved difficult. Instead of going to the library, Allison said, "Come on, we're going for a walk and talk about 'worst case scenarios'.

Sierra complied and somehow it did help as Allison asked 'what would you do' if various events might happen, such as: a rip in the seat of your jeans, lettuce stuck in your teeth, grease spilled down the front of your sweater. The discussion had them both in fits of laughter.

After school, Sierra joined Allison and Peter in the bleachers. Although she really didn't understand the rules of football, she did enjoy watching Luke on the field. She understood enough to stand and cheer with everyone else when their team made a touchdown.

"He's quite good," Peter commented, knowing Sierra had eyes only for Luke on the field.

When their team won, Sierra joined enthusiastically into the cheering. She thought of the times that Luke had watched her ride at a horse show, and how easily he had poured forth congratulations and comments on her ride. The team's victory and the fact that Luke had played in every quarter, would provide plenty for her to talk about.

After arranging where they would meet later, she said goodbye to Allison and Peter. In nervous anticipation she stood outside the team locker room to wait for Luke. Then as he emerged with his teammates from the locker room door, and his face lit up as he caught sight of her, Sierra's heart warmed in gratitude and she at last felt glad she had agreed to come.

"We won!" Luke exclaimed as he came up to her, his face split in a wide grin.

"You were awesome!" Sierra greeted him with an equally broad smile.

Luke took her hand as he led her through the crowd of happy kids; greeting his friends and receiving myriads of congratulations. Sierra noticed many eyes looking at her in surprise that she was with Luke, and even some envious glances from other girls. She could not help feeling a little smug and pitied the girls without dates milling around in groups.

He bought her a hotdog and soda at one of the many booths set up for the upcoming game, and then insisted she share a hot fudge sundae from another booth. How fun it was, the simple act of sitting side by side at a table, eating ice cream from the same dish.

When it was time for the varsity game, Luke guided her to a section of the bleachers where his teammates and their dates were gathering. Even the condescending looks from Crystal, sitting with Justin, could not dampen Sierra's spirits.

Luke had brought a fleece blanket that he wrapped around the both of them, and underneath the blanket, he held her hand. Their team played well, but Sierra almost resented every time they gained yards or when they scored a touchdown, for Luke jumped up and cheered, letting go of her hand. When the game was over and they had won, Luke hugged her exuberantly, picking her up off her feet.

"How did the dress rehearsal go?" Allison asked at the end of the evening and they were settled in the back seat of her parents' car.

"He is wonderful!" Sierra sighed out. "Allison, he held my hand all during the game. He is so considerate, and he is so easy to be with."

Allison laughed as Sierra gushed on about Luke all the way home.

That Friday was the first day Sierra had not gone to the stable since she had started boarding Fiel there.

Saturday, as Sierra and River finished sweeping the aisles (in frigid silence), he suddenly asked, "Where were you yesterday?"

"What?" Sierra frowned at him, startled and confused by the question. River hadn't said a word to her all morning; in fact had not spoken to her all week.

"You didn't come here," he stated, looking at her with an accusatory expression.

"It's homecoming, River," Sierra explained. "I planned on letting Fiel have the day off yesterday so I could go to the game."

"You went to a football game?" he asked incredulously.

"Yes, I had a date."

River stared at Sierra as if she had committed a crime. In spite of herself, she felt guilty, as if he were accusing her of neglecting her horse. Then he abruptly strode off to hang up his broom.

Sierra remained at the end of the aisle and leaned on her broom handle, trying to sort out what was going on with him. *What have I done wrong now, in his crazy opinion?* Not coming to the stable for one day certainly did not constitute neglect. She sighed in frustration and then made her way to the equipment bay. *I don't suppose he'll give me a lesson today.*

River was needlessly rearranging the pitchforks, shovels, and brooms and Sierra got the impression he was waiting for her. "Saddle Fiel and I'll give you a lesson," he stated with his eyes intent on straightening a pitchfork next to a shovel.

Don't order me around! Sierra wanted to yell at him. She wanted to grab him by the shoulders and shake him. Instead, she stared at him in helpless exasperation. "Just what is wrong with you?" she finally managed to ask.

He looked at her then, with an expression of such hurt that her frustration immediately vanished, and instead of wanting to shake him, she wanted to hug him. "Everything is wrong with me, Sierra, and it can't be fixed. Just go get Fiel." He walked away.

Okay, so he's in a self-pity mood today, and something about me not coming to the stable yesterday seems to have triggered it. With her anger dissipated, she did feel sorry for him; sorry about whatever was upsetting him now. She just didn't know how to help him and was too filled with her own happy anticipation of seeing Luke again tonight to be sucked into his gloom.

She brought Fiel in from his paddock, groomed and saddled him, and started her warm-up in the indoor arena. River emerged from wherever he had disappeared to, and as if nothing had happened, watched Sierra ride at walk, trot, and canter; in circles, serpentines, leg yields, and transitions. He told her what to do moment by moment with her seat, legs, and hands, and Fiel responded with energetic impulsion, working correctly from his strong hind end muscles. His ears flicked in concentration, in tune with Sierra's aids; his attitude relaxed and happy.

"You both look good," River said after about forty minutes of work. "Cool him out now." Then he left the arena.

"Thanks," Sierra said to his retreating back. The session had been the best ride she had had on Fiel all week. How nice it would have been to discuss it with River and let him know how much she appreciated his coaching. "Fiel, you are so awesome." She turned her attention to her wonderful horse, praising him as she gave him a long rein, and patted him on both sides of his neck as he stretched forward.

Sierra finished taking care of Fiel and then rode Silver, her assigned mount, around the trail. After the ride and taking care of Silver, then cleaning her tack, her work was done for the day. She could go home and concentrate on getting ready for tonight.

As she retrieved her bicycle from where she had left it near the back of the barn, she saw River in the paddock with the black horse, brushing him. *So, he's managed to win the horse's confidence enough to approach and touch him.* She felt a pang of remorse that she was not included in River's care of the abused animal.

The black snorted and shook his head as River walked slowly toward him. He murmured to his horse in a low, soft voice; pleased that the black held his stance as he came to stand in front of him. Slowly River reached out to touch his shoulder. The horse quivered his skin at the touch, but did not move away. Keeping one hand on the black's shoulder, River extended the flat of his other hand with a piece of carrot. Delicately, the horse snuffled at it and then lifted it with his lips. With the hand still on his shoulder, River began to gently stroke the black's neck and pull his fingers through the horse's thick mane.

It had taken patience and perseverance, but finally, three days ago, the black had allowed River to touch him. Today, he had brought a soft body brush. After stroking the horse on his neck a few minutes, he pulled the brush slowly from inside his shirt and let the black smell it. Starting low on the shoulder, River began to brush the rough, neglected coat. The black lowered his head, relaxed, and half closed his eyes as River groomed him.

"You've been brushed before," River murmured to him in Spanish, observing the black's state of relaxation. "I bet you had a good start before someone stole you." He took his time, gently but thoroughly grooming his entire body. Then he brought out a bucket of warm water and a sponge, and cleaned the sores with the shampoo Dr. Patterson had given him.

"*Está bien*?" The black actually turned his head to nuzzle at River's hand for more treats. River fed him the rest of the carrot, and with a final pat, quietly left the paddock.

8 HOMECOMING

It is not as much of an accomplishment to make an excellent military or dressage horse from a well-built, young horse, as it is to make a weak horse with irregular conformation into a conditionally useful, acceptable horse. - Gustav Steinbrecht

After finishing the evening chores, River and Manuel walked toward the lower paddock and Manuel's mobile home.

"Why are you not getting along with Sierra?" Manuel asked, their conversation in Spanish.

River ducked his head away shamefully, and then admitted to his friend. "It's stupid. I'm stupid. I got mad at her about something one of her friends did. It's not her fault. I should apologize."

"Why have you not?"

"I don't know."

Manuel shook his head sadly. "You apologize to that young lady. Do not waste your life holding grudges or holding on to what you think is your pride. She is a good friend to you."

"I know that."

"So?" Manuel persisted.

"I will, I will," River replied, annoyed. But it was himself he was annoyed with, not Manuel.

"Good; next time you see her…tomorrow."

"Okay."

Manuel smiled and clapped River on the shoulder. "Good work with that one." He raised his chin indicating the black as they neared the paddock. The black watched them warily but actually nickered softly at sight of River.

"Thanks."

Manuel watched as River gathered an armload of hay and entered the paddock. The black without hesitation followed the boy to the feed crib and tolerated River's hand stroking his neck as he thrust his muzzle greedily into his hay. Manuel called out, "*buenas noches,*" and left the boy and horse alone.

River stayed with his horse, talking softly to him, until the waning evening light faded to deep shadows. He quietly left the paddock, and whistled for Storm. But instead of heading for home, he turned onto the path that led behind Sierra's cottage. Maybe he would just see if there were lights on, and if he got up the nerve, maybe he would knock and try to apologize to her tonight…maybe. He approached the edge of her yard and looked with hope and longing at the light filtering out from the curtained cottage windows. He imagined Sierra and her mother inside, probably in the kitchen having dinner.

Headlights lit up the front yard as a car pulled into the driveway and came to a stop. River quickly slipped back into the shadow of a tree. A boy dressed in a suit got out of the back seat of the car, and knocked on the cottage door. When the door opened, he disappeared inside.

Of course, homecoming prom. He had forgotten. Knowing he should leave right now, River nevertheless shamefully waited and watched, feeling like a stalker. About ten minutes later, the front door opened and the boy and Sierra came out, followed by her mother. Storm barked once softly. River bent down, signaling her to hush, but Sierra must have heard for she glanced toward where he hid, squinting into the darkness.

The sight of Sierra momentarily took his breath away; then he gulped in air as his heart sped up, filling his chest with pain. Heaviness seeped into his muscles so that he could not move or pull his eyes away from staring. *She is beautiful!* The porch light lit up her bright face as she walked out the door, wearing a blue dress, her hair worn loose and cascading around her shoulders. The boy held open the car door and River gaped at a glimpse of bare thigh as she sat down. She slid over on the seat and the boy got in next to her. Sierra's mother had gone back into the house, the car engine started, and the driver backed up and drove away.

River sat on the ground, holding onto Storm until the sound of the car motor receded beyond his hearing. He squeezed his eyes shut, forbidding what felt like tears from forming. *Why does that girl make me feel this way?* He recalled the image of the well-dressed, handsome boy sliding into the car next to Sierra; the same boy, Luke or whatever his name, that hung around her at the championship. *Jealous? I can't be jealous. She's just a kid.* Even so, River folded his arms up and squeezed his fists as he thought about how he wanted to punch that boy in the face and shove him as hard as he could away from Sierra.

Storm whined and nosed at his folded arms.

"Let's go home." He hugged Storm and then pushed himself up to his feet. *Think about your horse.* He forced his thoughts around the progress he had made with the black. Tomorrow, he would try to get a halter on and then he would lead him out into the fields and let him graze. Through the months of winter he would just spend time with the horse; grooming him, letting him graze, and settle into a safe life, building trust. By next spring the black should have gained enough weight to think about starting him under saddle. Unbidden images of Sierra helping him with the black crept into his plans; how nice it would be to have a helper. Anguish flowed over him as he realized that she might not be willing to accept his apology (did he blame her?) or ever help him again.

As River rounded a bend and stepped into the short, rutted drive leading to his aunt's house, he saw a familiar pick-up parked in the yard. For the second time that night he drew in a sharp breath as his heart flipped; but for a very different reason. Cray Blackthorn, his father, was home.

"He's not supposed to be back for two more weeks," River said out loud, mournfully. His father, a racehorse trainer, had finished the local racing season and then took off to a track in California with an extended fall racing season. Something had gone wrong for him to be home early.

He fed Storm, and then in resignation walked to the back door of the house. He heard his Aunt Hazel's voice raised in scolding anger, loud enough to penetrate through the door.

"You had no right! He belonged to me," Hazel screeched.

"In name only; he was my horse and I could do what I wanted with him," his father shouted back, equally loud.

"The one good thing you had going for you and you couldn't even hold onto that."

"Just shut the…," Cray cursed angrily. "It's not my fault!"

"What possessed you to race him again? You should have kept him at stud."

Something happened to the stallion, River guessed from what he overheard. Curious now, he opened the door and stepped inside.

His father sat at the kitchen table, dejectedly curled around a whiskey bottle. His sister leaned back against the counter, arms folded tightly and her eyes blazing fire as she chastised him.

"Here's another one of your failures," Hazel spat out as River entered the kitchen.

Cray shifted around in his chair to focus his bloodshot eyes on River. It seemed to take him quite awhile to recognize him, but eventually he slurred out, "Hey, son."

"Hi," River replied. "You lost the colt?"

"Damn you, Hazel," Cray lurched back around in his chair to face his sister.

"Entered him in a claiming race," Hazel stated. "How utterly stupid is that!"

"I had no choice," Cray snarled back. "He lost his last two races. No one was going to want to breed to him. I needed a win."

"Someone would have; you'd just have to lower the stud fee," Hazel said through tight lips.

"You don't know anything so just shut your trap."

Hazel picked up a half empty beer bottle on the counter and flung it at Cray. A spray of beer flew in an arch across the table and the bottle smacked against his shoulder before it shattered on the floor.

Cray roared and shoved out of his chair to stagger toward Hazel. She stood her ground, screaming insults at him. Before he reached her, she pulled open a drawer, grabbed a butcher knife, and brandished it towards her brother.

River watched in horror. Both his father's and aunt's tempers ran hot and violent, especially when they were drinking. He foresaw bloody bodies, police, chaos, and his own world shattered.

"Cray, don't!" River shouted, trying in vain to stop his father's advance.

Cray flickered a glance toward River but did not alter his course; and shifted his focus back to the weapon in Hazel's hand. "You…" he swore violently, and sprang with surprising agility in his intoxicated state. He grabbed her arm wielding the knife, twisting. Hazel screamed and punched at him with her free fist. Ignoring the punches, Cray wrenched and twisted her wrist until she opened her fingers and the knife clattered to the floor. Then he raised his fist.

River sprinted across the room to throw all his weight against his father, unbalancing him enough that as he swung with his fist, he only grazed Hazel's cheek. She ducked and scurried away.

Roaring with rage, Cray turned on River, who was just regaining his own balance after the impact. Cray lunged forward and shoved forcefully so that River fell backward, hitting his head on the floor amid shattered glass. Sharp pain erupted in River's head and his vision went black. He struggled to take a breath as his father dropped down on him, shoving a knee into his chest as he grabbed with both hands at his throat. "Don't you ever dare interfere in my business," Cray growled through gritted teeth as he slammed River's head against the floor again and then again.

Another object flew through the air diverting Cray's attention. He stood and kicked River in the ribs before turning to chase after Hazel who had just fled, slamming the kitchen door behind her.

Alone in the kitchen, River lay still, gasping for air and with his head throbbing. He waited until his breathing slowed to normal before opening his eyes. Still seeing stars, he blinked several times until his eyes watered and his vision cleared. He pushed himself up in slow stages, assessing for damage that might increase with movement, and determined no bones were broken as he regained his feet. As he tried to stand up straight, the increased pounding of his head almost doubled him back to the floor. He left the house squeezing his palms against his temples, uselessly trying to stop the throbbing in his brain. Storm met him in the yard, whining in anxiety and trailed after him as he stumbled to the barn. He crawled up the stairs on hands and knees with his head tucked between his shoulders. At last in his room, he collapsed onto his mattress and curled into a tight ball while his body trembled uncontrollably and his stomach roiled with nausea. He let tears fall unchecked down his cheeks for there was no one here to see.

9 PROM NIGHT

Every training decision is based on how the rider can be the leader and the horse the happy, willing follower. - Richard Weis

Standing in front of the bathroom mirror, Sierra's stomach took a sudden flip at the sound of a knock on the front door. *He's here!* Her fingers trembled as she worked the last bit of a glossy gel into her hair to keep it smooth, and then combed through it one last time. She took a deep breath and smiled at herself in the mirror to see how that looked on her face. She had spent it seemed like over an hour carefully applying, wiping off, and then re-applying her make-up to get it just right. The reflection that smiled back at her seemed to be all eyes and in spite of the make-up, Sierra thought in chagrin, still looked like that of a little girl.

"Oh well," she spoke to her reflection, and then made her grand entrance into the living room.

Luke sat upright and stiff in the one easy chair, facing her mom sitting on the sofa. She had asked him not to rent a tuxedo, which would have been too formal for her dress, and she was relieved to find him dressed in a black suit and a light blue shirt, and had a light blue boutonnière attached to his lapel. He stood as she walked in and what Sierra hoped was an appreciative grin spread across his face.

"You look beautiful!" he exclaimed.

Sierra blushed and smiled. "Thank you; you look great!"

He stepped forward and proffered a clear box with a corsage inside. "Uh, here."

"Thank you; it's beautiful." Sierra took the box, feeling suddenly more shy than usual, and awkwardly removed the mum corsage made in their school colors of royal blue and gold.

"Shall I help you?" he offered.

"Sure."

Luke took the corsage and removed two long pins. With fumbling fingers he tried to attach it to the bodice of her dress without touching her inappropriately. He stood close enough so that Sierra could smell the freshness of his shampooed hair mixed with a spicy scent of his deodorant or maybe aftershave (although she doubted he needed to shave). His warm breath wafted against the skin above the neckline of her dress as he bent his head in over his task. The warm closeness of him, his smell, and feeling his breath, stirred her heart to racing and her breathing shallow. She flushed red with heat and feared the color would spread from her face down her neck where he'd surely notice.

Laughing, his own face flushed, Luke stepped back, unsuccessful in attaching the mum.

"Let me help you." Pam, also laughing, came to his rescue and expertly pinned on the mum.

"I guess we're ready," Luke stated and then recited to Pam the arrangements they had agreed on. "Mrs. Landsing, my parents are dropping us off at the restaurant and afterwards will drive us to the dance. Then my dad will pick us up when the dance ends at midnight, so Sierra should be home just a little after that." Then he handed her a business card. "Here's my dad's cell phone number in case you need to get a hold of him for any reason."

"Thank you, Luke, and let your parents know I appreciate this." Pam accepted the card graciously.

Weeks ago, Sierra had to explain to Luke about her mother's driving rules, afraid that this further evidence of her immaturity might cause him to back out of his invitation. But to her relief, Luke said lots of kids' parents had that rule, and not to worry, his parents wouldn't mind driving. She was very grateful now for the assurance he gave her mother, knowing it would also gain her mother's respect.

Pam followed Sierra and Luke outside, noting in approval how Luke held the door open for Sierra to get into the back seat. Luke's parents both got out of the front seat to come over and introduce themselves, and Pam thanked them again for driving. She waved goodbye and went back inside as Luke's parents returned to the car and his father started the engine.

Sitting next to Luke with his parents up front, Sierra's nervousness welled up in full force. The palms of her hands and under her arms felt moist and clammy while her tongue and throat felt dry as cardboard. She could not think of one single thing to say. She had never felt more awkward, or so like a child.

But thank goodness Luke was conversant enough for both of them and didn't seem put off by her trite responses to the questions from his parents. He supplemented her brief answers and then chattered with his father about the game last night. Sierra sat in awkward silence, for she didn't understand the plays they were discussing, nor did she have any opinions she could contribute.

"What do you think of Crystal and Justin getting chosen as freshman prince and princess?" Luke asked after depleting football as a topic. The homecoming king and queen were chosen from the senior class and the royal court consisted of three princes and princesses elected by their peers from the junior, sophomore, and freshman classes.

"I expected it," Sierra replied. "I'm sure they will both look very regal tonight."

"Just wait," he said with an impish grin. "There's a surprise after dinner."

"What is it?"

"Can't tell you; it's a surprise."

The fact that it sounded like this surprise was somehow tied in with Crystal and Justin filled Sierra with more foreboding, and her apprehension as to the outcome of this evening increased.

At last they pulled up in front of the restaurant reserved for the homecoming banquet. Luke gallantly jumped out and came around to open her door. After saying goodbye and thanks to his parents, they merged with other dressed up high school couples just exiting from cars, and entered the foyer of the restaurant.

Sierra and Luke were ushered into a banquet room with several long tables elegantly set with snowy white table clothes, bouquets of flowers in the school colors, and gleaming silver place settings.

"Luke, over here." Sierra's heart dropped as she saw Justin, standing up from his chair at a table where Crystal sat next to him. All the nearby seats were taken except for two empty chairs directly across from Crystal and Justin, obviously saved seats. The others at the table were all part of Crystal's elite group of friends; Gloria and her boyfriend, and most of the other girls with football player dates.

As the host steered them to the table, nausea roiled from Sierra's stomach to her throat. Dampness again exuded from her palms, armpits, and hairline. *I do not belong with this crowd!*

"Hello, Sierra," Crystal greeted in sugary tones and a smirk on her face as she overtly looked over Sierra's dress. She cocked her head to the side, and commented to Gloria, "How sweet." Gloria stifled a laugh as she also greeted Sierra.

"Hi," Sierra returned the greeting, her voice raspy from the dryness of her throat. She ducked her head to hide the flush she felt creeping up as she sat in the chair held out for her by the host, who then flipped open the white linen napkin and placed it on her lap. The formality of the banquet room and the service only enhanced her feelings of finding herself out of place. She could not help comparing her very plain attire to all the others; the boys in tuxedos and the girls in formal dresses.

If Sierra hadn't known, she would have mistaken Crystal for someone much closer to twenty years old than fourteen. She wore a strapless dress with a cream-colored bodice trimmed in tiny pearl beads that shimmered in the light whenever Crystal moved. The skirt of the dress was light blue chiffon, and she wore elbow length gloves in the same color. A diamond necklace graced her neck and matching diamonds sparkled where they dangled from her earlobes. Her hair had been professionally styled and adorned with the simple tiara of the freshman princess. The only accessory that seemed out of place was her mum corsage, identical to Sierra's own.

"Where did you get your dress?" Crystal asked, smiling.

"At the mall," Sierra replied feebly.

"Which shop?" Gloria inquired.

"Um…" Sierra couldn't actually remember; Allison and she had browsed through so many racks of dresses in countless stores. But she was sure her dress did not come from the same place as any of the girls at this table.

"Tell you what," Crystal leaned slightly forward and said in a loud whisper, "next time we'll take you shopping."

"Thank you," Sierra croaked back automatically, even though she knew the offer was only another way of insulting her dress. Fortunately, waiters arrived at that moment to fill water glasses and place baskets of bread and dishes of butter on the table, distracting attention away from Sierra. More waiters arrived to serve plates of salad.

Sierra picked at her salad. Next to her, Luke talked excitedly in between mouthfuls; glorying with his teammates over both the junior varsity and varsity victories last night. Crystal retained the attention of the girls as she related details of the other royal court's attire and accessories. By the time the entrée arrived, Sierra was actually a little bored, in spite of the continued niggling nervousness that took away any appetite for the fancy food. She thought about how hard it was going to be to wake up tomorrow morning to go work at the stable, which only reinforced her regrets that she had accepted this date. The atmosphere was way too formal and she did not enjoy the company. She resolved if she ever went out with Luke again, it would only be in more casual circumstances, like last night.

"Sierra."

She looked up in surprise, pulled back from her drifting thoughts.

"I hear you've finally realized what a jerk River is," Crystal said, "and you two aren't hanging out anymore."

The look of amicable conspiracy on Crystal's face reinforced Sierra's suspicion that Crystal's hatred of her stemmed from her friendship with River. "Um, well, I guess," Sierra agreed. *True, River has been a jerk.*

"We should ride together one of these days," Crystal suggested with a smile that actually looked sincere.

"Yes, all three of us could go out on the trail," Gloria added.

"Sure," Sierra answered, doubtful of their sincerity, especially since those two never rode their horses on the trail.

"I still can't believe Tess allowed him to buy that wretched creature he calls a horse," Gloria said, and she and Crystal laughed.

"What happened?" Crystal asked Sierra. "Weren't you with them that day?"

"They were going to take the horse to the auction where he would have been sold to meat packers," Sierra stated.

"So?" Crystal made a face indicating it wasn't an issue. "It would be a kindness to put that horse out of his misery."

Sierra shrugged, not wanting to openly disagree. "River thinks the horse has potential."

Crystal and Gloria both laughed derisively. "As if he would know," Crystal said contemptuously. "He doesn't even compete."

"He is next season," Sierra informed them. "It was part of the agreement Tess made with him to buy the horse."

"Oh my God." Crystal scrunched her face into a display of extreme displeasure. "I don't believe it." But she did believe it for she and Gloria spoke together in horror over the idea of River competing on the team.

Fortunately, they've forgotten to include me, their newly discovered friend and anti-River ally, she thought to herself sarcastically, but also happy not to participate in the discussion.

The entrée plates were removed and the waiters served dessert, a chocolate mousse with a raspberry sauce. Sierra nibbled at hers and enjoyed the rich flavor, but her nerves were still so tense she was afraid its richness would upset her jittery stomach. All she needed now was to have to vomit.

"You doing okay?" Luke asked after cleaning up his own dessert.

"Yes, do you want the rest of my mousse?" Sierra offered.

"Sure." Without hesitation he pulled her barely touched plate in front of him and dug in with his spoon.

Crystal and Gloria both got up from the table at the same time. "We're going to the ladies room; come along," Crystal said to Sierra. It sounded like an order.

Luke nodded and smiled at her through a mouthful of mousse. Sierra stood and reluctantly followed along with four other girls from their table, feeling excluded as they giggled together.

Inside the restroom was a cacophony of girls' voices and laughter, all talking at once and in loud voices in order to be heard. There was a line-up for the three stalls and another crowd at the mirror, touching up hair and make-up. Sierra got into the line, which moved quickly and she was in and out in no time.

"Sierra," Crystal called to her as she moved into a space near a sink to wash her hands. Sierra looked over her shoulder where Crystal and her friends huddled in a corner. She finished with her hands and joined them.

"Here." One of the girls handed her a clear flask half full of a golden liquid.

"What is this?" Sierra asked as she accepted the flask.

"Southern Comfort," Crystal answered, "it's bourbon."

"Oh, no thank you," Sierra declined politely and proffered the flask to Crystal.

"What's the matter, Sierra?" someone asked, speaking in a voice as if she were a little girl.

"Nothing...I just don't drink," Sierra replied, which seemed a stupid thing to say. *Of course I don't drink; I'm only fourteen. I've never even thought about drinking before.* Her answer sent all the girls into a fit of laughter.

"Sierra," Crystal said in a tone that indicated she was an idiot and she had to explain things to her in simple terms. "None of us 'drink'. It only takes one or two sips to relax you enough to really enjoy yourself; get loose. That's hardly drinking." She pushed Sierra's hand with the flask back toward her. "Just take a small sip."

"That's okay," Sierra answered and thrust the flask back.

Crystal frowned as she snatched it away, and tipping it, took a sip with her eyes narrowed on Sierra. She swallowed and then announced, "What a prude." Of course everyone laughed and Sierra heard other comments such as 'little goody two-shoes', and 'such a nerd'. Crystal screwed a lid onto the flask and dropped it into her purse. "Let's go." She led her followers from the restroom.

Sierra trailed behind, again feeling excluded and also very young.

It was time to leave for the school gym where the dance itself was held. Luke guided Sierra out of the restaurant with his hand at the small of her back. Sierra liked feeling his touch, and her mood lightened with him near. As they stepped outside, she heard kids cry out in surprise and whistles of appreciation as a white stretch limousine pulled up to the curb.

"Ever ride in a limo?" Luke asked.

"Never," she answered with eyes wide.

"Well, you're about to," he said with a laugh.

"What?" she asked incredulously.

"Crystal's father hired it for tonight and we're one of the couples she invited to ride with her and Justin," he announced, grinning.

"Luke, I can't ride in that!" Sierra said, thinking of her mother expecting his parents to drive them everywhere.

He looked at her in astonishment. "Why not?"

"Your parents are supposed to drive us. You told my mother they would be doing all the driving."

"Sierra, it's a professional chauffeur driving, not some kid. I'm sure your mother won't mind. I didn't say anything in front of her because I didn't want to spoil the surprise."

"It's okay with your parents?"

"Of course. My parents know all about it and we really don't have a choice because my dad isn't coming to pick us up."

"Come on, you guys," Justin called from inside the limo. Crystal and Gloria with her date had already seated themselves inside.

You do have a choice; you could call your dad. Sierra kept the thought to herself, again feeling so much younger than everyone else and foolish over her indecision. Maybe she was too much of a prude, and most likely her mother wouldn't mind at all. "All right," she agreed and allowed Luke to help her into the vacant seat.

Once inside, Sierra couldn't help but admire and enjoy the dreamlike luxury of the limo's interior with its cream-colored, buttery-soft leather seats. Each seat had its own controls for temperature, lighting, and seat position, as well as a computer screen. As she sank into her seat, the seatbelt clicked into place automatically. She joined the others playing with the controls and exclaiming how it was the 'ultimate in coolness'.

As the limo pulled up in front of the gym, Sierra noted the awed and envious expressions on other kids' faces; as if they were celebrities. Crystal and Justin were immediately whisked away to join the royal court. Kids crowded around Sierra and Luke, asking questions and making jokes as they moved with them into the decorated gym.

Luke answered questions and bantered back and forth with the crowd, most of them his friends. He grabbed Sierra's hand to keep her close for she noticed it was not apparent to the others that she was with Luke. But as he pulled her along with him through the gym, easily mingling with others, Sierra found all she had to do was smile and laugh at the jokes, and at last her tense nervousness ebbed away. She again became bored hearing the same congratulations and football comments and inane jokes. She amused herself by noting the curious looks that were cast her way, especially from other girls. This was more like hanging out with Luke last night, especially with Crystal and Justin gone.

"Sierra, that dress is absolutely adorable!"

Sierra turned as Katrina waved at her from behind. Her expression was warm and appreciative and Sierra believed it was the first compliment of her dress that was sincere. She waved back and called out, "You look spectacular!" Katrina, like Allison, had her own style, and both she and her date were dressed in a Victorian fashion that not many others could have pulled off. But Katrina had managed it.

The hired band appeared on the stage, picked up their instruments, and began to make last minute adjustments to the sound system.

"Let's get our picture taken before we get all sweaty," Luke suggested, and guided Sierra to a line of kids waiting to be photographed beneath the homecoming arbor.

"Sierra," Allison called from two places ahead in the line. "You look great!"

It was the second sincere compliment that evening, and Sierra was surprised how it helped her feel less conspicuous. "Thanks, you look fantastic," she returned the compliment. Allison wore a silver sheath dress with an open back. Other than a pair of silver earrings, her only accessory was her mum. Her simple style somehow seemed far more elegant and sophisticated than all the frilly, glittery, and over accessorized outfits of the other girls.

Booming music filled the air as the band opened with an attention-getting rift and played a processional tune in rock style as the royal court entered. The crowd cheered as the homecoming king and queen were presented, followed by the princes and princesses. The band bridged into a waltz, and the king and queen stepped onto the floor and danced solo for the first round of the song; then were joined in succession by the prince and princess of each class. When the last royal couple, Crystal and Justin, had joined in and danced a few measures, the band switched to a popular rock song, the signal that the floor was now open for everyone.

"Want to dance?" Luke asked, and without waiting for an answer, pulled Sierra with him to join other couples moving onto the dance floor.

Dancing, Sierra began to feel as if she were at last having fun. The knit fabric of her dress was much more suitable for fast dancing than the formal styles of her classmates, and she liked how it rippled around her as she moved. Luke danced in a loose, uninhibited style and she laughed at his antics, sometimes improvising her own steps to compliment him. The band slipped in a slow song for every two or three fast numbers. Luke pulled her against him for the slow dances, holding her around her back and waist and since he didn't take her hand, she had no choice but to put her arms around his shoulders. But she liked being held in his arms as he moved with slow steps to the music. They danced every dance of the first set.

"You're so cute when you dance," Luke said, leading her toward the tables of refreshments.

Sierra, already flushed from dancing, at least didn't appear to blush. "You are too."

"How's it going, dude?" Justin came toward them, carrying two plastic cups of punch.

"Great band," Luke answered.

"Here, you two look like you need these more than me right now." He handed over the drinks which they gratefully accepted. Justin winked at Luke before turning away.

"Mmm…good," Sierra commented after thirstily gulping her punch in just a few swallows.

"It is good," Luke agreed as he downed his own cup. "Hey, Tom!" He greeted one of his teammates waving at him from a group of football players. He grabbed Sierra's hand and pulled her along to join the group.

As they were pushing their way through the crowd, Sierra felt a sudden heat from her stomach rush directly to her head and spread throughout her body. She became lightheaded, her vision blurred, and the room began to sway ever so slightly making her feel nauseous.

They reached the group where Luke slapped hands with several of his teammates, and joined in the loud discussion of last night's game; many of the same comments Sierra had being hearing all evening.

"Luke," Sierra whispered, squeezing his hand to get his attention.

"Yeah?"

"Something's wrong. What was in that punch?"

Luke's eyes got big as he looked closer at her. Sierra's face had turned a pale greenish tinge. "Sierra, what's the matter?"

"I don't feel well. What was in that punch?" she repeated.

"Oh no," Luke said in a worried tone. Some of his friends were snickering and elbowing each other as they noticed Sierra's appearance. "Come on." He took her by her upper arm and guided her toward the side door of the gym.

It seemed to take forever to push through the crowd of kids. Sierra felt unbearably hot, stumbled frequently as Luke pulled her along, and afraid she was either going to throw up or pass out.

At last they reached the door that led to a cement patio outside. "Too hot in here." Luke smiled at the parent chaperon monitoring the door.

"Don't leave the patio," the parent answered.

"Right," Luke agreed.

They stepped out into the night, the coolness bringing welcome relief and Sierra gratefully gulped in the fresh air, swallowing hard to keep the bubbling contents of her stomach down. Luke led her to a corner of the patio, away from the couples who had also come outside to cool off.

"I can't believe that Justin," Luke said angrily. "He never said anything to me."

Sierra wanted to believe that Luke was not part of spiking the punch. "What did he put in the drink?" Her tongue felt thick and she slurred her words.

"I don't know…probably vodka; it's easier to hide the taste."

"Did he put some in your drink too?"

"I think so. I feel a little buzz. But it hasn't affected me like it seems to have hit you."

"I'm drunk!" Sierra moaned.

"Sierra, I'm so sorry. I had no idea," Luke said again.

"Can you call your dad? I want to go home." She fought back tears as well as nausea.

"Sure," he answered hesitantly. "But you'll be okay after a little while. You couldn't have drunk that much. You're just not used to it."

"Please, I want to go home," Sierra pleaded.

"Sierra, listen." Holding her hand in one of his, he reached up with the other to smooth her hair away from her face and gently stroked her neck, gazing into her eyes. "I'm really, really sorry. I'm going to kill Justin. But if I call my dad now he'll know you're drunk and I don't want to get anyone in trouble."

Sierra gazed back into his eyes in disbelief. "What?" In her opinion, Justin needed to get in trouble.

"Let's just walk around in the fresh air. Do you think you could throw up? You'll feel better if you do."

"You won't call your dad?"

"I will if you really want me to. But Sierra, think about what this will mean. Spiking someone's punch is a serious offense in the eyes of the school. Justin could get kicked off the team or even suspended. Besides, you were having a good time, weren't you, before this? Believe me, within an hour or so you'll be fine."

Disappointment settled into her stomach along with her nausea. *How could Luke cover for Justin?* It was bad enough to spike the punch at school, but to give it to someone without that person having a clue was especially low. Her feelings were in a whirl of confusion, and the alcohol was not helping her judgment.

"Hey, you've never had a drink before, have you?"

"No," she answered bitterly.

"I remember the first time I had a drink. I kind of made a fool of myself," he said, laughing at a memory.

"You drink?" Sierra asked incredulously.

"No, not really. Actually, it was at a party and kind of like what happened to you tonight. Someone spiked the punch and I didn't know."

"Luke, how can you be friends with kids who would do something like that?"

"It's all in fun, Sierra. Don't be such a prude."

For the second time that night she was called a prude, as if that were a bad thing. She wondered if she would outgrow her prudishness; if that was part of maturation.

"Come on, let's walk around and if you don't feel better after ten minutes I'll call my dad," he offered. "Hey." She had ducked her head away and with his fingers he gently tilted her chin to meet his eyes again. "I at least want to dance one more slow dance with you."

Sierra nodded, tired of the conversation and feeling despondent. She allowed Luke to take her arm and they began to stroll slowly around the edge of the patio. She actually did feel better, at least physically, by the time they heard the band starting up.

They returned to the dance floor, but the evening was irreparably ruined for Sierra. She avoided eye contact with Luke, and all she could manage was a weak smile when he asked if she was okay. Allison on catching sight of her, pulled her away to the girls' room to ask what was wrong.

"I'll tell you later," she said for she did not want to explain in the crowded bathroom where anyone could hear.

"Call me tomorrow," Allison insisted.

At last the dance came to an end and Sierra sat with Luke in the back seat of his parents' car. Luke held her hand, rubbing his thumb on the inside of her palm, while he answered his mother's questions about the evening. When they arrived at her cottage, Luke again jumped out to open her car door, and walked her to the front door.

"Thanks for being such a good sport," he said, taking both her hands as they stood on her doorstep. "I had a really good time."

"Thanks," Sierra replied but did not lie and say she had a good time as well.

Luke leaned forward and kissed her on the lips. "You are so sweet," he whispered.

"Good night," Sierra replied awkwardly, and quickly opened her front door and went inside, closing and locking it behind her. Moments later, she heard the car back away.

My first kiss. Sierra felt nothing at all, except very disappointed.

10 CORAZÓN

A canter is a cure for every evil. – Benjamin Disraeli

Storm barked once, soft and low, waking River. Still lying curled on his bed, he squinted in the light from the lamp and shivered, but this time truly from cold for he had not bothered with covers. The back of his head throbbed and his throat felt raw.

"River," a girl's voice hissed in a whisper from behind the door. He could hear the dull thumping of music with a loud bass coming from the house.

"Who is it?" he asked hoarsely.

"Laila; can I come in?"

"Yeah," he answered. He blinked at her as she stepped inside. Although she wore a different outfit, her gothic appearance was almost identical to the other night. "What do you want?" he asked, confused as to what she was doing here. He felt dazed from just waking up and maybe from the blow to his head.

"Are you okay? I heard about the fight."

He thought for a minute. "I think so."

Since he hadn't told her to leave, Laila came over to sit down on the edge of his mattress, looking at him intently. "Let me see," she said frowning. Very gently she touched the side of his head to turn it so she could see the wound at the back. She made a soft noise of exclamation as she discovered a large lump and blood clotted in his hair. "It's not that bad," she assured him as she pushed hair aside to inspect the source of blood. "It's just a scalp wound; they bleed a lot but I don't think you need stitches or anything. Is there any clean water in here?"

"No."

"I'll be right back."

River lay in a daze, listening to her steps recede down the wooden steps, and a few minutes later, coming back up, the pulsing of the bass in rhythm with her steps. She came back over to him with a bottle of water, several washcloths, and a container of antiseptic hand gel.

"This is going to sting, but try to hold still," she instructed as she sat down by his side and turned his head away. Gently she dabbed at his wound with wet washcloths, soaking away the crusted blood and picking out glass splinters. "You okay?" she asked.

"It's just numb," he answered truthfully.

When she had cleaned away all the blood, she used the hand gel as a final cleanser. "There, I think you're going to live."

"How did you find out...?"

"Steve got the story from your aunt. Your dad is passed out half way up the stairs. There's a lot of blood on the kitchen floor where you must have fallen, but nobody seemed worried about you so I thought maybe I should check to see if you were alive."

"Thanks," he said softly. "You've done this before, haven't you?" She had inspected his head and cleaned his wound like an expert.

"Many times…in my family, my brother got beat up; I got molested." She made her statement matter-of-fact, as if this were the norm in most households.

He pushed himself up on his elbow to look at her. "Even now?"

She smirked and with a short laugh said, "No, now I enjoy the benefits of a foster home." She rolled her eyes.

"Which is worse?" he asked.

"Believe it or not, I'd rather be back with my mother. My current foster parents don't touch me but there are other ways to beat a person; like making them feel like garbage."

"You're not garbage," he stated, looking intently at her thin, pale face with the thick make-up and many piercings, and thinking she looked soft and nice underneath it all.

"Thanks." She ducked her head away, embarrassed and then got up to bring back a saran-wrapped sandwich. Apparently she had gone to fetch more than just first-aid supplies. "Here, you must be hungry."

River sat up slowly so as not to increase his dizziness. He gratefully accepted the food and ate it hungrily. "What's Steve doing?" he asked between bites.

"He's already so loaded he doesn't even know I left the party. It's kind of pathetic; your father passed out on the stairs and your cousin passed out on the couch with everyone just stepping around them, trying to get equally loaded."

"Didn't you come to get high?"

"I only smoke enough to mellow my mood. Believe it or not, I don't like other drugs. I came here with Steve because I need a place to crash for the weekend. My foster parents think I'm at a church youth group retreat. Talk about punishment."

"Oh." River suddenly realized he did not want her to leave. "You can stay here if you want."

"Oh yeah, gay cousin?" she teased.

"Yeah."

"Why would I want to stay here?"

"I don't know...because you don't have anywhere else to go?"

"There's always somewhere else to go." She sat down next to him on the mattress and unzipped her boots, kicking them off. Then with her jade green eyes holding his own captive, she lay down and reached up to touch his cheek. "Give me a reason to stay," she whispered.

River woke from long habit a little after six a.m.; time to get up for work. In the darkness, he watched the shadowy outline of the girl sleeping next to him for a few minutes before he whispered, "Laila." She didn't stir. "Laila," he repeated a little louder and stroked her shoulder lightly.

"Umm," she replied.

"I have to go to work."

"Umkay," she muttered.

"Will I see you later?"

In answer, she reached out for him and pulled him back down on top of her.

A little while later, River rolled out of bed and dressed. The back of his head ached with a dull ache, and he had a wave of dizziness when he first sat up. *Concussion*, he thought. Well, he had been hit in the head before and knew what a concussion felt like. He'd be okay in a few days. For now, the dizziness had subsided after a few moments upright, and his headache was tolerable. He knelt and kissed Laila on her exposed cheek; she had already curled up on her side falling back to sleep. Then with Storm at his heels, he left for the stable.

The worst night of my life turned into the best night of my life, he mused and smiled to himself as he picked up a jog; he was going to be late. Without fail, today he would apologize to Sierra. He felt like he could face anything today.

The jangle of the alarm clock woke Sierra; the first time in ages that she didn't wake up on her own. She squinted through puffy eyes and her head ached. *I have a hangover and it's not my fault. So unfair!* She forced herself out of bed, dressed, and slipped out of the house for the stable.

Of all mornings, River, who was never late, showed up a half hour late. It didn't help Sierra's grumpy mood that she had to start chores by herself. She had fed all the horses their hay and was filling grain buckets when River finally showed up.

"Hi," he greeted with a smile.

Sierra glanced over her shoulder, a frown on her face. This was the first time he had said hi to her since their disagreement. And he was even smiling! Somehow, that made her angry, and she certainly did not feel charitable or forgiving today. She kept her back to him and continued to scoop up grain and drop it into a bucket.

"Sierra, I'm sorry," he blurted out.

She simply did not care and refused to answer. He had treated her very badly for weeks, and one 'I'm sorry' was not going to atone for that. She continued filling buckets and tried to shut out his presence as River began stacking the filled buckets in the back of the electric cart.

They stayed out of each other's way until time to clean stalls. Today, as she began mucking her first stall, he stepped inside, which prevented her from being able to toss manure and wet shavings into the cart.

"Sierra, you have every right to hate me."

She stopped, since she couldn't muck, and glared at him.

"I'm sorry. You did nothing wrong." He stood awkwardly, his hands running up and down nervously on the handle of the pitchfork he carried. "I want us to be friends."

"I don't," Sierra answered spitefully, and surprised how good she felt saying that. "Please get out of my way."

He sighed and left the stall to start mucking in the one next to her.

An aching lump of hurt and disappointment had settled in Sierra's chest last night, and she woke with the lump still there. She foolishly had promised Luke not to say anything to her mother, even though she had never lied to her mother or kept secrets from her. It had been so hard to keep her promise when Sierra found her mother asleep on the sofa, waiting for her. She awoke, ready to hear all about her daughter's first date, but all Sierra said was, "It was fine. I'm exhausted. I'll tell you about it tomorrow." She had hugged her mother and rushed to her room before she had to answer any questions. The one person who could have comforted and advised her, Sierra had to avoid.

Now Sierra felt bitterly angry that she had made such a promise to Luke. She was angry with River who had been treating her so unkindly and so unfair. At the moment, Sierra did not like boys at all. She was in no mood to forgive. Strange, how the lump in her chest was causing tears to form, and it was a struggle to hold them back. *I will not cry in front of him!*

She sensed River frequently looking over at her. She tasted the bitter-sweetness of revenge as she continued to work and ignore him. *How does it feel to be shunned, River?* she thought to herself vindictively.

Sierra worked harder and faster than usual, spurred on by her anger. The barn was full with twenty occupied stalls to clean, ten each. It took Sierra nine stalls before the lump won. As she stepped into her last stall she could no longer hold back the tears. She snuffled and brushed them away as the first few leaked from her eyes. Then one wrenching sob escaped and River looked up from his pitchfork.

The next moment, River was beside her, pulling the pitchfork from her hands and taking her into his arms. He held her close and whispered, "I'm sorry," and then, "please don't cry," which only caused Sierra to lose any remaining control and she sobbed helplessly against his chest. It seemed like for hours he just held her tight and let her cry.

"Did I hurt you so badly?" he asked when the sobs subsided to sniffles.

"It's not just you," Sierra said, muffled into his chest. "I had a horrible time last night."

"Tell me."

She did; even the part about Crystal befriending her because she thought Sierra and River were no longer friends. She told him about Justin spiking her drink and the promise she had made to Luke.

"No one should ever make you promise to hide anything from your mother. You have a great mom."

When he said that, the last vestiges of her anger toward him finally melted. "River, I'm sorry. I do want to be friends again."

"You have nothing to be sorry about. I'm so stupid sometimes."

"Yeah, you are," she agreed. She pulled away from his chest and looked up into his face with a tentative smile. The lump in her chest at least for now, was nearly gone.

River smiled back, his dark eyes warm and sympathetic, looking into hers. For a brief moment, it almost felt as if he wanted to kiss her, and somehow, Sierra actually wanted him to. But he dropped his arms, releasing her and they stepped apart.

A voice singing in Spanish warned that Manuel was on his way with the breakfast basket prepared every weekend by his wife Rosa. They stowed their pitchforks, washed their hands in the tack room, and joined Manuel at the observation platform of the indoor arena where he was setting out the food.

"Manuel," River called out as he and Sierra walked up to the platform. He said several sentences in Spanish.

"*Que gusto*," Manuel shouted out exuberantly. "Eet ees about time." He grabbed River and hugged him tightly and smiled over at Sierra. "Dees boy, finally find 'ees senses, no?"

Sierra nodded and laughed. Her mood shifted to an almost euphoric lightness. Her head had finally stopped aching. It felt so good to be friends again with River, and that Manuel cared about the two of them. These were her true friends. She resolved at that moment that she had quite enough of dating, at least for another year or so. Maybe she truly was just not mature enough.

After breakfast, they finished up the remaining morning chores and were ready to ride. "Can you give me a lesson tomorrow instead of today?" Sierra asked, for she didn't feel like she could handle the intense concentration needed for dressage. River readily agreed. The day was drizzly, so they put on rain slickers that spread out to cover the saddles, and rode out on the trail; Sierra on Fiel and River on a horse in training. It was the best hangover remedy and mood elevator that Sierra could imagine.

Later that afternoon, River took Sierra to the black's paddock. She watched in awe, impressed with how much progress River had made with the distrustful horse. As River entered the paddock, the horse stood facing him with his head arched forward and ears pricked, but Sierra could see him keeping one wary eye on her, where she remained at the paddock gate.

"He has been walking up to me," River told her in a quiet voice, "but I think he's unsure with you here."

"Should I leave?" she asked, but not wanting to go.

"No, I think this will be good for him. Other people need to be able to get close to him besides me." By this time, River had walked half the distance to his horse. The black, deciding that Sierra was not an immediate threat, lowered his head, emitted a soft whicker and took a few steps toward River. As they met, River offered the horse treats off the palm of his hand, all the time murmuring to him in low tones. When the treats were eaten, River held up a halter for the black to see and smell, and then with slow motions, buckled it on. He remained with the horse awhile longer, talking to him and stroking his neck before he picked up the lead rope and led him toward the gate.

"Turn slowly and start walking away," River told her, keeping his voice in the same low tone. "Head to the grass and we'll catch up with you."

Sierra obeyed, and soon she heard the sound of the gate opening and sensed River and the black approaching behind her. At one point, she heard them stop and the black snorted loudly. It was hard not to stop and look back, but Sierra resisted and kept walking slowly away. Within a few minutes, River came up along her right side, with the black on his right.

"If he starts grazing with you nearby that will be good enough for today," River said, still talking softly. He kept pace with her as they reached the patch of grass and then they all stopped. The black snorted a few more times, looking around warily and keeping an eye on Sierra. The two kids stood very still, waiting. Eventually, the black dropped his head to snatch a mouthful of grass and then bring his head back up. Before long, he dropped his head to graze uninterrupted.

They walked along with the horse as he moved through the grass at the end of the lead rope. Sierra listened as River softly explained his work with the horse and she noted how much better the animal already looked. Although still too thin, his bones were not as prominent and most of the sores had healed. His feet looked almost normal.

"You're performing a miracle," Sierra said softly, pleased that the black continued to graze, although she noted his ears flick at the sound of her voice.

"Let's see if you can get closer," River said. "Stay by my side, and just mimic my hands when I start to pet him." Again, Sierra complied, and as River kept a hum of low Spanish words, they both reached up to stroke his neck. The black didn't even flinch. By the time River led him back to the paddock, Sierra was able to reach up to occasionally give him a pat. When they released him into the paddock, they both held out their hands with a treat resting in the palms. The black quickly took the treat from River. Sierra didn't move, and waited patiently as the black studied her, flicking his ears, until he finally decided to reach forward and lip off the treat from her palm. He had accepted her!

"Have you thought of a name for him?" Sierra asked as she tossed hay into the black's feed crib and River followed with a bucket of grain and supplements.

"Not yet."

"You can't call him Demon."

"No, I've never called him that. I'm waiting to see what name might fit him."

"Maybe something with heart," Sierra said, "since he has that heart-shaped star."

"Maybe."

"What about Trueheart?"

"Hmm; where'd you get a name like that?"

"I don't know." Sierra didn't want to admit to him about her imaginary black steed that she had named Trueheart; the phantom horse that galloped alongside whenever she rode in a car.

Manuel walked by on his way to start bringing in the horses for the night, but he stopped and joined them at the paddock rail. They stood together, watching the horse contentedly chewing up his grain.

"We're thinking about a name for him," Sierra informed Manuel.

"*Peligroso*," Manuel said with a laugh, the name he called the horse ever since he had helped River bring him home.

"He's not so dangerous anymore," River replied. But the Spanish word gave him an idea. "What about *Corazón*?"

"What does it mean?" Sierra asked.

"Heart."

"*Corazón*," Manuel repeated, nodding his head.

"Corazón," Sierra tried out the word. "It's perfect!"

11 HOMEWORK

To these animals, the ability to intuit fear in a distant herd member and act on this feeling without hesitation is a lifesaving skill. Their innate aptitude for resonating with another being's trust, joy, or confidence is a life enhancing skill. – Linda Kohanov

River had few friends; he had always felt closer to and got along better with animals than with people. Since João had died, he really considered Sierra, Manuel, and Rosa his only friends, and maybe Dr. Patterson. He had never had friends his own age until Sierra, and then he had almost lost that friendship through his own stupidity.

Now River could not remember when he had felt so light-hearted or happy. Sierra had forgiven him and that forgiveness had lifted such a weight from his shoulders that only by its absence did he realize how heavy it had been; how much he had missed her. How stupid he had acted; and she was right, of course. Talking about people you cared about was okay. After all, he had talked about Sierra to João, and that had led to their friendship and the fact she now owned Fiel. It was just hard for him to believe that anyone talking about him could be saying anything good. He had imagined Sierra telling Allison how he wanted to drop out of school, how stupid, and what a failure he was. A wave of guilt washed over his bright mood when he thought about how badly he had treated her.

But she had forgiven him, and warmth spread throughout him as he thought about holding her in his arms. *Sweet little Sierra, mi angelita.* She had stayed around to help him and Manuel bring in the horses and feed, like she used to before he had been such a jerk. Then she had invited him over for dinner. He promised he'd come sometime soon, but not tonight. He didn't really expect Laila to still be hanging around but just in case…

Laila…to have a girl come to him and want him was such a strange and exhilarating feeling. She understood him. There was no sense of judgment or condemnation from her; just acceptance. She had been so tender in caring for his wounded head; and then so free and eager in giving herself to him. He didn't understand her, but he did want to see her again.

"Just remember, cousin," she had said. "I'm nobody's girlfriend."

"Okay," he answered. Laila was two years older than him, but seemed many years older in her experience and wisdom. She might not be his girlfriend, but he thought they could become friends.

Laila was not waiting for him, but his father was. River's heart sank as he entered the yard and the dilapidated truck was still there. Worse, his father leaned against it, smoking a cigarette. "River," he called out.

River gave him a nod and continued on to the barn. He heard his father scuff out the cigarette with his boot toe, and then follow behind him.

"Hey, son," Cray came into the barn where River was filling Storm's dish with kibble. "How're things?"

"Fine," River answered, keeping his attention on resealing the bag of dog food.

"School going okay?"

"I guess."

"Tess tells me you got a horse."

"Yeah."

"He any good?"

Just go away. River turned to face his father and shrugged.

Cray Blackthorn looked a different person from the drunk of last night. Showered and shaved with his hair neatly combed and dressed in well-fitting clothes and polished boots, he appeared a handsome, well-to-do man. Only the bloodshot corners of his eyes hinted at his recent binge. And as often the case, he seemed to have no memory of last night's fight.

"I bought a load of groceries and your aunt's cooking. Come on in and we'll catch up." He cocked his head toward the house and waited for River to make a move.

With a sigh of resignation, River started toward the house, his father falling into step alongside. "What happened to the colt?" River asked.

"He came up lame. I thought I had a good treatment plan for him, but he lost his next few races."

Yeah, a treatment plan of illegal drugs so you can race an unfit horse. River felt the disgust rising but kept his thoughts to himself.

They stepped into the kitchen and were met by the welcoming smells of a stew simmering in a pot on the stove. A pan of cornbread, still warm from the oven, sat on the counter. Aunt Hazel stood at the sink, actually washing dishes; that happened about twice a year. Usually River cleaned up the kitchen when he couldn't stand it any longer.

"That Walt Douglas, you know, Tess's partner; he knows a few breeders and he's invited them to a party tonight. Tess is going to introduce me." Cray continued his monologue as River dished up a bowl of stew, broke off a piece of cornbread, and sat down at the table. It always confused River that his father could talk to him like this; as if he were an equal, and then the next time around, beat him.

"So, just a few months and you turn sixteen. We'll be partners, how about that? You quit school and come work with me at the track."

It was an old line, and River just nodded as the easiest way to deal with his father.

"Oh, that's just great. Teach him to be another crooked horse trainer," his aunt commented without turning around from the sink.

"Shut up, Hazel," Cray said automatically and without force, keeping his attention on River. "What do you think?"

"Sure, Cray," River mumbled.

"River, why can't you call me Dad, huh? Would that be so hard?"

River shrugged and focused on his food. He could never bring himself to call this man 'Dad'. He had also refused to give up his mother's name and take Blackthorn, even though he had received a few blows over that.

The sound of a car's engine pulling into the yard and the tap of a horn interrupted his father's questions. "That's Tess; got to go," Cray said, jumping up from the table. He clapped River on the shoulder and left.

"Finish cleaning up in here," River's aunt ordered, throwing down her dish towel and stomping out of the kitchen.

River smirked to himself for he knew Hazel was jealous of all his father's girlfriends. He didn't understand that, nor did he understand how Tess kept going back to Cray. They had been in a relationship before River had been born. River had done the math and figured out that Cray must have been involved with Tess and his mother at the same time. Tess also figured that out when Cray had brought River home after his mother's tragic death in a horse race. He knew Tess had broken up with him then, but somehow, his father had wooed her back, and they continued in a stormy on-and-off relationship.

River's good mood had soured in the company of his father and aunt, but once they had both left, his food went down easier and he ate a second helping. He finished washing the dishes, scrubbed pots, wiped down the counters, and swept the floor with his thoughts on Sierra, Laila, and also Corazón, and his mood improved.

Finished in the kitchen, River climbed up to his room and with good intentions, spread his schoolbooks out on his mattress and his notebook on his lap. He hadn't decided yet whether to stay in school or not; although if he did quit, he definitely did not plan to work for his father. He would see how he did by the end of the quarter. If he could pass his exams; well maybe…for João's sake. As he looked down at his page, the throbbing headache that had abated while working at the stable now returned. His eyelids drooped as he tried to read, and he fell asleep.

"Hey, gay cousin," Laila spoke softly as she entered his room, jolting him back to wakefulness. Storm thumped her tail in greeting but didn't even raise her head, recognizing the visitor as welcome.

"Hi, not girlfriend," River smiled, very pleased she had come.

Laila plopped down next to him and leaned over for a kiss. "What are you doing?" she asked, picking up his notebook where it had fallen from his lap with his notes spilling out.

"Trying to do homework; I never get very far," he answered grimly.

"I'm not surprised," she murmured as she skimmed a page of his history notes, most of which were unreadable and didn't make sense. "The light is horrible in here." She flipped through a few more pages; his math problems and English notes. "You need help. Come on, we're going somewhere where the light is decent. I've got a car."

"Right now?" River asked, touching her shoulder.

"Well, maybe in a little bit." She let him pull her down onto the mattress, pushing the books aside.

After the disastrous prom, Sierra thought Luke would no longer have an interest in her. So she was surprised when he called her Sunday evening to ask how she was feeling.

"Pretty bad this morning," Sierra told him, "but I'm better now."

"I'm so sorry," he apologized again. "I just finished talking to Justin. I told him I didn't appreciate the dirty trick he pulled on you. He says he's really sorry."

"He should be," she said, however she didn't believe that Justin was sorry.

Luke laughed. "I think he's learned his lesson. While he was spiking other people's drinks he was doing the same to his own. He said when he got home he spent the night puking in the bathroom." He laughed again.

Sierra didn't find that funny; a fourteen-year-old drinking so much he was sick all night. She seriously doubted Justin had learned any kind of a lesson; especially if his friends all thought it was funny.

Over the next few weeks, Luke sought her out at school, called her in the evenings, and asked several times if she would stay for his JV games. He even asked her to the next school dance. But Sierra declined all his invitations. Her interest in Luke had simply died after the prom. She still liked him and considered him a friend, but his easy acceptance of what his friend had done to her and his desire to cover it up, somehow left her feeling devalued. The idea of being his girlfriend no longer appealed, and she definitely did not want him to kiss her again. Luke finally gave up, and Katrina told Sierra he had taken another girl to the school dance.

The time at the stable more than compensated for the loss of a boyfriend. River was consistently in a good mood; really the happiest Sierra had ever seen him, and working with him was the best it had ever been. He helped her with Fiel every time she rode him in the arena and she felt like she was back on track in developing her ability to communicate not only with Fiel, but with the other horses she rode as well. They spent time every day with Corazón; grooming, feeding him treats, and just being around him as they hand-grazed him. Soon, the black horse seemed as much at ease with Sierra as with River.

"Allison," Sierra said a few weeks after the prom. "Why don't you have your mom drive you to Pegasus after school? Then you can apologize to River and you can meet Fiel."

"Good idea," Allison agreed. Even though Sierra and River had reconciled, Allison still felt she needed to apologize to him, but they never saw him at school.

The next day, Allison and her mother drove into the stable yard just as Sierra came back from trail riding Silver, her assigned horse that day. Sierra waved and Allison got out of the car to walk with her as she led Silver into the crosstie bay.

"What a beautiful horse," Allison exclaimed. "Is this Fiel?"

"No, this is Silver, Gloria's horse. He's a Dutch warmblood, a different breed than Fiel, and he's also much taller," Sierra explained.

Allison timidly came forward to touch Silver on his nose and neck. "He's so soft and silky," she said in surprise. Silver snorted, spraying wetness from his nose and Allison jumped back with a small screech. "He doesn't like me!"

"He just snorted," Sierra laughed. "They do that a lot after a ride and it's a sign he's relaxed."

Sierra finished grooming Silver and then led him to his stall with Allison following. They passed the indoor arena where River was working Pendragon (nicknamed Penny), a warmblood bay gelding in training with Tess for dressage. At that moment, River rounded the upper corner of the arena and moved Penny into a left half pass to the center of the arena and then right half pass back to the rail. Penny arched his head gracefully as he moved laterally with legs crossing, his tail swishing rhythmically. On the rail with invisible signals, River moved him around the arena in medium trot, and then practiced the half passes again.

"Unbelievable," Allison breathed out on a sigh as she watched wide-eyed.

"Stay here and watch while I put Silver away." Sierra took Silver to his stall and then joined Allison back at the rail, her friend still mesmerized watching the horse and his rider.

River had transitioned up into canter and was riding figure eights with a flying lead change in the center of the figure. Sierra studied River intently, trying to detect when he signaled Penny to change the lead, but whatever communication River gave remained invisible to her eyes. He brought Penny from canter to walk and gave the reins, allowing the horse to stretch his head forward and low. Penny snorted, his ears flopping; a relaxed, happy horse. River reached down and petted him on both sides of his neck.

"I had no idea," Allison breathed out. "That was incredibly beautiful." She impulsively clapped her hands in appreciative applause.

River glanced at the girls and a frown darkened his expression when he noticed Allison.

"Oh dear," Allison said. "I probably shouldn't have made so much noise."

"No, it's fine; that's just River. Come on." Sierra pulled her away. "He's going to let Penny stretch and cool down; then he'll bring him to the crossties and you can talk to him there."

"What are you doing here?" River spoke sharply to Allison as he passed the girls, leading Penny into the crossties.

"River," Allison began. "I'm here to say I'm sorry and I was wrong for giving you test answers."

River finished pulling off the saddle and pad and then unfastened the splint boots on Penny's legs before he finally responded by turning to glare at Allison again. "Yes, you were," he confirmed.

"Please," she said again. "I'm sorry."

*River, if you make her beg, I'll…*Sierra thought but really didn't know what she would do.

River studied Allison, as if judging her sincerity. Then much to Sierra's relief, he nodded and said, "Okay."

"Can we be friends?" Allison asked.

"Why do you want to be friends?" River picked up a brush and began grooming Penny.

"Because you're Sierra's friend. You're very important to her."

"Okay, fine," he answered, though begrudgingly. He looked over at Sierra and when he saw the relieved look on her face, he softened his expression and allowed his mouth to slightly turn up into a weak smile.

And that was that; apology accepted.

Allison gushed to him about his fantastic ride; how much she admired him on the horse and that everything Sierra had told her didn't even come close to the reality of such beauty. She trailed after River and Sierra as they finished chores, and barraged him with questions. When River decided her inquiries were genuine, he lightened his attitude and willingly answered and even volunteered information, always at his most verbal when discussing horses.

"You know, I could help you with homework. It wouldn't be cheating," Allison offered just before saying goodbye.

"No thanks," River said abruptly.

River would never have accepted help with his homework from Allison, but he did find it a bit ironic that she had offered her help when he truly didn't need it. The night Laila had looked over his disastrous notes she had stepped into the role of his tutor. She had her own car now, and two to three nights a week she came up to his room, allowing him to pull her willingly into his arms and onto his mattress where they entwined eagerly together in insatiable, youthful lust. Then she drove him to a coffee shop near the university that had good lighting and an atmosphere conducive to studying.

Tonight they sat side by side at a table with River's books and papers spread out on its surface amidst coffee cups and napkins. Four other tables were occupied by college students plinking away on laptops, blending in with soft, unobtrusive music in the background.

"River, you are really irritating me," Laila said in exasperation. "Answer the question." She repeated the question, speaking slow and distinct as if to a child. "The first battle of the American Revolution took place where?"

"I don't..."

Laila made a noise meaning for him to stop, and shoved his shoulder. River had answered 'I don't know', so many times that she had devised a rule. "Either you use that underused muscle between your ears and come up with an answer or say, 'I'll look it up', or 'let me research that'. No more 'I don't knows'."

River leaned forward with a groan, grabbing his head. "Bunker Hill," he answered.

"You're guessing and that's as bad as 'I don't know'. River, you just wrote the answer; it's in your homework."

River sighed and sat up straighter. "I'll look it up," he said in resignation and shuffled through his homework answers.

Laila pressed her lips tight together, waiting.

"The battle of Lexington and Concord," he announced, finding where he had written the answer.

"And the date?"

"April 19, 1775," he read off his paper.

"Correct. I know Mr. Kennedy; he's a fair teacher. All the questions on his tests are in your homework. All you have to do is study your homework answers. I'm going to ask you these same questions the night before your test, okay?"

"Okay," he replied submissively.

"Good; I think you've done enough for tonight."

River breathed out in relief and gathered up his books and papers. His brain felt strained from Laila's aggressive coaching, but he also felt proud of what he had accomplished tonight, even though it had taken over three hours. For the first time in his life, he was consistently completing all his homework assignments.

"Why does Steve say you're gay?" Laila asked, switching from homework topics and leaning back in her chair.

"I don't know," he replied, zipping up his backpack.

"River," she said in an exasperated tone and punched playfully at his shoulder again.

"Ouch, you're bruising me, and that's not a homework question so it doesn't count," he defended himself, laughing.

"All questions count…so?"

"Let me think for a minute." He dropped his backpack onto the floor and took a sip from the dregs of his coffee cup. Her eyes that he found so startlingly green, watched him impishly from the blackness surrounding them. "Probably because I like horses."

"So?"

"And the way I ride."

"How is that?"

River thought for several minutes, finding it difficult to explain. "It might be different if I lived on the east coast or in Europe, but if guys around here like horses at all, it's usually because they want to be cowboys."

Laila nodded, waiting for more.

"I ride the way my mother taught me; dressage and jumping, and it's how I want to ride."

"Why do you want to ride like your mother instead of like a cowboy?"

"I don't…" he began but Laila scowled and raised her hand as if to punch him again. He laughed, pulling away defensively. "It's just better."

"That is not a satisfactory answer."

"Really, I don't…"

She kicked him under the table.

Laughing, River surrounded her with his arms and kissed her to stop her questioning.

Laila kissed him back enthusiastically, but when they had to stop for air, she persisted, "River, I want to know."

With a deep sigh, but keeping his arms around her, River said, "Let me think." He fingered the soft ends of her hair at the nape of her neck, the parts not caught up in her stiffly gelled, spiky hair. Closing his eyes, he thought about the times he spent on a horse's back. How could he explain how it made him feel? How could he put into words the awe he felt when a twelve hundred pound animal did what he asked through just the slightest shift of his weight or touch of leg or hand? No one would believe that sometimes he did nothing at all; just thought what he wanted and the horse knew. He didn't understand it himself, but it was the most incredible feeling of harmony and trust and always filled his soul with a sense of respect and love for his mount. It wasn't just riding either. The very sight of a horse or being near one filled him with calmness and a sense of rightness that he never felt anywhere else. He didn't know how to describe all this to Laila.

"Okay, the way I ride, I have to sort of think like a horse," he explained. "I have to somehow let him know I won't hurt him and that what we can do together is fun. It means I have to be aware of how my horse is feeling when I ride. If he's a little tired or sore, I have to be easy on him. If he's frightened I have to be patient with him. It's not a very macho way to ride, but I like how I feel when I get it right."

Laila leaned back in his arms and brought her hands up to the sides of his face. Looking deep into his eyes, she kissed him softly on his lips. "That's beautiful," she said.

Sierra thought the re-establishment of their friendship was the main reason for River's good moods. Then one day she discovered there might be another reason.

She was helping River and Manuel bring horses in for the night when a car drove up and a strange girl stepped out, looking around. Strange not only because Sierra did not know her, but her appearance was anything but normal. Sierra's first impression was of someone trying to look like a vampire. The girl's skin was pasty white and she had thick black eye make-up and spiky dyed black hair with a red and blue streak. She wore a black overcoat hugged tightly around her, its hem skimming the top of knee-high black boots. Light glinted off multiple piercings in her ears and on her face. The coat pulled tightly across her chest emphasized her well-developed shape.

The girl looked around in distaste and shivered. When she caught sight of Sierra gawking at her she called out, "Is River here?"

Just then River emerged from the lane leading Moose and when he saw the girl, he smiled and raised a hand in greeting. "Hi, Laila," he called out and still leading the horse, walked over to her. To Sierra's astonishment, River leaned in and kissed the girl on the mouth. Then they spoke in voices too low for Sierra to hear but she could tell River was talking about the horse. Moose waited patiently for a few minutes and then nudged his muzzle at River to remind him it was time to go in, pushing his way in between River and the girl. She actually squealed and jumped back. River led Moose into the barn and the girl got back into her car. Sierra saw her light up a cigarette, holding it in her hand out an open window.

Sierra caught up with River inside. "River, who is that girl?" she hissed at him.

"Just a friend."

"You kissed her." Sierra pointed out. "Is she your girlfriend?"

River paused a moment after latching Moose's stall door and then answered, "No, Laila's no one's girlfriend." He smiled and his color deepened.

"Laila?"

"That's her name."

"Like in the song?"

River laughed and nodded.

Sierra had been planning on inviting River to dinner, but when the horses were fed and Manuel was locking up the stable doors, River said goodbye to both of them and got into the car with the girl.

Sierra and Manuel looked at each other as the car pulled away, and Manuel raised his brow in a questioning look.

So River has a girlfriend; sort of. Sierra wasn't sure how she felt about that, but she definitely did not like that girl. *She smokes, and she's afraid of horses, for heaven's sake!*

Last Christmas, Sierra and River had known each other for only a few months and were still in the early stages of their developing friendship. It had not occurred to her to get him a Christmas present. But this year, they had been through so much together that she wanted to get him something special; something with meaning.

"Anything to do with horses would probably be appropriate," Allison suggested after Sierra had been musing out loud what to get him.

"I suppose I could get him something for Corazón, like a nice halter. I don't know though; I guess that's what I'll do if I can't think of anything better."

Sierra couldn't think of anything better so she ordered a bright red halter with Corazón's name stitched in black letters on the cheek piece. In addition, she bought him a pair of warm work gloves, for she had noticed River many times with his hands thrust beneath his armpits, trying to keep them warm. River had already agreed to come to the cottage for Christmas dinner, admitting there wasn't ever much of a celebration at his house, and Sierra planned to give him his presents then.

Christmas day landed on a weekday that year, and Sierra and River had decided to do the chores that morning as a Christmas present to Manuel. Sierra also baked cookies for both Manuel and Rosa and gave them a basket filled with gourmet coffee and two brightly colored coffee mugs, a package of smoked salmon, some cheeses, crackers, and chocolate.

They finished chores and walked the short distance to the cottage where Pam was already setting food out on the table. They stuffed themselves on baked ham, mashed potatoes, green beans from Pam's garden that she had put up in the freezer, homemade applesauce, and homemade rolls that Sierra had made the day before. For dessert, Sierra had also made her first pecan pie while in a baking mood yesterday.

After dinner, Sierra gave River his presents.

"This is perfect," he said appreciatively, holding up the halter. "The red will really look good with Corazón's black color." He tried on his gloves and thanked her again. They were sitting next to each other on the floor by the Christmas tree, and to Sierra's amazement, he leaned over and kissed her on the cheek.

She flushed with heat, but fortunately, he didn't notice for he had already stood up and walked over to where he had left his jacket. Pam noticed however, for Sierra could feel her mother's eyes from where she sat on the sofa, watching the kids.

River returned and sitting back down, handed Sierra a small red box with a gold ribbon. "Merry Christmas," he said.

Sierra blushed again and ducked her head to open the box. Inside was a stylized galloping horse fashioned out of metal. "River," Sierra breathed out. "This is so beautiful!" She set the horse in her palm to study it better. "Look, Mom." She held it up for Pam to see.

"River, how beautiful. How very thoughtful of you," Pam exclaimed.

River's own face deepened in color; he cleared his throat. "I made it in metal shop."

Sierra wanted to hug him, but somehow, after the kiss, she felt too shy. *Silly, it's just a brotherly kiss on the cheek.*

For River's birthday at the end of January, Sierra gave him a friendship bracelet braided out of hair from Fiel's and Corazón's tails; black and gray strands that she had pulled out a few at a time over several weeks.

"I like this," he said as he slipped it onto his wrist. "Thanks."

"You're not going to quit school are you?" Sierra had to ask the question. He had said no more about quitting but she wanted reassurance.

"No," he answered, relieving her worries. "I'm actually passing all my classes."

"River, that's great!"

"You don't have to act so surprised," he said.

The short, wet days of winter passed, and with the coming of spring, it was time to prepare for the upcoming show season.

12 TRAINING BEGINS

We shall take great care not to annoy the horse and spoil his friendly charm, for it is like the scent of a blossom – once lost it will never return. - De Pluvinel

An attractive rig and horse trailer pulled into the stable yard, bearing the name of a well-known breeding farm in the next state. Tess had been helping Crystal search for a new horse throughout the winter and a few weeks ago had finally found a promising prospect. Today, a Sunday in mid February, the horse arrived.

Sierra and River watched a pair of men step out of the rig and begin the process of unloading their equine passenger.

"Do you know anything about him?" Sierra asked River.

"Tess said she's a ten-year-old Hanoverian mare."

"Oh, a warmblood."

"Umhm," River replied, his attention focused on the tall, blanketed horse now backing out of the trailer. The mare stepped carefully down the ramp and then stood square on all four legs once she reached the level pavement, her head raised high and nostrils flared as she took in her surroundings. Her neck and legs, visible outside of her blanket, glistened a dark bay. She had a regal head with a white strip on her face from between her eyes to the top of her well-shaped muzzle. Her large, wide-set eyes looked around alertly; she appeared curious, not afraid.

The handler led the mare around in a small circle as River walked up to them. He spoke to River for a few minutes and then River nodded and took the lead from the handler. The other handler joined the first and together they pulled off the shipping blanket and boots, stowed them in the trailer and closed up the ramp, preparing to leave.

River walked the new arrival around the stable grounds, allowing the mare to see and smell her new home.

"She's beautiful," Sierra whispered as she approached quietly and fell into step with River. With her blanket and boots off, Sierra admired the mare's well-muscled body, her glistening deep red coat, her fine black mane and tail, four black stockings, and two gleaming white socks on her back legs.

River laughed and rolled his eyes. "Of course; it's what you say about every horse."

"But she really is magnificent, don't you think?"

"Yeah, this one's exceptional," River admitted. "Look at her deep chest and well-muscled neck and the slope to her shoulder, the straight hocks and nice slope to the pasterns. She has almost perfect conformation. She seems very level-headed. Look how she's taking everything in but without tensing up about anything."

"What's her name?"

"She's registered as Eager Encounter. Her handler said they called her Diva."

"Diva," Sierra repeated, and stroked the mare's fine neck. "I think it fits her."

River laughed but the mare snorted, and Sierra thought that meant she agreed with her.

That afternoon, Tess arrived; unusual for her to show up on a weekend but she wanted assurance that Crystal's new horse had arrived safe and sound.

"She's a proven horse; took regional championship at training level in an adult division last year. Walt paid more for this horse than any other he has bought for Crystal," Tess commented as Sierra and River stood at the paddock fence beside her, watching Diva. "It took some convincing for him to agree." Tess shook her head and mumbled to herself, "She whined enough; he gives her anything she wants." A few minutes later she said, "Since I'm here, come to my office. I want to go over the training schedule for the next few months."

They followed Tess into the office and took seats.

"There are ten riders in this year's clinic." Tess referred to a cross-country jumping clinic that she gave every year on the first weekend of March, officially starting off training for the eventing season. "River, I would like you to ride Moose first as a demonstration."

River replied, "Okay."

"Sierra, are you getting along with Minstrel on the trail?"

"Yes, he's good." Minstrel, a light chestnut, nine-year-old quarter horse gelding was in training with Tess, and had been assigned to Sierra for his conditioning work on trails.

"I've talked to his owner and she's anxious for him to compete this season and she's okay with a junior rider. We'll see how he goes in the clinic but I'd like to skip beginner novice and start him out at novice level. He's done hunter-jumper shows in the past, so if he handles novice level at a schooling show, we can move him right up to training level for the season."

"Okay," Sierra agreed. She looked at River and he nodded his approval; Sierra and Minstrel were well-matched.

"River, you're going to have to start out at training level this year. You need to compete in at least four trials before you can move up to preliminary."

"Sure."

Tess sighed, sounding annoyed. "If only you had started before now; you could take Moose preliminary this season."

River just shrugged.

"I'd like you to start riding Crystal's new horse this week. She wants to ride her in the clinic and I'd like her settled in before then."

"Is she even going to ride her before the clinic?" River asked.

"Of course; she will have her lesson on her this week. And she has ridden and jumped the mare when we tried her out, and got along with her very well."

"At least she's not a baby," River mumbled to himself.

Tess scowled at him; then changed the subject. "Here's a calendar of all the horse trials this season. The junior team will consist of the four girls: Crystal, Gloria, Katrina, and Sierra. River, you'll ride as an individual. I have one adult boarder competing, so her horse is included on the training schedule. I've highlighted the events I want Pegasus to compete in and which horses to go." She handed River several pages stapled together.

"In addition, I think it would be beneficial to attend a few dressage shows. Sierra, you said you wanted to compete in dressage with Fiel, and Katrina has expressed interest with Calliope. She thinks it will help her dressage scores in combined training and I agree. If you think you are up for riding two horses at the next dressage show, you can enter Minstrel at first level. The first level tests are similar to your training level tests in eventing. I'll let you and River decide what level for Fiel. Just note the closing date for entries and make sure you get yours mailed in on time."

"Yes, I'm up for riding Minstrel as well, and I'll send in my entry this week," Sierra agreed.

"What about Crystal and Gloria?" River asked.

"I wish I could get those two out here to ride more on their own, and I think they would also benefit from some dressage competitions; but it's doubtful they'll agree," Tess answered, "or, rather they will agree but then they always come up with some excuse."

Sierra was surprised at the annoyance she detected in Tess's tone, and the fact she was confiding this information to her and River. It had never occurred to her how difficult it must be for Tess to coach a student like Crystal, who furthermore was the daughter of her partner. She would always have to use tact and diplomacy, and avoid expressing her negative thoughts.

"River, I'm going to have you ride Felicity and Pendragon at the March dressage show. I want you to ride Felicity at training level. It will be her first show and it's an easy test that she can handle. I'd like to move her up to first level, test one, by the end of the season."

"She's a three-year-old," River protested. "Why are you pushing her? She shouldn't even start her show career for at least another year."

Tess's lips tightened and she answered with her irritation undisguised. "How many times do I have to explain to you that we are here to serve the clients? I have convinced her owner to only enter her in dressage this year. She's pushing me to start her right out in eventing."

"The owners aren't always right," River retorted.

"They are when they're paying the bills," Tess stated emphatically. "Now, Pendragon's owners are also very anxious to have him compete at FEI levels. That's why they brought him to me because he didn't perform very well with their last trainer at third level. You get along with him very well and I have convinced Mrs. Galensburg to allow you to ride him. She doesn't seem to care whether he's ridden by an adult or junior as long as he wins. I think you should be able to take him fourth level this year."

"What does he have to do?" River asked, already defensive for the horse's sake.

In answer, Tess produced a USDF member guide book, found the pages with the fourth level tests, and handed it to River. He scanned them over before he began his protest. "There are canter pirouettes at fourth level. He's just starting to learn those."

"They are not in the first test. And he's capable and I think will master them very quickly. We have almost a month before the first show. I need to send in the entries by next Tuesday."

"You're going to enter him in a class where he doesn't even know the movement?" River asked incredulously and with undertones of rising anger.

"Relax; I plan on entering him in third level, test three, for the first show, and then we'll progress him through the fourth level tests. I want him ready for FEI next year."

"You're…"

"River, this is a business," Tess interrupted him curtly. "My success is built on my willingness to push the horses and take chances. I know what I'm doing."

He turned back to the eventing calendar and Sierra noted the tightness of his jaw as he struggled to control his temper.

"What now?" Tess asked in irritation after a few minutes of watching him look over the calendar.

"Nothing," he replied in a tone that sounded very much like he had more issues.

"This is what you agreed to when I bought that horse," Tess reminded him with an edged look, daring him to challenge her over this.

"Fine, but I'm not going to ride a horse at a level I don't think he's ready for." He glared back, meeting her challenge. They stared at each other for a few moments.

Finally, Tess relented enough to say, "Let's just take it one show at a time."

River looked away with his arms folded tightly.

"Any more questions?" Tess asked, her own shoulders stiff in determination.

"Manuel is never going to get any days off with both Sierra and me gone almost every weekend through the summer," River grumbled, feeling very disagreeable.

"I've already talked to him and he thinks he can find someone to help him out. He's got a cousin or someone who just arrived in the country and hasn't found work."

"Okay," he mumbled begrudgingly. "Can we go now?"

"Of course." Tess turned to her computer before the kids had even risen from their chairs.

"Are you okay with all this?" Sierra asked as they walked back to the stable.

"She's going to kill me," River griped. "Cory (the nickname they had started calling Corazón) is worth it but competing every weekend is not quite what I expected."

"It will be fun," Sierra tried to convince him, for she looked forward to the upcoming season.

He shook his head in disagreement and stated with conviction, "If I were a trainer I would only take clients who would allow me to train as I thought best for the horse."

"River, you would be such a great trainer," Sierra stated, understanding his concerns. "Do you think you might want to as a professional someday?"

"I don't know…only if there are actual owners who care about their horse more than the ribbons and trophies."

"There's got to be," Sierra replied, "like me. I'd hire you."

He smiled at her and it seemed to help lighten his mood. "Maybe you should be a trainer."

"I'd love to, but I have so much to learn. It's hard for me to imagine it would be possible even by the time I'm out of school. I think I'll stick with my veterinarian plans. Maybe we could be partners; start our own barn with you as the trainer and I can take care of all the horses' vet needs."

He actually laughed good-naturedly. "Okay, partner. I'm thinking Cory is ready to start some lunge work. Do you want to help me?"

"Sure!"

A month ago Corazón had been moved up into the main barn as soon as a stall became available; to make room for a new colt his father had somehow managed to acquire. River, Manuel, and Sierra could all now approach him, halter him, and lead him without the black displaying aggressive or defensive behavior. They had to give him plenty of warning however, and make their intentions clear, for the horse still had a tendency to spin with his back toward any on-comer, ready to kick out.

But it was obvious that River had formed a tight bond with his horse. He spent time with Cory every day, bringing him to the crossties to groom him, and then leading him out into the fields to hand graze. Sierra noticed how Cory followed River with his eyes and would often reach out with his nose to touch River's arm. Whenever River approached, Cory whinnied and trotted up to him, whereas with Sierra or Manuel, he waited for them to come to him, his posture still wary.

As River brought Cory to the crossties, an unexpected shiver ran up her spine as a dark thought suddenly invaded from apparently nowhere. *I don't think River could bear to lose Cory.* She prayed a silent prayer that nothing would ever part the boy and horse – for either of their sakes.

Before she started to help with grooming, Sierra stood back a moment to study the horse. He had changed from the ragged, emaciated, and dangerous animal that had arrived last fall. He had gained enough weight to cover his ribs and hip bones. His sores had long ago healed. His feet were trim and in good shape. Picking up a brush, she ran it along his neck and side, noting his coat no longer felt brittle and course. Like all the horses, he was beginning to shed his winter thickness, and his black hair had a healthy luster and silky feel. She pictured him turned out each morning; how he took off running and bucking playfully, like a normal, healthy, and happy horse, glad to be free to move and full of energy. Fortunately, he had never shown any signs of lameness.

"He sure is looking good," her musings triggered her to say.

"Yeah," River agreed. "What do you think of him now?"

"He's beautiful."

River laughed and said, "That's what you say about all horses."

She made a face at him. "Well, tell me about a horse that isn't beautiful," she challenged.

"You got me there," he conceded with a smile. Then he said more seriously, "I've been putting a bit and bridle on him for the past few days. He's not too happy about it. I think he's been ridden before and I don't think it was pleasant for him."

"Hmm, I can imagine," Sierra said. She watched River take up a bridle with a plain snaffle bit, and very patiently, he coaxed Corazón into allowing him to put it on. The black tossed his head several times, his ears back, but River talked to him soothingly, stroking his neck and praising him until he finally stood still. He fed him a few bits of carrots to encourage him to chew on and taste the bit. Then with slow motions, he unhooked Corazón from the crossties and led him into the indoor arena. Sierra followed with a lunge line.

River led Corazón around the perimeter of the arena in both directions, letting him toss his head a few more times, snort, and look around; an exercise River had been doing with the horse even before putting him in the bridle, so the arena was not unfamiliar to him. Then River brought him to one end of the arena where Sierra waited with the lunge line. He hooked the line to the ring of the bit and then had Sierra stand on the outside of the horse with her hand on the outside rein. River led him in a small circle a few times, and then started to back away from him as he released loops of lunge line. Sierra's job was to keep Corazón walking on the circle and not allow him to follow River.

"Good," River said after a few rounds and then had Sierra halt Corazón as he came up to him, praising him lavishly. Then they repeated the exercise in the other direction. "Not bad," River exclaimed. "I bet he's done this before." They had spent less than ten minutes on this first lesson. River took him back to the crossties to remove the bridle, and then he led him out to the field to graze as a reward.

Sierra helped River the next few days, repeating the lunge lesson. Then River brought out the lunge whip. "I'm a little worried how he's going to react," River confessed as they were brushing Cory before the lesson.

"Yeah, me too." They both suspected the horse did not have good memories of whips.

River slowly brought the whip into view, letting Corazón sniff and snort at it, until he stood quietly. Then they started the lunge lesson with River merely holding the whip in a downward position. Eventually, River was able to lift the tip of the whip to encourage Cory to stay out on the circle, and Sierra no longer needed to hold on the outside rein.

A few days of independent lunging with whip in hand, and River felt Cory was ready for more disciplined work. He tried on a saddle pad with a lunging surcingle and at first, just had Cory wear it while he led him out to graze. When he left it on for a lunge lesson, it never became an issue. Then River added side reins to help keep Cory balanced and in a good frame. By the end of two weeks, he was able to work Cory for short periods of trot as well as walk.

River no longer needed Sierra's help with the lunge lessons, but she still hung around to watch, impressed with the horse's progress. Corazón now accepted the bridle without tossing his head; in fact, he dropped his head and opened his mouth willingly for the bit. On the lunge line, he remained on a circle in both directions, undisturbed when River raised the tip of the lunge whip, and responding to voice commands for walk, trot, and halt. Strangely, she often had to fight back tears as she marveled at how the abused horse had learned to trust River, all signs of stress or defensive behavior replaced with a curious and willing attitude.

13 DIVA

Love means attention, which means looking after the things we love. We call it stable management. - George H. Morris

"This doesn't look good." River stood at the opened grill of Diva's stall. The mare had thrust her nose out and he stroked it gently as he surveyed piles of uneaten hay strewn around her legs and mixed in with the shavings.

It was Saturday, and Crystal's new horse had been at Pegasus one week. Sierra tossed her armload of hay into the stall next door, and then joined River to peer in at Diva. "What's the matter?" she asked, as she also reached up to stroke the gentle mare.

"She didn't eat much last night. Look at all that leftover hay and she's only eaten half her grain."

"Do you think she has colic?" Sierra asked in a worried voice. With primitive digestive systems, horses have little ability to deal with intestinal maladies, and all horsemen fear colic which can disable and even kill a horse.

"It's possible, but she doesn't really act like it. She's not looking or biting at her sides," River answered, "and there's manure in the stall."

As if to answer the question for them, Diva pulled her nose in and took a mouthful of grain. Chewing noisily and with kernels of oats leaking from her mouth, she thrust her nose back out.

"Strange," River said. They watched Diva eat her grain. She took mouthfuls but thrust her nose outside the grate where the kids could pet her while she chewed. They waited until she finished, and then returned to feeding the other horses, neighing loudly and stomping in their stalls, unhappy with the delay in their breakfast.

"Let's not give her anymore feed this morning until I can talk to Manuel. I want to know how she's been eating all week," River advised, his tone worried.

"Right," Sierra agreed. "I sure hope she's okay."

When Manuel arrived with a basket of food, River questioned him about Diva.

"No, che no eat. Jus' a leetle; che no feenees anyteeng. I tell Mees Tess. Che call vet and 'ee come but 'ee no find anyteeng. I do not know." Manuel scratched the back of his head, his brow creased in a worried frown.

"She ate her grain while we were watching," Sierra said.

"Maybe she's lonesome, or homesick," River wondered out loud.

"*Quien sabe*?" Manuel shrugged.

That evening, alone in the barn after all the horses had been brought in for the night and fed and Sierra and Manuel had left, River stopped to peer into Diva's stall. She stood with her nose to the grate, looking out; her hay untouched and only part of her grain eaten. He stepped inside her stall and began to stroke her neck and shoulders while he studied her for signs of colic. While he stood with her, she thrust her nose into her manger and began to eat her grain. River stayed with her until she finished the grain and then moved to her pile of hay.

"Good girl," he praised, "eat all your food." He left the stall, but turned around when he heard Diva whicker after him. She had left her hay and stood at the grate, following him with her eyes.

Strange. He stepped back inside her stall. She rumbled a low sound and nuzzled at him with her head. "*Que pasa, linda? Triste*? Missing your old home?" he murmured. He began to stroke her again, pleased when she returned to her hay. Several times he tried to leave her stall, only to return when he heard her moving to the grate and ignoring her food.

This is going to take a while. Defying Tess's rule about no dogs in the stable while horses were inside, he called to Storm, and he and his dog kept Diva company while she ate.

It was after nine o'clock when River felt satisfied that the mare had eaten all but a few wisps of hay. As he and Storm left the stable, looking forward to their own suppers, Diva whinnied loud and longingly, watching him depart through the bars of her stall.

When Sierra arrived the next morning for work and flicked on the lights inside the barn, she was startled by Storm who came up to greet her, wagging her tail enthusiastically.

"Storm, how did you get in here?" she asked as she bent down to pet the furry head. "Where's River?"

In answer to her question, as she stepped around the first aisle of stalls with Storm at her side, she saw River getting up from a pile of horse blankets where it looked like he had been lying in front of Diva's stall.

"River, what...?"

"You woke me up," he said, blinking sheepishly, and rubbing at his face.

"What are you doing here?"

River explained what had happened last night; that somehow Diva seemed comforted to have a human nearby, and only then would she eat. After he left her, he could not forget the sight of her staring out of her stall and neighing after him, sounding so mournful. So after he and Storm had eaten at home, he decided to come back to check on her and ended up staying all night.

"Wow, and you were actually able to sleep?" Sierra asked, touched by how much River had been willing to do for the sake of a horse.

"Yeah. I'm going to try to contact her previous owners and see if they might have some idea about what's bothering her."

"Good idea. River…you are…" Sierra wanted to tell him how kind it was for him to stay, but the right words just didn't come to mind. Instead, she gave him a quick hug. From the look on his face when she stepped away, she thought he understood what she wanted to tell him.

"Come on, let's get these horses fed," he said, smiling. The sounds of horses whinnying, snorting, and stomping in their stalls echoed throughout the stable and diverted away any potential awkwardness that could have occurred in the moment.

After the horses had all been turned out, River went to the office to call Diva's previous owner.

"It's quite a story," River said when he joined Sierra mucking stalls. "I talked to Amy, the stable owner's daughter. Diva was her horse. She told me Diva's dam had some kind of an abscess or something and couldn't nurse her, so Amy took charge of the filly and bottle-fed her. They became really attached to each other. Amy started to cry when I told her about Diva's behavior and she thinks Diva is homesick and missing her.

"She said Crystal's father made a very generous offer for Diva, more money than her parents felt like they could turn down. Diva wasn't even for sale. Amy just happened to be jumping Diva in the arena when Tess, Crystal, and her father came to look at other horses they had for sale. When Tess saw Diva she was immediately impressed and then Crystal wasn't interested in looking any further."

"How horrible," Sierra empathized. *Imagine if I were forced to sell Fiel!*

"Yeah, I feel really bad for her. I promised her I'll stay with Diva as long as necessary and I'll stay in touch with her to let her know how she's doing."

"You're going to stay all night again?"

"I think I have to, at least for awhile…as long as it takes."

"Crystal is the one who should stay all night with Diva," Sierra stated emphatically, tossing a pitchfork-full of wet shavings into the cart.

River burst out laughing and Sierra joined in as an image of Crystal in silk pajamas fussing around in a pile of horse blankets with a look of disgust on her face, came to mind.

The following week, River slept every night outside of Diva's stall. For whatever reason, as long as she could see or smell his presence, she ate heartily, and finished all her grain and hay.

"She's only been back on her feed for a week," River grumbled. It was the first Saturday of March, and the day of the cross country clinic. He and Sierra were tacking up Diva and Silver in the crossties. Katrina was preparing her own mare, Calliope, in the third crosstie bay. Moose and Minstrel had already been tacked up and waited in their stalls. "She lost some weight and conditioning and they should not put her through this clinic."

Sierra half-listened, knowing he did not expect a reply. He had been grumbling all morning, in a foul mood. She was used to his ill humor, and knew him well enough now to know that it was usually triggered by his worry over a horse. She shared his concern and hoped with all her heart that no disaster would befall Diva or for that matter, any of the horses today.

The clinic would take place in the back fields of Pegasus where permanent jumps had been constructed; enough jumps to practice over full cross country courses from beginner novice to intermediate level. The jumps were typical of those found in eventing courses including logs, railroad ties, stone wall, chicken coop, a bank, ditch, and even a water jump. During the winter, Manuel and River reinforced or rebuilt jumps that needed repair, and replaced a few so there would always be some new obstacles. This year, they had built a preliminary level ramp and a flower box jump that had been filled with colorful plastic flowers.

It had rained all night and continued to drizzle. The footing would be muddy in places and visibility might be impaired. These were conditions that often occurred at events, so would provide excellent practice.

Loud voices mixed with laughter could be heard over the click of the heels of riding boots as a group entered the stable coming toward the crosstie bays. Crystal and Gloria came into view along with Justin, and Gloria's boyfriend, Greg. Luke was also with them.

"There she is," Crystal announced, pointing out her new horse to the others, who responded with the appropriate compliments they knew she expected.

"Sierra, you have the wrong bridle," Gloria stated as she came up to survey the preparations of her own horse. "I want the pelham bit with a running martingale." Sierra was buckling on Silver's usual snaffle bridle. Frowning, she slipped it off, and put his halter back on so she could exchange bridles.

"If you would quit yanking on his mouth every time you land from a jump, you wouldn't need that bit," River said, unable to control his irritation.

Gloria rounded on him. "Stay out of what isn't your business," she snapped back angrily. "Tess wants me to use the pelham. I am so tired of you thinking you know more than Tess."

River turned from tightening Diva's girth to glare back at her. He was about to retort when Sierra made a noise drawing his attention. She frowned at him, silently asking him not to cause trouble. River held his tongue and turned back to the saddle girth. Sierra took a deep breath of relief and slipped away to the tack room to change bridles.

"Sierra," Luke trailed after her into the tack room.

"Hi, Luke," she responded blandly. She wondered if he had come today as the friend of Justin and Greg, or if it was to see her.

"Are you riding today?"

"Yes," she answered, not offering him any encouragement. She hung up the snaffle bridle, took down the pelham, and a running martingale.

"Sierra, I…"

"Luke, I can't talk right now; I'm busy," she cut him off curtly. She had too much to do and concentrate on right now to make the effort to be polite when she was just feeling annoyed. She hurried back to the crossties, leaving Luke behind.

River had finished bridling Diva and handed off the reins to Crystal. Then he helped Sierra put on and adjust the new bridle and martingale on Silver. Gloria stood by with folded arms and tight-pressed lips, impatient and annoyed that Crystal and the boys had left, not waiting for her.

We're all in great moods today, Sierra noted to herself sardonically as she handed off Silver's reins. Gloria led him forcefully away to catch up with the others, jerking on Silver's mouth. He obediently followed but held his ears back.

Taking in deep breaths and rolling her shoulders to loosen up her own irritability, Sierra resolved to have a more positive attitude now that she could give all her attention to her own mount. She knew how much her emotional state would transmit to Minstrel.

"Those are two very tolerant and forgiving horses," River said, shaking his head as he watched the tail end of Silver and ahead of him, Diva. Sierra looked at him and their eyes met; and they smiled at each other, knowing they had been thinking similar thoughts.

At last all horses and riders were mounted and warming up around the perimeter of the field. Minstrel had picked up the atmosphere of excitement and his muscles bunched and tensed beneath her. His attention focused on the other horses, he fought against Sierra; shaking his head against her hold, and his gaits choppy with his neck stiff. *Is this what he'll be like at a show?* Sierra realized how fortunate she had been with Fala and Fiel, the only horses she had competed with; both who listened to her in spite of the distractions.

"Push him forward in trot." River came up alongside her on Moose. "Make him keep pace with us." As usual, River appeared to be melded onto his horse's back, the two of them moving as one; but Sierra knew he was in total control. "Every time you half-halt with the reins, push him with your legs…that's right." He rode alongside her, coaching every stride in a quiet voice. "Stay in two-point but use your center muscles to keep him from pulling you forward…good. Keep your weight in your heels."

Minstrel flicked his ears and dropped his head into the bit for the first time, tuning into his rider. With River's coaching, Sierra regained control.

"We're going to make a big circle around the next jump; once at trot, and then canter. But bring him right back to trot after one round. Just follow Moose; we're going to keep circling and changing gaits and directions so that he can't anticipate what you want. We're distracting him with work so that he has to pay attention to you."

Sierra followed River, pleased with the results of his strategy. She found that by pushing Minstrel forward rather than fighting to hold him back, it was easier to regain control. She remembered how River had once told her that a horse's reaction to stress is flight, and the best way to get horses to relax is to push them into exercises that work their muscles.

"Watch out for the mud just ahead," River called over his shoulder. "See if you can leg-yield him to the right and around the mud."

Sierra pushed her weight deeper into her right stirrup and pressed her left leg against Minstrel's side. He obediently moved laterally, and they trotted on safely past the slick spot.

"Good," River called out from where he had halted a few paces ahead. "You've got his attention. Let's gallop in a wide perimeter. If he goes too fast, remember to push your weight down and back, but keep your legs on him every time you use the reins."

Sierra nodded and watched Moose turn and jump into a gallop, as usual without an obvious signal from River. She allowed Minstrel to transition up and followed Moose two lengths behind as she concentrated on using her aids of weight and legs every time she used the reins. Finally, she felt like she was a partner with her mount.

"Slow down!" Tess called out through a megaphone. "Watch the footing. Okay, rein them in and back to me."

The riders brought their horses down to trot and then to walk with varying levels of difficulty and resistance and then milled around Tess at a walk.

"The conditions today are great for practice because this is often what you will find at an event. You all have got to learn to maintain control, so that's what we are going to focus on today. Cindy, you could have had a bad fall when you hit that muddy spot. You have to walk your course and know the conditions."

"I saw the mud," Cindy replied. "I just couldn't turn him away."

"Exactly, he was on the tail of the horse in front of you and that's also very dangerous. You have no business out on a course if you aren't the master." Tess surveyed the group around her, mentally adjusting her plan for the conditions and the amount of control she noted in each rider. "These are the jumps I want you to take for the first round." Tess described and pointed out eight obstacles. "They are all beginner novice to novice level jumps, so even if you are riding at a higher level this year, this is where we're going to start since most of your horses haven't jumped outside an arena since last fall. Any questions?" When no one had anything to ask, Tess said, "River is going to take Moose over the course first to demonstrate. I want you all to pay close attention to how he stays in control and rates his horse between the jumps."

River moved Moose away from the group and down a slight hill, picking up a posting trot. He circled and transitioned to canter half way around the circle and then headed for the first obstacle. Sierra marveled at how easy he made it look to ride the big thoroughbred that had terrified her when she had to trail ride him in the past. Moose's ears pricked forward and they galloped fluidly around the course, taking each jump well in stride and to all appearances, effortlessly. Tess kept up a running commentary, pointing out where River sat back to slow down for a turn, where he veered off to avoid the mud, and how he approached each jump for the correct take-off. River finished the course and then without any obvious signals, brought Moose down to a walk as he came back to the group.

The onlookers clapped in appreciation. "Wonderful ride," one of the observers said amid similar comments from the others. River smiled at Sierra as he brought Moose alongside Minstrel. Diva whinnied, looking at River as if to say, 'why aren't you riding me?' Crystal scowled and jerked a rein to turn Diva's head away.

"Thank you; good ride," Tess stated and then reviewed once again with the group how River had handled each obstacle. "Anything you want to add, River?"

"Um, watch the footing right after the coop," he said after thinking a minute. "Stay to the left."

"Okay…questions?" Tess looked around and then directed, "Sierra, you ride next; Katrina, after Sierra."

"Are you finished with me?" River asked.

"Yes, you may be excused," Tess said, turning her attention to Sierra, starting down the hill.

Sierra felt her nerves tighten, the same as an actual show, with everyone watching. Minstrel threw his head up and snorted loudly, as much as to say, 'you're nervous, so I'm wary.'

"Sorry, it's okay," Sierra murmured to him and blew out breaths in rhythm with his trotting stride as she descended the hill and started her circle. She circled twice, allowing both herself and her mount to settle, and as he dropped his head into the bit, she signaled for canter. She forgot about the others as she turned toward the first jump, concentrating on Minstrel and maintaining an even gallop. She completed the course, trying to duplicate all that River had done; sitting back to slow for turns, careful at the coop, and adjusting Minstrel's pace for correct take-off at each obstacle. As she returned to the group, the onlookers honored her also with applause.

But it was River's smile and his nod of approval that meant the most to her. He stood at Moose's head, having remained to watch her ride before he returned to the stable and chores.

"Good ride," Tess commented. "A little slow, however. You could have picked up the pace between the stone wall and the bank. But I'd rather see you err on the side of caution, especially in these conditions."

Sierra nodded in response to Tess's comments; pleased that she had nothing more negative to say.

One by one, Tess sent each rider around the course and commented on their performance. Katrina on Calliope appeared to take the jumps well in stride, but several times she needed to bring the mare all the way to trot to regain control. In spite of the harsher bit and martingale, Gloria still had a difficult time keeping Silver from rushing; a habit he had developed as he was faced with bigger jumps. Most of the other riders had at least one refusal or run-out, with Tess coaching them on how to correct the problems.

The only other clear round was achieved by Crystal on Diva. Sierra had watched River ride Diva and take her over jumps inside the arena, and recognized the mare's scope. But what surprised her, was Diva's tolerance of Crystal's heavy hands and how she managed to negotiate the course in fine style, in spite of her rider. It seemed at last Crystal had a mount that suited her.

"Okay, I've seen improvement in all your horses. I expect most of you will do very well this year," Tess announced two and a half hours later. Everyone had completed the initial course of jumps and then Tess had coached over individual obstacles. She finished the clinic by having each rider complete another round of jumps, adding more difficult obstacles according to each rider's level. "We'll debrief in the lounge after you have cared for your horses. And don't forget to pick up a copy of the competition calendar before you leave today."

Riders dismounted, milled around Tess asking questions and talking to each other, discussing the clinic.

"That was fun!" Katrina exclaimed as she dismounted and brought Calliope alongside Sierra, who had already dismounted and was loosening Minstrel's girth. "I'm really looking forward to training level this year. What level are you taking Minstrel?"

"Tess is going to have us start out at novice, but if he does okay, she'll move us up to training this season."

"Those last two obstacles were training level heights, and it sure looked like Minstrel handled them just fine," Katrina stated encouragingly.

"Yeah, it felt that way. Calliope didn't look like she had any trouble either. I bet you two are going to have a great season," Sierra countered.

"I hope. I'm kind of worried about the dressage test. We have to do lengthenings."

"I know. But I think it's great you're taking Calliope to the dressage show in two weeks. That's got to help."

The two girls led their horses back toward the stable, discussing the jumps in the clinic and what they might expect in the upcoming season.

"Shouldn't Crystal and Gloria dismount and lead their horses up the hill?" Katrina asked, just now noticing that those two were still mounted and passing the riders leading their horses.

"Of course they should," Sierra answered. Crystal was talking animatedly to Gloria, waving her hands around even though she held Diva's reins. Justin walked alongside Crystal's stirrup and Greg and Luke followed behind the two horses. Then she saw River descending the hill toward the group and even from this distance, she could tell he was not happy. "Uh oh," she said worriedly.

Katrina also noticed and added her own, "Oh dear."

River walked up to Diva and placed a hand on her bridle rein near the bit. "Get off," he ordered.

"Don't tell me…" Crystal started to retort.

"I know, I know," River interrupted in an acerbic tone. "Don't tell you what to do." He met Crystal's demeaning look. "Do you want me to take care of your horse or not?"

"Hey, you can't talk to her like that," Justin cut in.

River glanced at him with an icy and challenging look. Justin dropped his gaze.

Crystal looked like she wanted to kick him in the face. Then she took in a deep breath and huffed, "It's what we pay you to do." In a voice loud enough to be sure those nearby heard and would have no delusions as to who was in charge, she said to Gloria, "It's so hard to get good help these days."

Gloria laughed as she knew Crystal expected her to, and they both dismounted and flung their reins off to River. They proceeded up the hill with the boys behind them. Justin and Greg kept their eyes straight ahead, but Luke at least gave River a weak smile on passing.

"One of these days…" Katrina said in an ominous tone.

Sierra let out her breath in relief. "I thought for sure Justin was going to start a fight."

"Justin?" Katrina laughed. "No, Justin would never fight with someone like River. He's too much of a coward. I'm more worried about what mean, sneaky things Crystal will think up for him to do behind River's back."

"Yes, you're right about that," Sierra said in a pensive tone. "Do you remember how Gunsmoke reared and kicked out right before River's demonstration ride at the championship last fall? And how Fiel acted the same way right before our stadium jumping?"

"Yeah, that's right," Katrina replied. "I do remember that, and how strange it was for either of those horses to react that way."

"Right; I think it's because of something Justin did. I asked Luke and he said he didn't know, but he did tell me that Justin has this device he uses to give people electric shocks."

"Ahh; that explains a lot," Katrina said knowingly. "He has been going around school giving kids shocks…some joke."

The girls reached the stable and brought their horses into the crossties where River was grooming Diva. He had Silver in the wash stall to give them room.

"Do you think she could just once give a little to her horse?" River grumbled, although he kept the tone of his voice soothing as he brushed Diva's neck and gently down the length of her back. "Especially when she worked so well for her today."

"What do you expect from Crystal?" Katrina responded.

"It's not like Diva and Silver can't carry them up the hill. But why not dismount and lead them up as a reward? Let them know they did well?" River continued to complain as he bent down to start working on Diva's legs.

"Hi, guys," Luke greeted, coming up to the crossties. "Want some help?"

Both Sierra and Katrina looked up, but River remained bent over, ignoring him.

"No, we're fine…but thanks," Sierra answered, since Katrina looked to her for an indication of whether she wanted Luke around or not.

"Really, I'd like to help," Luke persisted, coming up to Minstrel and stroking his nose. "Just tell me what to do."

Sierra wished he would leave. But Luke stood there with an eager grin on his face, and she found she could not be outwardly rude to him. "All right, maybe you could carry the saddles and bridles to the tack room. Just set the saddles down on the pommel and hang the bridles on the cleaning hook."

"Sure, that's easy enough. What's the pommel?"

Sierra sighed inwardly and pulled Minstrel's saddle from the rail and showed Luke how to set it down. "Like this," she said.

"I can do that. Where's the tack room?"

"It's there." Sierra pointed to the open door over to the left.

"It's the room with the saddles and bridles in it," Katrina added glibly.

“Oh, I see it,” Luke answered unperturbed. He strode away with the saddle over his arm.

“He still has a crush on you,” Katrina said when Luke was out of hearing range.

“We’re just friends,” Sierra stated.

“Maybe you’re just friends…”

14 DRESSAGE

There are all sorts of tact in the equestrian field: that of the hands, that of the legs, that of the seat, and quite simply, the tact of the head. – Nuno Oliveira, *Reflections on Equestrian Art*

Training and conditioning for both horses and riders increased after the clinic. Tess worked out schedules for each competition horse that consisted of dressage work, cross country trail work on hills, and arena jumping. At the beginning of training, each horse had three days of flat work, one day of jumping, two days of trail work, and one day off to rest and recover. Within six to eight weeks, the schedule would increase to alternating one to two days of jumping per week, and three days of trail work.

Horses that stayed in training with Tess through the winter began the show season already in good condition; for she had Sierra and River ride them out even through the cold months. During the off season, most of the trail work consisted of walking up and down hills, but also occasional short intervals of trotting and cantering.

Beginning in March, Tess outlined for each horse how many minutes of walking, trotting, and cantering or galloping each one should do on the trail. By the end of two months, the very fit horses competing at training level or higher, might be up to two hours of trail work with up to six minute intervals of gallop. Horses brought to Tess for training at the beginning of the season usually were not as fit. Those horses might be kept to a walk for the first two weeks, and encouraged to stretch their necks forward and down as they climbed hills – great for building up muscles.

Mornings, Tess schooled the horses either in dressage or arena jumping. When River arrived after school, she had him work the horses she didn't have time for that day. He usually could fit in three rides each afternoon; either in arena work or on the trail. He saved the longer cross country rides for the weekend.

Sierra rode one assigned horse after school as well as Fiel. River continued to coach her at least once a week on Fiel in dressage, and if he had time, also on Minstrel, both in dressage and jumping. She and River tried to coordinate so they could ride out on trails together. It wasn't always possible after school, but every weekend, they planned their rides so they were mounted on horses of near equal fitness levels, and with similar conditioning schedules. Those rides were always Sierra's favorites.

Crystal and Gloria rode twice a week in lessons and at Tess's insistence, maybe would show up on a weekend to ride out on the trail. The conditioning of Diva and Silver ultimately depended on Sierra and River. Katrina rode almost every day, taking two lessons a week from Tess, and then working on her own on the flat and conditioning trail rides.

Sierra could hardly wait for the first horse trial of the season in May. In the meantime, there was the dressage show to anticipate.

Since turning sixteen, River had earned his driver's license, and Manuel had been taking him out to practice hauling a horse trailer. The Saturday of the dressage show, River drove the rig with Tess in the front seat next to him. Sierra and Katrina sat in the back repeating to each other their memorized dressage tests.

"Do you know where to turn?" Tess asked after directing River off the highway onto a side road.

"It's the second right coming up," he answered.

"Yes; don't forget to start slowing way before the turn," she instructed. "The idea is to never have to apply the brakes suddenly."

"Umhm."

"Watch the ruts…slow down!"

Why is she nagging him? Sierra wondered. She thought River was doing a great job driving, and he had already slowed and veered away from each pothole of the rough road, even before Tess said anything. *Perhaps she's nervous with him driving.*

River slowed way ahead of the turn, pulled into the show grounds and parked, all the while Tess kept up a stream of warnings and instruction.

The first thing Sierra noticed after they had unloaded the horses, was the very different atmosphere of a dressage show compared with a horse trial. Although an underlying sense of excitement still pervaded the air, there was nowhere near the bustle of activity and noise, and fewer horses. Competitors tended to trailer in with just enough time to prepare for and ride their scheduled tests, and then leave. At a horse trial, all the competitors arrived in the morning and remained for the entire day of the show.

Since Sierra, Katrina, and River were riding at several different levels, they would spend most of the day at the show, so had rented stalls for the five horses. They removed the shipping gear and settled the horses into their temporary quarters.

"You have enough time to hand walk Calliope, Minstrel, and Felicity once around the grounds before you need to get ready for warm-up," Tess announced. "I'll stay here to keep an eye on Penny and Fiel."

Calliope and Minstrel, both veterans of many horse shows, looked around with interest at their surroundings, exhibiting a heightened level of excitement, but well under control. Felicity however, a baby at three years old, snorted, pranced, and half-reared at the end of her lead. River patiently allowed her to express herself, as long as she didn't pull against him. He talked to her soothingly until she finally managed to walk instead of jig.

"You're going to have your hands full with her," Katrina warned, her eyes wide at Felicity's antics. Calliope had already settled down and lost interest in her surroundings; drawn more to the potential grazing opportunities of the grassy areas.

"She'll be okay," River murmured, talking to the filly rather than Katrina.

This was Sierra's first time out with Minstrel, and she was pleased that he had also readily settled down. She hoped he would remain this calm when she rode him at a horse trial.

By the time they returned to the stalls, Felicity had settled into an even walk. But as River finished grooming her and began to tack her up, she knew something different was about to happen, and she seemed to have lost her ability to stand still. She swung her body from side to side and stepped forward and back from where she had been tied to a ring inside the stall, and whinnied at every horse that passed by.

River never lost his patience with her, but continued to talk to her soothingly; and gently but insistently manipulated her to move where he wanted her as he put on saddle and bridle. At last he had her ready and led her to the warm-up area with the others coming to watch.

In the warm-up ring, Felicity threw her head up at every passing horse and shied in every corner of the ring. Tess called out instructions every time River passed near where they watched at the rail, but he kept his attention focused on the nervous filly, ignoring Tess.

"I don't see how he's ever going to get her through the test," Katrina whispered to Sierra.

But by the time the ring steward called River's number as on deck, he had the filly trotting with her neck forward and round, stretching into the bit, and at least appearing to be in a more relaxed frame. As he brought her back to walk, he gave her all the reins, encouraging her to stretch even more as he walked her out of the arena. Sierra doubted she would have had the courage to give the filly that much leeway. But Felicity did stretch forward, and River stroked the side of her neck, wet with nervous sweat, as he walked her to the test ring.

He was halfway there when someone walking by suddenly raised a hand carrying a whip to wave in greeting to someone beyond, and shouted out the person's name.

Idiot, Sierra thought.

Felicity half-reared and spun, preparing to take off at a run from the perceived danger. Sierra sucked in her breath in alarm and she heard Katrina gasp out. Other onlookers exclaimed their surprise and one woman unabashedly said, "Watch what you're doing," to the person with the whip.

But River had quickly gathered up reins, and mostly with his seat, brought Felicity back around and had her stepping forward. She snorted and jigged into the test arena.

"How unfortunate," another bystander commented.

But by the time River had walked Felicity half way around the outside barriers of the actual test ring, she had stretched once again into her bit, her ears flicking as she listened to her rider.

The judge rang a bell, the signal that River had forty-five seconds to enter the ring. He touched Felicity's neck and asked for trot. He continued around the outside barrier, and then entered the ring down the center line to halt at *X*, and salute the judge. After the judge's returning salute, River moved Felicity forward and into the simple movements of the test. She seemed a different horse from the flighty animal of minutes ago. Flicking her ears and swishing her tail rhythmically, she moved energetically and in a relaxed frame. She performed the simple movements of the test; twenty-meter circles in each direction at trot and canter, a ground-covering free walk, and stretched her neck generously in a trot circle when River gave the reins. Only once, when a movement at the judge's table caused the cloth to waver, did she lift her head slightly and roll her eyes. But River talked to her through his seat, legs, and hands and regained her attention.

A round of applause congratulated them as River gave the reins and Felicity walked calmly from the ring.

"Well done," Tess exclaimed as River rode up to where she and the two girls stood watching.

"She did very well," River agreed as he dismounted and patted her neck. "But she would do much better if you waited a year before exposing her to all this."

"She'll be fine," Tess scoffed. "It's good for her and each time out she'll be more settled."

"If she doesn't hurt herself or get an ulcer," he grumbled as he led her back to the stalls.

"River, that was so awesome," Katrina exclaimed as she and Sierra walked with him.

"Yes, she really settled down in the test and did great," Sierra agreed. "I don't think anyone could have calmed her down the way you did."

River nodded without further comment.

"Okay, girls, time for warm-up for first level tests," Tess stated after Felicity had been cared for and back in her stall. "River, you can hold Fiel while Sierra warms up Minstrel. Sierra, as soon as you finish Minstrel's test, give him to River and start warming up Fiel. And girls, remember to halt at *X* and salute the judge," she reminded them. "That's different from your eventing tests."

"Tess seems really up tight today," Sierra commented to Katrina, "more than usual."

"Yeah, I think it's because she expects Penny's owners to show up this afternoon for his test. I heard they actually had tickets for the last Olympics, and were really impressed with the dressage. Mrs. Galensburg especially wants to own an Olympic winner, and she thinks Pendragon might be a candidate. They have tons of money and I know Tess wants to do everything possible to keep them as clients."

"How do you know all this?"

"Actually from my parents; they were at some party with Crystal's folks and Mr. Douglas was going on about the Galensburgs. Well, catering to them can only help Pegasus financially."

"Hmm, I guess."

"I think Tess wants to get River to the point where he qualifies for an Olympic trial."

"Does he know that?"

"Probably not." They both laughed sardonically.

Riding first level, test one, was great practice for the similar dressage test they would ride for training level in eventing. In both tests, the circles were smaller, fifteen meters rather than twenty meters, which required more bend and balance; and in test one, ten-meter half circles at the trot. The horse would also be asked to lengthen the stride in trot and canter; pushing forward from the hind end as opposed to becoming faster in the gait.

It was the lengthenings that especially worried Katrina. She had been struggling with them in her lessons with Tess. Once or twice she believed she had achieved a few true strides of lengthening, but most of the time, Calliope just trotted faster, becoming unbalanced.

Sierra had an advantage in that Fiel was well trained in dressage movements all the way to the upper levels. He knew how to lengthen his stride and with River's coaching, all Sierra needed to do was learn how to ask him. When she worked Minstrel on the flat, she thought of what she did and how it felt on Fiel, and was able to get Minstrel to lengthen.

After riding Minstrel in test one, Sierra then rode Fiel at first level, test three. In addition to the trot and canter lengthenings, she also needed to ride leg-yields, and counter canter. Again, since Fiel knew these movements, it was Sierra who needed to learn the proper communication so that he understood what she wanted him to do.

They had finished caring for the horses and had a two-hour break before River needed to warm up Pendragon. He would be riding third level tests two and three. They sat in front of the stalls on canvas chairs, eating lunch. Tess had left to pick up their test results.

"Here she comes," Katrina announced apprehensively. "I don't know if I want to see my score."

Tess arrived and handed out the score sheets. "Not bad for your first dressage show," she said encouragingly.

Sierra looked first at Minstrel's score; not great at fifty-eight percent, but she felt it was fair. She knew he was leaning to the outside on the ten-meter trot circle to the right, and he had fallen onto the forehand in both canter departs. But at least they had done well in the lengthenings; a score of seven for the trot in both directions, and a score of six for the canter to the right and seven for the canter to the left. It looked like the judge thought they needed more impulsion at times (probably true), and Minstrel tended to fall onto the forehand in many of the transitions.

Then she looked at Fiel's test and broke into a smile at her score of sixty-five percent. The judge's comments were mostly positive and she had given them many sixes and sevens, and even one eight for the trot circle where she gave the reins to allow Fiel to stretch down into the bit. The negative comments were about maintaining the bend on her smaller trot circles; both scores of only five. One comment said, 'tilted to the outside', and another, 'stiff in back'. These were similar comments about her circles in Minstrel's test, and perhaps the problem was with her, the rider.

She looked up and noticed Katrina's crestfallen expression.

"It's what I expected," Katrina said mournfully. "Fifty-one percent; we got fours on our trot-lengthenings and fives on our canter. At least we got sixes for our last halt and for the free walk.

"You know what you'll need to work on over the next few weeks," Tess said.

"How did Felicity do?" Sierra asked.

In answer, River handed her his test.

"Wow, seventy-eight percent!" Sierra read out loud. "You got all sevens and eights, except for one six."

"When Felicity shied just a little bit at the judge's table," Tess said scornfully. "That's really splitting hairs for a training level test."

River placed first and far ahead of the second-place horse and rider. Sierra was pleased that she placed second on Fiel, and fifth on Minstrel. Katrina did not place at all.

"They are just finishing the second level tests now," Tess announced. "Time to get Penny warmed up."

Sierra and Katrina helped River groom Pendragon, and then tacked him up while Tess fussed over River's attire.

"Why didn't you get a haircut?" Tess complained as she used a clothes brush on River's jacket. "I told you to cut your hair."

"I did," he answered.

She snorted and said sarcastically, "Which hair?"

"I trimmed it."

"River, you need a professional haircut, and short; above your ears so it looks tidy underneath a helmet."

"I can pull it back," he argued, reaching up to grab his shaggy hair.

"Stop," Tess ordered. She pulled out a comb and aggressively went through River's hair before fastening it back in a short tail, ignoring his protests. Then she fussed with his shirt collar, straightened his tie, and smoothed the jacket lapels. "Appearance is very important in dressage; a well-turned-out rider compliments the elegance of the movements. River, you could look so nice if you'd put forth a little effort. You're very nice looking…like your father."

"I don't look like my father," River snapped back.

Tess huffed, "Yes, you do. Just because you don't get along with him is no reason to despise how he looks."

"I look like my mother," River stated in a tone that sounded like a warning.

Tess started to respond and then thought better of it. "Penny's owners will be here soon and I need you to make a good impression."

As she spoke, a couple strolled up to their group.

Tess greeted, "Hello, Mr. and Mrs. Galensburg. I'm glad you made it."

"Good afternoon," Mr. Galensburg politely responded.

His wife did not look at Tess or any of the others, but focused on Pendragon, coming up to stroke a gloved finger along his neck as if checking for dust. Dressed in tailored brown slacks with short, fur-topped boots, a burgundy wool vest over a silk, cream-colored blouse with a coordinated scarf, a brown leather blazer, and accented with expensive large-stoned jewelry; Mrs. Galensburg's wardrobe confirmed her moneyed status.

"How is Pendragon today?" she finally asked.

"He's ready," Tess answered with an ingratiating smile.

"I'm disappointed that he is entered only at third level."

"I'm sure he'll be ready for fourth level soon. I want him to have on record better third level scores than he achieved last year," Tess responded diplomatically. (She didn't tell her client that she wanted the scores for River as well, so that he could earn points for rider's awards.)

"So you've been saying," Mrs. Galensburg sniffed.

"Um, Mrs. Galensburg, this is River Girard. He's the rider I told you about."

The woman stared at River and her eyes opened wide in shock as her lips compressed and the corners of her mouth sank. "He's just a little boy," she declared.

"He won his class this morning with a score of seventy-eight percent," Tess defended.

"Then I expect a better score on Pendragon," she stated as she grabbed her husband's arm, turning him away and said without looking back, "we'll be watching from the stands. Come, Harold." The couple marched away.

"Horrors," Katrina breathed out.

"I'm ready," River said, sounding very calm and unperturbed.

"Never mind her," Tess said. She handed River a pair of white cotton gloves.

"I hate these clothes," he said under his breath as he put on the gloves and then took Penny's reins from Sierra to lead him to the warm-up ring.

"He is so handsome," Katrina whispered to Sierra as they trailed behind.

"Who...River?" Sierra asked and scrunched up her face at Katrina.

"Of course."

Sierra looked at her friend from the corner of her eye and noted the way she watched River with a look of worship on her face. *Oh my God; she has a crush on him!*

River warmed up Penny with a series of trot and canter circles, ignoring Tess's insistence that he at least execute a few flying changes of lead. When his number was called and he left for the test arena, Tess and the girls hurried to the stands and found seats behind the Galensburgs.

"Pendragon warmed up well," Tess informed them. Mr. Galensburg smiled blandly, but his wife ignored the comment. She fixed her eyes on her horse as he entered the ring.

When the judge rang the bell, River touched his fingers to Penny's neck and the big bay entered at a collected trot, his neck arched regally. After the salute, River moved him forward and into the movements of the test, all his communication invisible to the onlookers.

"What a magnificent horse," someone nearby commented. Sierra noticed Mrs. Galensburg lift her chin proudly.

When River completed the test and left the ring, the onlookers in the stands burst into enthusiastic applause, and Sierra heard more comments of 'talented horse', and 'beautiful ride'.

"What do you think?" Tess asked Mrs. Galensburg, smiling in expectation.

"I want to see the score."

Sierra could not believe the woman. Her horse had performed exceptionally well and the obvious appreciation of the audience confirmed that. If Pendragon had been her own horse, she would be rushing down to praise him right now.

They remained in the stands as there was only one horse between River's next test on Pendragon; third level, test three. It didn't seem possible for Pendragon to perform any better than his first test, yet the big bay seemed to have tapped into an inner source of pride and grace, for he and River danced through the movements in complete harmony. They finished the test again to the most enthusiastic applause given to any horse that day.

"We're going to help River," Sierra stated to Tess, and she and Katrina left the stands, leaving Tess to deal with her clients.

"That was so amazing," Katrina gushed.

'Yeah," Sierra agreed. "Can you believe that Mrs. Galensburg? Why do people like that even own a horse?"

"For the glory and recognition," Katrina answered logically. "It's sort of like art collectors. In a way, she's like Crystal."

"I think you're right."

They found River where he had dismounted amid a small group who had come up to compliment his ride and ask questions. He nodded at the girls and they joined him to take Penny back to the stalls.

Mrs. Galensburg didn't need to worry. Pendragon earned a score of eighty-five percent on his first test, and eighty-seven percent on the second, and won second and first place since both tests were in the same class. Sierra thought Mrs. Galensburg might at least come over to congratulate River, and maybe give Penny a pat and a carrot. She never came by, and Sierra caught a glimpse of the couple walking toward the parking area, proudly carrying their ribbons and trophy.

Later, with the horses loaded in the trailer and ready to return home, Sierra and Katrina dashed to the restroom. On the way back, Katrina said to Sierra, "You've only been riding two years but you already ride better than me."

The comment surprised Sierra, who had never really thought about how her riding compared with the others at the stable. She thought for a moment before she replied, "I've been very lucky to have two great teachers."

"Yeah, and I know you're not including Tess as one of them," Katrina said in a bitter tone. She stopped suddenly and grabbed Sierra by the arm. "Do you think River would give me lessons?"

"I don't know," Sierra answered honestly, but also surprised. She had always assumed that Katrina along with Crystal and Gloria, thought they had the best instruction from Tess, with her show career and reputation to back her up. "Why don't you ask him?"

"If I ask him I'm sure he'll say no. I was wondering if maybe you would ask him."

"Katrina, I…" Sierra wanted to say that Katrina just needed to speak for herself, but then she visualized the scene. She knew River still thought of Katrina as one of Crystal's friends and did not like her. But if she were to intervene on Katrina's behalf, explain that Katrina was not in Crystal's circle anymore, he might…especially if she pointed out that ultimately it would be for the benefit of Calliope. "Okay," she consented. "I'll mention it to him."

"Do more than just mention," Katrina pleaded.

"The thing is…" Sierra hesitated again. "Well, you'll have to work it out with Tess if you quit taking lessons from her."

Katrina had an almost sick expression on her face. "I know."

right leg over and settled gently into the saddle. Cory jerked his head up, his eyes wide; but otherwise he only flicked his ears and didn't move from where he stood. River immediately dismounted and both he and Sierra petted and praised Cory for his very good behavior.

From that time forward, River made rapid progress. After the first few times of only sitting in the saddle, he asked Sierra to lead Cory around. The next day, he asked Sierra to lunge Cory with him on his back. Then River gradually picked up the reins and gently began to use seat, leg, and hand aids. After another week and a half, River rode Cory independently around the arena.

"Are you riding Fiel out on the trail?" River asked Sierra as he brought Corazón into the crossties.

"Yeah, it's way too nice to ride inside," Sierra answered. It was Sunday in early April, and the promise of spring around the corner was evident in the clear blue sky, temperature in the mid-sixties, and birds singing their spring songs. She stepped back from buckling the saddle girth and looked over at River in the next bay. "You want to take Cory on the trail?"

He nodded. "Fiel is level-headed and should be a good influence for our first time out of the arena…if you're up for us coming with you."

"Of course, that's great!" Sierra helped River brush Cory and tack him up, and then they led their horses out of the stable toward the field.

Both horses held their heads high and stepped out energetically, enjoying the feel of spring as much as the humans. River whistled, and Storm trotted up with her nose quivering, looking forward to a squirrel chase.

"*No hay problema*, easy does it," River soothed his excited horse as he quickly mounted from the mounting block and moved him a few steps away while Sierra mounted Fiel. The black snorted and jigged and pranced in place, finding it difficult to stand still. River had his hands full as he played with the reins to keep Cory focused and sat deep in the saddle with his legs providing reassurance against Cory's sides. "You lead out," he asked Sierra, "do you mind keeping to a walk?"

"Not at all," she answered and moved Fiel down the incline across the field and onto the trail.

Fiel truly was the perfect horse to set an example for his excited and green companion. He walked with energy but calm manners, looking around happily with his ears flicking. When Cory jumped or shied at objects, Fiel laid his ears back and snorted, as if to say, 'don't be silly'. Sierra could feel how much Fiel wanted to jump forward into a trot or gallop, but he obediently responded to Sierra's half-halts whenever he bunched his muscles to increase the pace. Before they were even a third of the way around the trail, it seemed both horses had settled into a relaxed walk.

"He's doing great!" Sierra commented over her shoulder at how well Cory was now behaving.

"Yeah, he's smart and he figures things out pretty quick," River replied. "Trail riding is going to be the best thing for him; both for his mind as well as building up his muscles. I think it's all I'm going to do with him this summer."

"Sounds like a good plan," Sierra agreed. "He certainly seems happy now."

"Yeah, he does. I'll just keep him to a walk for a few weeks and then start adding some trot work. I bet by the end of summer we should be galloping around this trail!"

Sierra laughed as she agreed, "I bet you will." She enjoyed hearing River make plans for his horse.

By the time they arrived back at the field, Cory acted as if he had been out on trails for years. He stood calmly as River dismounted, and then immediately dropped his head to graze, a contented and relaxed horse.

Sierra studied the black gelding from a fresh perspective as they led their horses back to the stable. Out in the open air she appreciated how his body had filled out with weight and muscle tone, and how his coat gleamed with health. He no longer had a wary, suspicious look in his eye, but looked on the world with interest and curiosity. She studied the points River had been trying to teach her about a horse's conformation; the straightness of his legs with even hocks as she watched him from the back, and the slope of his pasterns. She moved up closer alongside and admired the ample slope of his shoulder and deep chest. He had wide-set, intelligent eyes, fine ears, and a handsome tapered muzzle. He held his head in a natural arch with a wide open throatlatch. River had seen all these features in spite of his emaciated appearance. Now she too could recognize his exceptional breeding. An uncomfortable feeling settled in her stomach as she reasoned the horse must have been stolen. She didn't want to think of the possibility of his previous owner showing up to claim him.

After taking care of Fiel and Corazón, Sierra and River again rode out on Minstrel and Moose; but this time trotting and galloping at the prescribed intervals for their conditioning program. Then while Sierra rode Fala on the trail, River rode Pendragon in the arena, working on exercises to prepare the horse for moving up to fourth level. After that he rode Felicity, and then lunged a horse in training.

With their riding assignments completed, Sierra and River cleaned tack together, and then helped Manuel bring in horses for the night. With chores done, Sierra joined River in front of Diva's stall. They watched the mare bury her nose in her hay without once looking up at them.

"She's more interested in her hay now than you," Sierra commented.

"I think she finally feels at home. I left her last night while she was eating and she didn't even raise her head to say goodbye. And her hay was all gone this morning. She doesn't need me anymore."

"She still needs you," Sierra laughed. "Think about who owns her."

He just shook his head as they turned and walked out of the stable. He whistled for Storm.

"So, if you aren't staying with Diva, do you want to come over for dinner tonight?"

"Where is Storm?" River asked, as he scanned the stable yard, distracted by the absence of his dog in her usual places.

Sierra thought back to when she had last seen her. "You know, I don't think she came back from the trail when we rode Minstrel and Moose." She furrowed her brow, trying to picture if Storm had trailed after them in the field. She clearly remembered seeing her as they started out on their second trail ride, but honestly did not think she had seen here since.

River whistled again, and then called her name.

"Do you think she's still in the woods chasing squirrels?" Sierra asked.

"Not usually…but it is spring time," he said in a worried tone. "I'm going to look there."

"I'll come with you," Sierra offered.

They walked down the lane past the paddocks, with River whistling every few minutes and both of them calling her name. When they reached the slope of hill down to the field, River cried out, "There she is!"

Storm walked slowly toward them, her tail tucked in tightly and shaking her nose side to side every few minutes.

"Oh no," River groaned, watching her behavior.

"What's the matter with her?" Sierra asked, but it became evident a few minutes later as Storm came within a few yards. "Oh, yuk, oh," Sierra groaned, putting a hand up to cover her mouth and nose.

"Storm," River said in dismay, pushing her away as she tried to come up against his legs. "Were you chasing a black and white squirrel?"

"Skunk!" Sierra stated the obvious. They both burst out laughing uncontrollably, covering their noses, for Storm looked so dejected and even embarrassed with her head low and tail tucked.

"What are you going to do?" Sierra asked, as they turned back to the stable with Storm following.

"I'll have to give her a bath. I think there might be some special shampoo left over from the last time she chased a skunk."

"She's done this before?"

"A few years ago; I thought she learned her lesson, but I guess she forgot."

In a supply cabinet, River found what he was looking for; a half-full bottle of commercial skunk odor removal shampoo. "You don't have to help," River said, but felt very grateful when Sierra insisted that she would. They donned rubber coveralls that were used for bathing and clipping horses and then took Storm into the wash stall.

Amid laughing struggles with Storm (who did not think a bath was the answer to her distress), and getting almost as soaked as the dog, they worked the shampoo into her fur, rinsed, and then again and again until they emptied the bottle.

"Still stinks," River said, tossing the empty bottle into the trash.

"Let's try some of that really fragrant horse shampoo," Sierra suggested.

"I think the smell is coating the inside of my nose. I can't tell if she is less stinky or not," River said after they used the horse shampoo.

"I know what you mean," Sierra groaned. She leaned back on her heels and released her hold on the wet dog. Storm shook herself vigorously, spraying water all around and soaking their already wet coveralls, and they both jumped up, laughing.

"Well," River glanced over at Sierra, and suddenly he found himself very aware of how she looked just then, standing in her splashed coveralls with soapy water dripping off the ends of her braids. She had smudges of dirt on her cheek and bits of wet dog hair clung to her clothes. Her brown eyes shown in the bright light of the wash stall, and her cheeks were flushed a warm, pink color. *She is very pretty!* Sierra met his eyes, laughing, and he suddenly felt his own face flush with heat. To hide his embarrassment, he scooped a clump of soap suds from Sierra's sleeve and playfully set them on the tip of her nose.

"Hey," she protested, laughing harder, and she scooped up a handful of suds and retaliated by putting them on his chin. Soon they were in a full-fledged soap bubble fight, laughing at each other and at Storm, who wagged her tail happily, feeling reprieved by their antics.

"Very cute," a derisive voice announced.

Sierra and River both turned in surprise, their hands full of soap suds. Laila stood in the stall entryway with arms folded and wearing a bemused expression. She was dressed in her usual assortment of pierced jewelry and a long-sleeved black jersey tucked into a short black leather skirt, black tights, and chunky heeled black shoes.

"Laila!" River greeted, and he felt his face heat up again. "Hi."

She cocked her head to the side, "Hi, River."

He smiled and stepped toward her, feeling somehow embarrassed in front of Sierra.

"Where have you been?" Laila asked.

"Here," he replied lamely.

"Your aunt thinks you ran away again."

"No, um…I've been horse-sitting," he explained. He glanced at Sierra from the corner of his eye. He could think of nothing to say.

"Uh, River, I better get home," Sierra said quickly, and she stepped past Laila. "See you tomorrow."

"Bye, thanks for your help," he said to her retreating back. He turned his attention back to Laila. "Um…"

She laughed. "So you'd rather spend time with a horse than with me." She sounded amused, not angry.

"No! No, I wouldn't. It's just…" he fumbled for an explanation.

Laila stepped up to him and lifted his chin with a forefinger so he would have to meet her eyes. She smiled. "I'm not your girlfriend, remember? It's okay. You didn't return any of my calls, and I was a little worried that you might have run away."

"No, um, I'm glad to see you."

"Are you coming home tonight?"

"Yeah, I was just getting ready to leave."

"Shall I take you home?"

"Okay, yeah…good. I just need to shut out the lights and lock up."

"I'll wait for you in the car." She turned to go but said over her shoulder, "You stink!"

Sierra pedaled her bicycle home, her thoughts in a whirl. It had been so much fun helping River bathe Storm; and it had really surprised her when he started the soap suds fight. That had been fun too. In fact, her best times were at the stable working with River. Allison was her best friend at school, but she really thought of River as an equal best friend, and even more, as her big brother.

So why does it bother me that he left with that weird gothic girl? He had said 'just a friend' when she had asked about her the first time she showed up at the stable. *But he kissed her!* She wasn't sure if what bothered her was that he might have a girlfriend, or that he kept it a secret. "I don't care if he has a girlfriend," she said out loud. *Just not that girl! She doesn't like horses, she smokes, and she's just plain creepy.*

The cottage came into view and Sierra sighed, trying to shrug off her confused feelings. As she wheeled her bicycle into the garage, she noted a strange car in the driveway. *Who could that be?* Sierra and her mother rarely had visitors other than River, their landlords, and their lawyer Mr. Tanglewilde. *That's not the lawyer's car.* Sierra stepped into the utility room through the back door. She heard voices talking in the kitchen.

"Sierra," Pam greeted as her daughter entered. Pam sat at the kitchen table across from a man who looked to be around her mother's age; a pleasant-appearing man of medium height with light brown hair and blue eyes behind glasses. Eyes that Sierra immediately noted looked warmly at her mother. "I'd like you to meet Ron."

"Hi, Sierra," Ron greeted, rising from his chair and stretching out his hand.

"Nice to meet you," Sierra responded automatically as she shook his hand, feeling bewildered by his presence here.

"I've been trying to get a date with your mom for months," Ron explained. "She finally agreed to let me come over for dinner tonight."

Sierra looked at her mother and thought she detected a guilty look in her eyes.

"He is very persistent," Pam said sheepishly. "Anyway, Ron brought pizzas and all we have to do is heat them up. I made a salad. We're just waiting for you."

"I'll go get cleaned up," Sierra said and fled to the bathroom. *Betrayed!* Twice in one day; first by River and now her own mother! Sierra's emotions were a turmoil of hurt, disappointment, and anger. *It's the secrets; that's what bothers me.*

She washed her face and hands and then went to her bedroom to change clothes, taking as long as possible to avoid joining the stranger ogling her mother. But as she heard their laughter from the kitchen, she could stand it no longer and left the sanctity of her room to see what was going on.

Ron was a pharmacist at the hospital where Pam had been training. He actually did seem like a decent enough guy, and obviously her mother had told him about Sierra for he knew things about her. He asked Sierra many questions about school and then Fiel and her riding experiences. His comments were intelligent and he seemed genuinely interested.

"You are a very special and unique young woman," Ron said at the end of the meal. "Your mother didn't exaggerate at all when she talked about you. I have enjoyed our conversation."

"Thank you," Sierra responded politely.

"Your mother is pretty special too," Ron added. Sierra nodded in agreement. "Do you think you would mind if I took her out to dinner some evening; you know, on a date?"

"Ron, that's not fair," Pam interjected.

"If my mom wants to then I don't mind," Sierra replied graciously. She had been watching her mother during dinner, the slight blush when Ron looked at her and the relieved look on her face when Sierra and Ron conversed amicably. *She likes him. My mother deserves a good friend and I'm being selfish to resent him.* But she did resent him.

After dinner, Ron helped carry plates to the sink and offered to wash.

"Okay, thanks," Pam replied. "I'll dry."

"I guess I'll go to my room and work on homework," Sierra stated, watching how her mom smiled at Ron as she handed him the dish soap and dishrag.

"Kitten, you can work at the table here," Pam assured her. Sierra and her mother usually worked on homework together, either at the kitchen table or snuggled on the sofa in the living room.

"S'okay," Sierra answered, and fled to her room. The thought of sitting at the table with that man next to her mother at their kitchen sink was somehow unbearable.

16 SCHOOL'S OUT, SUMMER'S IN

A man on a horse is spiritually, as well as physically, bigger then a man on foot. – John Steinbeck

April and May passed in a flurry of busy activity as Sierra juggled her time at the stable with her increased schoolwork as finals approached. The playful Saturday with River when they had bathed Storm, was the last full weekend they had together. Tess had him out competing every weekend, pushing him to qualify for preliminary level this season. He needed four qualifying rides at training level before he could move up, and she had entered him in two trials in April that involved traveling a longer distance than normal for the Pegasus team. The only other weekend in April she had him compete in a dressage show which took him away most of the day on Sunday.

In spite of his inexperience in competing, River placed first in all his classes.

The Pegasus team competed at their first event of the season, the first Saturday in May. Sierra rode novice level on Minstrel, and the other three girls rode training level.

For their first time out together, Sierra was very pleased with Minstrel and happy when they placed fourth. Minstrel went clean cross country and in stadium jumping, but his dressage score had not been very good. She had received many of the same comments given to them at the dressage show. Maybe she would ask River to give her a few lessons on Minstrel instead of Fiel, and work on some of her problems.

Katrina and Calliope placed sixth, and again it was their dressage score that brought down their points, for they had also finished clean in cross country and stadium. Gloria did not place at all. She actually finished with a better dressage score than Katrina, but Silver had trouble with the training level heights of up to three feet, three inches, and the more difficult combinations. He had one refusal cross country and took down two rails in stadium jumping.

Crystal and Diva came away with a solid first place win. Diva carried her rider flawlessly through the dressage test, and clean over the jumping courses. Crystal was unbearable; flaunting her trophy and reiterating how well she had done. Sierra listened quietly, amazed at how she gave very little credit to her horse, who was the true champion of the day.

River did not compete at the May show for he had ridden Moose the prior weekend, and Tess agreed Moose needed at least two weeks off between events. But he was back out the following week at another distant show, and again placed first. He needed only one more qualifying ride and Tess would push him up to preliminary. In only two months, River had earned a reputation as a formidable competitor, and the local eventing community had their eyes on him.

May passed into June and Sierra's freshman year wound down to an end. The hallways resonated with the gossip of proms and parties and end-of-year pranks. Sierra tuned it all out, concentrating on preparing for final exams or else thinking dreamily of riding after school.

Her interest in gossip did perk up when Katrina rushed into the cafeteria one lunch period and dropped her backpack on the table where Sierra and Allison were sitting.

"Did you hear about Crystal?" she asked as she slid into a chair.

"What?"

"She broke up with Justin. Stuart Kincaid asked her to the junior class prom!"

Allison smirked and said, "Score for Crystal."

Stuart Kincaid, a tall, husky jock, was the school's sports star, having outshone even his senior teammates in football, basketball, and now track. What a boost to Crystal's status to be going out with him. "Yeah, first prize," Sierra added her own sarcastic comment.

"Justin is in so much trouble," Katrina continued divulging the gossip. "He was going to get suspended but since it's the end of the year, he's going to have to go in for detention during the summer school session. And he's off of all sports next year."

"What did he do?" Sierra asked.

"Some kid finally had the guts to turn him in for using that electric shock thing he has."

"Good for whoever that was," Sierra stated with a feeling of vindication.

"But what really got him in the most trouble was he went into some kind of frenzy in the parking lot and he slashed the tires of the kid who turned him in, and also the tires of Stuart's car, and someone saw him. What an idiot!"

Yes, Justin is an idiot, Sierra thought to herself. *But he is also dangerous.* She wondered if Stuart would be as willing as Justin to assist Crystal in plaguing her enemies.

Sierra figured the best way to deal with Crystal was to keep out of her sight, and she often went out of her way to avoid her. Since the prom and her reconciliation with River, Crystal had glared at her with an iciness that penetrated the space between them. But so far she had done nothing worse than make derogatory remarks about her at school.

Luke still called Sierra at least once a week, and it was not too much of a surprise when he asked her to the spring ball, the last dance of the year for freshmen and sophomores. She was more surprised when Billy Bruber, the boy who had plagued her with his unwanted attentions in eighth grade, summoned his courage and called to ask her to the dance. But what really amazed her was when David Schulman, a freshman boy that shared many of her classes, cornered her in the hallway and suggested they go together. Sierra politely declined all invitations. None of those boys attracted her and she didn't want to waste her energy going through the stress of a date.

Sierra and Allison studied together in the library and a few afternoons the week before finals. They both finished their freshman year in the academic top ten of their class.

The back seats of the school bus were traditionally taken by the tougher kids of school, which was another way to say the losers, River always thought. He hunched into the corner of the last seat, gazing out the window. The kids around him left him alone. No one dared bully him.

River had been going to school with most of the same kids since the fourth grade when he came to live with his father and aunt. The bullies had quickly identified River as an outsider who was hurting; something bullies are keen at sensing. They started teasing with name-calling and then with minor torments such as tripping him on the playground or stealing his lunch sack. After three weeks, River put an end to their harassment. One day after recess when everyone had returned to their seats, River got up from his desk and deliberately walked over to the toughest of his tormentors and punched him as hard as he could in the face, giving him a bloody nose. Of course he was sent to the principal's office and he had to stay in at recess for a month. But that incident earned him the reputation as tough and crazy and nobody bothered him after that. A few other fights where he was the aggressor confirmed his reputation, and throughout grade school, middle school, and now in high school, he was still known as the messed up, crazy kid who could be dangerous. That suited him just fine because that meant they left him alone. He had not been in a fight since sixth grade.

He knew he was different. He didn't like the things normal kids enjoyed or liked to talk about. Television annoyed him, he didn't like to read, he didn't like to play games, and he thought most sports were boring. He had never had a friend his own age. Once in awhile he did enjoy a movie at a theater, which had a whole different feel from watching on a television set. He loved listening to music. Other than that, his life centered around horses and his only ambition had been to quit school as soon as he turned sixteen, and work full time at a stable or the track. He didn't care about money and would have been content to work as a stable hand, groom, exercise boy, or whatever for the rest of his life…so he thought.

But inside his backpack was his preliminary grade report. For the first time in his school history he had passed all his courses with at least a *C* grade, and most of them *B*s. He even had one *A* in metal shop. Okay, so he had repeated his freshman year since he had missed the last weeks of school last year when he ran away, but now he was a full-fledged sophomore. Maybe he wasn't quite as stupid as he had always thought. Maybe João had been right.

He had Laila to thank for his grades. With her teasing and coaxing, and using her body as motivation, she had kept him at his studies. He loved her for that and his heart was full of gratitude. He was proud of what he had accomplished, but also harbored some shame that Laila was the one who had managed to force him to study rather than João, who had wanted so badly to help him. He just hoped that maybe João's spirit might know and be proud of him…and his mother too.

Now, he seriously considered the possibility of taking advantage of the college fund João had left him. Could he possibly handle the studying required to be a veterinarian? He knew he would like that work. He thought about Sierra and smiled to himself at the memory of them talking about a partnership. *What if..?*

Well, he would have to deal with his father.

Ever since Cray had discovered his son had a talent with horses, he had used that to his advantage. A year after bringing River to live at his aunt's house, he sent River to work at Pegasus Equestrian Center in exchange for reduced board for the few race horses he had in the off season. Cray decided that River should quit school as soon as he was legally able and work with him at the track. Cray would no longer have to hire a groom or exercise boys, and if River's talent extended to training race horses, he might even make him a partner.

River had always agreed with the plan for it was the easiest way to deal with his father. Perhaps at one time he had seriously considered it. But River knew the last thing he wanted now was to spend any time around his father, least of all work for him. Since his sixteenth birthday last January, his father had been pressuring him to quit school but River had pleaded to at least finish out the school year. Cray had reluctantly agreed, but River knew he expected him to start working for him this summer and not return to school in the fall.

No, I won't do it.

The bus pulled up to his stop and River shoved his way past the two losers on the bench seat next to him, ignoring their glowering looks. He jumped off the steps and jogged along the gravel road that took him to his aunt's house. Storm bounded out of the barn to meet him, her tail wagging wildly as she jumped around him, expressing her extreme happiness that he was finally home.

"Hey, girl." River greeted her with pats on her head and the two hurried up to his room where he dropped his backpack happily onto the floor; *won't be needing that for three months.* With a sense of freedom, River quickly changed into work clothes and he and Storm retraced their steps back outside to head to the stable. He looked forward to telling Sierra that he had passed all his classes. And later tonight he would tell Laila. Laila had graduated, but not being one to participate in school activities, she had said she would pick him up tonight and they would go somewhere to celebrate.

As River stepped out of the barn, a red Camaro pulled into the driveway and parked. River recognized his cousin Warren, Steve's older brother, as he got out of the driver's side. Steve and two girls also climbed out of the car, carrying grocery sacks. They were all laughing and talking in loud voices, a party happening. River noted sardonically how both girls had their eyes on Warren.

Warren possessed the dark good looks of the Blackthorns; tall, muscular, and very fit. He wore a pair of camouflage fatigue pants and a tee-shirt with *Ranger* printed on the back. He walked with a swagger and exuded an aura of 'don't mess with me'. Steve, who might have been considered good-looking, was in contrast scrawny in build and had the sallow complexion of one who over-indulges in drugs and alcohol and rarely goes outside in daylight. *Too bad for the girl who gets stuck with Steve*, River thought with spiteful humor.

River smiled and waved a greeting. He liked Warren who unlike Steve, had always been friendly to him and had even intervened a few times when his father was on a drunken rampage. Warren had been arrested two years ago for some sort of brawl in a bar, but somehow had managed to enlist in the army rather than go to jail. The army suited him; especially since he had been accepted into Ranger training, and he now planned to stay in the army as a career. River guessed he must be home now on leave.

Warren waved back and called out," Hey, cuz." He never stuck 'gay' in front of the word the way Steve did. "How's it going?"

"Good, how about you?"

"Never better. Come on in and have a drink. We'll catch up."

"Later, I'm on my way to work, but thanks."

Warren nodded and then put his arm around one of the girls who had sidled up to him, and they went inside the house.

17 TRAINING LEVEL EVENT

At its finest, rider and horse are joined not by tack, but by trust. Each is totally reliant upon the other. Each is the selfless guardian of the other's very well-being. – Author Unknown

"Are you ever going to talk to River?" Katrina asked. It was the first week of summer vacation and Katrina had been coming to the stable every afternoon to ride Calliope.

"I guess I kind of forgot about it," Sierra admitted.

"Please, Sierra."

"Okay, I'll ask him today," Sierra promised. They were leading Minstrel and Calliope to the mounting block at the back field. Sierra was happy to have Katrina as a friend, someone who shared her love of horses. But when Katrina was around, River would find things to do elsewhere. Sierra preferred to ride with River and was beginning to dread a summer in which she would be torn between her two friends.

They rode together on a long loop of the trail with intervals of trotting and galloping. Then after untacking and rinsing the sweat off their horses, they led them to the field to hand graze while they dried off.

"I'll hold Minstrel for you if you go ask him now," Katrina offered. "I saw him working Penny in the indoor arena."

"Okay," Sierra agreed and handed Katrina Minstrel's lead rope. She might as well get it over with. "I'm not promising anything."

"All I ask is that you try."

Sierra went to the observation platform of the indoor arena and watched River schooling Pendragon. They were working on canter pirouettes, a movement required at the fourth and higher levels of dressage. Penny blew through his nose in rhythm with his collected canter as River brought him onto a smaller and smaller circle until he appeared to pivot around his deeply flexed inside hind leg in a half turn, or pirouette.

"*Bien*," she heard River murmur, and then he brought Penny down to a working trot, giving him the reins to allow him to stretch his nose forward.

"Was that a good pirouette?" Sierra asked, once he transitioned to a walk and as he passed by on the rail. Sierra had learned not to say, 'that's awesome,' or 'beautiful', because often River would laugh and then tell her all the things that were incorrect.

"Yeah, I'm happy with it for now," River answered. "We lost the rhythm on the first one but his second pirouette was better...still lost impulsion though."

Sierra accompanied River to the crossties asking questions about pirouettes. He answered willingly, always more verbal when it concerned horses.

"I have to ask you a question," Sierra began.

"Yeah?" River stood up from removing the wraps from Penny's legs.

"Katrina has been begging me to ask if you would consider giving her lessons."

"No," River replied emphatically. With Penny untacked, he clipped the lead rope to his halter and led him to the wash stall with Sierra trailing along.

"Um, why not?" she persisted.

"She takes lessons from Tess."

"She's figured out what I have about Tess's style and she is not happy."

River turned on the water and gently hosed the sweat from Pendragon. Sierra waited. Satisfied that he was rinsed off well enough, River shut off the water and sluiced the excess off of Penny with a sweat scraper. Sierra folded her arms and set her jaw. Finally River turned to face her. "Sierra, giving lessons is not what I want to do."

"Oh. So, giving me lessons..?"

"You deserved lessons and Tess was going to make you wait," River explained. "Besides, helping you doesn't feel like…well, with you it's just different."

The way he said that made Sierra feel like she was different in a good way, and suddenly she felt herself blushing. She ducked her head quickly. "Thanks. I guess I've never really let you know how grateful I am."

"Yes you have."

"River…" Sierra looked up. He smiled and she smiled back. "Thanks. Okay, I promised Katrina I would ask you; so now I've asked. I'll just tell her you said no."

"Good…and is she going to hang around here all summer?"

"What have you got against Katrina?"

"She's Crystal's friend."

"Not anymore. Haven't you noticed they're not hanging around? Crystal hates her."

"Oh." River thought for a minute, scrunching his brow. "I hadn't really noticed."

"Katrina told Crystal that you ride better than her and that she should listen to you."

"She said that to Crystal?" He clipped the lead to Penny's halter and led him outside to dry with Sierra walking at his side.

"She did. And you know Katrina cares about Calliope. She's always out here riding and she never asks you to groom for her the way Crystal and Gloria do."

"Okay, I give her credit for that."

Sierra kept silent, knowing River was mulling things over in his mind.

"I really don't have time to give her lessons," he stated after about five minutes.

"River, it's totally up to you, but you got to admit that the one who will truly benefit is Calliope. What if you just watch her ride on the flat one time and give her a few pointers?" Sierra suggested.

Again, he thought for awhile. Then with a deep sigh as if he had been given a formidable, unpleasant task, he relented. "Okay, just once."

Sierra smiled to herself. She suspected that if River started helping Katrina and if Calliope improved, he would probably continue to coach her once in awhile.

River kept his word and the next day when Katrina came to ride, he said he would watch her in the arena. Katrina listened intently and tried to follow all his instructions with the result that Calliope began to trot with more buoyancy and less stiffness as Katrina lightened her hands and focused on her core muscles.

"Thank you, thank you so much," Katrina gushed as she led Calliope over to where River and Sierra stood at the rail. "This is the best ride I've ever had on the flat…um…"

Sierra knew what she was going to ask.

Before Katrina could continue, River interrupted. "Look, Tess has me riding six to seven horses a day now, and with cleaning stalls and working with Cory, and taking care of lesson horses…I just don't have time to give you lessons."

Katrina's face fell and Sierra felt bad for her. "River, I would really like to have more rides during the summer. What if I ask Tess if I could take over some of your conditioning rides, on the horses that I can handle? And I really need help with Minstrel in dressage, but I don't want to give up the time with you on Fiel. What if you coached Katrina and me at the same time?"

"I'll clean stalls for you," Katrina chimed in eagerly.

Sierra's heart sank at Katrina's offer. Yes, it was only fair that Katrina should do something for River in exchange for lessons, but Sierra loved cleaning stalls with him. She didn't want to lose that time they had together. She glanced at River who had his eyebrows knit in a frown, so maybe he felt the same way?

"Okay, I guess we can work something out," River reluctantly agreed. Perhaps it was when Calliope nudged him with her nose that convinced him. "What are you going to do about your lessons with Tess?"

Katrina's eyes shifted nervously, as if she expected Tess to suddenly appear and overhear. "I don't know. I was thinking I would just keep taking them. The jumping lessons at least are good."

"You can't switch back and forth between lightening up on Calliope's mouth and then taking hold with Tess. It will confuse her and she'll resent you taking hold again once she gets used to a lighter hand," River warned.

"Maybe I can kind of not do what Tess tells me and think about your instructions. I don't want her mad at me."

Two weekends after school let out, the Pegasus team competed in their next event. Sierra, with River's approval, agreed to move up to training level on Minstrel. River would also ride on Moose, and Tess hoped this would be his final qualifying ride to move up to preliminary.

"It's going to be interesting to see if our dressage scores improve," Katrina said, as she and Sierra led Calliope and Minstrel to the warm-up ring. "I can't believe how much better Calliope is doing with River coaching us…at least at home."

"Yeah, we'll see, but I bet we both do better."

"Tess has already noticed a difference. She told me in my last lesson that I'm finally getting effective half-halts. What she doesn't realize is that I'm half-halting more with my weight and stomach muscles, and sometimes I don't even apply the reins. That exercise where River has us increase and decrease the tempo without touching the reins has been very effective. It still amazes me that it works."

"I know," Sierra agreed. "My friend João once told me that horses talk to us all the time and we just need to learn how to listen to them. They tell us when we are riding correctly by giving the correct response."

Katrina nodded; her expression pensive. "He was an amazing rider, wasn't he?"

"Yeah, and an amazing man."

They followed behind River leading Silver and Moose, and Tess leading Diva. Crystal and Gloria waited for their horses to be brought to them, standing near the warm-up ring's mounting block. Crystal nervously tapped her boot with her dressage whip, her expression tight.

Tess frowned a warning as she led Diva, who eyed the whip warily, parallel to the mounting block, and held the mare's head while Crystal mounted.

"Why doesn't Tess ever say anything to her?" Sierra complained.

"Boss's daughter, what do you expect?" Katrina answered in a sour tone.

"I thought her father was Tess's partner."

"Yes, but you know he's the one who controls the finances. The only reason he bought into Pegasus was for Crystal's sake."

"Hmm," Sierra mumbled.

Tess held Silver's head next while Gloria mounted, and then Katrina took her turn to mount up on Calliope.

Crystal walked Diva past where River waited with Moose. She sneered down at him and hissed vindictively, "You're going to lose."

River shook his head along with a short laugh.

"Why is that funny?" Sierra asked having watched Crystal's spiteful behavior.

"She is just so stupid; as if I even care. Go ahead and mount up." River indicated the vacant mounting block as Katrina walked off on Calliope.

He really doesn't care about winning. Sierra thought about that as she mounted up on Minstrel. *How much do I care about winning?* She walked Minstrel into the warm-up ring and began her relaxing regime of deep breathing and rolling her shoulders to loosen tight muscles. Minstrel held his head high and jigged as horses passed him, but she did not react to his tenseness. She sat deep and kept her legs softly against his sides, to reassure him she was there, but without pressure. With a series of gently squeezing the reins and a slight increase in leg pressure, she coaxed Minstrel to drop his head and then moved him into a working trot. As he stretched his neck into the bit, she reached forward to pat his neck to let him know, 'good'.

No, I don't care if I win a ribbon, Sierra realized, as a deep sense of satisfaction filled her when Minstrel responded to her communication. *Winning is when I effectively communicate with my horse, and then if we manage to place because we are working together as one…well that's just a bonus.* She recalled that João had said something like that to her some time ago.

One by one, as their numbers were called, they each rode their dressage test. Then after the horses were settled in their stalls, they followed Tess as a group around the cross country course; checking out the footing and distances, and listening to her advice on how to negotiate each obstacle.

"Are the dressage scores posted yet?" Crystal asked passersby as they returned to the stall area. Her obvious irritation when the answer was still no, resulted in the bearer of the news retreating from her prickly expression. Sierra was torn between wanting River's score to be higher and dread of being around Crystal if it was.

"Crystal, you are not going to know your score until after cross country," Tess snapped at her. "Now go get dressed for your ride." Crystal stomped away.

The cross country course was almost the easiest she had ever ridden, Sierra believed, even compared with the last novice level course. The heights were higher and the spreads were a little wider, but there were no tricky combinations or tight approaches. The one brick wall on the downhill was almost identical to a jump in the field at Pegasus, and she had practiced over it many times. She worried most about the water jump. So far, she had only faced water where they galloped through, but today she would have to ask Minstrel to jump off a low bank into water; something she had never done before. But Minstrel had never hesitated at water and she felt fairly confident she could urge him through. The footing was good; not too soft or hard. Scattered clouds and a slight breeze kept the temperature from becoming too hot.

Energized by the excitement around him, Sierra could feel Minstrel's muscles bunching, but he responded promptly to Sierra's aids during their warm-up. When she heard her number called, she brought him to a walk and headed up to the starting box. She loved the adrenalin rush as she walked Minstrel in a tight circle and then turned him to face the exit as the starter began the countdown. As the flag dropped, Minstrel jumped forward as Sierra gave with the reins. They were on course.

Minstrel took the first few jumps easily in stride; only once shaking his head as Sierra asked him to slow down after the downhill jump. When he responded obediently, Sierra felt confident to let him out to a full gallop on a long section of trail between obstacles. She slowed him again as they approached a chicken coop, jumped well in stride, and then it was on to the water. Sierra knew she had tensed up when she felt Minstrel's shoulder muscles stiffen and he brought his head up. "Easy," she spoke out loud to him and mentally to herself. She touched his neck with her fingertips and softened her fingers, pleased when he dropped his head back into the bit.

When Minstrel spied the shallow body of water coming up, he raised his head warily, and Sierra felt hesitation in his rhythm. "You can do it," she urged him out loud and increased the pressure on his sides with her legs. He flicked his ears back but then surged forward as she squeezed again more firmly. He took the drop into the water and then galloped on. Sierra whooped in glee. Two fences to go!

They galloped up the hill from the water and then an easy bend on course to approach a large log, typical of many they had taken and Sierra did not anticipate any problem. But this log was a bleached white color, and a sudden beam of sunlight through the clouds gleamed off the pearly smooth, bark-free surface of the log. Minstrel snorted and skid to a jolting halt, a few feet from the jump. Sierra was thrown forward onto his neck but quickly righted herself, circled Minstrel and brought him back to face the jump. This time she kept her legs firmly on his sides and with a tap of her jumping bat, pushed him onward. Minstrel responded by jumping high and wide, as if afraid of the log. "Good boy," she praised him and they galloped on to the last obstacle, a solid board fence. Sierra urged him probably faster than she needed to, reacting to his refusal. She sensed no hesitation as Minstrel took the fence in stride and they galloped through the finish flags.

At the end of cross country, River, Crystal, and Katrina all had clean rounds. Sierra had one refusal and Gloria had two refusals plus time penalties.

"I've never had a refusal before." Sierra felt devastated as she walked with River and Katrina back to the stalls.

"What happened?" he asked.

"I just didn't expect it. He spooked at it for some reason."

"But he took it the second time."

"Yeah, but you know, I think I lost focus; not really paying attention to the log and thinking we were almost done. I was so worried about the water and after we got through that I just thought the last two jumps were no-brainers."

"Yeah, I can see how that can happen," he replied.

"And lesson learned…there are no free jumps."

River and Katrina laughed at her almost-pun.

Back at the stalls, Sierra and Katrina quickly untacked and sponged off their horses and then helped River with Diva, Silver, and Moose.

The three of them led the horses to a grassy patch to graze and dry off, and to have a refreshing break before stadium jumping.

They had just returned the horses to their stalls when Tess, Crystal, and Gloria joined them with the dressage test sheets. Tess handed them out.

"Thirty-eight penalty points," Crystal announced and watched River's face smugly as he looked over his own score sheet.

He looked up at her and calmly said, "Good for Diva."

"River has thirty-nine penalty points," Crystal announced to the others. "I'm in first place."

"Can I see your test?" River asked, very politely.

"What for?" Crystal responded suspiciously.

"I want to read the comments."

"Only if I can see yours."

They traded their test score sheets and Crystal watched River as he read over her test results. He smiled to himself when he finished, and handed it back.

"What's so funny?" Crystal asked.

"Not a thing," River answered and turned away from her.

Crystal scowled and turned her attention to River's test. Sierra noted her expression darken as she read all the positive comments that Sierra was sure had been written.

Katrina was elated with her improved dressage score, and with her clean cross country round, was in fourth place.

Sierra also had a much improved dressage score, but with the one refusal, she dropped to eighth place. Gloria was in fourteenth place.

Stadium jumping went well for everyone except Gloria. Silver took two rails down. The others all jumped clean. Crystal remained in first place, River in second, and Katrina in fourth. The two riders ahead of Sierra had rails down and she moved up into sixth place. Gloria dropped down to twentieth place out of the twenty-three entries in junior training level.

At the end of the show and the final scores had been tallied for all the levels, Tess announced, "Those of you who placed, saddle up and get over to the stadium arena for the victory lap."

The loudspeaker squealed to life and several show officials walked into the arena carrying ribbons. "Junior beginner novice, first place..." The announcer began, calling out the name and number of each horse and rider pair that had placed in the ribbons. As those who placed heard their names, they rode their horses into the arena and up to the show officials, who clipped a ribbon onto the bridle if the horse would tolerate, or handed it to the rider if the horse shied from the ribbon.

After all six places had been announced from beginner novice through preliminary level; triumphal music blared from the loudspeaker and the riders moved their horses out of the line-up to canter around the perimeter of the arena.

Sierra completed one lap and then brought Minstrel down to a trot and left through the exit gate. Other riders followed close behind; traditionally the lowest placed riders leaving first until only the first place winners of each division were left.

She dismounted and waited for the others, prepared to take Diva's reins from Crystal to lead her back to the stall along with Minstrel. Gloria stood nearby watching, clapping her hands in obligatory applause for her friend, a rigid smile on her face that did not extend past the tight corners of her mouth. Sierra thought she looked like she was about to cry.

River exited and dismounted next to Sierra, followed by Katrina, beaming proudly with the fourth place white ribbon on Calliope's bridle. They waited for Crystal, who still cantered around on Diva, waving at her friends along the rail who were clapping and cheering for her. She was the last to leave the arena, stretching out her triumphant moment as long as possible.

Finally Crystal exited and rode up to the group. Her friends left the rail to come up and congratulate her. Sierra recognized most of them from school, including her new boyfriend, Stuart.

"You won!" Stuart called out as he walked up to Diva's side, his face beaming proudly for his girlfriend. "Awesome!"

"Thank you," Crystal answered, smiling sweetly at him, and then announced, "and I beat River. So who's the better rider, huh?" She turned to River who was loosening Moose's girth. He ignored her.

"He can't even face me; he's supposed to be so great and unbeatable. Well, I guess I showed him."

Sierra bit her lip to hold back her retort, her irritation rising to an uncontrollable level. "Get off, Crystal," she said, "so I can take Diva back to the stalls."

Crystal smiled down at Sierra. "I beat you too," she announced.

"Crystal, you did not win; Diva did. You were just a passenger, and you have River to thank for Diva's ability to carry you around," Sierra stated, loud enough to be sure all Crystal's friends heard.

The triumphant look on Crystal's face twisted suddenly into a violent contortion of hatred; her lips tight and her eyes narrowed beneath her glowering brows as she stared piercingly into Sierra's eyes. Then she looked away and smoothed out her face. Shrugging her shoulders, she stated smugly, "What a poor loser."

"What's she talking about?" Stuart asked.

"She's a little liar. She's making stuff up because she is just so envious," Crystal replied. She then dismounted and tossed the reins to Sierra without looking at her. River had already started leading Moose back to the stalls and Sierra turned to follow.

Stuart had his arm possessively over Crystal's shoulder as they started walking away in another direction.

"Just a minute," Crystal said, stepping out from under Stuart's arm. She retreated back to Diva. "I want my ribbon," Crystal demanded. Sierra obligingly unhooked it from Diva's bridle and handed it over. "You are going to pay for what you said," Crystal hissed in a low, menacing voice that only Sierra could hear. Then she spun on the heel of her boot and went back to Stuart.

"What did she say to you?" Katrina asked, coming alongside leading Calliope.

"Nothing worth repeating," Sierra answered, not wanting to acknowledge the tremor of fear that had traveled down her spine to needle into her stomach at Crystal's threat.

"I saw the way she walked away. Watch out for her," Katrina warned.

"Don't worry."

Tess helped ready the horses with their shipping boots and sheets, and then load them into the trailer. "Good riding today," she congratulated Sierra, Katrina, and River. Then she left, leaving River to drive the rig back to the stable.

"Anybody want something to drink for the ride? I'm going to the restroom and I can get them on the way back," Sierra offered as she helped River secure the ramp and check all the doors of the trailer.

"Diet coke," Katrina called from where she was stowing gear in the back of the truck.

"Regular coke," River said, "and a sandwich if they have any left."

"I'll just be a sec." Sierra took off at a jog and after the restroom, got into line at the concession stand.

"Congratulations," said a voice behind her as someone tapped her on the shoulder. Sierra turned to look up into an attractive face and the deepest blue eyes she had ever seen. A tall, lean boy wearing riding clothes grinned at her.

"I saw you in the victory lap," he explained, noting the confused look on her face.

"Thanks," she replied with a smile. "But you didn't see our refusal cross country." She felt she had to admit to that.

The boy laughed. "No, I missed that. But it happens to all of us."

"Did you ride?"

"Yeah, I'm trying to qualify for preliminary, but we had a refusal also." He made a face. "Actually, a few refusals."

Sierra laughed in sympathy. "Sorry to hear that, but it happens to all of us," she repeated.

He laughed with her and then said, "I'm Dean Clark."

"Oh…nice to meet you," Sierra answered and suddenly felt herself blush. He was certainly very good looking. *What's he talking to me for?*

"So, what's your name?"

"Oh," she said again awkwardly, "Sierra Landsing."

"Dean, come on, we already got the snacks," a girl called to him.

"See you around." He looked deep into Sierra's eyes and smiled a crooked smile that raised one side of his mouth, producing a dimple in that corner. He stepped out of line and Sierra watched him walk away, noting his purposeful stride and long legs that looked like they knew how to wrap around a horse. He held his shoulders and head high; a head crowned with thick, bronze-colored hair in a trim cut. Sierra thought he was probably the most attractive boy she had ever seen.

"I'm so sorry," Sierra said as River started the engine and moved the rig into the line of exiting trailers.

"What for?" he asked.

"You know, Crystal."

"Yeah," he said with a short laugh, "what a pain in the ass."

"How could she possibly beat you?" Katrina asked from the back seat in a mournful tone.

River glanced at both girls who watched him with looks of sympathy on their faces. He laughed out loud again. "I don't think of it as Crystal beating me," he stated. "Diva performed better than Moose in dressage. Diva will probably always do better than Moose. She has much better conformation for dressage than he has."

"But…" Sierra frowned.

"Besides, who trains Diva?" he asked. "I'm very proud of how she did today, in spite of her rider. Did you notice how she was overbent a few times in her dressage test?"

"No," both Sierra and Katrina answered honestly.

"Neither did the judge; there was no mention of overbent on her score sheet. I taught her to do that when she feels too much pressure on her mouth. It's a way for her to defend herself when Crystal holds on too tight and a lot of judges don't notice. It worked for her today."

Then Sierra laughed, thinking of the hours River spent schooling Diva and conditioning her on the trail. It was kind of ironic that River trained his own competition.

18 COLIC

God forbid that I should go to any Heaven where there are no horses. – R. B. Cunningham-Graham

Diva's ears pointed forward and her eyes wide as River guided her toward the three-foot-seven oxer of red and white rails on the first bar and blue and white on the second. He felt her hesitate, a slight stiffening of her shoulders and lagging in her stride. He touched her neck with the fingers of his left hand and increased the pressure of his legs until he felt her respond with a surge of energy. "*Buena chica*," he murmured to her and eased just a little of his leg pressure until two strides more and then, squeeze with his legs and forward into two-point. Diva leaped from her strong hind end muscles and cleared the two bars. She galloped on, grateful for the soft touch of the hands to her mouth – reassuring hands that talked to her gently, giving her confidence. She trusted this rider who always stayed in the right place on her back so that she didn't lose her balance, and never gave her sudden jerks of pain to her mouth; none of the unpleasant things that so often happened with the other.

River finished the course over a stone wall, and then sat quietly and allowed Diva to slow from gallop to canter to trot at her own will.

Then he kept her at trot around the perimeter of the arena, giving her the reins so she could stretch her neck, and finally to walk.

"Excellent!" Tess, who had been watching from the rail, exclaimed as River dismounted and led Diva from the arena.

"If Crystal doesn't get out here and ride more often, she should not move up to preliminary," River said.

"What are you talking about? Diva handled that course in excellent form."

"Yeah, Diva handled the course. Crystal hasn't jumped these kinds of heights or spreads. She needs more experience than she gets in one jumping lesson a week."

Tess snorted a laugh. "Someone finally beat you and now you're afraid of the competition," she stated.

"I don't care who wins," River answered in a cold tone. "I don't want to see Diva get hurt because her rider doesn't know how to handle the course."

Tess made a sound of derision. "You let me worry about what she can handle." She was tired of River's know-it-all attitude and she didn't believe for a minute that he didn't care about winning. Tess had grown up very competitive and it was inconceivable that others were not.

They reached the crossties. As soon as River had secured Diva, he turned to face Tess with folded arms and tight shoulders. "Do not let her kill another horse."

Tess stepped back, her own shoulders tightening in defense. "What happened to Magic was a freak acci…"

"No," River almost shouted, the word sharp with anger. He dropped his arms and lowered his voice when he sensed Diva jerk her head up behind him. "He was too green and she didn't have the experience to…"

"You weren't even there," Tess spat back.

"I didn't need to be." He turned his back to Tess and stepped over to Diva, stroking her neck to reassure her.

Tess stormed away.

After his argument with Tess, River's mood improved as he rode Cory and then his other assigned mounts. As he concentrated on each horse, he had been able to push his worry over Diva away. Crystal wouldn't move up to preliminary until next year, and a lot could happen between now and then.

He had hoped Sierra might invite him to dinner. He could talk to Sierra about his concerns for Diva and knew she would totally agree and sympathize with him. He didn't understand how that helped; he just knew it did.

But Sierra did not invite him, even though he had fished as best he could for an invitation. He asked about her mom and Charlie, but Sierra didn't take the bait. She had been sort of complaining lately to both him and Katrina about some man interested in her mother and hanging around many evenings. Maybe that was why she didn't invite him. Or maybe she had other plans or had invited someone else over…*that Luke guy, the boy always hanging around her?* He didn't like that thought.

Ill humor returned to waft into his being and end up as a burn in his stomach. Walking home, he kicked at a stick in his path, thinking about last summer, where it seemed Sierra and he spent all their time together until she got fired. Then after he introduced her to João, she began inviting him over for dinner. But now it seemed like Katrina was always around, claiming Sierra's friendship and attention. *Why does that even bother me?* He couldn't remember the last time he had been to her house; sometime before he had spent his nights outside of Diva's stall.

I need to see Laila. He hadn't seen her for awhile either. He pulled his cell phone from his pocket and pressed her number, hearing her voice mail…as usual. Most of the time he just hung up, but he decided to take a chance and left a message. "Laila, please, I really want to see you."

After graduation and since she was over eighteen, Laila had moved into an apartment with two roommates, leaving foster care forever. She worked full time at a metal rock fashion shop in the mall, and went to school at the community college at night. She told him she had a partial scholarship for the university in the fall, and she wanted to get a few classes out of the way that would transfer from the community college. She planned to major in psychology and become a counselor. He had never realized she was so ambitious.

"You're kidding," he had said when she described her plans.

She had made a face at him. "I want to do something useful with my life. You should go see that new counselor at school, Ms. Montoya. She's awesome."

"Right," he had answered, rolling his eyes. "They've made me go to counseling sessions a few times. What a waste."

"Most of them are," Laila had agreed. "Ms. Montoya is different. You haven't met her?"

"No, what's so great about her?"

She didn't answer right away, taking time to think. "She's…well, she understands things…she doesn't judge. I like her. I still call her sometimes for advice."

"Good for you," he had answered in a smart voice.

Then she had punched him playfully, the way she liked to do, and had laughed. "No, really," she had shifted to a serious tone. "I've hated all the other counselors. They're all so phony."

"For sure," he had agreed. "How is she any different?"

"Well…for example, the first time I went to see that other counselor, Mr…, whatever, I can't even remember his name. He made all these complements about my piercings and my tattoos, to show me how cool he was or to prove that he could accept me. But he couldn't get past my appearance. He would lecture me on how others perceived me and that it affected my ability to adjust, or whatever. He did a lot of talking and gave me a lot of inane, useless advice. He never listened to me. But Ms. Montoya has never said one thing about my appearance. I get the impression she really doesn't care how I look. She mostly just listened to me. And the way she listened and would ask me questions, kind of helped me work things out for myself."

"Good for you," he had repeated, annoyed.

"That's right, it was good for me. I mean it; you should go see her when school starts."

He remembered lying on his side next to her on his mattress, running his fingers along the contours of her clavicle bones, over her breasts, and down to her slightly rounded stomach. He had only half listened, his attention drawn to the marvelous design of a woman's body. *Great conformation*, he had thought bemusedly to himself. He had rolled on top of her and between kisses had asked, "You think I'm messed up?"

"Totally," she had laughed and tried to wriggle away. They had play-wrestled, laughing and kissing and touching each other.

She had come to see him only one other time since then. She refused to bring him to her apartment. "I don't want to get in trouble for messing around with an underage kid," she teased him. But he felt like she wanted to keep her real life separate from him. Things had never quite been the same between them since all the nights he had stayed at the stable to be near Diva. She had called him a few times, and he just never returned the calls since he didn't know how to explain he was staying with a horse. And even though she had said it didn't matter and always insisted she was not his girlfriend, he wondered if perhaps it might have hurt her feelings just a little.

Or, the truth simply was she no longer wanted to mess around with a stupid kid. She was so smart and ambitious, and their last time together she had left him abruptly and in anger when he had mentioned the college fund that João had left him.

"You have enough money to go to college and you're only thinking about going?" she had asked incredulously.

They had talked on the phone since then, and she assured him she was not angry, yet she never came over.

River arrived at the intersection to his driveway, and as he turned off the road he as usual looked around for Cray's truck; always wary as to when his father might decide to come home for a few days. He appreciated that Tess had somehow intervened for him, and had convinced Cray that River had to work one more season for her; to pay off the debt he owed for his horse. Otherwise, he imagined he would have been dragged off to the track as soon as school ended.

No truck, River noted with relief, but a red Camaro was parked in the yard. *Warren must be home again.* That did lighten his mood. He fed Storm, and then went inside the house.

"Hey, cuz," Warren greeted, and waved a bottle of beer at him. He lounged on one end of the sofa with one leg stretched out and the other hanging over the side. Steve slumped in a chair, smoking a cigarette, also with a bottle of beer in hand.

"What's up?" River greeted and smiled as he went over to Warren and they slapped hands.

"Shipping out next week," Warren answered.

"Where to?" River knew his cousin had already done a short tour in Iraq.

"Back to the desert, man," he replied.

"Iraq ? How can they make you go twice?"

"I volunteered; most of my outfit is going." He grinned back and River thought he looked excited. "Hey, we need to be where the action is."

Warren tossed River a beer from the six-pack carton near his feet. River caught it and sat down on the other end of the sofa, and listened as Warren talked about his life in the army. His phone vibrated, and he answered when he saw it was Laila.

"What do you need?" she asked.

"I know you say you're not mad at me and all that, but you never come over," he said. "Do you want to go get pizza or something? We can just talk."

"Is that what you want to do?" He could hear the teasing in her voice.

"I like pizza," he answered. "But…"

She laughed. "I have class tonight, but what if I come over after that. It'll be about nine-thirty."

"Thanks, I'll be here." He disconnected, feeling much better now.

"Hungry?" Warren asked.

"Always."

Warren drove River and Steve to a nearby café where they ate dinner. Warren had always been a good story teller and River liked to sit quietly and listen to him talk, finding his company relaxing. Steve sat sullenly, smoldering that his brother included River as part of the family.

On the way back to the house, River's phone vibrated again. *Tess?* He had no idea what she might be calling about except…a shiver went up his spine.

"River?" Tess said when he connected.

"Yeah."

"Manuel just called me and said something is wrong with Fiel. He is very upset and I can't understand him. I am at dinner with a client. Can you go see what's going on?"

"Yes," he answered, his heart suddenly pounding. He asked Warren to drop him off at Pegasus since it was on the way home.

"Ees no good," Manuel said as River hurried into the stable and up to Fiel's stall after Warren dropped him off. When he looked inside and saw the gray horse, his heart dropped like a rock into the pit of his stomach.

Manuel had the halter on and was holding the lead rope to keep Fiel from lying down. The horse stood with his head low. His neck was damp with sweat and his belly tightly distended. With each exhaled breath he emitted a mournful groan. Every few minutes he bared his teeth and brought his head up to try and bite at his side; but Manuel kept his head forward with the lead rope. Most of his hay ration lay in piles around his feet, untouched.

Colic! No question.

"Have you called Dr. Patterson?" River asked in Spanish.

Manuel shook his head and answered in Spanish that he had only called Tess. Fiel had tried to lie down to roll, and he did not want to leave him.

River felt so thankful that Manuel recognized the signs of colic and knew what to do. He pulled out his phone and with trembling fingers, scrolled through to the vet's number. When he got the answering service, all he had to say was, "I have a horse with colic," and quickly described the symptoms. The service immediately put him through to Dr. Patterson.

"I'll be right over," the vet said, alarm in his voice. "Keep him on his feet."

"We will," River assured him.

"Have you tried to walk him?" River asked. Manuel shook his head no.

"If we can get him moving, it might help," River suggested. He opened the stall door and both he and Manuel tugged gently on the halter and lead rope. Fiel took a few staggering steps and slowly, they started to walk him in the aisle.

"You call Sierra," Manuel said.

"I know; I need to." It was a call River dreaded. "I will, as soon as the vet gets here. How did you find him?"

"I was fixing that loose board out in the paddock and on my way back by the stable I heard loud pawing. I come in to check and everyone is still eating hay except Fiel. I think he had just gotten to his feet for he had hay on his coat, and it was him pawing and biting at his sides." Manuel explained in Spanish.

If he was down, did he roll? River wondered with increasing anxiety. He knew the danger of a colicky horse rolling and potentially twisting the intestines.

They walked one on each side of Fiel for a few steps, let him rest, and then moved him on down the aisle. The pain the poor horse suffered was evident as he pawed and tossed his head as if that might bring him relief, and frequently tried to bite at his sides. When he started to bend his knees to lie down, they would pull him forward to walk again.

It seemed forever, but was probably only fifteen to twenty minutes before they heard Dr. Patterson drive up. The veterinarian walked into the barn and observed the horse as River and Manuel led him down the aisle and then into the wash stall. "How has he been lately?" he asked.

"Fine," River answered through the lump in his throat. "Sierra rode him today on the trail in his usual work. She always cools him out thoroughly."

"I'm sure she does," Dr. Patterson said and then asked many more questions while he conducted his examination.

River answered all his questions in the negative: no, there had been no change in feed, work schedule, turn out, no unusual stresses, no new horses in the barn for two weeks, no change in the consistency or amount of stool cleaned out of his stall each morning.

"Definitely colic," Dr. Patterson said after he had checked vital signs, listened with his stethoscope over Fiel's heart and then his belly, and lifted his upper lip to press his finger against his gums. "Heart rate is up, I don't hear any peristalsis, and he exhibits all the symptoms."

"But you don't think he's twisted his intestines, do you?" River asked hopefully.

"I certainly hope not. Manuel, you stay with him here. River, you come with me and help me bring back supplies. Where is Sierra?"

"I didn't want to call her until you came," River answered as they went out to the vet's van.

"I think she would want to be here, don't you?" Dr. Patterson asked as he handed River a stainless steel bucket with rubber tubing and some other equipment stowed inside. He took some other supplies out of a storage chest and they returned to the wash stall.

"I'll call her now." River set down the bucket and pulled out his phone to press Sierra's number. He swallowed hard when he heard her voice answer. Then not knowing how to say it in any easy or gentle way, said, "Sierra, I'm sorry. Fiel has colic. Dr. Patterson is here now."

He could hear the tremor and fear in her tone as she asked, "How bad?"

"He's just starting to work on him. I don't know."

"I'm on my way." She disconnected.

Dr. Patterson gave Fiel an injection in his neck. "It will reduce the pain and relax the abdominal muscles," he explained. Then with River and Manuel holding the halter to assist, the vet inserted the rubber tubing through a nostril and into Fiel's stomach. He aspirated with a large syringe. "No food in the stomach at least, so the blockage is farther along the tract. Then he sucked up in succession from a large bottle of mineral oil and one of a milky substance into two very large syringes. He injected their contents through the tubing into Fiel's stomach. "Now, we walk him and wait."

Manuel and River took turns leading Fiel slowly in the stable yard, letting him stop and rest frequently, but moving him forward if he showed signs of wanting to lie down. River had the lead rope when Pam drove up in her car and Sierra jumped out. She rushed over to her horse and River's chest tightened at the ashen, anguished expression on her face. Pam followed close behind.

"Oh, Fiel." Sierra touched his neck and looked into his suffering eye. "How is he?" she asked, looking from River to Dr. Patterson.

"He's not trying to bite at his sides now," the vet answered. "He seems willing enough to walk and he's not trying to lie down."

"Is that good?"

They stopped to allow Fiel to rest while Dr. Patterson explained to Sierra and her mother Fiel's symptoms and the current treatment plan. "I have given him a dose of mineral oil and a laxative. The walking will help encourage stimulation of the intestines. I hope before too long we will see results."

"What if it doesn't work?" Sierra asked desperately.

"The worst case scenario is he will need surgery if the intestine has twisted and is strangulated, or he simply cannot pass the blockage." Dr. Patterson was never one to hold back information. "But I don't see symptoms drastic enough for that yet."

For three more hours River and Sierra took turns walking Fiel. As the temperature dropped, they covered him with a horse blanket to keep him warm. Several times Dr. Patterson listened with his stethoscope over his abdomen. Finally, around midnight he announced, "I hear some rumblings, and something should happen soon!" Everyone felt as if heaviness in the air lifted a bit with his news.

River encouraged Manuel to go home and sleep. Manuel left but came back with Rosa, who brought a basket with cookies and fruit, made a pot of coffee in the lounge and brought out mugs of coffee or tea to those who wanted it. Then the couple went back to their trailer; Manuel promising to return in a few hours.

"Mom, you might as well go home too," Sierra said. "I know you have school tomorrow and there isn't anything you can do here." Pam refused to leave but did agree to go lay down on the sofa in the lounge. Dr. Patterson repeated the doses of mineral oil and laxative, and then he reclined in the front seat of his van and dozed, warning Sierra and River to notify him immediately of any change for the better or worse.

Shortly after three a.m., the blockage broke loose. With an explosion of gas, Fiel produced the first few plops of stool. He let out a long sigh, snorted, and tugged at the lead that Sierra held, stretching his nose toward the grass at the side of the stable yard.

Sierra hugged him and burst into tears.

Her sobbing woke River, who had been dozing on a bench in front of the stable, where he and Sierra had been resting in between their turns walking Fiel. He jumped up with his heart racing, fearing the worst. When he arrived at Sierra's side, she pointed to the three green balls on the pavement and smiled through her tears. He took the lead rope from her and she fell against his chest as he pulled her into his arms.

"He's going to be okay," she cried, hugging River tight around his chest. "He's okay!" They broke apart and grinned broadly at each other.

Dr. Patterson awoke, hearing their voices, and came over to examine Fiel. As he did, Fiel produced another small pile of droppings, and the veterinarian grinned broadly in satisfaction.

"Excellent!" he exclaimed. "Don't let him eat," he instructed, noting Fiel pulling at his lead toward the grass. "Offer him some water now; he can have all the water he wants. Then continue the walking with breaks for another hour and if he continues to produce stool, then I think we're out of the woods."

"River, you take him, I'm going to tell my mom," Sierra said.

After another hour and several more piles of droppings produced by Fiel, Dr. Patterson decided it was safe for him to leave. "There is an extraordinary amount of grain in the stool," he commented. "How much grain do you feed him?"

"Fiel's an easy keeper," River answered. "He only gets a half scoop morning and night." He furrowed his brow as he also noted how much grain appeared in the droppings.

"Hmm…well, continue the walking for about another hour or so, and if he continues to stool and looks this comfortable, then I would just turn him out in a paddock with plenty of water but no food. Mid-morning, you can give him a bran mash. Keep an eye on him throughout the day and call me if any symptoms return. I'll swing by to check on him this afternoon and advise when and what to resume feeding."

"You should come home now, Sweetie, you're exhausted," Pam advised after Sierra and River determined it was safe to leave Fiel in a paddock.

Just then Tess drove up; very early for her to arrive since it was just after six in the morning. She had called River once last night and when he told her what was happening, determined all was being done that could be done and she didn't need to come to the stable.

"How is he?" she asked.

River gave her the news.

"Good, I'm very relieved." She studied Sierra and River, noting Sierra's tear-streaked face and the deep shadows beneath both kids' eyes. "You two go home; take the day off from work. I'll call Katrina to see if she can clean stalls this morning with Manuel."

"I'm afraid to leave him," Sierra stated.

"All of us will check on him. You can come back, but at least get a few hours of sleep."

"Come on, Sierra," Pam said, and took her daughter by the shoulder. "I need to get home and shower right away. River, can I give you a ride home?"

"Yeah, thanks." He followed Pam as she shuffled Sierra to the car.

River asked Pam to drop him off at the intersection to his driveway. He felt embarrassed for them to see the condition of the house where he lived. "I guess I'll see you later this afternoon," he said to Sierra. "I doubt if I'll sleep more than a few hours."

"Me either," Sierra replied. "River, thanks so much."

He nodded and waved and watched their car pull away before he turned to walk up his driveway.

He was half way to the house when he remembered, *Laila!*

19 SEASON ENDS

It is not sufficiently appreciated that artistic horsemanship is not the ability to make horses perform particularly difficult movements; it is purely the attainment of complete accord between rider and horse, and it is by the measure of this accord that every performance has to be judged. – Brigadier General Kurt Albrecht

Storm trotted up to River as he came into the yard. She spoke to him in her canine language, a range of low howls and whines, asking, 'where have you been?' She was used to River leaving her during the day when he went to school, but he had never left her all night long.

River bent down to hug her, ruffle her fur, pat her sides, and allowed her to lick his face. "Hey, I missed you too," he said. He felt grateful for her health, and the health of Cory, Diva, and all the other horses…so thankful that Fiel was going to be okay.

Then he noticed Laila's car parked next to Warren's Camaro. *Still here?* He hurried into the barn and up the stairs to his room, but slowed before pushing through the door in case she was sleeping. He was met by his empty mattress. *Not here.*

He went back outside, wondering where she could be. At the sight of her car side-by-side with Warren's, it hit him like a rock in the chest – *no, she wouldn't!*

Inside the house, he took the stairs with weighted feet. He stopped outside of Warren's closed bedroom door. *Do I really want to know?* He hesitated a minute, then turned the knob silently, and opened the door enough to peer in. He stared. He should just turn and go. He stood there and stared, swallowing down the angry scream that rose to his throat.

"River?" Laila said, her voice croaky with sleep. She lifted her head from the pillow where she lay next to sleeping Warren.

He violently pulled the door closed and fled to the bathroom, slamming that door shut as well and locking it. He braced over the sink, gulping in deep breaths, feeling a violent rage bubbling up from his core into his brain and turning the atmosphere around him black. *How could she? How could she? How could..?*

"River, open the door," Laila called to him, rattling the knob. "Open. The. Door," she insisted. "We need to talk." She rattled the knob again. "If you don't open up, I'll have Warren break this door down."

He reached over and unlocked the door.

She pulled it open and stood in the doorway, wearing only Warren's camouflage shirt wrapped around her.

He turned and leaned back against the sink; arms folded tightly, and glowered at her.

"Where were you?" she accused. "We had a date, remember?"

He should have called her; but in his worry over Fiel he had totally forgotten Laila. Some of his anger shifted into guilt. He did not like to feel guilty, and that made him angrier; both at her and himself.

"Well?"

"I was with a sick horse. Didn't Warren tell you?"

"He only said he dropped you off at the stable…that's all."

It was true he had not told Warren why he wanted to be dropped off at Pegasus. "I've been up all night walking a horse dying from colic while you were here…" His tongue tied up in his painful rage until he ineffectually accused, "You and Warren!"

"How was I to know that? Did I receive a phone call?" She cocked her head, her mussed hair falling around her face, and the morning light glinting off her eyebrow stud. She looked how he had seen her so many times in the morning. And standing in that camouflage shirt…she looked so sexy. He felt himself responding to her in spite of his exhaustion and his anger.

Her eyes dropped to look down at him and the hint of a smile crossed her face. He noticed it even though she looked back up to meet his eyes with a very serious expression. "Now you listen here, River Girard. I am not your girlfriend. You know that. I waited for you until after midnight. Warren and I talked and talked and I like him. I like you. What happened tonight is no secret. I do what I want. Do you have a problem with that?"

He did have a problem with that, but what could he say? "Do you…are you Warren's girlfriend?" he asked lamely, and regretted it the moment the words left his mouth.

"Of course not; how many times do I have to tell you I am no one's girlfriend? You can accept that fact or not. We can be friends or not…your choice."

He looked down at his feet, not knowing what he wanted or what to say. His anger had drained away; replaced by confusion and a feeling of betrayal and hurt. "I'm tired. I'll talk to you later." He pushed past her and started down the hall to the stairs.

"Your choice…" Laila called after him.

He fled to his room and collapsed on top of his mattress. He buried his face in the pillow and thumped with his fists next to his head, trying to pound away the heaviness in his heart. He felt Storm nose at the nape of his neck, whining. Relaxing his hands, he allowed her to crawl next to him, and with a hand clutched in her fur, fell into an exhausted sleep.

Fiel acted like his normal, healthy self when River returned to the stable late in the afternoon. Sierra was already there, just hanging out with Fiel in the paddock, brushing him from time to time, and talking to him. They had given him a bran mash and celebrated when he produced stool within a half hour of consuming the feed. Dr. Patterson returned and pronounced him cured.

"I would like to know what caused this, however," he said, as he studied Fiel standing in the wash stall crossties, looking alert and hungry.

"We don't feed him that much grain," River said. "Do you think it's just been sitting and accumulating in his intestines?"

"That would be rather unusual…maybe he's not drinking enough water."

"It seems like he drinks as much as the other horses. The trough in his paddock is always down a level when I bring him in," Sierra said.

"It is strange…well, grass hay only and half ration for the next few days; no grain at all. I'll come by in two days and check on him again. Turn him out every day but I would recommend no work for a few days and then begin again gradually."

Dr. Patterson left and Sierra and River began helping Manuel bring the other horses in for the night.

"Reever, I talk wid you," Manuel said after the horses had all been fed. River said goodnight to Sierra, and followed Manuel into the feed room. Manuel closed the door behind them, and spoke to River in Spanish.

"Some strange things," Manuel began. "Last night after we feed, there was enough oats in the bin to fill half of the buckets for this morning's feed. When I feed this morning, the oat bin was almost empty. Where did the oats go?"

River's stomach lurched as suspicions of what might have happened entered his mind.

"Last night I went to the trailer and Rosa and I, we have our supper. After that, I come back to fix the loose board. I see a car leaving the driveway as I come up. I recognize the car. I have seen a friend of Crystal's come here in that car before. I think it is strange because that girl never comes here except for her lessons. Why is she here now? But, nothing wrong with that, I don't think. I go fix the fence. And I have already told you what I hear when I come back near the stable."

"Crystal!" River said through clenched teeth.

"That one has a mean spirit," Manuel said, shaking his head.

"Thank you, Manuel, for telling me."

"You tell Tess; I don't have good enough English to explain to her."

"Yes, I will."

They left the feed room and locked up the stable. River sat down on the bench outside. He shivered, in spite of the summer warmth of the early evening, and pressed Tess's number on his phone. "I need to talk to you now," he said when she answered.

"Go ahead," Tess said.

"In person," River insisted.

"River, I am having dinner; tell me what is so important."

"Finish your dinner, but I am waiting for you here."

He heard her sigh over the phone. "All right, I'll come in a few minutes."

A half hour later, Tess drove up and parked, and then she and River went into her office.

"Crystal tried to kill Fiel," River stated.

Tess's face creased into a frown, but River noted she didn't immediately refute his accusation. "Why do you think so?" she asked.

He related to her all that Manuel had told him. Again, Tess showed no signs of doubting his story.

"What are you going to do?" he asked in a tight voice.

Tess closed her eyes and took in a deep breath that she let out on a long sigh. With her shoulders slumped, she opened her eyes to look back at River with an expression of regret. She leaned her arms on the desk and hunched forward toward him, looking down at a stack of papers. "River, let me explain to you my situation. I half own Pegasus because Walt wanted to give his daughter the best facility for her horse, the best instructor, and every opportunity that she could want. This partnership with him only exists because of Crystal. I cannot survive financially without his backing. Unfortunately, that forces me to deal with Crystal very delicately. This business is my life and I am not going to do anything to jeopardize it."

He stared back at her in disbelief. "Even if it means killing a very good horse?"

Tess closed her eyes again and pressed her thumb and index finger into the corners. "River, try to understand. I am very sorry about what happened to Fiel. We just have to do everything possible to protect the horses in the future."

Anger rose, along with frustration. River bit back the words he wanted to shout at her. He studied her slumped posture, trying to understand. "Can't you buy him out?"

With a humorless smile that flashed quickly and then disappeared as Tess looked up, she said, "First of all, he would refuse as long as Crystal wants to ride. Secondly, the money I might have had to buy his shares, I loaned to your father."

River leaned back in his chair. His jaw dropped open and he shut it quickly with clenched teeth. "What?"

"How do you think he got the money to buy his colts? Your father is quite the talker, and I believed the loan was a good investment. It was looking to be a good investment last year. He had a good stallion and he could have paid me back with the stud fees. But you know what happened to that horse. Why he thought he needed to race him again…"

Iciness coursed through River's veins, numbing his limbs and filling him with a sense of useless waste. "So you're going to just let her get away with it?"

"I have no choice."

Choice…Laila had told him it was his choice. Why did he think of that now? The situations were not at all the same. He rose slowly, still feeling numb. "Tess, if anything happens to Fiel, or Cory, or even Diva…any of the horses…"

"I will take measures to keep them safe," she stated.

River left the office.

The next day, Tess called a locksmith to come out and put a keypad lock on the feed room door. All the boarders knew the combination to the back door of the stable, but only she, River, Manuel, and Sierra knew the combination to the feed room. That was Tess's measure to keep the horses safe.

River never told Sierra the exact details of the cause of Fiel's colic. But he did tell her and Dr. Patterson that he believed Fiel had somehow received an extra measure of oats. They had a right to know, so that they wouldn't think there was something wrong with Fiel's digestive system.

Sierra pressured River for more details but soon gave up. She was used to him telling her only what he wanted. But she had her own suspicions, remembering the threat from Crystal at the last show.

Fiel was back on normal rations and into his usual work within two weeks, and it seemed as if he had never been ill at all.

The summer fell into a routine. Katrina came on weekends and two to three weekdays if she could, to help clean stalls; her payment for lessons from River. When she came, it freed River to begin riding, leaving Sierra and Katrina to do the mucking.

River rode Cory out on the trail every day, and was starting to do intervals of trotting. It pleased him how much Cory seemed to enjoy the rides, and how quickly he was gaining fitness. Most of the time, Sierra rode with him on Fiel, for the two geldings seemed very compatible, and these rides were often the best part of his day.

Much to his surprise, River actually enjoyed coaching Sierra and Katrina, and looked forward to the weekly lesson he gave the two girls together. Katrina listened with rapt attention, trying very hard to do all he asked. It pleased him more than he would have ever thought, to see the girls get what he tried to teach them; the bright expressions on their faces when Minstrel and Calliope responded to the correct use of their aids.

The Pegasus team competed in two more horse trials over the summer. River had moved up to preliminary level on Moose, and won both his events; and qualified to compete in the Pacific Regional Championship. Crystal won first place on Diva at both events, and Sierra and Katrina both placed. Katrina took a fourth and third consecutively, and Sierra took a fifth and then surprisingly, second place at the last event. They also qualified for the championship.

Because of Fiel's bout with colic, Sierra decided to keep him home for the remainder of the summer, and she did not take him to any more dressage shows. She and Katrina continued to show Minstrel and Calliope at first level with improved scores each time out.

Pendragon did very well at third level with River as his rider, earning consistent scores above eighty percent. He placed first in all his classes at the dressage regional championship and Mr. and Mrs. Galensburg were thrilled when he also placed second in the nation-wide Horse of the Year awards for third level.

Felicity also qualified for the dressage regional championship, but River pleaded with Tess to convince her owners not to enter the filly. The championship was held at a facility over twelve hours away from Pegasus and he felt it would be too stressful for the filly at her young age to travel that distance. Since the owners were more interested in Felicity eventually competing in combined training, they relented.

For the Pacific Regional Combined Training Championship event, Sierra's mother again came to watch and support her; and this time they had João's old camper to stay in. Bittersweet memories enshrouded Sierra over the three days. At some moments, the loss of João seemed as acute as a year ago; for he had died right after the event. But at other moments, she felt his presence so intensely fill her spirit that she believed he rode with her, and she heard his voice coaching her in her mind.

It was no surprise when Crystal took first place at junior training level, and River took first place at junior preliminary level. Katrina finished in third place and Sierra in fourth; both girls pleased that their horses had performed the best they could.

Out of curiosity, Sierra looked for the name *Dean Clark*, on the list of entries at preliminary level, remembering the handsome boy who had been trying to qualify. His name was not there, so she guessed he never did achieve a qualifying ride.

Neither did Gloria; who attended the championship as a spectator and as Crystal's friend. Her expression contained a fixed, tight smile that never extended beyond the corners of her mouth during the entire show.

20 SOPHOMORES AND A SENIOR

The dressage rider should be deeply rooted in the horse. Movements and shifting of weight should be invisible to the onlooker. – Susanne von Dietze, *Balance in Movement*

"I can't believe just a few weeks ago I was complaining of boredom and wanted school to start. With all the homework they've piled on us, I wouldn't mind a little boredom," Allison complained on Monday morning as she and Sierra trudged forth from first period biology. It was the end of September, the horse show season over, and school had been in full swing for a month.

Sierra murmured agreement, her head bowed over a thick packet of handouts and her brow furrowed as she surveyed the daunting list of plant and animal classifications they were supposed to memorize.

"Oh my!" Allison's tone suddenly altered from complaining to a low sound of appreciation. "Who is that?"

The change in tone caught Sierra's attention and she looked up to where her friend blatantly stared. They were pushing their way through the main hallway to get to their next class, and were approaching the administration offices. A boy had just stepped out of the heavy glass doors marked *Administration*, where he hesitated, frowning at the sheaf of papers in his hands.

Something familiar about him caused Sierra to also stare, trying to place him in her memory…a tall, long-legged, slender boy, with trim reddish-brown hair. He wore name-brand slacks, a light green polo shirt with a soft-looking, tan leather jacket; clothes that fit him well.

The boy looked up and met the stares of the two girls, out of a pair of deep blue eyes.

The eyes confirmed his identity. "Dean?" Sierra greeted, smiling.

The furrows in his brow deepened into a scowl; he looked angry and there was no sign of recognition on his face. He looked away and stepped into the flow of students going in the opposite direction.

"Do you know him?" Allison asked, glancing over her shoulder at his retreating back.

"He looks like someone I met last summer at a horseshow, but he didn't seem to recognize me so I could be wrong," Sierra answered.

"Hmm," Allison mused. "He's going to cause a stir." They both laughed and hurried on to class.

Usually oblivious to the gossip that always hummed throughout the school, Sierra found her ears pricking to the rumors…new boy, a senior, hot! And then the more intriguing information…expelled from some private prep school...for drugs?..involved with a teacher? She heard his name, Dean Clark, which confirmed he was the boy she had met last summer…only once, so obviously he didn't remember her. *Why should he?* She thought of her own face as ordinary and easy to forget. But he had looked so angry. *What was that all about?*

Activity at the stable slowed down after season's end. Sierra and River returned to their school year schedule of cleaning stalls on weekends, and then working after school. Katrina only had time to ride one or two days after school and weekends, and Sierra felt a little guilty how glad she was to have time alone again with River.

River and she were just returning from the trail. River rode Felicity, beginning her slow conditioning work to prepare her for eventing next season. The filly seemed to delight in shying at every leaf, stick, and shadow on the trail. River enjoyed the youngster's antics, telling Sierra that Felicity used shying as an excuse to play. Sierra loved how River calmed the young horse without tensing or becoming frustrated at her antics, sometimes even laughing at her silliness.

Sierra rode a ten-year-old bay gelding, Magnificent, sent to Tess for retraining. He had done well at beginner novice, and novice levels of eventing, but his owner had not been able to qualify at training level last season. He was refusing jumps more often and taking rails down in stadium, and the owner hoped Tess could remedy these faults. River thought the horse had been pushed too hard and needed a break – very much like Crystal's last horse, Galaxy. For once, Tess actually listened to River and the plan was to trail ride only through the winter and not face him over jumps until next spring.

Sierra didn't particularly enjoy riding Max (so nicknamed). He always laid his ears back, exhibiting his displeasure when she groomed and tacked him up, stating clearly that he was not looking forward to a ride. She had to carry a whip to keep him moving. Even with another horse, he showed no desire to move beyond a plodding walk. He was however, the perfect companion for Felicity, for he remained sedate and steady no matter how much the filly snorted and jumped around.

"With my luck, Tess will assign me Max as my mount next season," Sierra complained as they reached the field and dismounted. Minstrel's owners had taken him away after the championship, their training contract with Tess completed. It had been hard to watch the horse van receding down the driveway the day he left, for Sierra had grown quite attached to him.

"Poor Max is so broken I don't know if he'll ever regain any spark," River said. "Look at him; his whole attitude is depressed and bored. I think he had been campaigned on the hunter/jumper circuit before his owner tried him at eventing."

Sierra patted the bay's neck as his ears finally pricked up with the scent and sight of the barn. "He still enjoys his oats and sleeping in the sun," she commented, laughing. "He'd be good for some little girl as a backyard horse or maybe a therapy horse."

"Yeah, maybe," River agreed.

As they came up into the stable yard and passed the outdoor arena, Sierra noted Tess giving a lesson to an unfamiliar horse and rider. Another figure dressed in riding clothes watched from the rail. *New students.* Sierra didn't recognize them or the trailer parked in the yard. Another man was untacking a bay horse tied to the side of the trailer. The bay tossed his head impatiently and stomped his front leg as the groom pulled off the saddle and began to brush him.

"Good horse," River commented as they walked by. "Needs ground manners."

They finished caring for Max and Felicity, and River left to get his next assigned mount. Sierra was done for the day, having ridden Fiel earlier. She would hang around to watch River school, always a pleasure, and often she learned something just watching and asking him questions. Then she would help bring the horses in for the night before going home.

She wandered back outside and watched Tess giving the lesson while she waited for River. The student was a young girl riding a gray mare over a course of jumps in double combinations. The jumps had been set up so that she had to ride figure eights and change leads before each combination. Tess was working with the student to get the mare to change leads without losing her balance and falling onto the forehand. The rider appeared competent and experienced at jumping.

"Good," Tess called out after the mare changed to the correct lead after the first loop. The mare cleared the double and then into the next loop, made another flying lead change. "Excellent," Tess praised. "See how keeping your outside aids helps with the change?"

The rider nodded, bringing her horse to a trot and then a walk. Then she rode over to Tess and dismounted, and they discussed the lesson in voices too low for Sierra to hear. With the lesson over, Sierra turned back to the stable.

"Hey," a boy's voice called out behind her.

She turned around and squinted into the afternoon sunlight, seeing the silhouette of a boy walking toward her. As he came closer she recognized Dean Clark.

"Don't I know you?" he asked, smiling.

"Not really," she answered, returning his smile. "We met once at a show last summer."

"Oh yeah, that's where I've seen you," he replied, although he still had a look on his face as if trying to place her.

"We go to the same school too," she said, and to help him out, added, "I'm Sierra."

"Sierra…of course. I'm Dean Clark."

"I know," she said, and felt herself flush.

"Is this where you train?"

"Yes, and I board my horse here."

"Cool, my sister and I have decided to join the enemy since we can't beat him."

"The enemy?" Sierra asked, confused.

He laughed. "You know; the competition. My father always says the way to win is to know your enemy. I figured I needed to start taking lessons from my enemy's coach."

Sierra squinted at him, still bewildered. "I don't understand. Who is the enemy?"

"Him of course." He cocked his head in the direction of River, leading a horse into the stable.

"River?"

Dean laughed again. "Yeah, 'Mr. Unbeatable'. I'm sick of hearing at the club about this newcomer who's never competed before and winning everything he enters. Where did he even come from? I decided I need to take lessons from whoever trained him, so here I am." The humor had faded from the tone of his voice.

Sierra did not bother to explain that River had not learned to ride from Tess.

The girl who had finished her lesson led her horse up to Dean. "She's good," she commented, cocking her head toward Tess who was walking in the other direction toward her office.

"I told you," Dean said. "This is my sister Caroline." He introduced the girl, who appeared to be Sierra's age. "I met Sierra at one of last summer's events."

"Nice to meet you," Sierra smiled at Caroline, always happy to meet another horse enthusiast.

Caroline mumbled a response, barely acknowledging her. "Let's get going, Dean; I'm starving."

The groom walked up and took the reins of the gray mare. "Did you have a good lesson?" he inquired politely.

"I'm satisfied," Caroline answered. Relieved of her mount, she strode off toward a sporty BMW parked near the trailer.

"Gotta go." Dean smiled at Sierra and then walked off after his sister. They both got into the car, Dean behind the wheel, and drove away, leaving the groom to care for the mare and then load up the two horses.

The gossip and rumors concerning Dean Clark remained the hottest topic at school for over a week. Sierra overheard the same emphatic statements about his good looks, mostly from girls, and what an amazing sports car he drove, mostly from boys, and how rich he was, from both. It seemed to be a confirmed fact that he had been expelled from a very expensive, private prep academy, but the rumors as to why, ranged from drugs to cheating to involvement with a teacher.

Sierra admitted she was very curious as to why he had been expelled. He seemed like such a nice guy.

Apparently everyone else at school thought he was a nice guy as well. Within the first few days of his arrival, he had risen to the status of one of the most popular boys of the senior class.

Friday, the day after she had met Dean at Pegasus, she and Allison were finishing lunch in the cafeteria and getting ready to leave for the library. Allison suddenly grabbed Sierra's arm and gasped. "He's coming over here!" she exclaimed in a harsh whisper.

Sierra turned and saw Dean with three senior boys approaching. He said something to his friends, who all laughed and then left him for their usual table. Dean continued on toward Sierra.

'Hey, Sierra," he called to her. Heads turned.

"Hi, Dean," she greeted, smiling and blushing.

"So, we go to the same school."

She had said that to him yesterday. "Yes," she answered.

"Cool. Hey, you want to sit with me for lunch?"

Sierra flushed an even deeper color, astounded at what he had just asked. *Did he just ask me to sit with him?* "Um, lunch?" she replied, feeling suddenly tongue-tied and dense.

"Yeah, you know, put food in your mouth, chew, swallow, it goes to your stomach? Nourishment?"

Those sitting at the nearby tables laughed.

Sierra laughed as well. "Thanks, I just finished eating. We're on our way to the library," she explained. She rubbed her palms on the thighs of her jeans, to dry their sudden dampness.

"The library?" Dean responded in a tone that sounded as if he had never heard of the place. "You're kidding." He grinned at her.

Sierra found herself entranced by the dimple at the corner of his mouth. "Yes, well you know, I need to work on homework so I have more time to ride after school."

He raised his eyebrow at her quizzically; then shrugged his shoulders. "Okay, maybe another time."

"Um, sure…thanks." She turned to go, catching a very amused look on Allison's face, mouthing to her the word 'go'.

"Hey, maybe we can ride together sometime," he called after her.

She turned back, and smiled broadly at his beautiful face. "Yeah, I'd like that."

"Give me your number," he said. He pulled his cell phone from his pocket and held it ready to enter the digits.

Sierra gave him her cell number, giggling and turning deeper and deeper shades of red…and very conscious of the spectators watching the unbelievable act of the most popular boy at school asking for the number of a very insignificant sophomore. Inside, her stomach twisted and churned, threatening to project up her just eaten lunch, and her heart palpitated. She felt humiliated! She hated giggly girls. She felt so out of control of her own body as a silly giggle came out of her mouth once again.

"Got it; catch you later." He winked at her and headed over to where his friends waited expectantly.

"Whoa," Sierra whispered as she and Allison retreated from the cafeteria.

"Oh my God," Allison whispered back. "Sierra, he's interested in you! Why didn't you go sit with him?"

"I couldn't! Allison…he can't be. Maybe he just wants to be friends because we both ride."

"Right, that's why he asked you to sit with him in the cafeteria, in front of all his friends."

"How could he possibly be interested in me?"

"Because you're beautiful and very sweet," her friend answered with conviction.

Sierra scrunched up her face in disbelief and laughed. But oh how she wanted to believe.

21 DEAN

A horse can only understand corrective guidance that shows him what to do, not the kind that shows only what not to do. – Charles de Kunffy, *The Ethics and Passions of Dressage*

The rest of the day Sierra struggled to keep her mind focused and pay attention in class. But inevitably, she would find thoughts and images of Dean slipping in between the (so boring in comparison) teachers' lectures. Then her face would flush and she ducked her head, trying to appear intent on writing notes. Staring at her paper, she saw his deep blue eyes, the dimple when he smiled, and admitted to herself, *I am very attracted to him.*

After supper that night, Sierra worked on her remaining homework at the kitchen table while her mother worked on her own nursing school assignments. Her cell phone rang and Sierra caught her breath as her heart suddenly raced in anticipation. But it was only Allison on her caller I.D.

"Did he call you?" Allison asked.

"No, I really don't expect him to," Sierra replied, trying to conceal the disappointment in her voice. They talked a few minutes longer and said goodbye.

Twenty minutes later when her phone rang again, she experienced the same breathless palpitations, and again let-down when it was Katrina.

"Tell me all the details," Katrina demanded.

"There's nothing to tell; I'm sure you heard what happened. All he did was suggest we ride together and asked for my phone number."

"All he did…Sierra, he hasn't asked for any other girl's number at our school."

Sierra did not know that. They talked a few minutes longer and then disconnected.

"Do you have an admirer?" Pam asked, having tuned into her daughter's conversations with maternal radar activated.

"I don't know," Sierra said pensively, and then told her mother what had happened. "But he's a senior and he's already hanging out with the popular kids; so I think his asking for my number really is just because of our interest in horses."

"Hmm," Pam said thoughtfully. "Are you attracted to him?"

Yes, very much. But Sierra did not want to admit the words out loud. For some reason, she felt expression of the words would change the whole essence of what had happened. She didn't really understand the meaning of what had happened. "Well, he is very handsome, and he seems like a very nice, friendly person. I do like him…" She flashed her mother a smile and ducked her head to turn pages of her textbook and hide the flush spreading up from her neck.

Pam studied her daughter, noting the flush of her cheeks. She had sensed the anticipation that Sierra must have been feeling each time her phone rang, and also the disappointment when it was not the boy. She smiled to herself, thinking of her own first crush in high school, and didn't pry for more information.

"Enough of this," Pam stated, and yawned, closing her textbook firmly. "I'm going to veg out and watch some mindless television." She stood and stretched, gathered her books and papers and stuffed them into her backpack. Coming up behind Sierra, she hugged her shoulders and kissed the top of her head. "Having an attractive, older guy pay attention to you can be a heady experience. Keep your wits and your common sense sharp, my darling daughter."

Sierra leaned into her mother and looked up into her face. "Don't worry," she reassured. "We both just like horses, kind of like me and River. River's older than me too."

Pam kissed her head again. "Perhaps; at least I believe River would never want to hurt you."

"I don't think Dean will hurt me," Sierra said.

"I certainly hope not." Pam left her alone then, and Sierra heard the sound of the television in the living room. A few minutes later, she heard her mother's cell phone ring. Sierra could tell by the tone of her mother's responses, even though she could not hear the actual words, that she was talking to Ron.

Shame settled onto Sierra's shoulders as she thought about her resentment of Ron, and her own selfish desire to have her mother's attention all to herself. How selfish she had been! Now that she found herself interested in someone, she recognized the unfairness of her behavior.

She tried to be polite when Ron was around but she couldn't help wishing he would leave whenever he came over, which was two to three nights a week. He brought pizza or some other take-out food, and always left soon after they ate; Pam insisting she needed to study. Sierra realized that answering Ron's questions in as few words as possible, and never asking any questions of her own, and then leaving the kitchen as soon as she had eaten, had been almost as obvious as saying, 'I don't like you'. Her mother certainly understood her behavior, although she never scolded her for it. Sierra knew Ron wanted to take her mother out, and it was probably because of her resentment that her mother never accepted a date with him.

She resolved to let her mother know she was okay with Ron coming around, regardless of what happened between her and Dean…because obviously, nothing was going on between her and Dean…it was almost nine, and he hadn't called. *Why hasn't he called?* She gave up trying to do homework and packed up her books.

"I'm going to get into bed and read for awhile," she said to her mother, giving her a quick goodnight kiss as she passed through the living room to her bedroom. She tossed her school backpack onto her desk and undressed before running into the bathroom for a short shower and brushing her teeth. Once back in her room, she couldn't help checking to see if she had received any calls before connecting the phone to its charger. Usually, she turned her phone off at night, and now she made no excuses to herself for leaving it on. *Maybe he'll call in the next few minutes…it's not that late yet.*

Sierra's eyes drooped after only two sentences of her book. She dropped it on the floor and shut out her bedside light. The mental intensity of school and the physical activity at the stable resulted in her almost instantly falling asleep every night as soon as her head hit the pillow.

Something pulled Sierra's consciousness from her dreaming state. She lay in the dark a few moments trying to clear the fog from her brain. A noise across the room on her desk…she glanced at her bedside clock, 11:22…*it's my phone!* She heard it again and lunged out of bed and grabbed up the phone, still plugged into the charger. "Hello?" she spoke in a sleep-husky voice.

"Hi, Sierra."

She recognized his voice immediately. "Dean," she whispered.

"Hi," he repeated. "Were you asleep?"

His voice sounded funny and she heard noise in the background; like music and laughter. "Yeah, well it's almost 11:30."

"Oh…(a pause)…really?"

"What do you want?" she whispered, holding the phone close to her mouth. She did not want to awaken Pam.

"I wanted to hear your voice. I've been thinking about you."

Sierra felt herself flush, even in the solitude and dark of her bedroom. "Dean, where are you? Why are you calling me now?"

Definitely she heard laughter in the background. It also sounded like Dean just laughed. But his voice was serious when he said, "I'll call you tomorrow, okay?"

"Okay…" The phone went dead. Sierra stared at its outline in the dark for a few moments, and then turned it off. *Weird!* Calling this late at night didn't seem quite right. Nevertheless, he had called her! *He's thinking about me!* She crawled back in bed, her mind and emotions whirling. It seemed hours before she was able to go back to sleep.

Dean did not call her the next day. Sierra usually left her cell phone in the bag attached to her bicycle; but today, she stuffed it into her pocket, waiting for his call. She and River fed, turned out the horses, cleaned stalls, took their break, and started their riding assignments, and still Dean hadn't called. She put the phone back in the bicycle bag when she and River brought their first horses in to ride. Between each horse, she slipped away to check messages. There were none.

"Are you okay?" River asked after the first trail ride together.

"I'm fine, why do you ask?"

"You seem somewhere else today."

"I'm fine," she reassured him. "I've got a big project for biology that's been on my mind (*partially true*), and I stayed up too late studying. I don't think I got enough sleep." *Why am I lying to River?*

He accepted her explanation and didn't ask any more questions.

At the end of the day, she helped Manuel and River bring in the horses, and then went home, her feelings dejected. *He'll call me tonight. Nobody calls in the middle of the day.*

He did not.

Sierra didn't carry her phone around on Sunday, but she couldn't help but check it for messages a few times. There were no messages, and Dean did not call Sunday night either.

Sierra did not want to admit to herself and definitely not to any of her friends how disappointed she was. She had reasoned to herself, considering the strange sound of Dean's voice and the background noise, that he had been drinking at a party, and probably didn't even remember calling her. The fact that he would have drunk enough to be in a state of forgetting bothered Sierra, and she told herself he was not the kind of guy she wanted to get involved with.

But on Monday, between second and third period when Sierra heard Dean's voice calling her name in the hall, her heart flipped violently, her face heated up, and she quickly turned around.

"Hi," he greeted her sheepishly.

"Hi," she answered, and smiled in spite of herself.

"Did I call you late at night over the weekend?"

He doesn't remember? So, he had been drunk. "Yeah, you did, like at 11:30. You don't remember?"

"I kind of do." He ducked his head and smiled up at her sideways. She felt her heart melting at the sight of the dimple at the corner of his beautiful mouth. "I had the flu over the weekend, and I think I had a really high fever. But I kind of remember getting out of bed and calling you. I fell asleep watching T.V., and I didn't have any idea how late it was."

Possible…the laughter and music could have been from a television show. Sierra suppressed all her suspicious feelings. She wanted to believe him. "Oh, I see," she answered lamely. "You're better now?"

"Yeah, I kind of slept the weekend away. I didn't get out to ride at all."

"Wow, that's harsh," she said in genuine sympathy.

"So, uh…you want to try to get together to ride?"

"Sure, I'd like that."

"What about today; is there a horse I can ride at Pegasus?"

Sierra was a little taken aback. She thought he would trailer over with his own horse. She thought for a minute. Since he was taking lessons from Tess it would probably be okay for him to ride on the property. She could ask Tess if it would be okay for him to ride one of her assigned horses, but of course…he could ride Fiel. "You could ride my own horse…he's very nice."

"Great, can I give you a ride after school?"

Another problem; she knew her mother would not allow her to ride in a car with a teenage driver. "How about if we just meet at the stable, around 3:30?"

He winked and gave her his dimpled smile. "It's a date."

At lunch, Sierra could hardly wait for Allison to join her, bubbling over with her news. She waved when she saw Katrina, who occasionally joined them before they left for the library. Katrina had her own group of non-horsey friends and she alternated her lunch time between them.

"What's up?" Katrina asked, scooting into a chair.

"Guess who's coming to the stable today to ride with me," Sierra asked with a broad grin.

"Oh my God…Dean?" Allison had come up behind and overheard the question.

Sierra nodded and her two friends squealed in their excitement. Then Sierra told them all about the weekend, the late night call, and his explanation in the hall this morning.

"He said he had such a bad fever that he didn't realize he had called you at 11:30 at night?" Allison asked suspiciously. "You believe that story?"

"Sure, why not?" Sierra replied defensively, but her few bites of sandwich started to clump in her stomach. It did seem strange. But why would he lie? He didn't even know her very well.

Allison raised her eyebrows and Katrina said, "Weird."

Arriving at the stable that afternoon, about 3:15, Sierra looked around hopefully for Dean, even though it was a little early. River had already arrived, for Storm lay in her usual shady spot and she looked up and thumped her tail as Sierra parked her bike. Sierra stepped inside and found River saddling Diva. He smiled as Sierra walked up, and suddenly a wave of guilt rushed over her as she realized he was waiting for her.

Awkwardly, she explained, "Uh, I'm going to wait for a bit. You know that guy who was here taking a lesson from Tess last week?"

"What about him?"

"He's coming over today to ride with me. I told him he could ride Fiel while I ride Max."

"You what?" River gaped at her incredulously.

Another wave of guilt hit Sierra. "So, we're going to ride on the trail together," she repeated.

River stared at her a few moments, his brow creasing into a deep frown and his eyes narrowing. Then without another word, he led Diva away.

"He's mad," she stated into the vacant space.

It was after four when Dean finally pulled into the yard in his BMW…actually, almost 4:30. Sierra had both Fiel and Max ready in the crossties, feeling miserable. She feared River would return from the trail and find her still waiting, and now without enough time to ride two horses. She would feel like a total fool if that had happened.

"Hi," Dean greeted cheerily as he entered the stable, coming towards the crossties. He was dressed in tan riding breeches, polished brown field boots, a tailored royal blue pullover, and carried a helmet. *He is so beautiful!* Her frustrated, hurt, and angry feelings almost completely dissipated at sight of him; just a niggling dark feeling that she pushed into a back corner of her heart. He had come, and that was all that mattered now.

"You ready to ride?" she greeted him with a smile. "We don't have a lot of time."

"Let's go then," he replied as he came up to her. Then to her astonishment, he leaned down and kissed her on the lips as if that was the most natural way to greet a friend.

Sierra flushed a deep red and turned quickly away to grab Fiel's bridle from a nearby hook. "This is Fiel," she said, turning back around once she felt she had her color back under control. She handed him the reins and then adeptly bridled Max. They each tightened their saddle girths and then led the horses out.

With trembling fingers, Sierra held onto the reins, as she mounted at the field mounting block, thankful she had chosen Max to ride. He was so placid he would not react to her nervousness. Her mind felt numb and besides her trembling fingers, she could feel her face constantly flush and her armpits damp. It didn't help when River passed by leading Diva, having finished his ride. He glanced at them with a stony expression and Sierra noticed Dean watching River's back as he led Diva up the hill, a deep frown on his own face.

Dean chattered almost constantly; talking about his own horse, past horses and wins, his other many accomplishments, and a little school gossip. His manner was so easygoing that Sierra at last relaxed, especially since he did enough talking for both of them. All she had to do was make appropriate responses, and kick Max or tap him with her whip to keep him moving forward and close enough to Fiel that she could hear. In moments of silence, she let Max lag back, and she studied with admiration Dean's elegant posture in the saddle. How handsome he was and how competently it seemed he handled Fiel, who stepped out with his ears pricked, untroubled by the unfamiliar rider.

He hadn't apologized for being late, and Sierra had already forgiven his tardiness; happy that he was here with her now.

After the trail ride, Dean helped her untack and groom both horses before they took them to their stalls for the night. Manuel was already bringing horses in and the stable aisles echoed with the sounds of horses nickering for their anticipated supper.

"Want to go get something to eat?" Dean asked as they stepped outside of the stable. He put his hand on her elbow, as if to guide her over to his car.

"I usually help bring horses in before I go home," Sierra told him.

"Is that your job?"

"No, I just like to help out."

"Can you skip it today? I know this great little café that makes exceptional pizza." He looked at her pleadingly with his lovely blue eyes.

How she wanted to say yes. "Thanks, Dean, but my mother doesn't let me ride in cars with teenage drivers," she answered truthfully, feeling like she needed to get this rule out of the way. But she felt herself blush, and felt so immature.

"Does she have to know? I can have you home in two hours."

Sierra's mind actually began to think of excuses that she could tell her mother…*I'll be home late, another horse has colic…Fiel threw a shoe on the trail and I need to wait for the farrier.* "No, really, I can't; but I appreciate the offer." She smiled up at him, hoping he would understand. How badly she wanted to go with him! How romantic to sit at a café table, just the two of them. She imagined a red-checkered tablecloth and candle light, just like in the movies. "Um, but would you like to come to dinner at my house?"

"Nah," he said, offering no excuses. "At least let me give you a ride home."

"I can't, my mother…"

"Okay, little girl," he said teasing, but she thought it sounded slightly irritated. He flicked his finger down the tip of her nose.

Will he kiss me again?

"See you tomorrow." He did not kiss her, but sauntered away to his car without looking back.

22 GOING OUT

Beauty is often the perception of the least amount of energy being spent to produce a desirable outcome – a soap bubble whose glistening shape is defined by the perfect equilibrium of pressure inside and out, the brilliance of horse and rider defined by a common intent, giving their best. – Jill K. Hassler-Scoop, *Equestrian Instruction*

Is this love? Sierra wondered. Every time she caught sight of Dean, or saw his name on her phone's caller I.D., or even overheard someone mention his name; her heart raced, her stomach fluttered, her breath caught in her chest, and heat flushed throughout her body, not just her face. Her mouth and throat became dry as her palms and armpits dampened; her hands and knees trembled, and her brain froze. Thoughts of Dean were the first to enter her consciousness when she awoke and the last to fade away as she drifted to sleep. She used to enjoy school lectures, especially from the more talented teachers; but now all seemed incredibly boring since she had to force herself to pay attention and not think of Dean. She had no appetite, and ate food without interest, just to appease her stomach when it growled and grabbed at her insides to get her attention.

Is it also love that causes the sharp pain in her heart every time he doesn't call, every time she sees him talking to another girl, every time he passes her in the hallway as if he doesn't see her? She had not expected love to ever be so painful.

She did not know what their relationship was supposed to be – just friends, his girlfriend? Other sophomores seemed to think they were going out; she overheard the buzzing gossip. Katrina seemed to think so, asking when they were going to ride together, and what they were going to do on the weekend.

When he did pay attention to her, it was so amazingly wonderful; so grand that she always forgave him in her heart for past neglect…never actually saying so to his face, for he never asked for or acted as if he needed forgiveness. *It's just his way*, she told herself. *His mother has never taught him consideration for others.* Because when they were together, he said the sweetest things – told her he always thought about her, he missed her, she was so special, different from other girls.

When she was with him, it was easy to believe every word. When they were apart, she tried to find excuses for him so she could still believe.

Sierra didn't hear from Dean for a week after their trail ride together. His sister Caroline had come for her lesson alone and Sierra didn't feel as if she could ask her about Dean. She had just reconciled to herself, through many a wet pillow at night, that he had decided she was too much a baby, or she bored him, and he wasn't interested in her.

Then, he suddenly called her the following Friday night (at nine o'clock), asking if she wanted to catch a movie. She made her excuses, knowing her mother would never let her go.

On Monday, he found her in between classes and walked with her to her next class, as if he did it all the time.

The next day, he approached her at lunch where she sat with Allison and Katrina, and invited her to sit with him.

"Come on Sierra, I promise I won't bite, just my sandwich." He raised his eyebrows in a comical way, imitating a villainous look, which caused her to giggle. "You come too, Allison. Ashley's dying to meet you." Dean cocked his head in the direction of his table where Ashley Brown, another senior and considered to be very hot, stared at them with an expectant expression. Crystal also sat at that table next to Stuart. The knowing smile she wore on her face raised Sierra's suspicions.

Nevertheless, Sierra had been about to say yes, for the last time he had invited her, Allison had told her she should have accepted. Both Allison and Katrina had encouraged her friendship with Dean…then. But now, when he blatantly excluded Katrina, she froze in her response. Things were going on that she did not understand…and she feared it had something to do with Crystal. She wondered if the obvious exclusion of Katrina had to do with Crystal and Katrina's broken friendship. *But why is it okay for him to invite me, then?*

"I'm not interested in meeting Ashley," Allison replied in a cool tone. "Go ahead if you want," she said to Sierra, but she kept her narrowed eyes on Dean.

"Thanks, I'll stay with my friends," Sierra answered meekly.

"It's okay, Sierra," Katrina encouraged. "Go ahead."

Sierra knew it was not okay with Allison. "Dean, I'm going to the library," she said firmly.

He laughed and turned away. She could not see the expression on his face, but whatever it was, it caused an uproar of laughter at his table.

He didn't speak to her again for the rest of the week, almost as if in retaliation. Sierra told herself she had already gotten over him once, to forget about him. But whenever she saw him, it felt as if razor sharp needles were puncturing holes in her heart.

Then the next week he came with Caroline for a lesson. He rode first, and then while his sister had her turn, he found Sierra working

Fiel in dressage exercises in the indoor arena. He watched from the rail silently. His presence disturbed her, and as she felt stiffness in Fiel's responses she knew she had tensed up. She could not seem to ignore his presence and calm her nerves, so she gave up and gave Fiel the reins to stretch, ending her ride.

"You're a very good rider," he complimented, coming up to her when she dismounted.

"Hi, Dean," she greeted him, wishing he would go away…but also wishing he would stay and say he was sorry.

He walked with her to the crossties, commenting positively on her ride, and at least what he said didn't sound like flattery. Fiel had been giving her correct shoulders-in, moving on three tracks along each long side of the arena, when she had first noticed Dean at the rail. He had seen her riding canter figure eights with a simple change of lead at the center, and Fiel working correctly off his hind end. So when he complemented her on those movements, she believed him sincere.

After that day, he called her almost every night, usually after nine o'clock. They talked for up to an hour; or at least Dean talked. But in amongst talking about his day, his problems with certain teachers, and his distrust of certain of his friends, he threw in what he thought of her – how understanding she was, he trusted her, and other sweet things. Sierra started leaving her phone on vibrate and moved her charger onto her bedside stand so she could grab the phone when he called and burrow under her covers so that her mother would not hear.

He walked with her in between classes they had close together. He came up to her table at lunch to say hi, although he didn't invite her to sit with him again.

It was after that week that rumors started to buzz that they were going out.

"Has Dean asked you to homecoming yet?" Katrina asked one day after announcing she had accepted a date with Kelly Ivers, a popular sophomore boy who Sierra thought was very nice.

"No, he hasn't said anything," Sierra confessed. She had been wondering if he would ask her soon, for homecoming was currently the hot topic at school. Allison was going again with Peter.

Another week went by, and if Dean wanted to take her, she needed to know. She didn't want to wait until the last minute this year to shop for a dress, and she wanted something more grown-up than last year.

The next time he called her, she summoned her courage to ask, "Are you going to homecoming?" She knew it was an obvious, loaded question.

He laughed through the phone. "School dances are not my thing," he said.

"Oh," she also laughed. "Yeah, I guess they are kind of dumb."

"Sierra, did you want to go?" he asked in a surprised tone.

"No…I went last year and I had a horrible time."

"That's because you weren't with me," he said teasingly.

"Maybe, but it was pretty boring."

"You do want to go," he stated.

"No, I don't," she said, feeling ridiculous.

"Tell you what, I'll think about it."

And that's what Sierra told Allison and Katrina, that he was thinking about it so they probably would go. She joined them one evening to shop for dresses and accessories, confident that Dean would end up taking her.

But homecoming came and went, and Sierra sat at home; her new satiny, dark green dress hanging in her closet.

She told herself all weekend that she had never really wanted to go, reminding herself of her date last year with Luke. How stupid for kids to dress up in grown up clothes that were uncomfortable to dance in; just to show off to everyone…how foolish. She tried to feel smug and mature that she had grown above such nonsense.

Nevertheless, she felt an aching loneliness inside as she listened to everyone talking about the banquet and the dance all during the week after.

"You know," Allison said, "if you would sort of make it known that you're not actually going out with Dean, some other boy might ask you out."

Sierra laughed, trying to sound nonchalant. "I'm not interested in anyone, and I agree with Dean. School dances are pretty stupid."

"Peter and I had a good time. Do you think we're stupid?" Allison asked pointedly.

"No, of course not…that's not what I meant," Sierra answered, flustered and her face reddening. She felt like she had just insulted her friend.

"Sierra," Allison said in a softer tone. "We're best friends, right?"

Sierra nodded, her throat tightening.

"You don't have to make excuses or try to convince me that everything is okay with you and Dean. Tell me the truth, if he had asked you to homecoming, would you have accepted?"

"Yeah, I guess if he had wanted to go." Sierra's stomach felt uneasy with these questions, for she knew how perceptive Allison was.

"But did you want to go?"

"I didn't have a very good time last year, remember?"

"That wasn't the question. Last year's bad experiences didn't really have anything to do with the prom itself but having to deal with Crystal and Justin, and Luke not really coming through for you."

Sierra ducked her head, and after a pause, looked her friend in the eye with the hurt transparent on her face. "It's not so much that I wanted to go to the prom, but that I wanted to go out with him."

"Has he ever asked you out on a date?"

"Yes, well sort of. He asked me if I wanted to get something to eat after we rode together. But you know how my mom feels about me riding in a car with a boy. And he asked me to the movies once."

"But he's never come to your house to meet your mother, or made arrangements for his parents to drive so you could go out."

Sierra shook her head, looking at her lap.

"I think your mother is right and you should never ride in a car alone with Dean," Allison warned in a very serious tone.

Sierra looked up at Allison, feeling pressure building up behind her eyes. "What do you mean?"

"Okay, I've tried to keep my mouth shut about this, but you are my best friend and I have to tell you what I think. Dean is a total jerk."

"You don't know him," Sierra defended. "It's not like he's ever said anything like a commitment to me, or that we're anything but friends. Why should I expect him to take me out?"

"Everyone in school seems to expect it."

"But they don't know anything."

"Sierra, how do you feel about him?"

"I like him. I like being with him." Sierra could not say even to Allison what she wanted to shout out, *I love him; I'm only happy when I'm with him.*

Allison's expression softened and she gave Sierra a hug. "I don't want you to get hurt," she whispered.

It was bad enough that Allison didn't like Dean, but River's attitude was unbearable. Ever since Dean rode with her, River had been cold and aloof. He coached her in lessons, but afterward, walked away or talked with Katrina, who always had questions.

Then Dean suggested that they ride together again. "I asked Crystal if I could ride her horse, and she said, 'anytime'."

Sierra dreaded how River would react to that.

"He's going to ride Diva?" River had said incredulously when Sierra arrived at the stable, and told him the plan.

"Crystal said he could ride her," Sierra answered, feeling somehow traitorous. River spent many hours working with Diva, conditioning her on trails and schooling her in the arena. It did seem unfair that Dean could ride the mare on his own whim.

"He can't!" River exclaimed.

"River," Sierra said in a calm and reasonable tone. "She is Crystal's horse and she gave him permission. I don't think he'll hurt her. He's a good rider."

River's expression reminded her of the way he had looked when Crystal had demanded that her horse Magic be put down after his injury. It cut into her like a sharp knife, and her first reaction was to agree, that Dean should not ride Diva. But when his expression shifted to one of contempt and anger, she became defensive, and her jaw tightened firmly as she glared back.

River spun away and she did not see him the rest of the day.

He is way over-reacting, she told herself, but nevertheless remorse and guilt slipped in alongside her anticipation of Dean's arrival.

Dean actually arrived only twenty minutes late, and his attention and chatty cheerfulness quickly overshadowed her guilt, and she forgot about River. They rode out together; Dean on Diva and Sierra on Fiel. She watched him in the saddle, and could see nothing wrong with how he rode or in Diva's behavior.

"Let's take a few jumps," Dean suggested as they left the trail and walked onto the field.

"Tess has her on a schedule for what days she should jump, so I don't think that's a good idea," Sierra replied, thinking that was a bit much to ask of a horse he was riding for the first time and didn't belong to him.

"Just a couple low ones; nothing challenging." He smiled disarmingly, and without waiting for her to say no again, he nudged Diva away and into a canter. He guided her over a two-foot section of the rail fence, then a low stone wall, a ditch, and finished over a coop before bringing Diva down to a trot and rode her back to where Sierra waited. Diva snorted and trotted up energetically, obviously not damaged in the least. Dean beamed at Sierra and patted the mare's neck. "How was that?"

"You looked good," Sierra replied, smiling at him, but thinking to herself in relief, *no harm done.*

The following Saturday, as they were cleaning stalls together, Sierra tried to reason with River. "I don't think Dean does any harm riding Diva. He's a good rider."

She didn't expect him to answer, accustomed as she was to his cold silences. But she needed to get this out in the open between them. "River, what is up what you? Are you mad at me or something?"

"Why should I be mad at you?" he answered in a bitter tone.

"You don't talk to me. You won't even look at me."

He looked up at her then. "I'm not mad."

"You act mad."

River maintained communication silence, mucking vigorously.

"If you're not mad, what is wrong then?"

He scowled at his forkful of wet shavings. "I don't think you should hang around with that Dean guy."

"Why?" she challenged.

River shook his head.

"What's wrong with him?" Sierra persisted.

"There's nothing right about him."

"River…" Sierra said, exasperated, "that's ridiculous. How can you say that? You don't even know him."

"I know enough."

"That's unfair. He's a nice person," Sierra insisted.

River dumped his forkful forcefully and then stood with his arms folded around the pitchfork. "He's too old for you, he's using you, and he'll hurt you."

Sierra squeezed the handle of her own pitchfork as tight as possible to hold in her exploding emotions. She had thought the same things, and it hurt so much to hear that expressed out loud. But River couldn't know, anymore than she, and now it was River hurting her. "You're wrong," she stated, struggling to keep the tremor out of her voice.

River shook his head again and turned his back as he returned to mucking.

"I don't get you," Sierra said to his back. "Dean is fun to be with. He likes horses. He thinks you're a great rider. (Dean had never said that to her, but he had inferred it when he talked about River as the competition.) I think you and he could be friends."

River made a derisive sound. "I will never be friends with him."

"Why not?"

"He doesn't like horses. He uses horses…like Crystal."

"How can you say that? I've seen him around the horses and he shows a lot of affection. He's not at all like Crystal."

"I've seen him around horses too, and he doesn't care about them."

That statement made no sense at all. She had never seen Dean do anything harmful around a horse. *Of course he likes horses.* "You just don't know him." They returned to mucking in thick, bitter silence. After a few more forkfuls, Sierra shot out, "And he's not too old for me."

"Yes he is," River insisted.

"What about that girl you were seeing? Laila or whatever her name is. She's way older than you," Sierra demanded.

"That was different."

"I don't see how."

River faced her again. "Exactly; that's why he's too old for you."

"That doesn't make any sense."

He turned away and dug in forcefully with his pitchfork.

"And it's really none of your business," she added spitefully, although in her heart, she felt it might be his business if they were friends.

"Right. So forget it."

"Fine."

They finished the last few stalls in cold, brittle silence.

When Dean and his sister came for their lessons, he would find Sierra and talk with her while Caroline rode. She anticipated his arrival on their scheduled day, and delayed her rides so that she would be at the stable when they pulled up in his BMW, the groom driving the trailer behind them. Sometimes it meant that she cut her ride short on Fiel, though she always made sure she accomplished the allotted time on her assigned horse for that day. But she grasped at all the short intervals of time she had with him – walks between classes, a few minutes in the cafeteria, and a full forty minutes or so during Caroline's lesson. Dean and Caroline always left as soon as both their lessons were finished, leaving the groom to take care of their horses.

Then one evening as she pedaled her bicycle homeward, she found Dean sitting in his car, almost hidden in a stand of trees near the Pegasus driveway.

"Sierra," he called to her.

"Dean! What are you doing here?" Sierra rolled her bike alongside his car, smiling in her happiness to see him.

"Waiting for you." His tone was serious and he didn't smile.

"What's wrong?" Sierra's heart jumped as she imagined a tragic accident to their trailer with the horses in it.

Dean breathed out a long sigh as he stared straight ahead, his arms extended in front of him with his hands gripping the steering wheel. "I try not to think about you. I know I shouldn't be interested in you. I'm too old for you; that's what all my friends say."

Sierra could not think of a response. Her mind filled with the idea that he talked about her with his friends. She stood awkwardly, squinting in at him.

He turned his head to look at her, his eyes dark in the shaded light. He studied her face, his expression serious and unsmiling. It made her feel vulnerable and self-conscious and she flushed a deep red.

"Could you just talk with me for a little while?"

"Okay," Sierra answered, confusion mingling with the pleasure of seeing him; unsure of why he was here.

Dean leaned over to open the passenger door. "Sit down," he invited. When Sierra hesitated, he did smile and coaxed, "I'm not going to drive away with you. I just want you to be comfortable."

"Um, okay." Sierra set her bike down and got in the car. *I'm not disobeying; he's not driving.*

"I can't stop thinking about you." Dean picked up her hand, stroking her fingers and then lacing his own fingers with hers. "Do you have any idea how special you are?" he asked in a husky voice.

"No," she replied in a whispered squeak. His words sent thrills down her spine. His touch sent heat surging up her arm. Her heart pumped with such force that she feared Dean would hear it. She stared down at the hand holding hers.

He began to run a finger, feather-light, up her arm. "I'm obsessed with you. I can't concentrate in class or on my homework because you are always in my mind. I can't eat. I can't sleep. I toss and turn every night wondering what you look like in your bed."

Sierra looked up to meet his penetrating gaze, speechless.

He dropped her hand and sat back from where he had been leaning in towards her and covered his face with both hands.

Is he going to cry? This entire situation felt surrealistically weird.

"Sierra," he said in a muffled voice. "Do you care about me?"

"Yes," she croaked through her dry throat, coughed and said again in a clear voice, "yes."

He scrubbed his hands down his face, turned to face her again, and reached out to touch her cheek with his thumb. He picked up one of her braids and rolled it between his fingers. His other hand reached forward and cupped her chin as he slowly leaned in with his eyes on hers. He kissed her softly on her parted lips.

Sierra closed her eyes. When he pulled her against him she did not resist. He kissed the top of her head, then her forehead, her nose, and when he reached her mouth again, she kissed him back. She put her arms up around his shoulders and allowed herself to melt against his chest, feeling the thump of his heart and thinking it beat in time with hers.

He stroked her shoulders, her neck, traced her ears, her jaw line, and then when she lifted her face, he pressed his lips to hers more firmly, but oh so sweet.

But when his tongue probed into her mouth, Sierra's eyes flew open and she pulled away in shock.

Dean broke away and held her by her shoulders, gazing into her startled eyes. He smiled and touched his finger to her lips and traced them gently. "Never been French kissed before?" he whispered.

She shook her head.

"You didn't like it?"

"I…I don't know. I think so…"

"I liked it," he continued in a seductive whisper. "You taste like honey…sweeet." He drew the last word out on a whispered breath as he leaned in and kissed her softly; then traced her lips with his tongue. "So sweet," he repeated. This time he closed his eyes and kissed her deeply.

Sierra kissed back, losing herself in the warmth of his embrace and the eagerness of his mouth. She did like it!

He broke away from her mouth to whisper, "I want you," and then kissed her again. And now his hands were rubbing her shoulders, and between her shoulder blades. It felt so wonderful. He stroked over her shoulder and down her neck, to trace her collar bone, and then down her chest.

His touch seemed to draw heat from her deepest core to spread throughout her body…her body that tingled mysteriously in places it never had before…a mystery she wanted to unfold, but…*not here, not now*! "Stop, Dean," she asked him. He did not and she pushed his hands away.

"Please," he pleaded, looking mournfully into her eyes.

"I can't." She shifted and moved herself away.

His expression shifted into a frown. "You're not very nice." He almost sounded angry.

"Please," Sierra pleaded in turn, not liking how he glowered at her. She felt a little scared. "I'm not ready for this."

He stared back coldly.

"Don't be mad at me."

His expression softened to one of wistful reproach. "Why are you rejecting me? Do you know how that hurts me?"

"I'm not rejecting you…" she started to explain, but he interrupted by leaning in to kiss her again. As he tried to take her back into his arms, she pushed them away. "No. I don't ever want to hurt you, but I can't."

"Okay." He moved back away and dropped his hands onto the steering wheel. "Goodbye." He didn't look at her as he reached forward and turned the ignition key and the engine purred to life.

For one frightened moment, Sierra feared he would drive off with her. But he waited, his hand on the gear shift, still looking straight ahead.

"Dean…" When he didn't move, she opened the door and got out. As soon as her door closed, he drove off. She stood forlornly watching him drive away.

The next day at school, Dean acted as if the incident in the car had never happened. Sierra, feeling very inexperienced, confused, and embarrassed to ask what it had been about, pushed the whole thing to the back of her mind.

23 JUMPING

The essential joy of being with horses is that it brings us in contact with the rare elements of grace, beauty, spirit and freedom. – Sharon Ralls Lemon

I am not jealous. I just don't want to see her get hurt.

River tried to convince himself that was his only concern, whenever he saw Sierra with Dean.

River never thought about love; it was not something he felt like he needed or that would ever happen to him. Of course he had loved his mother and he had loved João. He loved Storm and the horses…*but that is easy love.* He probably had loved Laila, although he didn't think he had been in love with her. He never expected to fall in love.

He did not like the way Sierra invaded his thoughts, or the fact he found himself having imaginary conversations with her in his mind; conversations where he convinced her to stay away from the biggest jerk in their school. All the pleasant memories of things they did together - riding, working, cooking in her kitchen, playing with Storm and Charlie - now only caused an acute sense of loss. He missed her, *but that doesn't mean I…*

I am mad at her. How could she be such an idiot? He tried to think of all the things he didn't like about her. But honestly, there was only one thing - the fact she had chosen Dean over him.

He had seen them together in Dean's car and that had inflicted a wound more painful than any beating he had ever received from his father.

Yesterday on his way home, he saw the parked BMW, almost hidden next to the driveway leaving Pegasus. Storm had barked once, and maybe her warning had triggered him to slip into the foliage to clandestinely peer into the front seat…a couple making out.

He recognized the back of Dean's head, and quickly looked away, because he already knew who the girl was. But he had to look; and when he saw part of Sierra's face, her eyes closed with that jerk's mouth on hers, it felt as if a giant fist punched him through his chest. His vision momentarily went black and he dropped down to the ground, squeezing his fists against his tightly folded arms to hold in the screams that ricocheted within his heart and mind. He couldn't move until he heard a door open and close, the car drive away, and Sierra pushing off on her bicycle.

I hate her! I don't care about someone who is so stupid. But he did care, and he did not hate her; he… His emotions vacillated between jealously and anger to profound feelings of wanting to protect and care for her.

Boys' locker room banter did not interest him and most of the time he tuned it out, but when he heard Dean's name and something about a bet, he did listen. He had missed the details but understood that it involved a contest between Dean and two other seniors, and it had to do with girls. Even then, he had a bad feeling that Sierra might be a target of this bet. He had wanted to warn her, but had nothing definite he could warn her about.

Don't hurt her! If you hurt her I will tear you apart, he threatened Dean in his mind. He knew he could take him on. The guy might be slightly taller, and maybe carried twenty more pounds; but he was a wimp without muscle. The guy obviously never stacked hay bales, repaired fences, or dug drainage ditches; all the things that had given River firm chest and arm muscles in spite of his thin build. *I could pulverize him…and her! No*, he never wanted to hurt Sierra…*ever!* He wanted her to open up her beautiful brown eyes and see the truth about Dean.

Of course, if Dean did hurt her badly, she would give him up and she would need someone to comfort her and… But that was not how he wanted things to happen. He did not want Sierra to come to him on the rebound with a broken heart.

No real food in the house, no hot water when he took his shower, a night of thumping his pillow as he tossed and turned, left River in an extremely foul and bitter mood the next morning with the weekend ahead of him. He knew better than to try anything new or difficult on his rides today; he did not want to project his despondent feelings onto the horses. He trail rode Penny, Moose, and his other assigned horse; and lunged Felicity in the arena. Then he went out to a corner pasture where Corazón had been turned out.

His horse whinnied and trotted up as River stepped inside the gate. The sight of the beautiful animal with his mane flowing and his black coat glistening in the afternoon light; at least temporarily lifted his mood. A horse moving in freedom with head and tail held proudly, had always thrilled River's spirit, transporting him to a place unhindered by the problems of the world.

"*Hermano*," he greeted his horse and reached up to touch his nose and stroke his neck. The black nuzzled at his chest, and then at his pockets. River fed him a carrot, and allowed Cory to lick the salt flavor from his palm.

The shadow of a hawk passed overhead, followed by its piercing cry. Cory snorted and shied away from River, tossed his head and kicked out with his back legs, then returned to face the boy, standing squarely with head high. He blew out one loud snort and stomped a front leg.

River laughed. It seemed obvious that Cory wanted out for a run. With so many horses assigned to him every day, he often didn't have time for his own horse, and it had been two days since he had last ridden the black. He did make sure he worked him at least four times a week, either on the trail or twenty to thirty minutes of basic dressage exercises, to maintain his fit condition. Cory's gleaming coat, prominent veins, and rippling muscles confirmed he was in top form.

"*Bueno, vamos.*" River walked over to the gate and picked up Cory's halter, his horse following close behind. He fastened the halter on the black's head, looped the lead rope around his neck and tied it to the halter ring, forming reins. He led him outside the gate and glanced surreptitiously around to be sure no one saw, although this part of the property was not visible from the stable yard or the back field. Tess would have a fit if she found out he rode without bridle, saddle, or helmet. He swung himself up onto Cory's bare back, picked up the rope reins and guided him onto a path that edged the lower part of Pegasus and intersected with the network of trails.

Cory jigged impatiently as River tried to keep him to a walk to at least attempt a warm-up. He gave up after a few minutes and allowed him to break into a lengthened trot. As soon as they reached the intersection to the trail, he let go, and Cory leaped into a gallop.

They raced up and down the hills of the trail, the speed clearing River's mind of troubles and soothing his aching heart. He couldn't think; only feel…Cory's muscles bounding beneath his seat and between his legs felt like they belonged to his own body. The wind from their speed whistled in his ears, silencing the world around. He only heard Cory's deep breathing in rhythm with his galloping stride, and the pounding of his hooves. His eyes watered, blurring the vision of Cory's black head moving rhythmically in front of him. His spirit melded with his horse and they moved together as one animal, filled with pure joy. He never wanted to stop.

But they had to stop, and when the trail led them to the back field, River sat deep and quiet and 'spoke' to Cory to slow down. The black brought his hind end muscles underneath to slow from a gallop to a canter and then trotted off the trail onto the field. He pricked his ears, snorted, and turned his head to look at a log jump to their right.

Has he ever jumped? Recklessness suited River's mood, and impulsively, he turned Cory to face the log. *If he goes straight, we'll take it; if he veers, I will guide him to the side,* River decided.

Cory jumped back into a canter and moved confidently toward the log, took off at the correct spot, and sailed over, galloping on toward a low stone wall straight ahead of the log. River let him go, and he took the wall boldly. *Awesome!* He turned him toward a rail fence; it seemed all he needed was to point the black where he wanted, and his horse soared over.

"*Está bien.*" He guided Cory to the perimeter of the field and down to a walk. He leaned forward and hugged him around his neck, patting and stroking his chest and shoulders. Cory dropped his head and snorted, relaxed and happy. River slipped off his back and hugged him again, his heart bursting with pride and exhilaration. *Cory can jump and he likes it!*

A figure walked toward them, waved and then called out, "That was so amazing! Incredible!"

River looked up, startled, and recognized Katrina. *Uh oh, caught in the act.* "Hi, Katrina," he greeted. "What are you doing here?"

"I dropped my whip coming back from the trail and I was just coming down to get it when I saw you. River, I have never seen anything so beautiful; you should have seen the two of you…and bareback!"

"Yeah, this guy can jump," River grinned, unable to hide his pride over his horse.

"How can you possibly have the courage to jump bareback, and you only have a halter on him," Katrina exclaimed.

River shrugged, but he was pleased by her gushing praise. "They're not very big jumps."

"Still…"

"Please don't tell Tess," he asked conspiratorially. "She gets mad when I ride bareback."

"No, I won't, but where's your helmet?"

"I just sort of got on him without thinking," River admitted. "Don't tell her that either; you know I always ride with a helmet."

"You could have been hurt," Katrina chastised him with a genuine look of concern on her face. She walked with him and Cory back to the stable, chatting away, mostly in words that emphasized her admiration of him.

River thought it was quite nice having someone look up to him and want to be with him; kind of how it used to be with Sierra.

Corazón truly loved to jump; and when he did, he jumped big and bold. River (using bridle and saddle), started jumping him once or twice a week in the outdoor arena or over a few field jumps. He started with low heights in easy combinations, but Corazón exhibited so much enthusiasm and natural ability, that River gave in to the temptation to challenge him with bigger fences, tricky combinations, and tight turns. Cory's eagerness matched that of his rider as he boldly faced each new obstacle with what appeared to be little effort.

Anyone at the stable when River jumped Corazón, found themselves drawn to stand at the rail and watch in awe; for the horse's natural ability seemed dauntless.

"I never would have believed it the day you brought that animal here," Tess said; her eyes bright, thinking of the possibilities. "Did you know he could jump?"

"No, I just saw the potential," River stated proudly.

After that, Tess pushed River to try Cory's limits and see how high and wide he could jump.

"Give him time, he's only around six years old," River replied, and refused to jump him more than three feet for the first month, even though Cory cleared three feet as effortlessly as most other horses cleared a foot.

But River was curious as well, and one afternoon, relented when Tess offered to set jumps for him to challenge Corazón to higher heights. She and one of her adult students set up a course of four jumps with two even strides between obstacles; simple cross-rails for the first two, a narrow oxer, and a final cross-rail. She set the cross-rails and the first rail of the oxer to start at two-foot-six, and the second rail of the oxer at three feet.

After twenty minutes of dressage exercises to warm him up, River took Cory through the line. As expected, he cleared them easily. Then Tess raised the height of each rail by four inches.

An audience drifted over to the arena to watch; Sierra, Katrina, and another boarder. It was the afternoon of Dean and Caroline's lessons, and they had just arrived. As Caroline got out of the BMW, she saw Corazón take the four jumps in a clean go.

Tess had just raised the highest rail to four-foot-six.

"Who is that?" Caroline, who rarely noticed anyone at Pegasus, hissed at her brother.

Dean looked askance at his sister and his brow creased into a frown at the admiration in her expression. "That's my competition, sister dear," he said with a sneer.

Instead of going directly to the trailer where the family groom waited with her horse saddled and ready for her lesson, she strode over to join the group of spectators. Dean reluctantly followed, but he wanted to see just how good this horse was as well.

"This time will be five feet," Tess called out as she and her student raised the rails another four inches.

River trotted a circle with the reins long, encouraging Cory to stretch his neck in between jumping rounds. "Okay, but this will be the last go." He picked up the reins and signaled for canter. Cory snorted and lifted his head. "Tired?" River spoke to his horse and relaxed his aids to test his eagerness to continue. Cory maintained his energetic gait, pricking his ears toward the row of obstacles. "Okay." The pair turned down the line and jumped as easily as the last round.

The spectators clapped and cheered, and Tess grinned broadly. "Just one more round," she called out. "Let's just see if he can go over five feet."

River knew his horse could, for he had sensed Corazón judge the height and gather and bunch his muscles just enough as he negotiated and cleared each rail. He was certain his horse had more jump still in him. But he had done enough for today. "Tess, he can," he told her with finality. "But this is all I'm going to ask of him today." He brought Cory down from the trot to a walk and let him stretch his neck as he cooled him down, walking along the rail.

"River…" she started to protest, but his back was already to her as he rode off on the black, and she gave in. Nevertheless, she was very pleased.

"What do you think of Corazón?" Sierra asked Dean, who had moved to stand next to her.

"The horse can jump," he said flatly, watching River through narrowed eyes. "Where did Tess get him?"

"He's River's horse; the one he rescued over a year ago."

"Really," Dean said, almost to himself and not as a question.

Caroline studied the black horse with an intent expression on her face. Then without speaking, she strode off to the trailer to mount up for her lesson.

"That was amazing!" Katrina called out as River and Cory rounded the top end of the arena and approached the group of onlookers on the rail.

Sierra smiled up at River and their eyes met for a brief flash of understanding. Like parents sharing a moment of love and pride over a child, they shared their love and pride over Corazón.

But then River's face creased into a frown and Sierra suddenly felt Dean put his arms around her shoulders, and kiss the top of her head. She flinched. A gesture that at any other time would have thrilled her, she instinctively recognized was not a spontaneous moment of affection for her, but aimed at River…*to make him jealous*? She did not like it and pulled away from him.

"Nice horse," Dean said.

Okay, he complimented Cory and maybe he just wanted to demonstrate to River that I belong to him (do I belong to him?); sort of a male dominance gesture or whatever. As Dean playfully tugged on one of her braids she found she had already forgiven him.

"What are you doing now?" Dean asked. He kissed the top of her head again.

"I've got one more horse to ride and then I'm done for the day," Sierra answered.

"Take a break and hang out with me until it's time for my lesson."

As usual, she readily agreed.

But instead of remaining at the rail to watch Caroline, he said, "Come on." He grabbed her hand and led her away. They walked past the entrance to the stable and Sierra caught a glimpse of Katrina helping River untack Cory. A pang of remorse momentarily tightened her chest as she realized that Katrina was doing the things with River that she thought of as hers…*mine?...ridiculous.*

Dean guided her to the hay storage barn. Inside, he pulled her down next to him into a pile of loose hay, surrounded by stacked bales that hid them from anyone who might venture in. He immediately started kissing her face and neck, and then pressed his lips against her mouth, probing with his tongue. His hands roved over her shoulders and back.

He just wants to make out! Well, that's what she knew most girls at school did with their boyfriends. And she did like it…sort of. She liked feeling his hands touching her, and his warm, velvety lips on her own. But the tongue? *...Not so sure about that.* But she did like the passion he obviously felt for her; that she interpreted as affection. Sierra couldn't imagine such intimacy unless you were really attracted to the person.

But when Dean pulled her tee-shirt out from where it was tucked into her breeches, she froze and stiffened in his arms.

"It's okay," he broke off the kiss and murmured against her cheek. "I'm not going to do anything bad." He brought his hands up to hold her face as he resumed the kiss, and she relaxed again. But a few moments later, she felt his hand moving up underneath her shirt, touching the bare skin of her abdomen.

"Dean, no," she pulled away as if she had received an electric jolt.

"I just want to touch you." He gazed deep into her eyes. "How can it hurt anything? Don't you like me?"

"I just don't want you to touch me there," she insisted. She knew with certainty that she was not ready for this level of intimacy, but she also knew she did not want him to know how flat-chested she was; as if he couldn't tell just by looking.

Dean sat up and moved away, sighing, and just as he had in his car, acted hurt and a little angry. "I better start warming up my horse." He stood up and walked away.

Sierra felt humiliated and very immature. *What was I supposed to do?* She jumped up and hurried after him. "Dean…Dean, wait," she called to his back.

But he didn't wait or even look around.

24 COLD WEATHER, COLD RELATIONSHIP

In training the riding horse no exercise effects a full measure of usefulness unless it be conducive to the ultimate improvement of free forward movement. – Henry Wynmalen, *Dressage: A Study of the Finer Points of Riding*

The weeks of autumn slipped into winter. Sierra and Katrina helped River and Manuel clip the shaggy coats of the horses so they could continue in work throughout the winter months without sweating and becoming chilled. The horses wore heavy, waterproof blankets for turnout and warm, quilted stable blankets at night. When the temperatures dropped to near freezing or below, the riders used quarter sheets under their saddles when warming up; and often the cold, wet weather forced riding in the confinement of the indoor arena. It was the time of year for breaking the ice in the outside water troughs and wearing rubber boots to lead horses in and out as the many passing hooves churned the lane into mud. The horses received warm bran mashes two to three nights a week.

Happiness for Sierra, something she had taken for granted all her life, now only completely filled her when working directly with or riding a horse.

She forced herself to focus on the lectures at school, and was diligent in completing her homework. At lunch, she discussed with Allison history, English reading assignments, and debated over math problems, as if she cared; laughing at jokes and feigning interest in news and gossip. Whenever Sierra allowed her thoughts to take their own course (which occurred often), she thought of Dean. Then her insides twisted in agony. How she wished she could command herself to forget him, evict all the feelings she felt for him, and return to the trouble-free, happy life she had known pre-Dean.

Allison seemed to be growing more and more fond of Peter; talking about all his good qualities and his quirky habits, and even his faults, in endearing tones. Peter called Allison every night and they spent time together every weekend. Sierra appreciated that Allison at least hadn't given up their lunch time together to spend it with Peter.

Katrina didn't seem to be interested in anyone in particular, but many boys were interested in her. She went out almost every weekend but rarely with the same guy. She turned down as many dates as she accepted.

What would it be like to have a boyfriend who called her often, took her out, and wanted to be seen with her? Dean walked her to a few classes and called her maybe once or twice a week, and usually after nine or ten o'clock at night; and pulled her away to make out during Caroline's lesson. That was the extent of their relationship.

I should break up with him. But how do you break up with someone that you're not even sure you are going out with?

"Sierra, you don't have to pretend with me," Allison said one day in a soft voice after she had asked Sierra when she had last talked to Dean (which had been over a week), and Sierra had answered in a bright tone that she couldn't remember.

The sympathy of her friend really didn't help, and Sierra choked back what felt like a sob. *I will not cry.* Then she admitted, baring her raw feelings, for after all, Allison was her best friend. "Maybe I do have to pretend."

At one time, she could have confided to her mother all her hurt and confusion. But Pam seemed so happy and somewhat distracted lately, which Sierra blamed on Ron. Blame or not, she didn't want to infuse her hurt into her mother's blissful state.

So she continued with the pretense of going out with Dean, because she wanted it to be true. She knew he was playing with her. A smart girl would tell him to leave her alone, would hang up when he called, and would laugh at him when he said all the endearing, affectionate things that made her feel special and like he really did care. But Sierra recognized that she was book smart. She was definitely not boy smart. She felt helplessly and hopelessly in love.

Dean did not call her for two weeks after the incident in the hay barn. For those two weeks, Sierra's eyes roved the hallways and cafeteria hoping for the sight of him walking toward her with his endearing half-smile. Her heart tumbled into palpitations every time her phone rang, and dropped into despair when it was not him.

But one morning, at the end of that two weeks, she awoke thinking about her ride on Fiel yesterday, and then about her latest homework challenge before she thought of Dean. She walked with Allison and Katrina between classes and her mind did not drift away from their conversation. That night, she shut her phone off completely and moved the charger back to her desk across the room. *I'm over him…mostly.*

A few days later, Sierra grabbed her phone on her way out the door to school, barely glancing at it, and was just about to shove it into a pocket of her backpack, when she noted two messages from Dean, both asking: *call me*, and *call me, I need to talk to you.* Then a text message: *Sierra, I'm sorry. I've tried to leave you alone and get you out of my mind. I'm too old for you. But it's hopeless. I miss you. Please forgive. Meet me at the back door after last period. Please.*

I won't. I'm over him. But she did meet him, telling herself she was just curious as to what excuse he would have. But when he looked into her eyes with his own that seemed sincerely filled with passion, it all began again.

Allison persisted, "Sierra, I'm your best friend, right?"

Sierra nodded agreement, her stomach knotting for she knew what Allison was going to say.

"Forget him. He's turned out to be the absolute worst creep we've ever had in our school."

"I know, I know. Allison, what can I do? I tell myself every time he calls I'm not going to answer. Sometimes I actually ignore one or two calls, but then I give in. Every time he comes up to me at the stable and looks into my eyes with those beautiful, deep blue eyes of his, that just smolder with his passion, I lose all my resolve. I let him take my hand and we go make out somewhere. I'm such an idiot!" Sierra laughed to keep from crying.

"No you're not," Allison said. "You're someone with the capacity to love true and deep. He's the idiot." She hugged her friend sympathetically.

Two weeks before Christmas break, Sierra received an invitation from David Schulman, the boy who had asked her to the spring ball last year, to go with him to the Christmas ball; the last school event before the end of the term. She politely refused, and then fell on her bed to sob silently into her pillow, for she believed his asking meant that nobody assumed she and Dean were going out together…and they weren't. But it was like a knife probing a raw wound.

"You really should go with him," Allison encouraged. "It wouldn't hurt for Dean to have some competition; might even make him jealous."

"It wouldn't be fair to David," Sierra replied.

"Sierra, you don't have to be in love with a guy to go out on a date. You like David, don't you?"

"Sure, he's a nice guy. I'm just not attracted to him."

"But you could go with him as a friend and have a good time…get your mind off creepy Dean."

"I'd be bored and probably make him miserable," Sierra persisted. When Allison shrugged and rolled her eyes, Sierra changed the subject. "At least Billy Bruber didn't ask me, now that he has a girlfriend."

Billy had recently latched onto a new freshman girl, Charlene Pickering, and the couple was the subject of much derisive gossip around school. Charlene was a bit on the simple side; probably just intelligent enough to not attend special needs classes. She was slightly overweight, but had a well-developed figure, and an attractive face. Her wardrobe consisted of bright colored tee-shirts with pictures of cute animals. But she was a happy person who laughed readily at everyone's jokes, even when the joke was on her. She had a generous nature; always willing to loan out pens, paper, and even money. A sweet girl, Sierra and Allison both agreed.

Allison smiled and said, "I think they're a cute couple. He is certainly devoted to her."

Sierra agreed. How nice it would be if Dean treated her half as nice as Billy treated Charlene. Billy's mother drove the two of them back and forth to school. They arrived together holding hands, Billy waited for her between classes to walk her to her next class, and they sat together at lunch eating from the same tray. Billy gazed at her adoringly, playing with a lock of her hair, giving her a quick kiss, and always holding her hand or had an arm around her.

Dean should take lessons from Billy; well, not that Dean didn't know how to be nice, Sierra supposed. He simply chose not to.

Over Christmas break, Dean called her only once, and after ten at night. His speech was slurred and Sierra could not doubt that he had been drinking. He suggested they ride together the next day. Sierra wasn't surprised when he did not show up, and at least she hadn't wasted time waiting for him.

On a whim, she invited River over for Christmas dinner, remembering how sweet it had been last year; and she wanted to let him know she held no grudge against him. She really did miss their friendship. But as she expected, he refused. River hardly spoke to her anymore.

The holidays passed, the New Year came, and they were back in school for winter quarter.

"The whole school is invited; everyone," Crystal announced as she tacked up invitations on all the bulletin boards around the school. She had talked her father into sponsoring a senior class fundraiser, she claimed for Stuart's sake, by hosting a Valentine's Ball at his country club. It soon became the most anticipated event so far that year.

Sierra and Allison stood in front of one of the invitations while Allison wrote down the details, for she and Peter planned to go.

"Has Dean asked you?"

"No, you know how he feels about school dances."

"Which is totally stupid. But he might ask you since it's not actually hosted by the school and he is good friends with Crystal."

"I don't really want to go," Sierra said, although she kind of hoped Dean just might ask her.

A whiff of a familiar aftershave and then sensing someone behind her, she turned to find Dean coming up to them smiling. As much as she tried to suppress her physical responses, she could not prevent the rush of color to her face or the acceleration of her heart. "Dean!"

"You don't want to go?" he asked mischievously, having overheard her last words.

"Do you want to go?" she countered.

"Sure, if you'll go with me."

Sierra gaped at him, astonished. "You don't like school dances."

"It's not at the school," he winked at her. "So do you want to go?"

Sierra continued to stare at him awkwardly, aware of Allison watching.

Dean picked up her hand. "I want to take you; please go to the Valentine's Ball with me." He smiled his disarming smile.

"Okay, I'll go," Sierra agreed, her color deepening even more.

"Great, I'll pick you up." He winked again, and turned to go.

He was so casual, as if they went out all the time. And of course, he pretended that he didn't know she wasn't allowed to ride in his car. "Um, Dean…"

He turned back. "Right, I forgot, your mommy won't late you ride with me," he said in a mimicking baby tone. "I guess you'll have to get her to drive you."

"We can pick you up," Allison said, her eyes narrowed at Dean. "Peter's folks are driving."

"Great, I'll meet you at the club. Will that work?" Dean suggested.

"I guess so."

"It's a date then." He flicked his finger under her chin and then up and over her lips before he turned away again and left.

Sierra breathed out slowly.

Allison turned her narrowed eyes to Sierra. "I thought you didn't want to go," she said pointedly.

Two days later after school, Sierra and Katrina saddled Fiel and Calliope for a trail ride, taking advantage of a day with clear skies. Sierra never rode out with River anymore and she sometimes wondered how it had happened that it was now Katrina who spent time with River. He still gave both of them lessons once a week, and was coldly polite to her when they cleaned stalls on weekends. It wounded her that her interest in Dean should ruin the friendship between them. They had gone through so much together, and she really missed him. She tried often to re-establish their former easiness together. She asked him questions about the horses and riding which he answered politely enough but with minimal detail. She still helped him and Manuel bring in the horses at night, but Katrina also helped on the days she came to the stable. She noticed how Katrina tagged around after River and he did not seem to mind.

"I hear you're going to the Valentine's Ball with Dean," Katrina said as they led their mounts to the field.

"Where did you hear that?" Sierra had told no one, but maybe Allison had told Katrina.

"It's all around school," Katrina answered.

"Really?"

"Yeah. So, I was wondering…" Katrina hesitated.

"What?"

"You wouldn't mind if I asked River, would you?"

Sierra could not hide the shock on her face as she gaped at Katrina. At least Katrina didn't know her insides froze in objection.

"I mean, I know you two are friends, but…I thought since Dean, well…"

Sierra composed her features and smiled weakly. "Of course I don't mind. I think it's sweet." *River will never agree to go*, she assured herself.

Katrina sighed audibly in relief. "Oh, thanks…I mean, well…"

"Katrina, I don't own River. Why should I mind?" *And why do I mind?*

"I just thought…well, thanks."

They reached the mounting block, mounted up, and Sierra let Fiel step out in front to lead onto the trail. She struggled with her feelings. *I shouldn't care if Katrina and River start going out. It would be nice for both of them. River is like my older brother. I should like that a nice girl like Katrina is interested in him. She's certainly much nicer than that other creepy girl he was seeing. Katrina is very pretty, popular, and she genuinely loves horses. I should be happy if River likes her.*

Fiel tossed his head in irritation, drawing Sierra's attention to how tightly she gripped the reins.

"Sorry, boy." She patted his neck and released her hold, allowing him to move his head freely with his walking stride. *Where is all this resentment coming from and why am I so possessive? I've been resentful of my mother's interest in Ron, and now River?* Somehow, Sierra thought if Dean would change into the boyfriend she wanted, that her resentment would disappear. She felt ashamed.

"River?" Katrina found him in the wash stall with one of the horses in training, applying cold soaks to a swollen fetlock. Her heart raced and her palms were damp with nervousness.

"Yeah?" he answered without looking up.

"I was wondering…well, you know the Valentine's Ball?" Katrina waited but when he didn't say anything, she continued, rushing her words. "I was wondering if you might like to go with me." She gulped and bit her lower lip to keep it from trembling.

River sat back on his heels and squinted up at her, plainly surprised. "I don't usually go to school dances," he answered.

You never go to school dances. "I know, I was just hoping that maybe…well, it could be fun."

River started to shake his head no, but something in the wistful expression on her face stopped him. For a fleeting moment it reminded him of how Sierra looked when she first started working at the stable; innocent, vulnerable, so hopeful. When had she lost that sweet expression to the one she wore so often now; sad, as if she hurt? He suspected it had to do with Dean, and River did not want to do to Katrina what Dean was doing to Sierra. Besides, he had heard Dean was taking Sierra so she would be there and… "Okay," he consented.

"You'll go?" Katrina's face brightened, her eyes wide in disbelief.

"Yeah, what time do you want me to pick you up?"

As River walked home with Storm, he already regretted having agreed to go to the ball. He really didn't want to go…it was Crystal's party, what was he thinking? Maybe he had accepted because he didn't want to hurt Katrina; but maybe it was more because he knew Sierra would be there. How would she like seeing him there with Katrina?

"Not a good reason to go," he said out loud. Storm looked up at him and emitted a soft whine. River laughed and leaned down to ruffle her fur. "Come on." He broke into a run and Storm raced past happily.

Usually running, like riding, could block out his thoughts. But today, even as his lungs began to cry out for oxygen causing his chest to ache, he could not stifle the confusion in his mind. He had no idea Katrina was interested in him.

How did he feel about Katrina? He used to despise her when she was Crystal's friend. But that was a long time ago. He had gotten used to having her around and it really wasn't so bad. He had been so fixated on Sierra that he just hadn't noticed Katrina. She was a beautiful girl; and he vaguely knew she was popular at school and that guys talked about her in admiration.

He felt flattered that an attractive, very nice girl was interested in him. Maybe he should try to like her. Maybe that would help him deal with his confused feelings about Sierra. Okay then, he would look forward to this stupid dance. Maybe he could kiss her goodnight; that would be something to look forward to. It seemed like forever since he had been with Laila.

Most of the day, his work with the horses absorbed his attention and he could push thoughts of Sierra out of his mind.

It was at night that anguished feelings over images of Sierra and Dean together overwhelmed him as he tried to sleep.

25 VALENTINE'S DAY

Making a horse defensive is really a simple matter; anyone can do it, just work him too hard. – Michael Schaffer, *Right From the Start*

"You look incredibly beautiful!" Sierra exclaimed as her mother twirled in front of her in her new red dress. It was true; with her hair down instead of pulled back into a knot the way she wore it for school, her face carefully made up for the evening, and the sleek lines of the dress flattering her slender figure, Sierra, who took her mother for granted, acknowledged that she was still a very attractive, young woman.

Another wave of guilt spread over Sierra, thinking about how selfishly she had behaved in allowing her resentment for Ron to be so obvious, so that her mother had not encouraged his attentions. Well, she still kind of resented him, but she tried hard not to let it show. She greeted him now in a friendly manner and spent a little time with him and her mother when he brought them dinner. She encouraged her mother to accept his invitations out.

Tonight, February fourteenth, was a school night, but being the actual Valentine's Day, Ron was taking Pam out to dinner.

"Do you think this dress is too revealing?" Pam asked as she turned back to the mirror to study her reflection in profile.

"No, it's a perfect dress," Sierra complimented from where she sprawled on her stomach on her mother's bed, providing moral support during the preparations.

A knock on the door caused mother and daughter to both suck in their breath, and then they both laughed. Sierra followed her mother to the living room and greeted Ron, who wore a suit and presented Pam with a bouquet of red roses. As he stepped in the door, he kissed Pam on the cheek. Sierra noted how her mother blushed. *So that's where I inherited my affliction.*

"Wow," Ron exclaimed, "you look incredible!" Then he turned to Sierra. "How's the horse rider?" He handed her a package wrapped in shiny, red foil paper.

"Fine," she answered politely. "For me?"

"Happy Valentine's Day," he announced. Sierra took the package, knowing without opening it that it was a box of chocolates.

"Open it," Ron encouraged.

She politely complied, and appropriately exclaimed over the fancy chocolate truffles inside. "Thanks." She picked one out and took a bite to demonstrate her gratitude. "Umm, exquisite."

Pam hugged her daughter and kissed the side of her head. "You sure you don't mind?" she asked in a whisper.

"Of course not; I've got tons of homework. I won't even know you're gone," Sierra assured her. "Have a good time."

"Okay, I'll probably be home before ten. Call if you need anything at all," Pam said over her shoulder as they stepped outside.

"Don't worry, I'll be fine," Sierra waved and watched as her mother and Ron crossed the yard to his car, then shut the door and went to her room to tackle her assignments.

The ringing of her phone awoke Sierra from where she had snuggled in her bed with her biology text book. Socrates curled next to her pillow and Charlie lay across her feet. Groggily she glanced at her clock – 9:18. "Hello," she answered, her voice cracking.

"Sierra." His voice sounded tremulous.

"Dean?"

"Is your mom home?"

"No, she's out with her boyfriend."

"Sierra," he repeated and she heard a choking sound. "I just found our cat." The choking sound again. "She was hit by a car."

"Oh my God!" Sierra exclaimed.

"She's dead. I found her." His voice trailed off in a tremor.

Is he crying? "I'm so sorry."

"Sierra, can I come over?"

Sierra was not allowed to have boys over when her mother was not at home. "Um… Dean…"

"I need to see you. I knew you would understand. Nobody in my family understands. My sister says she's just a stupid cat; a stray that wandered into our barn five years ago."

"I do understand, and I'm so sorry…"

"Please," he interrupted her.

Sierra looked at the clock again, 9:20. Her mother would be home any time and at the latest, within forty-five minutes. Surely her mother would understand. This was an unusual circumstance, and he sounded so forlorn. "Okay," she consented.

"I'll be there in a few minutes." He disconnected.

Sierra jumped from her bed, pulling off her pajamas as she ran to the bathroom to wash her face, comb her hair, and make herself presentable. She pulled on clean clothes, her favorite dark green tee-shirt that she thought was a good color for her. She had taken her hair out of braids for the night and now pulled the sides back with a clip. She had just finished re-brushing her teeth when she heard a knock on the door. *How close does he live?* It had been barely ten minutes.

When she opened the door, Dean gazed down at her silently with a mournful expression on his face. At least his eyes weren't red and puffy from crying. That would have been hard to see.

"I'm so sorry," Sierra said sympathetically and stepped aside for him to come in.

Dean walked over to the sofa, sat down and held his arms toward her. "Can I hold you?"

Sierra joined him on the sofa and allowed Dean to pull her onto his lap and into his arms. He held her tightly with his face against her hair and gently rocked back and forth. He started to stroke her hair and then pushed his hand underneath to fondle her neck.

She tried to think of something comforting to say. "What was her name?"

"Who?"

"Your cat." It surprised her that he didn't know who she meant. Wasn't it his cat he was thinking about now?

"Oh…Tabby," he answered after a pause. He took her shoulders to turn her toward him and leaned in to kiss her on her mouth.

Sierra closed her eyes, enjoying the closeness of him and the feel of his lips on hers. But the kiss went on and on and he began to use his tongue, making sounds of pleasure.

"Dean," Sierra pulled away in surprise. "How can you do this right now?"

"I need you, Sierra," he spoke nuzzling against her neck. "I need you to take my mind off poor Tabby." He leaned away to look deep in her eyes. "I found her in the road." His face scrunched up as he moaned, "Blood and guts all over the road. It was horrible! I need to get that sight out of my mind." He pulled her against him, holding tight and Sierra sympathetically put her arms around his shoulders to hug him back.

It must have been awful! Again, she struggled to think of something soothing to say, but really, words never helped much. Instead, she found herself stroking the back of his head as he nuzzled against her chest and she kissed the top of his hair…until a hand went underneath her shirt.

She pulled away in shock that he could do this while in mourning. "Dean, don't do that."

"Please, Sierra…I need you. I lie in my bed at night seeing your face and imagining how wonderful it would be to hold you; to touch you like this. His hand had moved underneath her shirt again to grope at her chest.

It did feel good…but it also confused and scared her. She pushed his hands away and said firmly, "Don't."

With a deep sigh, he dropped his hands, but reached up to pull her close again and kiss her deeply. "Please," he begged in between kisses. "I need you so badly…you are so beautiful."

Sierra kissed him back until his hands started roving again. Then she pushed him away and sat up, moving a few inches from him. "Dean, I said no. I don't see how this is helping you."

"That's it? That's as far as you'll go…just a kiss?" He looked as if she had physically wounded him.

Sierra nodded meekly.

His wounded look turned to anger; his brow furrowed and his eyes narrowed to slits as his lips tightened into a snarl. "Thanks for nothing." He pushed himself off the couch violently and stormed toward the door.

Sierra sat frozen, stunned by his behavior. *Is this how he deals with grief?*

She watched his shoulders heave up and down with his back to her. Then he spun back around and with his face scrunched in an expression of sorrow, walked back to her and gently took her hands to pull her to her feet. He kissed her, just a soft kiss with closed lips. "I'm sorry," he whispered.

His behavior totally baffled her; one minute sad, then amorous, then angry, and then contrite. She had no idea how to respond to him.

"Do you forgive me?" he asked, tilting her chin up to meet his eyes. His voice was gentle and beseeching.

"Of course," she answered. "You better go. My mother will be home any minute and I'd rather you weren't here."

"Okay," he whispered and then kissed her hard and passionately before turning to go back out the door. A few minutes later she heard his car backing away and the sound of its motor receding.

Sierra remained standing a few moments, feeling numb with confusion. Is he truly grieving or is he manipulating me? She glanced at the clock, a few minutes before ten. At least she wouldn't have to explain why she had broken a rule. When she had allowed Dean to come over she had expected a tearful, unhappy boy in need of consoling and she thought her mother would understand if she came home and found him mourning for his cat. But his actual behavior, if her mother had come home, would not have been so easy to explain.

A car scrunched slowly up the gravel drive. Her mother was home. Sierra darted to her bedroom pulling off her clothes as she ran, frantically put her pajamas back on, and jumped into bed. She wasn't ready to explain anything to her mother tonight. She would tell her tomorrow, after she had a chance to sort out her thoughts.

She heard whispered voices and then the door closing and a few moments later sensed her mother hovering at her bedroom door. Sierra feigned sleep until she heard her mother's soft footsteps as she went to her own room.

"Did somebody come to our house last night just before I got home?" Pam asked the next morning as the two of them were getting ready for school.

So Dean and her mother had passed each other in the driveway, as Sierra feared would happen.

"Yes, Dean came by. I was going to tell you about it tonight because it's kind of involved."

Pam looked up with a quizzical expression. "Nothing bad happened, did it?"

"His cat got run over by a car. I'll tell you everything tonight."

"Okay, tonight." Pam slipped on her jacket over her scrubs, grabbed her bag and kissed her daughter on the cheek as she passed her on her way out the door. She did not like the seed of worry that settled in her stomach about what Sierra might be going to tell her.

At school, Sierra told Allison what had happened.

"How can you have any doubts that he is playing games with you?" Allison asked, sounding incredulous.

"I know it sounds strange, but if you could have seen him; I mean he really did seem very upset," Sierra said, trying to defend Dean's behavior.

"Hmph," Allison snorted. "He's a very good actor."

"That's unfair, you didn't see him."

"Tell you what; why don't you ask his sister about their cat the next time you see her?"

"Okay, I will," Sierra said belligerently, not liking how Allison's suspicions enhanced her own doubts.

Sierra's mother was equally skeptical about Dean's excuse for coming when Sierra explained everything while they were eating supper.

"You could have called me to at least let me know he was coming over," Pam said after hearing Sierra's story. "Ron and I were just lingering at the restaurant. We could have come home right away."

"Mom, I'm sorry," Sierra said for about the tenth time. "I didn't think of that and I knew you'd be home soon anyway. I thought he would still be here when you got home."

"Okay, enough said, but don't let it happen again. If you ever have doubts as to whether I will mind or not, you should call me."

"I will, I promise."

After supper, they cleaned the kitchen together, and then settled onto the sofa to work on homework.

"Momma," Sierra said in a pensive tone, shutting her biology book that she was getting nowhere in reading; too many distracting thoughts whirling in her head. "Give me reasons why I shouldn't have sex now."

Pam sat bolt upright and gazed at her daughter with a look of panic.

Sierra quickly assured her, "I'm not having sex and I don't want to either; don't worry. I just want to hear reasons other than you can get pregnant or a bad disease, because everyone knows there are ways to have safe sex."

"This boy is putting a lot of pressure on you, isn't he?" Pam asked softly.

"It's nothing I can't handle," Sierra proclaimed boldly. "It's just that everyone at school talks about sex and I know some girls even younger than me who are already having sex with their boyfriends. They talk like it's no big deal."

Pam thought for awhile before replying. "First of all, there is no such thing as safe sex and I'm not talking about pregnancy or diseases. Sex is powerful. It is an act of such intimacy where your physical body is literally part of another. Both men and women use and abuse sex to get things they want; you know, things like status, money, power over other people. When sex is part of a loving relationship, it is the most pleasurable and ecstatic experience. Sex at its worst will give some a distorted sense of dominance and superiority and others will feel degraded and dirty, or will even suffer physical harm. There are good reasons why societies develop moral and religious rules about sex."

"So when is it okay to have sex?" Sierra persisted.

"That's a good question. I guess I'm kind of old-fashioned, but I believe first of all you should be in love and ready to commit to your partner. I don't know about men, but for women, sex is very tied up with emotions. You need to be mature enough to examine your own feelings honestly and not mistake physical attraction for love. I don't think most high school girls are ready to deal with the emotions tied to sex. I am sorry there is so much pressure on girls today to do something they are not emotionally prepared for."

"I guess that makes sense."

"Sierra, could you make me a promise?"

"Probably…it depends on what you ask."

"When you think you might give in to a boy, could you try to at least put him off until you can talk to me?"

"What if I talk to you and my feelings are that I still want to. Are you going to say no?"

"I will probably try to talk you out of it," Pam said honestly. "If you can promise me this, I promise not to get mad if you disagree with me. I promise to talk to you woman-to-woman."

"Okay, that's fair. I promise."

Later that night after Sierra had gone to bed, Pam stayed up alone, working on homework until her eyelids drooped; but also mulling over her worry about this boy Dean. She did not have good feelings about him; even before the unlikely excuse he had given Sierra last night. She did not trust him one bit, even though she had never met him. Well, that was part of the problem, why hadn't she met him? In her opinion, a decent boy always took the trouble to meet the parents of a girl he was genuinely interested in and respected. She had been trying to give her daughter warnings; that it was unusual for a senior to be interested in a sophomore and to take with a grain of salt all the compliments and sweet things he said to her. "Actions speak louder than sweet words," she had cautioned, but couldn't help regret it when she saw the strained look on Sierra's face. It broke her heart to see how her face fell when her phone rang and it was not Dean, but it was just as hard to see how her eyes lit up and her smile shone the few times he did call. Her daughter was infatuated with someone taking advantage of her! She felt so helpless as a mother. She could forbid Sierra to see him, but she knew how fruitless that could be and certainly wasn't going to change the feelings in Sierra's heart. All she could do was set and enforce rules that she prayed might protect her. She thought of all the worst things that Dean might have tried to do last night with Sierra, and bitterness filled her mouth as so many unpleasant images came to her mind. She could not suppress the animosity she felt toward him; this boy she feared was going to destroy Sierra's faith in love, and her innocence.

With an aching heart, she shoved her books aside and got up to go to bed. On the way to her room she quietly opened Sierra's door and peered in at the shadowy outline of her daughter sound asleep, cat and dog snuggled next to her. *So innocent!* The love that welled up for her daughter at that moment brought a painful ache to her heart, accentuated by the fact that she could not protect her from the evils of the world. She gently pulled the door closed and quickly got ready for bed with tears falling unhindered from her eyes.

26 THE BALL

Dressage training is exactly like the tango. It's an entirely improvised form of dance in which the rider needs to listen to the horse and understand exactly what the horse is feeling. – Richard Weis

Peter's parents, with Allison and Peter in the backseat, picked up Sierra and drove them to the country club. Sierra's mother would pick them up at midnight when the dance ended.

Sierra, Allison, and Peter walked into the ballroom of the country club, and all three stood in awe of the beautiful room – a room out of a fairy tale. Crystal chandeliers hung from the cathedral ceiling that rose up into a glass-sided dome. Gilded floor to ceiling mirrors were mounted at intervals on every wall, and reflected the light from the chandeliers and wall sconces. Marbled alcoves leading to small balconies broke up the exterior wall, and a highly polished hardwood dance floor in the middle of the spacious room was surrounded by many long tables loaded with refreshments. All the décor, the table linens, flower arrangements, and other accessories, were in bright red and snowy white.

"Where is Dean supposed to meet you?" Allison asked as they scanned the milling crowd.

"He didn't say. I really don't expect him to be here yet; he's not the kind of guy who shows up early or even on time." She laughed, hoping it sounded light and amused. "I'll just find a place to sit where I can watch while I'm waiting."

Allison and Peter walked with her to a row of cushioned chairs along one wall, and Sierra settled herself on one with a view of the entryway. She declined Peter's offer to bring her refreshments. "It's too early. I'm fine. You two go dance."

Sierra watched couples arrive, mill around, and move onto the dance floor or stand around in groups at the refreshment tables. Most of the girls wore red or pink dresses and the boys wore suits; some even in tuxedos. Sierra's own dress was light pink in a silk-like fabric. It had delicate white lace trim around the neckline, waist, and hem, and the flared skirt swished in what she thought was a very feminine way when she moved. Her shoes were flat, black ballet-style slippers. She didn't want any heels to trip over when she danced with Dean.

Crystal arrived; the princess of the evening. Her friends flocked around her as if they were her royal court. She was dressed in a strapless sheath in bright red satin, its shape hugging her slim figure, and the hem at mid thigh. Her high-heeled pumps matched the same shade of red of her dress. Stuart wore a white tuxedo, a pink ruffled shirt, and red cummerbund.

Billy was there with Charlene. He looked even fatter, stuffed into a gray tuxedo with a pink cummerbund. Charlene wore a pink dress printed with bright red hearts and a bright red velvet sash at the waist. Sierra thought it was probably the only dress that was more little girlish than her own. But Charlene's face beamed in a constant smile and Billy grinned from ear to ear. They were on the dance floor and Charlene giggled every time Billy stepped on her toes as they awkwardly danced in their own space. A wave of envy spilled over Sierra watching them. They looked so absorbed in each other and obviously were having a very good time.

The minutes dragged on. Allison and Peter joined her when the band took a break, their faces glowing and damp with perspiration.

"Dean still hasn't shown up?" Allison asked the obvious.

Sierra shook her head and smiled weakly, afraid her voice would give away her hurt and trepidation that Dean might stand her up.

"Let's check out the food." Allison grabbed Sierra's arm and propelled her toward the refreshments.

In spite of having no appetite, Sierra picked out a few hors d'oeuvres to place onto a small red paper plate, and picked up a bottle of water. Allison and Peter loaded their plates, sampling and exclaiming over the delicious assortment.

The three walked around; greeting friends, exclaiming over each others' dresses, the food, the band, and what a great party it was.

Sierra pasted a smile on her face, feeling alone and miserable. *He's not coming.*

When the band started to play again, Allison told Peter to dance with Sierra while she went to the ladies' room.

"It's okay," Sierra protested, feeling like a wallflower receiving a charity dance.

But Peter did not give her a choice, pulling her onto the dance floor. She moved her feet and smiled, trying to look like a person having fun. The last thing she wanted right now was to dance with Allison's boyfriend, but at least it was less conspicuous than sitting along the wall… alone…stood up.

When the dance finished and Allison rejoined them, Sierra excused herself to go to the ladies' room herself, not that she needed to, but to pass the time. A crowd of girls filled the small space, chattering and laughing as they lined up for the stalls and touched up make-up at the mirror.

"Sierra," one of her classmates called over the heads of several girls. "Are you here with Dean?"

"He's going to meet me here later," she replied, hoping it would turn out to be the truth.

"He is so hot," the girl exclaimed before stepping into the next open stall.

Sierra finished in the bathroom and made her way back to her seat. Halfway around the room, she caught sight of a couple from the corner of her eye. When she looked their way, her heart seized up in her chest. *Katrina and River!* She sucked in a deep breath, and her heart pounded painfully as her stomach knotted.

Katrina looked so beautiful in a red print dress, her rich brown hair cascading down her back with red ribbons interlaced through her thick tresses. Her face glowed radiantly, her eyes focused on her partner.

But River! She almost didn't recognize him. He wore black jeans and a long-sleeved white shirt (probably his show shirt) open at the throat without a tie. He had combed his hair back away from his face, and its rich blackness shone in the crystal light, framing his face. Less dressed up than all the others boys, he stood out, and in Sierra's mind, he stood out as the most handsome of them all.

She watched, mesmerized as he danced with Katrina, holding onto her waist and her hand rather than apart, even though it was a fast song. Of course he would be a good dancer; why wouldn't anyone who rode harmoniously with a horse not also move in harmony to music? He danced gracefully, moving shoulders, hips, and feet rhythmically in time with the music but with some interesting steps thrown in, as he guided Katrina around the floor. Sierra noted how the couples around watched him with sidelong glances; the boys looking envious and the girls in admiration. Katrina wore a gloriously happy expression.

Sierra watched River's face as he listened to Katrina chattering, and occasionally smiling at something she said. *He likes her!*

A sob rose in Sierra's throat and hot tears pushed at the back of her eyes. She turned away and fled back to the hallway leading to the restrooms, finding a quiet nook where she huddled alone until she managed to regain control of her emotions.

To see Katrina in River's arms had slammed against her senses as *so not right.* It shocked her that her first thoughts had been, *that's my place! That's where I belong.* She recalled the many times River had held her against his chest while she cried, comforting her. She could imagine the feel of the cloth of his shirt against her face and the scent of him. With her eyes closed, she saw very clearly his dark brown eyes looking deep into her own. She remembered how once she thought he was going to kiss her, and that she had wanted him to kiss her. *It's River I want! It's River 's kisses I want!*

She was such a fool; a blind fool! It was as if blinkers in front of her eyes had been suddenly torn away. How could she have been so naïve and stupid to become infatuated with someone like Dean? His self-centered, inconsiderate behavior suddenly seemed so transparent…so cruel! He was a jerk, just as Allison had been trying to tell her…just as River had tried to tell her.

Breathing deeply and swallowing down her anguish, Sierra returned to the ballroom, her outward appearance serene and calm, and a stern look on her face. She looked at the gilded clock; just after nine; three hours before her mother came to pick them up. Dean was an hour late, if he was even going to come.

The evening dragged on painfully. Peter danced with Sierra once each set. She sat, she walked around, she drank water and punch, counting the minutes until she could escape this purgatory and go home.

It was after ten and the band had just returned from a break, and Peter took her hand for the first dance of the set.

"Thanks, Peter, but I've had enough dancing," Sierra declined his polite insistence. She shooed Allison and him back to the dance floor. "I'm going to walk around some more."

"Sierra," a girl's voice called behind her. Sierra turned to find Crystal waving at her with one arm, the other looped through Stuart's as she dragged him along with her.

"Hi, Crystal," Sierra greeted her in a flat tone; dreading the inevitable question about where was Dean.

"Dean just called me. He says to tell you something came up but he's on his way." Crystal smiled at her with a crinkle of her nose, and then turned, pulling Stuart back to the dance floor. "You are so lucky," she added over his shoulder.

It was like the final clue in a mystery. Dean had been playing games with her and somehow, she knew Crystal was in on the game; perhaps even the one making the rules. What else could it mean that Dean had called Crystal and not her?

"Sierra."

River! Sierra froze with her heart in her throat. *How can I turn around and face him?*

The touch of fingers, light on her shoulder, impelled her to turn. "Do you want to dance?" River asked, his dark eyes shadowed, and his expression unreadable.

"Uh…" How she wanted to fall into his arms. *Comfort me! Care for me!*

"Come on." He cupped her elbow, not waiting for an answer, and guided her to the dance floor. With fingers lightly on her waist, he turned her to face him, and picked up her right hand; leaving her no choice but to place her free hand on his shoulder. The hand that held hers was warm, rough with calluses, strong, and held hers within a firm but gentle grip. How unlike Dean's soft hands that had never known work.

"Where's Katrina?" Sierra asked in a weak voice. Could he feel the dampness of her palm in the hand he held?

"She went to the restroom."

"Does she know you're..?"

"She told me to dance with you," River interrupted.

"Oh." How painful to realize it had not been his idea to dance with her. She had heard the expression of wanting the floor to swallow one up, and that was exactly how she felt. How humiliating that the boy she wanted to dance with more than anyone else, was dancing with her only because his girlfriend, who felt sorry for her, had told him to do it.

In silence, River led her rhythmically to the band's music, as graceful on his feet as he was in the saddle. Sierra closed her eyes, allowing herself to forget the reason she was in River's arms; and at least for a few moments enjoy the closeness of him, the exhilarating sensation of moving together in rhythm. It seemed he had pulled her in just a little closer, or did she imagine it?

She opened her eyes, and the brief moment of pleasure ended as the visual impact of reality surrounded her. "How did you learn to dance so well?" she asked in a nervous, high-pitched voice, feeling the silence had become awkward.

"I had to take ballroom dancing like everybody else in eighth grade."

"So did all the other boys, but they don't dance as well as you."

River merely exhaled on a short laugh, and turned her gracefully, back into an eddy of silence.

"I believe that's my date you're dancing with." What timing; Dean had finally arrived! He placed his hand on Sierra's shoulder and pulled her away from River.

River immediately dropped his hands, scowled sideways at Dean, but did not even look at Sierra as he walked away.

No…how could you finally show up at this moment? Sierra looked up at Dean's smug expression, and suddenly, his handsome face only looked petty and mean. How could she have ever thought him attractive? She narrowed her eyes at him angrily and turned away, striding purposefully from the dance floor.

"Sierra," he called as he followed her and when he caught up, grabbed her by the upper arm to slow her down. "I'm sorry. I don't blame you for being mad."

"I'm not mad," she answered truthfully. "I've just lost interest in this ridiculous party. I want to go home." She shrugged her shoulder out from underneath his hand and continued walking.

"Oh…okay, that's fine. I'll take you home." He continued to trail after her. "Sierra, what is wrong?"

Sierra tried to quicken her pace to get away from him, but it was impossible within the swarm of kids. She looked around desperately for Allison and Peter, and finally catching sight of them dancing, pushed her way through to reach them.

"You finally made it," Peter commented as Sierra came up with Dean on her heels.

"What's the matter?" Allison asked, immediately noting the fixed, tight expression on Sierra's face and how she ignored Dean.

"Do you two mind if I call my mother to pick us up now?" Sierra pleaded. She did not want to spoil Allison's evening, but she simply could not bear spending another moment in Dean's presence.

"Sierra," Dean broke in. "I said I'll take you home. What is the matter? Just tell me." He caught Allison's eye and raised his brow in an expression of 'I don't know what's wrong with her'.

Rage suddenly rushed up Sierra's spine as her mind filled with all the neglect, abuse, and aggressiveness she had endured from Dean, filling her chest with blackness. She pivoted on her heel to face him. "Get away from me!"

"Sierra…" Dean's eyes flew open in shock; for he had been sure he could sooth her anger and placate her, as he had always done before.

"You heard her," Allison said, with her own eyes blazing. "Come on, Peter." She linked her arm with Sierra's and with Peter following close behind, as if he were a protective shield, they moved out of the ballroom, ignoring the stares and buzz of comments of all those who witnessed the scene.

Safe at home, Sierra sobbed into her pillow. Pam sat on the side of her bed, rubbing her shoulders and smoothing her hair, giving what little comfort she could. Sierra had poured out her emotions and told her all; her infatuation with Dean, her jealously of Katrina, especially when she suddenly realized in an epiphanic moment, how she truly felt about River.

When her last sobs subsided and Sierra's breathing evened out into a soft snore through her stuffed nose, Pam rose and went to her own bed. Her heart ached in sympathy with her daughter's heartache, and anger filled her soul at the ruthlessness of a good-looking and charming boy who used his gifts to abuse and hurt her daughter. A suppressed memory rose to the surface and for once she did not force it away from her thoughts. A handsome boy, full of charm, wooing her with delicious words that made her feel beautiful and special. The same boy had lured her into his bed, but like a brick wall, had repelled her when she told him about her pregnancy. Somehow his parents found out (not from her), and forced him to marry her; a marriage full of pain as he left her every night to party with his buddies. She had no regrets, and only a little guilt, when his life ended after he crashed his car, drunk and stoned. She had never told Sierra the truth about her father; only that he had died in a car accident, withholding the details of his drunken and selfish lifestyle. The daughter did not need to know the worst of her father. She had maintained a relationship with his parents who were decent enough, although distant, and kept in touch with their granddaughter mostly through birthday and Christmas cards with an occasional small check enclosed.

The night her husband died had freed Pam from her worst nightmare. If Sierra's experience with Dean had taught her caution, well then, perhaps the pain she suffered now would be for the best; maybe prevent her making a future mistake. But how Pam hated the boy who had stolen her daughter's innocence.

When Tess learned that River was taking Katrina to a dance, she insisted on loaning her Lexus for the evening. Now River escorted Katrina from the country club's ballroom to the parking lot, and held the door for her. He watched as she slid gracefully onto the passenger seat, noting her attractive curves outlined by the clingy dress she wore, and the view of her legs as she swung them in – shapely legs, with strong calf muscles; *the legs of a girl who rides*, he noted appreciatively. He walked around the front of the car, and as he got into the driver's seat, Katrina smiled at him demurely.

"Every girl at the dance had her eyes on you tonight," Katrina stated.

"I think it was their partners looking at you," he countered.

Katrina giggled. "No, their partners were looking at you too; jealous that their dates were watching you."

River laughed, but he could feel his face heat up at the complement and was glad for the darkness. He had to admit, he liked how Katrina looked at him with admiration in her eyes. It was nice to be sought after. He started the engine and moved the car into the line of exiting partygoers. Katrina chattered almost nonstop; gossiping about everyone there; for she knew everybody and quite a few tidbits about the different relationships. River only half-listened; he wasn't interested in the others there, until Katrina mentioned Sierra, and then he paid full attention.

"Sierra really let Dean have it tonight. Did you see the look on his face when she walked away from him? Good for Sierra! He's been taking her for granted and maybe he'll appreciate her a little better now. I don't blame her one bit; I mean, he was over two hours late! I'll bet next time they go out he'll be on time."

River hoped there would be no next time.

Then Katrina moved on to gossip about another couple. *She sure talks a lot*, River observed, her chatter like background noise that allowed him to think his own thoughts; all of which were of Sierra.

She had looked so unhappy and forlorn tonight with a frozen smile on her face, and every few minutes looking toward the ballroom entrance. As much as he hated Dean, he had found himself wishing the jerk would show up; just to relieve the painful expression on Sierra's face. He wanted to ask her to dance but didn't know how he could, since he was with Katrina. His heart warmed toward Katrina when she saw Sierra walking with slumped shoulders, alone, and she had told him to go ask her to dance. He thought that was very kind of Katrina.

Dean had hurt Sierra. He was glad Sierra had the sense to be angry with him, and he had broken out in a smile when he saw her walk away from that jerk. He had felt like cheering. But was Sierra over him?

Would she forgive Dean and take him back if he begged her for forgiveness?

He pulled into Katrina's driveway and shut off the engine. Katrina at last quit talking, and looked up at him sideways with a wistful, expectant look on her face. Should he kiss her now? Her house was dark except for the front porch light. It didn't appeal to him to walk her to the door and kiss her in that light.

"River," Katrina spoke barely above a whisper. "Thank you…"

Okay, here in the car. He leaned in and cradled her cheek with one hand as he gently kissed her open mouth, and pleased when she kissed him back. She emitted a sound of pleasure and shifted closer to him; clearly an invitation. He put his arms around her and she immediately reached up with her own arms to encircle his shoulders with her hand at the back of his neck and her fingers playing in his hair. They kissed, long and passionately.

It felt good to kiss a girl again and his body stirred with yearning as her soft lips, slightly parted, pressed against his own, and he could feel her breasts rising against his chest with each inhalation. His own fingers caught in her hair and with his other hand he caressed her shoulder and neck, moving his fingers to trace down her lovely throat and across her collarbone…and then daringly across her breasts. Katrina murmured a soft sound, and it seemed her breasts rose to meet his touch.

Katrina broke away from their kiss to ask, "Do you want to go somewhere?"

"Like where?"

"Anywhere that we can park and be alone. My parents don't wait up for me."

River sensed that she would not protest if he tried to make love to her…in fact, seemed to be asking him to. And he certainly wanted to…sort of…physically, he definitely wanted her. It had been quite awhile since the last time with Laila, and it would be so lovely to undress this beautiful girl, run his hands over her smooth, bare skin, and kiss her all over, starting with the tip of her nose to her chin, down her throat, to…

But there was innocence in Katrina that he had never sensed in Laila. Laila had made all the first moves and had made it very clear that she wanted pleasure from him but nothing more. They had both taken equal pleasure in their lovemaking; Laila took as much as she gave.

Katrina was different. She seemed to like him very much; maybe loved him? He cared for Katrina, and he had already admitted that it felt good to have her like him; a bit of balm in his lonely life. But he was not in love with Katrina. He instinctively knew it would be wrong to make love to her unless he shared her feelings. He did not want to take advantage of her.

He leaned in and kissed her again. “Not tonight,” he said, and with genuine regret in his tone. He moved away and got out of the car. He opened her door and held out his hand to help her out, and then with his arm affectionately around her shoulder, walked her to her door.

“Thank you,” she whispered and she reached up to take his face between her hands, and kissed him softly. “I had the best evening of my life.”

27 THE BET

Through the days of love and celebration and joy, and through the dark days of mourning – the faithful horse has been with us always. – Elizabeth Cotton

The morning after, Sierra had the hardest time dragging herself out of bed that she could ever remember. Her head throbbed and her eyes were still puffy from crying herself to sleep. Pam suggested she call the stable and tell them she was sick today. Sierra considered it, but decided getting out would be the best remedy. "I think it would be worse to lie around. If ever I needed to be around horses, it's today," she explained, but she did consent to her mother's offer to drive her to the stable.

Now her entire body dragged through the morning chores. With each heart beat, her head throbbed and seemed to echo in her brain, *lub, dub; lub, dub; lit-tle-fool-girl.* She knew River watched her from the corner of his eye, as if he heard her thoughts.

Half way through mucking the first aisle of stalls, he asked, "Are you okay?" in a gentle tone without spite.

Sierra had expected, 'I told you so'. She was prepared to admit her mistake and take whatever River chose to dish out. She knew how much he despised Dean and what an idiot he must think she was. Well, she had been a total idiot. She gulped down her humiliation and decided to make a full confession.

She halted her pitchfork action and leaned on its handle for support. Looking up to meet his eyes that she found filled with concern; it was a little easier to swallow her pride as she admitted, "Actually, I'm not okay. I've been very stupid and blind. Dean has been playing games with me and I was too infatuated to figure it out. Last night was the last straw and I suddenly saw the real Dean." She tried to keep her voice matter-of-fact. Nevertheless, she couldn't prevent a slight quaver to her last few words.

River listened, sensing her inner struggle to hide her emotional state. For a fleeting moment he felt triumphant, but then his heart wrenched in his chest at the look of dejection she tried to hide from her face and the heavy slump to her shoulders. He wanted to toss his pitchfork aside and rush to her side, take her in his arms. *Should I..?*

"Good morning," a cheerful voice called out and moments later, Katrina walked into view, smiling brightly. "Hi, Sierra." She waved to her as she passed the stall where Sierra stood, and then walked confidently up to River, stepped into his stall, and gave him a kiss.

He kissed her back…I saw it. Sierra turned away so that she could fight back her tears, and returned to mucking with more vigor than she had exhibited all morning.

Grabbing another pitchfork, Katrina hung around to help, chatting almost nonstop and oblivious to the fact that neither Sierra nor River said more than the occasional 'uh huh'.

With chores finished, Sierra and Katrina saddled Fiel and Calliope for their usual Saturday morning lesson. Sierra focused all her attention on River's instructions, and realized that she really hadn't been concentrating the way she should have for the past few weeks, her mind always drifting to thoughts of Dean.

"Leave the reins alone," River called out to her, just a slight tone of annoyance in his voice. "All you need to do is weight your inside stirrup and let that turn your hip slightly. You should feel him under your inside seat bone. Try that to turn him onto a small circle. You can squeeze a little with the outside rein, just to help him keep his balance."

It was hard not to press on the inside rein and reach with it to the inside, but Sierra tried closing her eyes and then consciously repeated River's instructions in her mind. She pushed down on her inside seat bone and stirrup, and to her delight, felt Fiel's inside hind leg move underneath him as he bent his body onto the circle. She opened her eyes and kept the aids to complete the circle; with only a squeeze of the outside rein!

"Beautiful," River complimented.

A grin of accomplishment split her face and she looked over at River, who smiled back as their eyes connected.

After the lesson, and as she and Katrina talked about what they had each learned and what they were still struggling with, Sierra suddenly realized she had not once thought of Dean; not since she had focused all her attention on Fiel during the lesson. She stroked her horse's neck in gratitude for his gentleness, patience, and consistently forgiving nature. She almost felt happy and was glad she had not stayed at home feeling sorry for herself. Her emotions still felt painfully raw and exposed, but Fiel and the other horses would provide the perfect medicine to help her heal.

"Sierra," River walked up to the crossties, frowning. "Tess is here and wants to meet with us in the office."

"I'll be there as soon as I put Fiel away."

"How old are you now?" Tess asked as she leaned back in her chair and scrutinized Sierra sitting next to River.

"Fifteen."

"Hmm, good; you're old enough to ride preliminary, and you have enough qualifying rides at training level to move up this year.

"She's not ready for preliminary," River interjected.

Tess glared at him. "Let me finish. It's simply something to keep in mind." She turned her attention back to Sierra. "Gloria has found a new horse and he should be coming in a few days. She is not interested in continuing to ride Silver, so I would like you to compete on him at training level to keep him active and give him exposure until he sells. It should help find a buyer."

"Okay," Sierra agreed after glancing at River and not noticing any signs of disapproval.

"If he sells, we will then look at another horse for you to compete…at training level," she finished, glaring at River before he could protest.

Glancing at a list, Tess continued, "Moose's owner is very excited to see him go intermediate this season. You need one more qualifying read at preliminary, and then I don't see any reason why he shouldn't move up. Do you?"

"No, I guess not. He might have a hard time with the dressage."

"It will give you something to work on," she said sarcastically.

Sierra glanced sideways at River, trying not to smile. Conversations between him and Tess were always laced with static.

"Mrs. Galensburg asked if we would be showing Pendragon at Prix St. Georges this year, and I assured her that was the plan." Noting his frown, she snapped at him, "River, part of running a business is diplomacy. I made no promises, but I don't want to dash her hopes either. If you show him at all three of the fourth level tests, we might be able to try him at Prix St. Georges at the end of the season. You earn your scores and then there is no reason not to move up."

"Maybe," River begrudgingly agreed.

"Also, I suggested a musical freestyle at third level, and she seemed quite enthusiastic."

River actually perked up with a look of interest. "Really? I'd like to do that. You'd help me find music and design the ride?"

"Of course; I already have a few selections that I think would suit Penny." She handed River a CD with a homemade label. "Listen to these and let me know if any of them appeal to you. I firmly believe the rider has to feel inspired by the music as well as it needs to fit the horse."

River took the CD and nodded.

"Sierra, are you interested in competing in dressage again?" Tess asked.

"Yes, at least on Fiel. I want to try second level this year."

"Good, I think you're both capable. Okay, now for eventing. River will take Moose intermediate. Crystal and Katrina are both taking their horses preliminary. Gloria will start out with her new horse at training level, and Sierra, you'll take Silver training level. River, I'd like you to take Felicity beginner novice." She raised up her hand before he could protest. "One or two schooling shows and maybe one rated event; her owners are satisfied with that."

"I guess…"

She scowled at him, but then shifting back in her chair asked, "What about Corazón?"

River looked up, startled. "He's my horse…"

Tess interrupted, "Don't get so defensive. I'm just asking if you're interested in showing him. It's up to you."

"I hadn't thought about it…maybe beginner novice."

"River, come on," Tess said derisively. "He'll walk all over a beginner novice course. He could easily handle training level and you know it. He's already capable of a preliminary course."

"I'll think about it."

"I've never seen a horse take to jumping the way he does, so it's not like he wouldn't enjoy competition…just think about it." She raised her hand again when River opened his mouth.

Tess looked at her list and then reached for a three-ring binder with a separate page for each horse in training. She reviewed with them the conditioning schedules she had outlined and handed them an assignment calendar. "I'll have this posted in the tack room, so check in there for any changes. You know how an injury or loss of shoe can alter the schedule."

They both nodded as they looked over the calendar.

"The cross country clinic is in two weeks. Sierra, I'll have you ride Silver. River, as usual, I would like you to demonstrate first over the course. I thought you might like to ride Cory; give him a taste of having strange horses around to see how he might react at an event."

"Okay."

"Any more questions?"

They both shook their heads but River mumbled under his breath, "If Crystal is going to ride Diva at preliminary she should get out here and ride more often."

Sierra looked at River in surprise, but then she realized his concern was for Diva.

"I heard that. River, you let me worry about Crystal," Tess snapped at him.

"It's not Crystal I'm worried about."

Tess scowled but then rolled her eyes. "One more thing; I thought you might like to see this." She handed River a regional dressage publication opened to an article. "Do you remember that lady who interviewed me at the dressage championship?"

River held the magazine so that Sierra could read along with him. The article had a couple paragraphs about Pegasus Equestrian Center and mentioned River, who had amazed the dressage community as well as eventing circles last season.

...unheard of for a rider as inexperienced in competition to out-perform veteran competitors. Teresa Holmes, part owner of Pegasus Equestrian Center and the young rider's coach, told our interviewer, 'River literally began riding before he was born. He is the son of Renee Girard, a jockey killed in a tragic racing accident. River has probably spent more hours on the back of a horse than he has on his own feet.' His years of riding and a natural ability certainly became obvious as he wowed spectators at the region six championship on Pendragon...

The article went on to talk about Pendragon's breeding, training, and competition history and also quoted a statement from Mrs. Galensburg about how proud she was of her horse.

"Wow," Sierra breathed out and smiled at River when he caught her eye. He smiled back.

"This is the kind of publicity that will keep us in business," Tess said when River handed back the magazine. "I'm very proud of you."

"Thanks," River said somewhat begrudgingly. "Is that all?" He started to get up from his chair.

"Yes, but I want to talk to you alone for a few minutes if you don't mind."

He shrugged and sat back down and Sierra left the office.

As soon as the door closed behind Sierra, Tess stated, "I've broken up with your father; for good."

Startled, River looked up to meet her eyes, wondering why she was telling him this. Tess never talked about her relationship with his father. Nevertheless, he knew she had broken up with him several times over the years, only to forgive and take him back. "You've broken up with him before," he said flatly.

"I realize that has been a pattern, but believe me, it is really over now. It affects you because your father will no longer bring his horses here for the winter. There will be no board for you to work off."

River shrugged. "Cory is boarded here."

"Yes, but I have another offer for you."

"Like what?" River frowned, studying Tess's face for what she was really after.

"You're not planning on quitting school and going to the track with your father this summer, are you?"

"No. That's what he wants me to do but I don't want to work at the track and I especially don't want to work for him."

"Good, that's a smart decision. How many more years of school do you have?"

"Two, after this year."

"What do you plan on doing after you graduate?"

"I'm thinking about going to college. João left me some money for school."

"Here's something else for you to consider. I want to change your duties here. Your talent is wasted cleaning stalls and doing chores and I am planning on hiring an additional stable hand to replace you. I want you to spend your time helping me train the horses. It would be an apprenticeship over the next two years, and I am prepared to offer you full wages as well as free board for your horse. If the stable continues to profit as it is now and you can prove your worth, Walt and I would offer you a position as assistant trainer with a salary much higher than you make now."

River could only stare at her, not at all sure what to make of the offer.

"You can also teach some lessons." Noting his frown Tess continued, "I know you've been teaching Katrina."

"But…"

Tess interrupted, "You're doing a good job. I realize her improved dressage scores are a result of your coaching."

River could not believe what he was hearing and looked at Tess with an expression that displayed his disbelief.

"Well?"

"Um, this is kind of unexpected, but yeah, it sounds okay…I mean the apprenticeship part. I still don't know for sure what I'll do after I graduate."

"Fair enough." Tess pressed her palms down on her desk and pushed herself up to her feet. "I'm going to ask Katrina if she wants to clean stalls on weekends in exchange for reduced board. Sierra gets full board because she also helps with conditioning rides. Manuel has a cousin who needs work and will clean stalls during the week days and assist Manuel in the other chores and maintenance that you've always helped him with. He can start next week."

River nodded and stepped out of the office, thinking about Tess's offer. He had never minded doing chores, but giving them up to ride more often sounded like a really good deal. One of his first thoughts however, was that he would miss the time he and Sierra spent cleaning stalls together; especially the times before Katrina started hanging around. But then he realized it had been quite some time since he and Sierra had really gotten along together, so what was he really going to miss?

For now, working as Tess's apprentice trainer would be okay. He'd have to think hard though, as to whether he would want to continue to work with her after he graduated. They had too many differences in how they viewed the proper training of a horse and rider. And maybe he would go to college; or now that he apparently was making a reputation for himself, maybe he could work for another training stable that might manage their horses more in line with his own beliefs.

For the first time in his life, River felt like he had options for a future…that he could actually have a future to look forward to. He smiled to himself, thinking he had always seen himself as mucking stalls and grooming horses at the track for the rest of his life.

He had much to think about and time to make decisions; but one thing he did know for sure. He was not going to quit school. He would never work for his father.

Only his father still did not know that, and he dreaded the confrontation when he told Cray.

The moment Sierra arrived at school Monday morning, she felt the charged atmosphere of some significant event that had everyone in an uproar. Some groups whispered together and others talked in loud animated voices.

Allison caught up to her before first period. "Sierra, I've been trying to call you all weekend. Where were you?"

"Oh, I guess I left my phone off. You know, after Dean showed up so late as if nothing was wrong, I just didn't want to hear him call with his lame excuses. I never checked messages."

"That's what I wanted to tell you…about Dean!"

Sierra studied Allison's troubled expression. "What?" she asked, a lump of dread balling up in her stomach.

"Come on, we have almost ten minutes. We need to sit down." Allison grabbed Sierra's arm and guided her to a bench seat outside the administration offices. Sierra did not think she was going to like what she was about to hear.

"After we left, Dean cut in on a dance with Billy's girlfriend Charlene. He kept dancing with her and ignored Billy when he tried to cut back in. Then Dean left with Charlene. Maryann Jacobs called me on Sunday because she heard the rest of the story from her brother, who's a senior. Ashley Brown, Manny Arkenstone, and Dean had a bet going as to which of them would be the first to get a virgin into bed. Dean apparently had picked you. Ashley was bragging he was sure to win for he's been taking Sarah Chambers out for months and she had essentially promised him that the night of the Valentine's ball, well... When you walked out on Dean, he was desperate for a way to win the bet. I don't know if you've noticed, but he doesn't take losing very well. I think he thought you were going to be a sure thing, but when that didn't happen, he picked the easiest target he could think of...Charlene."

"No," Sierra gasped in a whisper.

"Charlene is a sweet girl but not very bright. You can imagine..."

A wave of nausea and dizziness swept over Sierra and she pressed her hands over her mouth. Yes, she could imagine the sweet, convincing words Dean would use; the same words he had said to her that had stolen her heart; the passionate kisses and caresses. She felt fresh humiliation, but also a deep sense of compassion for poor Charlene.

"To prove he won, he had to get a picture and tape record everything said during the act. Maryann said Dean got a picture of Charlene with his cell phone, and had a small tape recorder hidden somewhere. He's shared it all with his buddies, and nobody doubts he won the bet."

It could have been my picture, my words... if Dean had been just a little more faithful in his promises and consistent in his attention to her she really didn't know if she eventually might have...She shuddered.

It felt like every eye fixed on her as she walked into homeroom. She stumbled into her desk and kept her eyes focused on pulling out her notebook and supplies from her backpack.

Throughout the day, friends came up to her, offering sympathy. At first, Sierra only felt further humiliation, but eventually began to take comfort as she realized no one seemed to think she had been a fool or thought she had been gullible. "He seemed so nice," many of the girls said. "Everyone thought he really liked you." She hadn't been the only one fooled by Dean's charm.

Charlene did not come to school that day; nor did Dean. But Billy came, and in the middle of English as they were discussing Jane Austin's *Sense and Sensibility*, he burst into blubbering sobs and fled the room. Sierra raised her hand and received permission to follow him.

Outside the nearest boys' restroom she could hear Billy sobbing. Since everyone else was supposed to be in class, she entered and found him slumped against the wall hunched over his knees, with his head buried in his arms.

"Go away," he blubbered, hearing the door open.

Sierra ignored the command and sat down next to him, putting an arm around his shoulder. He turned to her and continued to cry against her, soaking her tee-shirt with his tears. When he subsided to sniffles and hiccoughs, Sierra tried to explain.

"There is a magical charm about Dean that is almost irresistible. I can imagine how Charlene is feeling right now and she probably feels worse than you do."

"Nooo," Billy groaned. "How could she do this to me?"

"She didn't do it to you, Billy. She was swept away by a boy from a dream. Dean can make a girl forget reality, forget herself, and believe all the lies he tells. I know; I believed him too."

"You're his girlfriend," Billy declared in an angry tone.

"I thought he was my boyfriend but I was never his girlfriend. He enchanted me, just like he did Charlene."

"I loved her!"

"Don't you still love her?"

"How can I after what she did?"

"Billy, I bet Charlene has never had a boyfriend before you. I bet she is totally naïve to the ways of lecherous guys. I think she loves you too, but I think in her innocence, she was temporarily blinded by a very handsome and charming boy. I know how Dean can get into your face and convince you of his sincerity."

"She picked him over me."

"Well, first of all, she doesn't really have that choice. And, second, maybe she picked him for a brief enchanted moment. But believe me, his charm eventually wears very thin. If he hadn't dumped her after that night, she would have come back to you in time." Sierra didn't really know that, but it seemed like a good thing to say.

"He ruined everything between us."

"Only if you let him, and he is so not worth ruining a good thing. I've noticed you and Charlene together. You have something sweet and special between you. Billy, I know how hurt you feel because that is what Dean did to me. So I also know how hurt Charlene feels. Maybe you can't today or even this week or next; but Billy, try to forgive her. I think you both can learn and grow from this experience."

"Forgive her?" He spat out the words.

"Yes, forgive her. If you really love her, you will understand. You will know how she is also suffering and how sorry she is. Forgive her."

"She's been calling me and saying how sorry she is," Billy admitted.

"Have you talked to her?"

"No, I can't."

"If you can't talk to her and forgive her, then both of you will go on suffering."

"Sierra, it hurts so bad." He brought out a handkerchief and blew his nose loudly.

"I know, Billy, I know."

Dean returned to school on Tuesday but Charlene remained absent for the rest of the week. Sierra caught sight of Dean a few times in the hall; laughing and joking with his friends as if nothing unusual had happened. Perhaps for Dean and his friends, humiliating and hurting another person was nothing unusual. Sierra avoided him, unable to face him with the hatred and disgust she now felt.

However, the next time Dean and Caroline came for a lesson, Sierra approached Caroline while Dean rode.

"I'm sorry about your cat," Sierra said.

"What cat?" Caroline glanced at her with a look of annoyance.

"I heard your family's cat got hit by a car and killed."

"You're mistaken. We don't have a cat; my mother's allergic to cats."

"Not even a barn cat?"

"No," Caroline replied irritably, and turned her attention back to Dean's lesson.

When Charlene returned to school the following week, it was with Billy. She hung onto his hand and arm wherever they went, avoiding everyone else. Her ready smile and easy laughter were gone, and it broke Sierra's heart to see the change in her. She hoped time would eventually restore some of Charlene's innocence, and had no idea her mother hoped the same for her.

28 COMPETITIONS

…all work – whether in-hand or ridden – always starts with basic gaits and a clear rhythm. Once the horse is in rhythm, he can begin to relax. Once he relaxes, he can begin to take contact. With contact begins impulsion. A horse can only be straight if he has impulsion, and with straightness comes collection. In other words, collection happens. – Jorgen Koschel

Even River had to admit that Corazón loved an audience. His lovely black horse arched his neck proudly and waved his tail triumphantly; trotting in a big forward moving trot, almost passage, as River rode back to the group after his demonstration round for the cross country clinic. It was as if Corazón knew the cheering and loud applause honored him.

With strong encouragement from Tess, Sierra, and Katrina; River agreed to start Corazón at training level rather than novice.

At the end of March, Pegasus riders participated at their first competition of the season, a schooling one-day event. River won two first places; on Felicity at beginner novice level and Corazón at training level. Gloria had also entered in the schooling show at Tess's insistence, since it was her first competition on her new horse. Four Score, a ten-year-old chestnut Holsteiner had been shown by his previous owner at preliminary level. Gloria had a hard time hiding her disappointment when she only came in fourth place at training level. Like Crystal, she did not get it that an expensive, well-trained horse did not guarantee winning. A good horse needs a good rider to perform its best.

The following weekend, River competed on Moose at preliminary and took first place; and earned his last qualifying ride in order to move up to intermediate.

Dressage came next, the second weekend of April. River again took first place on Pendragon, riding fourth level. Sierra decided to start out at the same level she and Fiel had shown at their last show the season before, and rode first level test three. To her delight, she scored a sixty-nine percent, and won her class. Katrina also rode Calliope at first level, test three, a test very similar to the preliminary level dressage test. She was pleased with her score of sixty-five percent, and second place.

Not all of the local events offered an intermediate level of competition, so the following weekend, River and Tess traveled some distance from Pegasus so that River could compete on Moose at intermediate. Again, he took first place, although as he had predicted, Moose did not score as well at this level in dressage, and they won only because the horse that had scored above them in dressage had a refusal cross country.

The last weekend of April arrived and the first local rated event of the season with five riders and horses from Pegasus entered: Diva and Calliope at preliminary, and at training level, Silver Knight, Four Score, and Corazón.

Sierra and Katrina arrived early in the morning to help River and Manuel ready the horses and load them into the six-horse trailer. Manuel's cousin, Enrique, would take over the chores at the stable that day so that Manuel could help out at the show.

With the show season underway, and ramped up training schedules at the stable, Sierra found all her free time centered on caring for and riding horses. It was the best cure for her broken heart, for the needs of the horses occupied all her attention and she hardly ever thought of Dean.

It also seemed that her relationship with River had somewhat re-established to its previous easy camaraderie and sharing their tacit love and respect of the horses. Sierra could have been content enough with friendship with River, at least for now, except for the possessiveness of Katrina. She could not suppress her jealous feelings as she watched her friend hover around River, grabbing his hand or kissing him on the cheek. She knew she had no right to resent Katrina, and guilt niggled in next to her jealousy. Her only consolation was that she never noticed River initiate a kiss or holding Katrina's hand.

So it was in high spirits that Sierra arrived with the others at the show grounds for her first combined training event of the year.

Crystal and Katrina rode their preliminary dressage tests first.

"Diva should place first if the judge overlooks the two times she was overbent," River said as he and Sierra watched their tests. "If she would just let go of her mouth…" He mumbled something derogatory and Sierra made a sound of agreement.

Katrina had a decent test on Calliope and beamed proudly as she rode her mare out of the test ring, especially when River smiled at her and said, "You two did well."

Then it was time for Sierra, River, and Gloria to warm up for their training level tests. Sierra had been riding Silver in dressage at home as well as cross country, and thought they were well prepared. He was such an even-tempered guy, who did perk up with more energy at a show but never felt out of control. River had told her that dressage was much more Silver's talent than jumping, and if Gloria competed him just in dressage, would probably have a lot more success. She trotted the big gray, now on the bit, asking him to collect and then lengthen his stride and very pleased at his prompt responses to her aids.

Silver suddenly pinned his ears and stiffened his back as another rider came up behind them, *riding way too close,* Sierra thought, *and did he actually flick Silver with his whip?* The rider passed without looking at her, but Sierra knew it had been done on purpose when she recognized the rider…Dean! Darkness seeped into her spirit at sight of him. But of course he would be here. He had started taking lessons from Tess because he had failed to qualify for preliminary last season, even though he owned a very talented horse. She had stood at the rail watching so many of his lessons that she knew his horse, Calculator, had been refusing fences. Tess had been working with Dean on rating his stride and helping him place his horse at the correct take-off; and then re-schooling him over countless low courses in many different combinations to build Calculator's confidence. They had made progress for there had been almost no refusals in the lessons of the past two months.

I will not let him ruin my time here, she said to herself with a bitter taste at the back of her throat. She knew he needed one more qualifying ride to move up to preliminary, and she hoped he would earn it today. Then he would be competing against Crystal and Katrina, not her.

After everyone had finished their dressage tests, Tess led them around the cross country course, coaching the preliminary and training level riders at the same time. Now in her third year of competition, Sierra was pleased that the grounds were familiar to her, and although the course varied from year to year, she would still be facing many familiar obstacles.

"Silver will have the hardest time with the bank and again jumping downhill at the log. He really doesn't like jumping down, so use your whip if you feel any hesitation," Tess warned Sierra. She nodded in agreement, for the few times she had a refusal from Silver in their practice at home, had been at the bank. But she had gotten him down it each time, and in her last few jumping sessions, he had not refused.

The training level riders would ride stadium next while the preliminary riders rode cross country and they had just enough time to walk the stadium course right after returning from the cross country course.

Then it was time to get back in the saddle and warm up for stadium. Again, Silver responded promptly to her aids as she trotted and cantered him around the warm-up area, and then over a cross rail jump. She watched River on Corazón whenever she had a chance to glance his way. She could detect Cory's pent-up energy and excitement in his arched neck with bulging veins, but she couldn't detect if River was having any difficulty in controlling him. River rode two rides after her, and she was glad she would be able to watch them.

She heard Gloria's number called, and watched her ride out of the warm-up area over to the stadium. "We're next," she spoke to Silver, and brought him down to a stretching trot, to help him relax but stay warmed up. When the ring steward called to her that she was on deck, she brought Silver to a walk and headed over to the stadium.

Gloria had a clean round, but with two time faults. She rode out of the arena with her expression tight, and she threw a searing glance at Sierra as they passed each other on their way in and out. Sierra moved Silver into a beginning circle at a trot, picked up the canter, and started the course. They cleared all twelve obstacles and had no time faults.

"Good boy!" she praised Silver enthusiastically as they left the arena. With her attention focused on Silver, she avoided having to look at Dean, who rode next.

"Good ride," River said to her and smiled as he came up on Corazón, for he was after Dean.

"Thanks; he tries really hard."

"He does," River agreed.

They both turned to watch Calculator. Sierra realized what an aggressive rider Dean was, for he used spurs and raised his jumping bat before each obstacle, not even waiting for Calculator to take the jump on his own. They finished the round clean and Sierra noticed how Dean left the stadium, his eyes looking over to someone, and never even a pat on the neck for his horse that had done very well. How could she have ever thought he cared about horses? Well, River had been right about that too. Sure, she had seen him pat Fiel and then Diva on the neck when they had ridden together; but that was with her watching. But all the times after he had finished his lesson at Pegasus, she thought back to how he tossed the reins off to the groom, never looking back at his horse, never going over to him with a carrot or some other treat.

"Cory, go wow them," Sierra said, turning her attention back to River as he stepped away to enter the ring. He raised a hand in acknowledgement but had his attention focused on his horse and did not turn around. Once in the stadium, River moved Cory into the beginning circle and then on course. Sierra watched how fluidly the two of them galloped on and floated over each obstacle in harmonious accord. River did not wear spurs and didn't even carry a whip. It was a joy to observe the eagerness that Cory displayed as he jumped in a beautiful arc over each fence, to land and gallop on off his hind end, and effortlessly change leads as he made turns. It was a flawless ride, although a few seconds slower than Calculator.

Applause and cheers from the spectators greeted each rider as they completed their round, but Sierra noted how the cheering seemed more enthusiastic for Cory, and how people laughed and commented as he pranced proudly out of the stadium.

"Lunch break," Tess announced as Sierra and River arrived back at the stalls leading their horses. "Eat light but drink plenty of water."

"How was cross country?" Sierra asked Katrina who was using a hose to fill up the water bucket in Calliope's stall.

"We went clean," Katrina exclaimed happily. "She was so good, even through the water and…" Katrina chattered on about different obstacles on her course while Sierra and River untacked and brushed down Silver and Cory. Finally she finished describing her ride and asked, "What about your stadium rounds?"

"We all went clean but Gloria has time faults." Sierra led Silver into his stall and Katrina passed her the hose so she could fill the water bucket. "Guess who's here competing at training level."

"Dean, I know," Katrina answered.

"You knew that already?"

"He's hanging out with Crystal over at the snack stand."

"Really?" Sierra asked, although not really surprised.

"Yeah, and Gloria looks like she's ready to kill someone. What's up with her?"

"Who knows? I think Four Score is not turning out to be the sure winner she thought. Too bad; if she'd spend a little more time riding and getting to know him they might actually do well. River says he's got good breeding and has had some good training."

"Where's the food?" River asked, stepping out of Cory's stall. Sierra and Katrina had packed lunches so they wouldn't have to buy food, and they began to pull out sandwiches and drinks from a cooler.

They had two hours before time to warm up for their last ride and they wandered over to the show office to pick up their dressage test sheets, and then Katrina asked River to walk her stadium course with her one more time. Sierra tagged along, interested to check out a preliminary course.

At one point, Sierra looked up and noticed Crystal and Dean standing near the course postings, talking together about something very intently, and then they both looked over where River was walking with Katrina. Sierra hesitated, watching them watch River, noticing the deep frown on Dean's face as Crystal spoke to him. *What are those two plotting?* Her suspicions churned in her stomach, upsetting her just-eaten lunch, as Sierra recalled Justin giving shocks to Fiel and Gunsmoke. It looked to her like Crystal had a new accomplice.

As if sensing someone watching her, Crystal jerked her head to stare back at Sierra, her lips curling into a snarl. Dean also turned, and smiled at Sierra, a smile full of spite.

"Here we go," River whispered to Cory as they sprang forth from the starting box. Cory's ears pricked forward as he reached with his forelegs in a gallop as his powerful hind end propelled him on; as eager as his rider. They covered the straight stretch to the first obstacle, a three-foot brush jump; not difficult but River knew he would need to make a fairly sharp right hand turn very quickly. Cory sailed over and as

River looked to the right, Cory also turned in that direction, just as River's left leg touched his side. River delighted with their harmonious communication. It never ceased to amaze him how often it seemed he only needed to think of what he wanted to do next for his horse to already respond. They galloped on over a roll top obstacle and then up a hill to a rail fence at the top.

River had been surprised to discover how much he actually enjoyed competing, especially in combined training. It wasn't the tallying up of scores at the end of the day and winning first place. He truly found no satisfaction in that, for he admired the horses ridden by the other competitors, and loved each one for the willingness and courage they displayed in spite of some very bad riding. And there were some good riders too, which pleased him even more when he saw a pair in harmony with each other in a partnership made of love and respect.

What River loved the most was the cross country jumping; the thrill of riding a course that his horse had never seen before and feeling the anticipation, excitement, and sometimes even fear, as they galloped around taking the obstacles together.

With Moose the challenge had been to overcome the thoroughbred's desire to only run as fast as he could, and to help him overcome his spookiness of the strange obstacles; to trust his rider, and slow down to a competent speed and then jump without rushing.

Riding Cory however, was almost no challenge, as the horse's love of jumping and eagerness to gallop outside in an open space matched his own. Moving with the rhythm of Cory's gaits was pure joy; a joy shared with his horse. On Cory's back, the world contracted to just the two of them, or rather the two of them merged into one being with a mutual purpose – to be wild and free.

After the rail fence they had another straight stretch and then a turn at the crest of a hill to take another log and then descend down a steep slope; a tricky jump, for River immediately needed to sit back and communicate to Cory to gather himself underneath and slow down to a canter to take the slope safely. At the bottom, River let him stretch out again and they galloped on and into the water. Cory laid his ears back because like most horses, he did not like to get his feet wet; but he never hesitated and galloped in with the shallow water splashing up to his knees and spraying his belly, and then jumped up and out over a railroad tie bank.

Cory faced each obstacle courageously, encouraged by the enthusiasm of the rider he trusted, until he came to the twenty-first fence, with only three to go. River suddenly felt Cory tighten his muscles as he raised his head and snorted suspiciously at the fence, made to look like a railroad crossing with a red and white diagonal-striped board between two poles with round disks at their tops. He shortened his stride and even pulled to the right as if he wanted to flee.

"*Que pasa*? What is it?" River talked to his horse as they approached the jump. He could feel the tightened muscles of fear, and the hesitation; something he had never experienced with Cory before. *He's going to run out!* Making a snap decision, River turned Cory to the left, brought him down to a trot and made a wide circle. Since they had not come close enough to have actually presented the jump to Cory, it would not count as a run out or refusal, but he was sure to receive time penalties.

River completed the circle, feeling a slight easing of Cory's tightness, yet he continued to snort nervously. *Well, here goes.* He turned Cory to face the jump, urging him with his legs and his heart, speaking to him, "*Tu puedes*, you can!" He pushed him on, back into a canter and Cory leaped into a gallop, rushed at the jump, and trusting his rider, leapt over the frightening obstacle with a foot to spare, and galloped on at breakneck speed. River whooped out loud as he praised his horse, reaching forward to pat his neck and allowed him a few more strides of full out gallop before he sat back and eased him to a more controlled pace. They took the last three jumps in Cory's usual flawless style, and finished the course. They had no jumping faults but had two time penalties.

"What was that all about?" River spoke out loud to his horse as he brought him down to trot and then to a walk to cool him down.

Something about that diagonal-striped board had really panicked Cory. Had he been hit with such a board in the past, or come close to a real railroad crossing and experienced a train rushing by? He would probably never know; but he was bursting with pride for his horse. Cory had trusted him enough to approach and jump over something that obviously terrorized him.

"Cory must have done well," Sierra greeted River as he walked back to the stalls, now leading Cory. It pleased her to see the happy expression on his face. River looked up to meet her eyes and smiled with such genuine warmth that her heart ached with a longing for him to always look at her that way.

"He did very well," River said. "How did Silver go?"

"Clean! I didn't even need a whip at the bank; I just pushed him harder with my legs and cheered him on." Sierra turned back to pat Silver on his silky neck where she had just brushed his coat.

"You're getting along well with him," River said.

Sierra quickly turned to give Silver another few strokes with the brush as she felt her face heat up at the compliment.

River told her about the fence that had spooked Cory but that the big black had taken it anyway; how proud he was of him. They talked for a few minutes about the course; which jumps had been difficult and which ones had been especially fun. Their conversation was easy and relaxed…like old times.

The pleasant interlude was too soon interrupted by the return of Katrina leading Calliope and Manuel leading Diva back from stadium jumping. "Katrina looks happy," Sierra commented, noting the smile on her face.

Trailing after the horses came Tess, Crystal, and Gloria. Tess carried a handful of dressage score sheets and with a grim expression on her face. Crystal wore an expression of extreme satisfaction while Gloria looked as if she wanted to cry.

"I'm first in preliminary," Crystal announced. "Dean won in training. He beat you." She looked at River expectantly, hoping for some sign of humiliation.

"Dean won?" Sierra said, the disappointment thick in her tone. The image of Dean's face with the smugness of having placed ahead of River was like vinegar seeping into her veins, leaving a very bitter taste. She had thought that even with time penalties, River would still have won.

"What happened?" Tess asked River as she passed out the score sheets.

River didn't answer until he had looked over his score sheet, and then looked at Tess in confusion. "What do you mean? Cory has a great dressage score."

"I'm not talking about his dressage score. What happened cross country that slowed you down?" Sierra thought Tess's obvious disappointment that River had not won equaled Crystal's pleasure that he hadn't.

"He did great cross country," River defended his horse, with irritation rising. He didn't feel like he needed to justify Cory's performance to Tess, nevertheless, he told her how he had spooked at the railroad crossing jump and he had given him a chance to calm down by circling.

"You should have ridden him straight on and used a whip," Tess retorted angrily. "How many times have I told you to carry a whip? That circle cost you first place!"

"Right, and do you think he would trust me next time? If I had used a whip, it would have confirmed in his mind that the jump was dangerous," River replied with equal anger. "I am more proud of how he did today than at the last show where we won." He pivoted away from her to step back to Cory, picking up a brush, the act of grooming helping to calm his ire.

Tess huffed out in frustration, and Sierra noted her clenching and unclenching her fists. "You have twenty minutes before the victory round," she stated before she stormed away.

In the final placings, Crystal took first and Katrina took fourth at preliminary level. Dean took first in training and River second; his time penalties causing him to drop in spite of a better dressage score than

Dean. Sierra took fourth on Silver, and Gloria, with one refusal cross country, came in eighth.

At the end of the day as they were getting the horses ready to load into the trailer, Katrina continuously reiterated her disappointment that River had not won, saying over and over how sorry, and how unfair, until River finally stopped what he was doing to face her and state, "Katrina, stop it. Cory showed me his courage today; his willingness to face something that terrorized him when I asked him to. What makes you think we didn't win?"

"Oh," she answered, abashed. "Oh, I hadn't thought of it like that."

She doesn't understand River, Sierra thought to herself, *not that I do, but I know him much better than she does.* Whatever significance that might have, it pleased Sierra.

Later, on the way back to Pegasus, Katrina whispered to Sierra, "Gloria wants to quit riding. She was crying in the restroom and Crystal was rubbing her back and telling her she can't quit."

"Why does Crystal care if Gloria rides or not?" Sierra asked.

"Who knows? I mean she was saying that they were best friends and she wanted her best friend to share with her, stuff like that. Poor Gloria; I don't think she has ever really liked riding; she's just always done it to please Crystal."

"It makes no sense," Sierra whispered back. She retreated into her own thoughts, not understanding so many things. First of all, she could not imagine anyone not loving to ride but she understood how everyone was attracted to and turned on by different things. But secondly, she could not imagine doing something you didn't like just to please your friend; and what kind of friend would insist on it? She could not imagine Allison insisting she take ballet lessons or her insisting that Allison take up riding.

On Monday, Sierra brought the subject up while Allison, Katrina and she were eating lunch.

"I don't know," Katrina said, "but I've been going to school with those two since kindergarten. I remember in first grade how most of us girls talked about nothing but horses and how we longed for a horse of our own. I had never heard Crystal talk about liking horses when we were in kindergarten and she really didn't seem all that interested when the rest of us were dreaming about owning a horse. But the next thing I know, her daddy bought her a pony and she's taking lessons. And of course the rest of us are very envious. I didn't get to start taking lessons until I was ten. Then in second grade Crystal has a new pony, Muffin, and she's showing in hunter/jumper shows and coming to school with blue ribbons for show-and-tell."

"Muffin was her pony?" Sierra asked, surprised.

"Yeah, he was already a champion when Crystal got him. That was about the time that her father formed the partnership with Tess, so that Crystal would have the best place for her pony and the best instruction. When she outgrew Muffin, he stayed at Pegasus as a lesson horse."

"Interesting," Sierra mused.

"When she got her first horse after Muffin, that's when she pushed Gloria to start taking lessons. It's interesting that she never pushed me, even though I moaned all the time about wanting to learn to ride. Well, Gloria started taking lessons in third grade and by the end of the year her parents had bought her a pony. I had been saving my money and begging my parents but it wasn't until fifth grade that they finally consented and I got to start lessons. I didn't get Calliope until seventh grade."

"Hmm, I can sort of understand how with so many girls envious of her that it would motivate her to ride," Allison said thoughtfully. "But why she has to force poor Gloria to also ride, and then see her not doing well…interesting. Perhaps it has something to do with the power she holds over other people; taking pleasure from making them do things they don't want to. She didn't push you because it was obviously something you wanted…I don't know."

"Oh no," Katrina groaned, dropping her head over her tray of food. "Look who's coming over."

Sierra, sitting opposite Katrina, turned her head to meet the eyes of Dean walking toward her. He smiled at her, the smile that dimpled the corner of his mouth; the smile she used to think so adorable. "Sierra," he said, not even looking once at Allison or Katrina. "How's wonder boy, huh?" His beautiful smile twisted into an ugly sneer. He moved in so that his face was close enough for Sierra to feel his breath as he hissed, "I'm going to smash him at the championship." Then he turned and walked back to his friends.

Staring at his back in disbelief, Sierra watched him strut back to his table of friends, where Crystal sat looking very satisfied.

The following weekend, River showed Pendragon in dressage, taking first in his fourth level test and also competing in a third level musical kur and taking first as well. Sierra rode Fiel at first level, test three, and this time added second level, test one. She took a second in her first level test and third in her second level test, and happy with both scores.

The last weekend of May, River rode Moose at intermediate level, as well as Felicity at beginner novice at her first rated show; and placed first on both horses.

The first weekend in June, the Pegasus team competed again, and this time River came in first on Corazón, winning with a wide point margin above Dean in second place. Sierra came away again in fourth place, and this time Gloria actually placed in the ribbons, in sixth place. Crystal won at preliminary and Katrina took third.

Why didn't Dean ride preliminary? Sierra wondered, for he had certainly qualified after the last show. The only reason she could think of was that he wanted to stay at training level so he could compete against River.

29 FATHER AND SON

The one best precept(;) the golden rule in dealing with a horse is never to approach him angrily. Anger is so devoid of forethought that it will often drive a man to do things which in a calmer mood he will regret. - Xenophon

"He is truly amazing," Tess stated in a respectful tone as she watched River massaging liniment onto Cory's legs. Tess held her keys in hand, ready to leave the stable; but noting River still here after the long day at the show, she had deviated her course.

River glanced up and flashed a rare smile at Tess. "He did well," he stated proudly.

"I've never seen a horse as bold or eager as this one. He seems to love a challenge; so…" Tess said hesitantly, "Next time out?"

River stood up and stroked Cory's neck and shoulder before he turned to Tess. "He could do preliminary, but what's wrong with letting him stay at training level? Why rush him?"

With a sigh of resignation, Tess wisely decided not to push it. One more year wouldn't make that much difference. River would turn eighteen next year and he would be able to compete on Moose at advanced level. Perhaps on Moose they might qualify for an Olympic trial in the next year or so. But if he didn't qualify with Moose, she was positive he could on Corazón. And unlike her past attempt with Gunsmoke, she was sure River would make the Olympic team. It would assure the success of Pegasus Equestrian Center…would assure her own future.

"Good riding today," Tess complimented as she turned away.

"Thanks," River replied automatically, his attention already back to Cory. He bent down again to resume massaging the black's legs as the sound of Tess's car faded into the distance. He added standing wraps for the night, and then finished with one last brushing, focusing on the spots Cory loved to have brushed and scratched. Finally, he put on Cory's stable blanket before leading him to his stall and his waiting hay.

He stood at the stall door, watching Cory thrust his muzzle into his hay, and his heart filled with contentment at the sight of his horse enjoying his feed. He thought back to the frightened and aggressive animal he had been, and marveled at all the positive change that had come from patience and good care. No, he would not rush him. He did not want to take any chances of destroying his horse's current enthusiasm for jumping. He smiled to himself, recalling how Cory had exploded like a bomb from the starting box, and eagerly galloped on in anticipation of the first jump, as much as to say, 'what have we here today for me to conquer?' River had been able to sense how Cory calculated and adjusted his strides for each distance and height, clearing each with inches to spare, yet not over-jumping; sensible in not expending energy where he didn't have to.

As River's stomach growled and Storm pushed against his legs, he whispered goodnight, and then made a quick tour down both aisles to make sure all horses were contentedly eating and looking well. Then he turned out the lights and locked the doors.

On the way home, Storm frolicked about, sensing River's happy mood, and laughing, he play wrestled with her and then tossed sticks for her to chase as they walked along.

Only one thing could dampen River's euphoria, and the sight of his father's truck parked in the yard brought his high mood crashing back down to reality. The last time Cray had been home, River had managed to avoid him completely. That might have been a mistake, for he heard from Aunt Hazel that Cray had been furious. With only one more week of school, he had no more excuses for not going to work for his father this summer.

He can't make me go, he told himself but with doubts pushing at the edges of his determination. He filled Storm's dish with kibble and then her water bowl; and waited for her to finish eating, stalling for time. "Stay here," he told his dog after they went up to his room and he changed from his riding clothes to jeans and a sweatshirt. *Might as well get this settled between us.* With reluctant steps, he climbed down from his loft and went into the kitchen.

His father sat hunched over a bottle at the kitchen table; unshaven, red-eyed, and stains on his shirt. *Not good…*

River had learned to recognize the two levels of drinking for Cray; a mellow drunk and a despondent drunk. When mellow, he showed no outward signs of intoxication except for a whiff of his breath if he came too close. His appearance would be immaculate and his eyes bright, even if red-tinged. When River had first come to live with his father, he had enjoyed being with him when in his mellow state. Cray would hug him spontaneously, ruffle his hair, and tell him what a great kid he was. Often he told stories about horses he was training at the track and about owners, jockeys, and other trainers. Or he would talk nostalgically about the ranch the Blackthorn family had owned before it went bankrupt. He could tell a story so that the listener felt like he was there seeing the events as they unfolded. In those early days, River almost understood how his mother and Tess had succumbed to Cray's charms, and in those days, the mellow drunk was his usual state.

But over the years, as his success at the track waned, his father more often drank himself into a state of despondency and a tendency to volatile anger. River had learned to stay out of his way, but too many times, he could not avoid a confrontation that ended in his father lashing out at him with fists and kicking him with heavy boots, and peace only came when his father passed out.

River was about to make a quick exit when his father looked up and slurred out, "River." Ignoring him, he pushed through the back door even as he heard the scuffle of Cray's chair and the stream of swearing as he stumbled after him. "I'm talking to you," Cray yelled.

River sprinted for the barn and up to his loft, hoping his father was too drunk to negotiate the steps. From his loft window he watched him stagger across the yard, swearing as he weaved, and then suddenly, halfway to the barn he paused, looking around as if he had forgotten something, and then lurched for his truck. It took him several attempts to pull open the driver's side door and crawl up onto the seat.

I should stop him, River thought guiltily, but made no move to do so as the truck's engine burst to life and with a spray of dirt and gravel, his father negotiated a wayward track out to the road. River threw himself onto his mattress in relief, and waited for his pounding heart to slow to normal, taking in deep breaths. Storm nosed her way onto his chest with a comforting whine, and he hugged her tightly until his inner trembling subsided.

Later, he returned to the house for a quick shower, and to scrounge a peanut butter sandwich and half a bag of pretzels, and then returned to his room to study for his finals next week; trying to keep up with the study habits he had learned from Laila. But after his long day, his eyelids drooped and he fell asleep hunched over a book.

The sound of tires coming too fast into the yard woke him. He sat bolt upright and froze, listening as the truck door opened with a screech of un-oiled hinges and the sound of boots scuffing…then silence. River held his breath, hoping to hear the sounds of the back door opening, indicating his father had forgotten him and gone into the house.

"River," Cray roared at the top of his voice from the middle of the yard. "Get y'bagshs packed and get y'ass down here…now!"

His heart accelerating, River remained still, as if any movement would bring Cray immediately in front of him, and with each breath, wishing, *go inside, go inside.*

"Y'hear me, boy? Git'sh down here!" Silence for a few moments. "Don't make me drag you down here!" Footsteps moved toward the barn.

Closing his eyes tight with one last hopeful prayer, River forced himself to get up. "Stay here," he said to Storm who sat as tensely alert as River felt. He left his room, descended the stairs and went outside to meet his father. He wanted to get this settled once and for all.

Outside, Cray stood in the middle of the yard, wavering on his feet, staring up at River's window. As River stepped out of the barn, Cray turned to face him, almost falling backwards.

"Cray, I'm staying here," River said, trying to keep his voice from shaking and hoping his father could not see how petrified he felt.

"Boy…" Cray spat out in fury, and then staggered forward and swung with surprising coordination and strength for his inebriated state. River managed to duck and sidestep away and the punch only grazed his shoulder. Enraged, Cray turned again, tripping over his own feet and falling flat.

River watched him struggle and then went over to help him to his feet. *He can't hurt me tonight,* he thought in relief. "Come inside," he said, trying to propel his father toward the house. "We'll talk about it tomorrow."

"Talk, 'bout now," Cray slurred, resisting River's efforts to pull him along. River gave up, and let go of him, stepping back and away.

"Cray, forget it. I am not going with you," he said again, and then turned away, wondering if he should go back to his room, or run off into the woods and hide until his father passed out. With relief, he heard his father moving away, crunching gravel back towards the house. Maybe it was safe to go to his room. He would be gone to the stable long before Cray ever woke up tomorrow. River started for the barn.

He heard the creak of the truck's door. *Is he going to try to drive off again?* River turned to look, and saw his father with one hand holding onto the truck's door for balance as he reached for something inside the cab. When his father pulled back out and turned to face him again,

River froze in horror, looking into the muzzle of a handgun waving at him in his father's hand.

"I mean what I shay," Cray growled thickly, and cocked the gun.

Shaking his head in disbelief, River said, "Don't do it." He wanted to turn and run but he forced himself to stand still. "Cray, put the gun down."

His father wavered with the gun swaying in front of him in a small arc, all aimed at a part of River. He frowned, staring, and suddenly dropped the hand holding the gun to his side.

"Dad, we'll talk tomorrow, okay?" River said, trying to placate him. His father slumped forward, his arm with the gun dangling, and River thought best to quickly get out of his sight. He turned and started walking away.

"River!" He heard his name a split second before the explosive crack of the gun; just another split second before he felt the jolt of a searing, excruciating pain into his left side. *What?* He kept on walking, not looking back, not believing his father would actually…until he stumbled forward, his vision going black. He lay still, a roaring sound filling his ears, the sound of his own blood pulsing; pulsing out of his body; and very faint, the sound of the truck's engine receding away.

He lay still; he couldn't do anything else. *He shot me! I'm going to die!* He couldn't move, but tears filled his eyes; tears of regret for his future, his horse, Storm, his life…for Sierra…he never told her…Suddenly Storm was there, whining pathetically and licking at his face. *I'm not dead yet. Still breathing…*for each labored breath he took caused pain to shoot throughout his chest, and brought him no sense of getting oxygen. *Need help!* He tried to move his fingers and surprised himself when he could. Forcing his arm to move, in spite of how it seemed to shock and jar everything inside, he brought it to his back pocket and grabbed the rim of his cell phone. He couldn't feel it in his fingers but as he forced his hand up to his face, and opened his eyes, he could see its blurry outline. Without looking, he moved his finger down the screen and to the place that should be his contacts. He tried to look; yes, the list had come up on the screen. He pressed the first one and heard it ring.

"Hello?"

"Sierra," he spoke her name in a croaky whisper, and it seemed most important that she know how he felt about her, before he...

"River, what's the matter?"

"Sierra, I...you..." He licked his lips, tasting blood. "Been shot!" he said, as if surprised, and passed out.

"River...River?" Sierra repeated, but he didn't answer. She heard a sound like the whine of a dog. "Storm?" she called through the phone, and Storm barked, hearing her voice. "River!" she tried again. She looked over at the clock, 11:10. Pam had gone to bed around 9:30, but Sierra had been too wound up from the show and didn't feel tired. With finals next week, she had made herself comfortable on the sofa, her books spread around her, and with plenty of snacks. But she must have fallen asleep when the ringing of her phone inside her backpack woke her up.

"Something is very wrong," she said out loud, and heard Storm bark again. River was not answering. She pushed her books aside and went to wake up her mother.

"We have to go over there," she pleaded after explaining the phone call and that River was not answering.

Pam sat up groggily in bed, pushing her hands through her tousled hair, trying to make sense of what Sierra was going on about.

"Mom, please, I think he's in some kind of trouble. Maybe his father..."

Pam suddenly felt very awake. "Okay, get dressed...oh, you are dressed. Okay, let me get dressed. Do you know his address?"

"No, I only know his driveway where we dropped him off that day after Fiel had colic."

"Yes, it's not very far from here," Pam said; now out of bed and pulling on her jeans and a sweatshirt. "We could try calling 911, but we don't know the address."

"I'll call," Sierra said, needing to do something. "I can describe to them about where it is."

"Good," Pam called over her shoulder as she dashed to the bathroom.

Sierra made the call, and found the operator not very helpful since Sierra couldn't tell her exactly what the trouble was or an exact address. Sierra pleaded with her that she suspected child abuse, which did get the operator's attention, and she said she would dispatch a car to the general area.

"Let's go," Pam called as she came out from the bathroom with keys and purse in hand. They left the cottage, quickly got into the car, and sped away to about where they thought River lived.

"This is the driveway, don't you think?" Pam asked as they cruised the road they had taken to drop River off.

"Yes, I remember that mailbox on the other side, painted like a cow," Sierra said, squinting into the light provided by the headlights of the car. Pam turned onto the driveway, and they slowly maneuvered up the gravel road that ended at the yard of a very large old house in extremely decrepit condition. Pam stopped with the motor idling, and they both scanned the area.

"There!" Sierra shouted, noting a figure on the ground near an old barn. "It's River!" She saw the shadowy form of a dog near the lying figure. She had her hand on the door handle to jump out, but her mother grabbed her arm, holding her back. "Mom, it's River."

"You are not getting out of this car, we don't know what happened here," Pam said firmly.

"Mom," Sierra tried to pull away.

"Sierra," Pam said again in a tone that Sierra hardly ever heard. "It won't help him if you or I get hurt also. I'm calling 911 again."

Even as she said the words, three patrol cars rolled up behind them. Four officers stepped out of the car with guns in hand, two of them moving cautiously up to the house and two of them going toward the body. Sierra could see another officer inside one of the cars on a radio, and then a sixth officer came up to Pam's window. She pressed the button to roll it down and began explaining what had happened so far.

The rest of the evening became a blur to Sierra. Neither her mother nor the police would allow her out of the car. She watched as the police forced their way into the house when no one came to the door. Shortly after, they came out with a woman and a young man, both handcuffed and pushed into the back seats of two separate patrol cars.

An ambulance had been summoned. Storm would not allow the strangers to approach River, growling menacingly with teeth bared. Sierra had called out to them that she knew the dog, and only then was she allowed out of the car with a policeman on each side of her. Storm came to her when she called, whining pathetically, and Sierra held on to her while paramedics rushed over to River. She didn't know if he were dead or alive, and suspected the worst at the sight of all the blood pooling at his side. Relief flooded over her when she saw them doing things that must mean he was alive: starting an intravenous needle, putting some kind of tube into his mouth and down his throat, checking his blood pressure over and over, and finally, carefully lifting him onto a stretcher and loading him into the back of the ambulance. One police car with two officers followed the ambulance away. Another policeman escorted Sierra back to her car and she got in with Storm.

"Just a few questions and we'll escort you home," the officer said. More patrol cars were arriving with their lights flashing; Sierra never knew how many. She and her mother answered his questions, adding information they thought might be helpful. At last a patrol car escorted them home, where they settled Storm in with Charlie, and then left on their own for the hospital.

The officer explained that almost at the same time they had placed the 911 call, a patrol car had discovered where Cray had driven his truck into a ditch. The police found him clutching the steering wheel, sobbing, a loaded gun next to him, and saying over and over, "I killed my son." With the information from the 911 dispatcher and the address on his driver's license, they had arrived at the scene just moments behind Sierra and her mother.

The tiled corridor seemed endless…and dizzying. Sierra focused on each green tile placed at intervals along a row of yellowish tiles in a wall of dull beige tiles…a sea of tiles; very ugly tiles. *This is Mom's world,* she thought, clinging to her mother's arm as she led her daughter from the emergency room where they had entered the hospital to the surgical waiting room. *What a horrible place; I do not want to be here.* Only holding onto her mother's arm connected to her solid and confident presence leading the way, kept Sierra moving forward on her trembling knees. *Even the smells…*really not what she had expected; not a clean, fresh smell, but an acrid, antiseptic smell that tried to smother the odor of sickness and death. *River does not belong here! He belongs with me at the stable with the smell of horses…*

They reached glass doors that Pam pushed open. Inside, the room offered several green plastic sofas, chairs, and tables piled with crumpled magazines and leftover coffee cups and food wrappers. It was after one a.m., and apparently nobody else had a loved one in surgery, for the room was empty of people.

They sat down to wait…and wait. They had been told by the nurse in the emergency room that River had been taken to surgery and she could tell them nothing more; except he was still alive when the ambulance arrived. She had steered them over to an admitting desk and they had given what information they knew, which wasn't all that much. "We should call Tess," Sierra suggested. "She probably knows more about him than we do." She gave the clerk Tess's number, who punched it in on her desk phone. They waited until she made a connection, and then the clerk nodded at them in dismissal, telling them to go to the surgical waiting area.

Pam left once to go to a bank of vending machines and came back with cups of bland coffee for both of them. It gave them something to do. Sierra leaned against her mother where they sat on one sofa, and tried to sleep, but as gritty as her eyes felt and as lightheaded as she was with fatigue, she could not doze off.

Tess arrived about thirty minutes later, her face pale and taut. Sierra let her mother explain what they knew while Tess sat on a chair with rigid posture, fingering over and over a plastic figure of a jumping horse and rider on her key chain.

"I feel so guilty," Pam said after explaining and answering Tess's questions. "We suspected his father of abuse, and we never did anything about it. Maybe we could have prevented this."

Tess shook her head, but not in disagreement. "I know he was sometimes rough on River, but I never, never in a thousand years could have thought him capable of trying to kill him." Sierra suspected she held onto a rather large measure of guilt herself.

The wall clock electronically ticked away the minutes and then hours. They fell into silence, and Sierra believed she might actually have fallen asleep for a few minutes at least.

Finally, a side door to the waiting room opened and a surgeon, still in light blue scrubs, walked over to them. As one, they sat up straight, their eyes full of hope and fear.

"I'm Dr. Hoffman. Is anyone here a parent or relative?" the surgeon asked.

"I'm his employer," Tess spoke up, "and these are close friends of his. His mother is dead and his father is the one who shot him." Tess did not mince any words. "His aunt is his legal guardian, but I believe she has been taken into custody."

The surgeon's eyes flashed open wider in surprise, and sympathy? He cleared his throat and then proceeded, "I see."

"How is he?" Sierra blurted out. She wanted to scream, very annoyed with all this useless, preliminary banter.

"He is doing well," the surgeon answered, and that seemed to draw him back to his role of giving the news. "He is a very lucky young man. The bullet missed his heart and large blood vessels, but nicked part of the left lung, and resulted in a hemothorax." He cleared his throat again and explained, noting the baffled expressions on everyone's face except Pam's. "What I mean is there was bleeding into the chest around the lung, causing its collapse. He lost quite a bit of blood, but the paramedics got to him in time and with their resuscitation efforts, probably saved his life. I was able to remove the bullet and I did have to remove a small amount of lung tissue. I believe however, that he should heal well and regain near normal lung function. He's just going to need some time."

There was a collective sigh of relief. Tess asked, "Can I see him now?"

"We've moved him to the intensive care unit for now. His condition is serious, but stable, and I want to rest him on the ventilator overnight…well," he glanced at the clock, "until later today. If you wait here just a little longer, the nurses are settling him in, and one of them will come and get you, probably in about twenty to thirty minutes. He'll be sedated. We won't let him wake up until we are ready to remove the endotracheal tube." Again when he noted their expressions he explained, "It's a breathing tube into his lungs."

Pam asked a few more specific medical questions, and then they sat back in their seats to wait again.

Finally, a nurse summoned them to River's bedside, but she would only allow two at a time. Tess and Pam went in first, and then Pam accompanied Sierra into his room.

River lay in a bed with a tube inserted in his mouth and attached to thick plastic tubing connected to a square machine; the ventilator, the nurse was explaining. Sierra stared into his face, looking so peaceful right now, yet washed of color. How could someone with brown skin look so pale? She had never noticed what long and thick eyelashes he had, but now above his cheeks, they looked like black smudges. There was crusted blood on part of his teeth that she could see around the tube in his mouth. Her eyes went from his face to his body covered with white blankets. A tube the size of a garden hose protruded from beneath the covers to drain into a square plastic container hanging at the bottom of the bed. Thick, red fluid dribbled down the tube – *blood?*

Bags of fluid hanging from poles and with thin, clear tubing threaded into the mechanisms of machines and then continuing on into a needle in the side of his neck and another into a vein in his arm, dripped in, as she watched briefly, drop after drop.

"You can take his hand," the nurse said to her kindly, "and talk to him."

"Can he hear me?" Sierra asked, her voice a squeak.

"He is sedated, but we never know what our patients are hearing, even if he doesn't remember later."

Sierra stepped closer to the bed and found River's hand beneath the blanket. A cloth restraint had been wrapped around his wrist and tied to the bed frame.

"It's in case he wakes up suddenly, and not knowing where he is, could accidently pull out his breathing tube," the nurse explained.

Taking his fingers and encasing them within her palm, Sierra spoke softly, "River, it's Sierra; I'm here. You're going to be okay." Then her voice cracked and she turned to her mother as tears came in a rush.

Pam rubbed her back and asked, "Are you ready to go?"

"Just a minute," Sierra gulped, forcefully trying to regain control. When she thought she could trust her voice she turned back to River's bed and took his hand once more. "Don't worry, Storm is with me and I'll watch out for Cory, too." It almost looked like his eyelids flickered but then maybe it was just her imagination. She squeezed his fingers gently, and then let her mother lead her away.

30 THE MARSHALLS

The best riders in the world have their horses totally under control, but from the half halt – not from strength. – Dr. Reiner Klimke

"Take the day off," Tess said, glancing at her watch and then confirming the time of almost six a.m. on the wall clock. "I'll call Manuel to let him know what happened and he or Enrique will help Katrina with the chores." She had just come back from seeing River once more, and now fumbled through her keys for the one to her car.

Sierra nodded in agreement and she and Pam also left the hospital. They drove home in silence, too exhausted to think, much less talk. Sierra crawled into bed and fell instantly asleep.

Four hours later, her eyes popped open, sunlight penetrating through her bedroom curtains. *River.* Her mind reeled over all that had happened, and she knew there was no chance of going back to sleep. Leaving a note for her mother who did appear to be sleeping soundly, she left for the stable.

Katrina and Manuel had finished the morning chores and Katrina was brushing Calliope in the crossties when Sierra arrived. "How is he?" Katrina froze with her brush in hand the moment she caught sight of Sierra, her face pale and drawn with evidence of recent tears.

"They say he's going to be okay," Sierra told her.

Katrina's face screwed up as she tried to hold back her tears. She dropped her brush and she and Sierra fell into a hug of mutual comfort. "I thought…I thought," Katrina gulped.

After regaining control, Katrina, sniffing through her stuffy nose, picked up her brush and returned to grooming Calliope while Sierra gave her more details. Katrina brushed as she listened, and then when Sierra finished, continued brushing in silence until she suddenly leaned her face against Calliope, her shoulders shaking as she cried again.

"Katrina, I'm sure he's going to be okay," Sierra reassured her.

Katrina nodded but then turned her face to look at Sierra. "It was you he called," she said in a choked voice.

Sierra's mouth dropped open in stunned surprise. *Katrina is jealous! Ha, if she only knew how jealous I am of her!* But she did not believe Katrina needed to worry and she explained, "Of course he called me. I live close to him and he knows my mother is a nursing student. Katrina, he could have died! He needed help quickly."

"It's not just that," she sniffed. "I've seen the way he looks at you. We ride on the trail together but he's never really asked me. I just always try to be ready when I know he's going out. He's never asked me to help him with Cory."

Sierra's heart jumped. *The way he looks at me?* How badly she wanted to ask Katrina what she meant by that. And she realized that what Katrina told her was true. She had thought Katrina was doing all the things she and River used to do together, but it did seem now like it was mostly Katrina tagging after him. He didn't ask Katrina to help with Cory or to help out when the shoer or the vet came. And last week he had asked Sierra to hold a horse for him while he treated a swollen leg according to the vet's instructions. Still…but then she thought back to seeing River's pale face with blood on his teeth, and connected to so many frightening machines and she prayed with all her heart, *just let him be okay, even if it's Katrina he cares about; I just want him to be okay…and happy.*

"Katrina…" she started.

"I love him!" Katrina cried out, turning her face back to Calliope and now sobbing uncontrollably. Sierra watched a few moments as her own heart seized in almost unbearable pain; aching for what she knew Katrina was feeling, aching for her own feelings, and how much it hurt to be rejected by the one you thought you loved. She moved forward and put her arm around Katrina's shoulders, hugging her again.

Giving Calliope the day off, Katrina rode Fala and Sierra rode Fiel on the trail together; both understanding the time with horses was the best way to soothe their troubled spirits. Then Sierra decided to go ahead with her assigned horses for the day even though Tess had given her the day off. It was far better than moping at home, waiting until her mother woke up so she could take her back to the hospital.

When she arrived home, her mother told her she had called to check on River; that he was stable, off of life-support, and doing well. They planned on moving him out of intensive care in the morning.

"Sierra, I am too exhausted to go back to the hospital tonight," Pam said to Sierra's pleading. "I'm sorry; I will take you tomorrow when I get home from school."

Somehow Sierra managed to review her notes for the two final exams she had tomorrow, and although she woke up several times during the night, managed to get several hours of sleep. In a way, the exams were a blessing, giving her something to forcefully focus her mind on, and off of her anxiety over River. She felt like she passed and probably did well on both tests. She completed her work at the stables, and then suffered through her mother wanting to eat dinner before they finally went back to the hospital.

When they entered through the main lobby, her mother led her to a different area than where they had been yesterday. Pam checked in at the nurses' station for River's room number.

"He's in 401, but the police are talking with him now."

"We'll wait in the visitor's room," Pam said, leading Sierra to an alcove with a few chairs and the usual tables piled with old magazines.

"The police! Why the police?" Sierra asked in alarm.

"Someone shot him, Sierra," Pam stated. "That's a crime."

Of course, Sierra realized and then other thoughts bombarded her mind. What now for River? His father in jail and the other people who lived at his house also arrested; was there anyone at home for him? Would he have to go into a foster home? How little she actually knew of his life beyond the stable.

From the alcove they could see the nurses' station and the elevators. When they saw two policemen walk to the elevators and press the down button, they got up and went to River's room.

He lay in a bed with eyes closed. Green plastic oxygen tubing delivered oxygen through two small prongs inside his nose. The same large hose draining blood emerged from the covers to the container below the bed. Intravenous tubing draped from a pump and dripped fluid into a vein in his arm, secured with tape.

Pam set a folding chair beside the bed and indicated Sierra should sit there. "I'm going to ask his nurse how he's doing," she said and left the room.

Sierra sat down, watching River until his eyes flickered open and he looked at her, his expression unreadable.

"Hi," she said, feeling very shy.

"Hi," he whispered back, his voice hoarse.

"Are you..?" She didn't know what to ask. Are you okay seemed a stupid question.

"I'm okay," he answered.

"Storm is with me," she told him quickly. "Charlie is keeping her company."

He nodded and closed his eyes again.

He must feel awful, she guessed. She sat awkwardly, wishing she could think of something comforting or reassuring.

"Are you in pain?" she asked.

He opened his eyes again to look at her. "Not too much."

"Oh, that's good."

He closed his eyes again, and she wondered if he was getting drugs; pain killers or something, that made him sleepy.

"Cory's fine, I checked on him today," she said, trying to say the things he would want to hear.

"Thanks," he whispered, and opened his eyes once more to meet hers. "Can you lunge him a few days a week? He's doing so well; I hate for him to lose conditioning."

"Of course." When River managed to keep looking at her she blurted out, "River, what happened?"

"My father shot me."

"Why?"

"We got in a fight." He looked away to a point across the room.

"What's going to happen?"

"I don't know. The police told me he's in jail. They arrested my aunt as an accessory." His eyelids drooped closed but he continued to explain, "She didn't have anything to do with him shooting me though. I told the police that. She's just a drunk."

Sierra watched his face tighten into a frown. She could think of nothing to say.

Pam came back into the room, followed by Katrina.

"River!" Katrina cried out at sight of him.

Feeling embarrassed, although she didn't know why she should, Sierra quickly got up and let Katrina have her chair.

River opened his eyes and smiled at Katrina. "Hi," he greeted her.

"Oh, River," Katrina choked back her sobs and grabbed his hand. Sierra noted he did not pull away.

Pam placed her hands on Sierra's shoulders, signaling they should leave. "It's so good to see you awake, River," she said.

"Thank you. Thanks for coming," he said, noticing Pam taking out her keys. "Thanks for taking care of Storm and Cory," he said to Sierra.

"Of course. Um, I'll come see you tomorrow."

He nodded, his eyes closing again.

"Don't stay too long and tire him out, dear," Pam cautioned Katrina as she and Sierra left.

Every evening after supper, Pam took Sierra to visit River for the week and a half that he remained in the hospital, and they would stay until visiting hours ended. Tess came for a few minutes every evening; and Sierra wondered at the deep circles under her eyes and the deeper creases by her mouth, as to what guilt or anguish kept her looking so haggard; surely not just her concern for River. Manuel and Rosa visited the evenings that Rosa did not have to work at her restaurant job. Allison came by once, bringing horse magazines and homemade cookies; and even Dr. Patterson stopped in. Sierra was at least spared seeing Katrina and River together, for Katrina visited him right after school.

River's room filled with cards and flowers, mostly from owners that knew River worked with their horses. Even the Galensburgs sent flowers, actually the largest and most expensive arrangement, and with a card that said the usual 'get well soon', but also, handwritten, 'looking forward to you back on Pendragon'. Jane Fayette, the owner of Moose, actually came to the hospital and assured River not to worry about this show season. She just wanted him to get well. "No other rider could have taken him along as fast as you have; not even Tess," she told him. "I wasn't sure he would even make it to intermediate level, and the way you two are going…well, don't worry, next season. I feel confident you'll be able to move him up to advanced."

Then one evening he had another visitor that bothered Sierra even more than Katrina.

She stood at the doorway watching while Sierra was telling River how Cory had behaved on the lunge line that day. When Sierra noticed River's eyes look up over her head and grow wide, she looked over her shoulder to see the girl; still in black, her clothing accented with chains, studs, and many piercings, and spiky, multi-colored hair.

"Laila!" River said; a surprised timbre in his voice but also a note of gladness, and a smile spreading across his face.

Sierra shoved away in her chair and quickly stood up as the girl came over to River's bedside and stood looking down at him.

"Hey, gay cousin," she said.

When River's smile widened, clearly indicating his happiness to see her, Sierra backed away to take the only other vacant chair in the room, by the window.

"I'm sorry, please forgive me," he said quickly as if trying to get something out of the way. "I acted a complete jerk."

"Yes, you did," Laila said and leaned over to kiss him on the mouth before she sat in the chair and took his hand. "Still, I've missed you."

"I've missed you."

"How's school?"

"I was hanging in there; mostly *C*s. They're going to let me take my finals this summer when I'm better."

"Need help studying?"

"Yeah, I could use your help."

No, I don't believe this! Sierra's heart cried in anguish as she watched.

"How did you know I was here?"

"I ran into your cousin last night and he told me."

"Oh, so they released him…that's good…and my aunt?"

"Yeah, she's home. She and Steve were never actually charged with anything. Your father made a full confession and Steve said they asked him a lot of questions about drug dealers and stuff, but still let them go after a few hours at the station. Your father's trial is in two weeks."

As Laila told him the news, River's brow creased into a frown, his eyes closed tightly, and his mouth closed in a grim downward curve; as if a dark shadow passed over him. When Laila finished, she watched him for a few moments and then leaned down to whisper, but Sierra heard. "You won't ever have to see him again. You're free of him." River nodded, not opening his eyes, as if trying to control his reaction.

But as Laila remained leaning close, holding his hand and smoothing hair off his forehead; his expression slowly softened and his features smoothed into neutral.

Sierra recognized they shared something profound, and she felt very left out and inadequate.

At last River opened his eyes and looking at Laila said, "That's Sierra."

Laila turned and with a smirky look said, "Hi Sierra. I'm Laila."

"Hi," Sierra said weakly, and now feeling like she should leave. "Um, I guess I'll see you tomorrow, River." She rose from her chair. Her mother had gone to another floor to get some information on a patient she needed for a homework assignment. She would wait for her in the alcove.

"Okay," River said, not asking her to stay. "See you tomorrow?"

"Of course." Sierra left the room feeling as if her heart would burst through her chest, exposing her feelings for all to witness.

Many evenings, it was just her and River. She would sit quietly at his side after she had told him about the horses and Storm, and watch him retreat into his own thoughts, withdrawn from her. But when she thought he had fallen asleep and she would get up to go, he usually opened his eyes and asked, "Do you have to go?"

"No, I can stay as long as you want me to; until the nurses kick me out," she answered, her heart filling with warmth at the thought that he wanted her to stay. She longed to take his hand the way she had seen both Katrina and Laila do, but never quite had the nerve. She was too afraid he would pull away.

One evening when Sierra and Pam arrived, Tess was already there, and pacing in front of the window. River sat propped up in bed with a tight expression.

"River has agreed to see his father," Tess explained. "The police are bringing him."

"Should we go?" Pam asked.

"No," River stated, emphatically. "Stay."

Shortly after, Cray arrived, handcuffed, wearing an orange jumpsuit, and accompanied by two policemen. Sierra hardly recognized the wreck of a man that she had seen several times at the stable.

Cray burst into tears as soon as he sat down at the bedside. "I didn't mean it, I swear, I didn't," he repeated through his choked sobs.

"You shot me in the back," River said through a tight mouth, unsympathetic to his tears. "You tried to kill me."

"I didn't," Cray denied. "It was an accident, I swear. I only meant to shoot over your head to get your attention, but I lost my balance. You know how drunk I was. I didn't know what I was doing."

"Right," River retorted and turned his face away.

"Please, forgive me," Cray pleaded.

"Can you take him away?" River asked the officers.

"Time's up," one officer said, pulling Cray to his feet and propelling him toward the door.

Tess, who had watched in disgust, suddenly said, "Cray."

He turned his head toward her.

"If you ever touch this boy again, I'll kill you myself."

Sierra looked at Tess in shock, that she would make such a statement in front of the police. But one of the officers actually showed signs of a smile at her words. She guessed a man who had shot his own son would not find much sympathy with the law.

When River was finally discharged, Sierra was surprised to discover all that Tess did to help him. She had immediately contacted her own lawyer and also Mr. Tanglewilde, the lawyer in charge of River's inheritance from João. When she met resistance at her offer to take River as a foster child, she petitioned for him to become an emancipated minor. River would turn eighteen in about seven months; already had a job at the stable, and as it appeared he had essentially been taking care of himself for years, the petition was granted. Tess had the empty floor above the stable lounge cleaned up and furnished as a room for River. He would have the bathroom with a shower downstairs in the lounge, as well as a refrigerator and microwave. It was certainly a step up from where River had been living.

The social worker assigned to River at the hospital, insisted however, that River stay in a foster home after discharge, to be sure his medical needs were met and his injury well-healed before living on his own. She also insisted and had approved in the conditions of his emancipation, that he see a counselor once a week until he turned eighteen.

River stayed in foster care six weeks.

Riders from Pegasus participated in two competitions while River convalesced; one dressage show and one horse trial. Fiel did very well in his two second level tests. Tess rode Pendragon at fourth level, and placed fourth in the class. Sierra couldn't help feeling proud for River when Mrs. Galensburg's only comment to Tess was, "When is your boy going to be able to ride again?"

At the horse trial, Dean again came in first at training level, and Sierra took third on Silver. Gloria had time faults and one refusal cross country on Four Score, and did not place in the ribbons. Crystal, to no one's surprise, came in first at preliminary, and Katrina came in fifth, dropping from third place when Calliope took a rail down in stadium.

As they were returning from the victory round, Sierra heard footsteps behind her, and turned to find Dean walking up, carrying his first place trophy. "So the famous golden boy of the Pegasus team couldn't face me today," he said, smiling as he gestured with his trophy.

Sierra glared at him. She knew Dean must know what had happened to River, for the whole school during finals week had been buzzing with the news.

"Shot by his father, tsk, tsk," Dean said in a mock sympathetic tone when she didn't answer him.

"Go away," Sierra said flatly, and turned her back, stepping up her pace as she led Silver back to the stalls, her neck turning red and her spine prickling at his derisive laughter that followed her.

"Come on, River, let's go for a walk." Laila shoved at River's shoulder where he lay on top of his bed, facing the wall.

"I don't feel like it."

"I don't care; I do. Come on."

"Since when did you become the exercise nut?" He begrudgingly opened his eyes and glanced over his shoulder at her, since she wouldn't quit bothering him.

"Since you need to get off your pathetic ass and walk."

"Go away," River groaned into his pillow.

Laila ripped away the quilt that River hibernated beneath. "Quit feeling sorry for yourself and get up."

River rolled onto his back to face Laila, glowering at her. "I'm not feeling sorry for myself. I just want to sleep."

"That's all you've done for the past week. The Marshalls tell me you lie here in bed all day. You hardly eat anything at all. The more you sleep and do nothing, the less your body wants to do."

"When did you get to be the medical expert?"

Stepping back, Laila controlled the retort she wanted to shout at him in exasperation. All that kept her standing in place with her arms folded across her chest in determination was the memory of another person who hadn't given up when she had gone through her own suicidal period. That person had saved her life. She didn't think River was suicidal, but he was definitely depressed. And he certainly didn't get it that he could not sleep away his days until he was allowed to return to the stable.

"I am not leaving. I am going to stand here until you get up and walk with me."

River glared at her without moving. When he closed his eyes and started to roll back away she ordered, "Don't you dare." She reached over and grabbed his shoulder, preventing him from turning.

"Okay," he groaned in resignation, and sat up abruptly. Then he groaned again, hugging his side where his wound still ached and burned whenever he moved too quickly. He looked up at Laila, expecting sympathy, but she merely retained her militant posture with her determined expression unaltered.

"It hurts," he whined.

"Of course it hurts. Your damn father shot you in the back. He tried to kill you. Now, are you going to let him kill you for real?"

River's eyes widened at her blunt words. Then he hunched over himself to escape her disgusted look, and hugging his side, complained, "I hate it here. The Marshalls won't let me go to the stable. They won't let me keep Storm here. All I'm allowed to do is go for walks and watch television. I hate television."

Laila gently pulled at his shoulder and said in a softer tone, "Get up; let's go for a walk and talk about it."

Surrendering, River sat up, ran one hand through his snarled hair, and looked around for his shoes. Laila brought them over to him and then helped him put them on, tying the laces for him. "I can't even dress myself," he continued to complain.

"Quit being such a whiny baby," Laila admonished him. "You can't dress yourself because you've been lying in bed doing nothing so your muscles are getting stiff. You'll heal much faster if you just move. Now get up." She took his hand and pulled him to his feet and steered him through the house to the front door. "We're going now," she called out.

Mrs. Marshall peeked around the corner of the kitchen, smiled and waved. Laila met her eyes and Mrs. Marshall silently communicated her thanks.

The Marshalls, a couple in their fifties, owned a large four-bedroom house in one of the better neighborhoods of Firwood. Their own children grown, they now took in temporary foster children, 'to help fill the emptiness of the house', and maybe help out a few less fortunate children than their own had been.

"The Marshalls are great people; you're very lucky," Laila told River as they walked out the front door and onto the sidewalk.

"I never said they weren't."

"They're doing what they think is best and they're following your doctor's orders. Believe me, it could be a whole lot worse."

"I don't know how," River grumbled to himself, but he did feel guilty for in his heart, he knew the Marshalls were trying to do what they thought best. He just didn't agree with them.

"Well..," Laila started, and frowning, looked off into the distance. "At least they don't make you kneel on the bare kitchen floor in your underwear when it's freezing cold; to ask forgiveness for your sins. Especially when you don't even know what sin you are supposed to be guilty of."

River glanced at her, confused. "What?"

"Like turning on the radio and a song plays that they don't approve of, like I chose the station's playlist. Or when I came home with a book from the school library; a book that was on my English teacher's recommended list, but it's one that their church had banned. Or my choice of outfits. That was my last foster home. The one before that, well, my foster father used to come into the bathroom to pee every time I was in the shower. There was no lock on the bathroom door. I'm not going to tell you what happened after that." She shuddered at the memory.

River stopped and turned to look at her. Laila ducked her head. Shame filled him. He pulled her into his arms and she let him hold her for a few minutes. "I'm sorry," he apologized.

She made a choking noise and then pushed out of his arms and looked up into his face defiantly. "River, your father tried to kill you…but he didn't succeed. Yeah, you're laid up for a bit, but you will recover if you do the right things. You could be dead. You could be paralyzed. You could be in a very different kind of foster home."

"Okay." He reached for her hand but she yanked it away.

"Be glad about what you do have and quit making everyone around you miserable."

"Laila, I'm sorry. You never told me…"

"I'm sorry too, but it's in the past and I'm over it. Believe me, physical hurt is the easiest to deal with."

They started walking again, and when River took her hand a second time, she did not pull away.

"You have so many people who care about you," Laila said after they had walked in silence for half a block.

"Like who?" River wanted to be more agreeable but still hadn't totally thrown off his self-pity.

"Me, for one."

He looked at her and when she smiled, he smiled back and then impulsively kissed her on the cheek. "Thanks, I care about you too."

"I believe you do." Then she continued, "Your boss cares about you; Tess or whatever her name is. You have her to thank for getting you emancipated."

"Okay, she cares some, although with Tess it's probably more she doesn't want to lose my cheap labor."

"She cares," Laila said emphatically. "Nobody is completely selfish, including you."

"I never said I…"

"Never mind. You also have two pretty girls madly in love with you."

"Right, like who?" River laughed in disbelief.

"Those two girls from the stable; the one who gushes over you and the brown-eyed, petite one that you're in love with."

"What are you talking about?" River's heart flipped at her words.

Laila laughed and squeezed his hand. "Don't act like you don't know it."

"I don't…Laila, why do you say that?"

She scrutinized him for a moment. "You really don't know, do you?"

"I just want to know how come you think so."

She laughed and said, "Never mind, I just know."

"Come on, tell me what you think," he asked, his thoughts churning in a turmoil of hope and doubts as they turned the corner of the block. She looked at him with a smug expression. "Laila, why do you think Sierra likes me?"

"Umhm, just as I thought. You like her, don't you?"

"Okay, I admit it, I do. I think she likes me as a friend. She just broke up with some guy at school, so I can't see how she can like me that way."

"What way?"

"Laila, don't tease me. You know how I mean. Do you think she likes me more than just a friend?"

"River," she assured him, "I'm positive she does."

"How can you tell?"

"It's the way she looks at you; it's really very simple."

"Hmph," he huffed. "It's not so simple. Do you think she's looking at me, like on the rebound?"

"Probably; I personally can't see any reason why a girl would love you."

"Thanks a lot," he responded, recognizing the teasing in her tone. They walked on and then River asked more seriously. "Laila, how come you didn't ever want to be my girlfriend?"

"What makes you think I didn't?"

He studied her face, unsure if she was joking again or not. But when she laughed and punched him playfully, he smiled.

"River, if you were older, or had been more experienced with girls so that you knew when you had a good thing…I don't know. I could have fallen in love with you, but you weren't ready for a girl like me."

"I knew you were a good thing…"

"Besides," she interrupted, "you were already in love with your little stable mate."

"I was not!"

Laila made a noise of disbelief. "Tell me truthfully, who were you thinking of more often than not when I was in your arms?"

"You."

"I'm sure you did some of the time; but who was in your heart? Think about it before you answer."

River looked down at his shuffling feet, not knowing how to answer. As he thought back to all the times with Laila, he had to admit how often he had wondered what it would be like with Sierra.

Laughing, Laila said, "River, it's okay. I'm just trying to help you understand your own feelings."

"I do love you, you know."

"I know, and I love you too…the same way. You're maybe the best friend I've ever had."

They rounded the block and returned to the Marshalls' house to see Sierra getting out of her mother's car. She was halfway up the walk when she heard their footsteps and turned to look their way.

"See the look on her face?" Laila said. "She is not at all happy to see you with me."

To River, Sierra's expression reminded him of how she had sometimes looked at Dean as he walked away from her…wistful and hurt. *Could Laila be right?*

"Hi, Sierra," Laila called out and waved, smiling wickedly. "Well, I gotta go." She turned to River and kissed him on the mouth. Then she waved at Sierra again and skipped off to her own car.

"Laila," River hissed under his breath after her. Then he walked up to Sierra, and feeling very shy, said, "Hi."

After his walk with Laila, River did feel his spirits lifted, and he determined to make more of an effort to speed up his recovery. He forced himself to get up as soon as he woke each morning and go outside to walk. He made himself sit down at the table and eat the good food Mrs. Marshall prepared for him, thanking her with sincere gratitude. The Marshalls had one other foster child living in their house at that time. Todd, a ten-year-old boy, stuttered whenever he tried to say more than two words, and jumped at any sudden noise. *His story is probably much worse than mine,* River realized, and also noticed the kindness of both the Marshalls as they tried to make the boy feel safe and wanted. They really were very fine people.

Laila came almost every morning for two hours before she had to leave for her job at the mall, to help him study for finals. Four weeks after his discharge from the hospital, Mrs. Marshall drove him to school two days in a row, and he completed his final exams. A week later, he learned that he had passed; actually with an *A* on his geometry test, the first *A* he had ever earned in an academic subject, and a few *B*s, and squeaking by with a *C* minus in world history, never his favorite subject.

Best of all, Laila must have said something to the Marshalls, for a few days after his walk with her, and he was demonstrating an effort to help himself, Mrs. Marshall drove him and Todd to the stable so he could visit the horses. Sierra had been bringing Storm to the stable with her every day, and when Mrs. Marshall observed the reunion of River with his dog, but also the fact that Todd seemed to really enjoy petting her and whispering to her in sentences without one single stutter, she consented to let River bring Storm back to their home.

"Sierra, while I'm here, do you want to ride Cory?" River asked after watching her lunge his horse.

Sierra's eyes opened wide with surprise and a smile split her face. "You would let me?"

"Sure, he knows you almost as well as me."

Sierra saddled Corazón, and River watched her ride him in the arena, coaching her, and very happy with how well the two seemed to get along. "It would be great if you could get him out on the trail a few days a week," River said as Sierra brought Corazón back to the crossties, and he stroked his neck while his horse nuzzled at his chest.

"No problem! I would love to take him out; he's so willing and responsive. I can ride him at least five days a week."

"Thank you," he said, and the gratitude and relief in his smile caused a strange full feeling in Sierra's heart and a desire to hug him. *He trusts me.*

When Mrs. Marshall invited Sierra for dinner, and then Sierra helped her cook, it became a routine. Sierra figured out the bus schedule and went to the Marshalls every evening after she had showered and changed clothes from working at the stable. She helped prepare dinner and clean up afterwards, and then hung out with River until her mother came to pick her up. They saved a plate for her mother, who usually stayed a short while visiting with Mrs. Marshall.

One evening, Sierra and River were sitting on the back porch, watching Todd play with Storm, when Allison appeared.

"Allison, hi!" Sierra greeted happily, welcoming her onto the porch and offering her a chair.

"Hi," Allison returned the greeting. "Hi River. I just stopped by to give you my news; well, okay, I'm showing off a little. I got my license today and I drove over here."

"Oohh!" Sierra gave a little squeal of delight and gave her friend a congratulatory hug. "Did you get your car?" Allison's parents had been taking her used car shopping ever since she had turned sixteen this summer.

"I did, you should both come and see it."

"Take care of Storm," River called to Todd who smiled and nodded; and then followed Sierra and Allison out front.

"Of course I don't plan to go drag racing against Crystal who's driving all around town in her brand new Porsche," Allison said as she demonstrated the features of her ten-year-old Subaru wagon.

"Yeah, smart. But I like this; it's very cute. Hey, Katrina just got her license too. She doesn't have her own car but she gets to use her parents'," Sierra informed her. "Well, when I finish drivers ed first quarter of school, my mom says I can drive João's truck that he left us. She thinks he really intended it for me."

"It's a nice truck," River said. Then he smiled. "I guess I get my father's beater truck. He won't need it where he's going."

Sierra and Allison both looked at him in surprise and when he laughed, they joined in.

"Is his trial over?" Allison asked hesitantly.

"No trial; he plea-bargained, and they dropped the charge from attempted murder to attempted manslaughter. He still has to serve at least four years and part of that is for his DWI."

"How do you feel about that?" she asked as they started walking back to the house.

River shrugged his shoulders. "I'm okay with it. Mr. Tanglewilde explained how it saves the state money if they can avoid a trial and get a quick conviction. By the time he gets out, I'll be an adult, done with school, and there's nothing he can do to me. Part of the deal is that he never tries to make contact with me unless I initiate it."

Allison nodded as if in agreement. "Hey, I hear you passed all your finals. Congratulations."

River frowned at her. "Why is everyone so amazed that I passed?"

"River," she chided him, "I'm paying you a compliment. Why do you have to turn it into an insult?"

Sierra breathed in with relief when River laughed and conceded Allison's point. The relationship between them was still a bit prickly and Sierra always felt a little nervous with the two of them together.

"All of us are juniors now!" she said. "Can you believe we're half way through high school?"

They returned to the house and into the kitchen where Mrs. Marshall served milk and cookies; very traditional in what she thought children needed. Allison brought out a book she had finished reading to give to Sierra, talking about what she liked about it, and they went on to discuss other books.

River relaxed in his chair, listening to the girls' discussion, and although he hadn't read any of the books they talked about, found what they were saying quite interesting, almost to a point where he might even want to read one of those books (almost). *They're smart, like Laila,* he thought, and realized that he liked being around smart girls.

"Oh yeah," Sierra said after Allison had left and her mother had called to say she was on her way. "I almost forgot to tell you. Gloria found a buyer for Silver. Somebody made an offer for him after the last event, and her parents accepted it. He's leaving in a few days."

"Oh," River said, interested. "I hope it's a good home. He deserves it."

"Me too. And now Four Score is for sale. I think Gloria wants to find a horse like Diva."

"Gloria and Crystal both need to learn to ride," River mumbled.

Six long weeks passed. Mrs. Marshall drove River to the medical clinic, for what he hoped would be his final check-up.

"You're doing well," Dr. Hoffman said after his examination, and looking at a chest x-ray on his computer screen. "You still have a little fluid collection in the pleural space but it is greatly decreased from two weeks ago. It will all go away in time, but that's why you still get a little short of breath. I'm willing to give you a clean bill of health to return to all normal activities, as long as you take them up gradually and don't push yourself. Get plenty of rest; eat well; call me if you experience…" Dr. Hoffman proceeded to recite a list of symptoms that River should report immediately if any should occur.

"I know this is good news, River," Mrs. Marshall said as they left the clinic, "and I'm very glad you're healed, but I can't help feeling sad at the thought of you leaving us."

"Thank you," River replied in a voice filled with gratitude.

"You don't have to go, you know," she added.

Surprisingly, River realized that as eager as he was to move into his own place, he would miss the Marshalls and Todd…a lot. For the first time in his life he felt like he belonged to a family; and that was a very good feeling. Not since his mother or João had he felt so cared for. It was almost tempting to stay, but…

"I don't know what Todd will do without Storm," Mrs. Marshall said, watching the young boy walking ahead. Todd scuffed his feet, looking at the ground with slumped shoulders, for he knew who would be leaving with River.

"Well…" River started to say as they got into the car. Mrs. Marshall looked at him, and they both grinned, knowing they had the same thought. Instead of going home, they detoured to the county animal shelter.

They let Todd choose the dog he wanted to bring home. Mrs. Marshall thought he might pick one of the adorable puppies in a litter of six; all in a pen together and eagerly yipping out to 'pick me, pick me'. But she wasn't surprised when Todd picked an older mongrel dog with coarse, nondescript patchy brown fur, very sad, runny eyes, and missing a back leg. "This is the one," he announced, without a stutter. And that was how Brownie, destined for euthanasia, found the best home of his sad life.

"You don't have to leave," Mr. Marshall repeated the offer after dinner. River remained at the table with the Marshalls, talking about his plans. Todd, who had wolfed down his food so he could be with his new dog, was out on the back porch with Brownie and Storm.

"Thank you; I do appreciate all you have done for me."

He stayed with the Marshalls for the rest of the week, teaching Todd how to take care of his dog, and letting Mrs. Marshall take him shopping for the things she thought he would need in his new home. When he moved in on the weekend, he felt as if he had good friends that he could call on if he needed help or advice. They made him promise he would come over for dinner at least once a month; a promise he was glad to give.

31 RIDING CORY

A rider must have passion. Without passion, how can a rider feel? – Lisa Wilcox

"You can't let her do it." River hugged his side, anger causing his wound to throb. Tess, her countenance equally defiant, stood next to him at the rail of the outdoor arena where Crystal had just finished a course of jumps and now walked Diva on a loose rein.

"You are being ridiculous. Diva did not have to recover from an injury like you. Don't project your own lack of conditioning on her," Tess retorted.

"I agree she is in better shape than me, but she has lost conditioning. Can't you see it?" River insisted. "Why did you depend on Crystal to keep her in shape? Sierra could have taken Diva out on the trail."

"It so happens, in case you've forgotten, Diva does belong to Crystal. She told me she did not want Sierra riding her horse. I'm disappointed that she didn't keep her word and ride the mare herself, but I can't force her to do anything."

"But you can advise her. She needs to scratch this show."

"You haven't been here. She came in a strong first at her last event while you were in the hospital."

"Yes, over a month ago when Diva was still in condition."

"It may challenge the mare, but I think she will still do very well. What is it you found wrong with the way she jumped today? Her form was perfect."

"Right, she did her best and she jumped well. But look at her. Can't you see how she's breathing too fast? She should have recovered her breath by now. Can't you see how tired she looks?" To River, it was obvious the mare was drained of all her energy. She plodded at the walk, barely picking up her feet, her head low with fatigue, her body slick with too much sweat for the amount of work she had done on a day not that hot. The honest mare had cleared every fence of a very difficult preliminary level course, using all her heart and strength. A less willing horse would probably have dragged the hind end, taking rails down.

While River had been laid up, Crystal declared she would take responsibility for Diva's conditioning rides. She had come out twice the first week, but after that, had only shown up for her lessons. Diva's exercise program diminished from six days a week to usually only two. Some weeks, Tess managed to fit in a twenty-minute session on the flat, but her own schedule was crammed fitting in rides on all the horses that had been assigned to River. She had been able to add two of them to Sierra's schedule, and even Katrina had picked up one extra horse; otherwise, she probably would have had to hire a temporary rider.

When two weeks went by where Crystal only showed up for lessons, Tess had tried to convince her of the wisdom of letting Sierra ride Diva, but Crystal had been adamant. It had been over a month since Diva had been trotted or galloped on the trail or jumped an outside course.

Now Crystal planned to show Diva at the upcoming event this weekend.

River foresaw disaster.

As Tess stormed away to meet Crystal at the exit gate to debrief, he swore under his breath and shuffled toward the stable with his shoulders hunched, his eyes on the ground, and feeling impotent in his ability to protect the horses. Anxiety exacerbated the tightness already in his muscles from his anger, causing achiness from his wound throughout the left side of his chest, forcing him to take short, painful breaths.

Suddenly, the muscles along the left side of his rib cage knotted into a spasm of pain, doubling him over, and he had to stop in his tracks, clutching at his side, sucking in air, until finally the spasm subsided.

Tess wanted him to ride Cory in the event this weekend, and thanks to Sierra, his own horse was still in top condition. But even more than Diva, River realized he was not in any shape to compete. Finally, the spasm subsided and he could stand up straight and continue walking slowly to the stable.

His frustration and anger were not just because of Diva. He had been back to riding for over a week. Not just his wounded side, but every muscle in his body ached. He tired after just a few minutes of grooming a horse. Sometimes bending over to pick out their feet, he felt like he might pass out. He needed a few minutes to rest after tacking up his horse before he could summon the energy to mount into the saddle. Within ten to fifteen minutes of riding, his body wanted to quit; nevertheless, he pushed himself to ride for at least twenty minutes and earlier today, made it to a half hour. He knew he needed time, just like rehabilitating an injured horse. It was just hard to feel so weak and incapable. River couldn't remember ever being sick, other than once or twice having a head cold. He had always possessed a healthy appetite and plenty of energy and endurance. Now he was so tired at the end of the day that he had to force himself to eat something before he dropped onto his bed and almost instantly fell asleep.

"River, are you okay?" Sierra met him on her way to take Diva from Crystal and cool out the mare. She had seen River doubled over.

"I'm fine," he stated curtly, so tired of people asking him that, but then immediately felt ashamed of the rudeness in his tone. His frustration at his weakness and the humiliation for her to see him was no excuse to snap at her. It certainly wasn't her fault. He looked up and more shame washed over him at the look of hurt in her eyes. "Sorry," he offered. "I still get spasms in my side sometimes."

"That must be awful." Sierra tried to keep her tone neutral and hold back all the sympathy she felt. She understood how much River needed to hide his frailty. She quickly changed the subject, but it disturbed her to note his ashen look and the glistening line of perspiration across the top of his lip and across his brow. *He's pushing himself too hard.* "Did Tess tell you that Silver's new owner is picking him up today?"

"Yeah, I've been keeping an eye out so I can help get him ready. Has Tess assigned you another horse yet to compete on?"

"No, she mentioned Felicity, but I think she's too flighty for me. She needs you to ride her until she has more experience."

River walked alongside Sierra back toward the arena where they saw Tess leading Diva toward the stable and Crystal walking off toward her car. He waited while Sierra continued on to take Diva from Tess. He didn't want to confront Tess again just now. Then he walked back with Sierra to the crossties, noting to himself with wry humor, *here goes a drained horse and a drained human.* Then he had a thought. "Sierra, Tess hasn't scratched Corazón yet, and there is no way I'm going to be ready to ride. Why don't you compete on Cory?"

Sierra looked at him in amazement. "You would let me show him?"

"Why not? You're the one who's been keeping him fit. And he does love to get out and show off."

They reached the crossties and Sierra led Diva in. "River, that would be so awesome! You know I'd love to, but I've never jumped on him."

"Don't tell me you've never taken him over the log on the trail." He smiled at her with a knowing look.

"Well sure, but that's not much of a jump."

"Okay, how about right now?"

Sierra slipped off Diva's bridle and on with her halter, thinking furiously. *Could I do it? He's such a great horse…I don't know… but it's training level; what I've been riding all season…* She turned to face River who waited for her answer. "Okay," she agreed, her face breaking into a very enthusiastic smile. "I'd love to."

"Let me finish Diva. Go get Cory and take him around the short loop of the trail to warm him up, and I'll meet you in the back field."

Sierra nodded, too excited for more words, and skipped off to the paddock for Cory.

When Sierra brought Corazón back to the field after trotting and a short gallop on the trail, River was there waiting. He waved and she walked Cory up to him.

"Take him around a few low obstacles, whichever ones you want. Just point him at the jump, and keep yourself balanced and quiet. That's all. He knows how to rate himself. Let him decide where to take off and just be ready for him," River instructed.

Sierra nodded, and scanned the field, picking out some easy novice level obstacles. "I'll do the log, split rail, coop, and how about the in-and-out fence?"

"Good choices."

"Okay, Cory," Sierra spoke to the black, who already sensed that jumping was coming up and she could feel the bunching of his muscles beneath her seat. She turned him onto a beginning circle and then pointed him at the log. *Easy.* It was only an inch or two higher at its lowest spot than the one on the trail. They galloped toward it, Cory's ears pointed at the jump. She kept herself balanced in two-point position with her weight slightly back until she felt him a stride away gather his hind end. She shifted her weight forward as he sprang off his hind legs, letting his momentum move her over his withers, and as he cleared and landed, came softly back into the saddle. "Good boy!" She turned to the right on the same lead, to the split rail, a jump six inches higher. She didn't think about its height, and again stayed balanced in the middle of the saddle until she felt him gather for the thrust, and then let her weight move forward as he jumped, and in mid air, she touched the left rein, and Cory landed onto his left lead as she turned him back to the coop. He soared over the coop, and then took the in-and-out, adjusting his stride competently. Just as River said, all she had to do was stay balanced on his back and not interfere.

"He is so awesome! He's the easiest horse I've ever jumped on!" Sierra exclaimed enthusiastically, riding back to River.

"You were perfect on him," River praised. "Sometimes it's just as hard not to control the horse as it is to control him correctly."

She nodded in understanding, still wearing a euphoric grin.

"Take him down the bank; see how that feels," River suggested, knowing she had experienced some difficulty with Silver at the bank.

Jumping down the bank proved no more difficult for Cory than the upright fences.

"Try the ramp," River said next.

"The ramp?" Sierra knew the ramp was three-foot-six-inches, a preliminary level jump.

"You should be able to jump at a level above the one you're competing at," he said. "It's not a difficult jump, just a little higher than what you've done before. Don't think about the height. Ride just like you've been riding and Cory will take care of you. I know you can do it."

Sierra nodded, and before she could think herself into a state of fright, she moved Cory back onto the field at a trot, circled well in front of the ramp, turned him in its direction and let him gallop on. Cory carried her over as competently as he had the lower jumps, with no idea his rider had never jumped this high before. Sierra whooped out loud, and praised Cory enthusiastically, stroking his neck as she rode back to River, her face split in the widest grin possible.

"Well?" River asked her, also grinning.

"This has been the most exciting day of my life," she answered.

River's heart filled with warmth as he felt like he and Sierra had gained back some of their past close friendship.

The next day, River watched Sierra ride the training level dressage test on Cory, correcting her in a few movements, but for the most part, satisfied with how she rode with her core muscles, seat and legs, and keeping her hands very soft.

Two days before the weekend, he coached her over a stadium course. "You two can do it," River declared. Then Friday he told her to just ride Cory at an easy walk and trot on the trail.

A two-day event, Sierra rode dressage and stadium jumping on Saturday. She had been apprehensive of riding Cory in his excited state, the way she had seen him prance under River as he showed off. But to her surprise, even though he jigged and pranced on his way to the warm-up areas, he remained obedient and light in her hands, seeming to understand that he was not yet in a test.

For as she entered at *A*, down the center line for dressage, he rounded his neck and shoulders into her soft hands, and trotted energetically in a forward moving trot, and responded obediently to her aids as she asked for transitions and changes of rein, and responded promptly when she asked him to lengthen his stride both at trot and canter, and obediently transitioned back from his hind end muscles when she asked him to come down to working trot.

When the standings were posted late in the afternoon, Sierra was in first place for training level, having the highest dressage score and a clean stadium round without time penalties. Dean and Calculator were in second place and Gloria in tenth.

"I know Diva is a much better bred horse than Calliope, and there will always be better horses out there. I'm just so proud of Calliope that she consistently places among all these really expensive horses,"

Katrina said as she and Sierra read the postings, and as expected, Crystal was in first place in preliminary and Katrina in fourth place.

"You should be proud. River is proud of you," Sierra declared, having heard the faint note of bitterness in Katrina's tone. "Can you imagine what would happen to Calliope if someone like Crystal rode her?"

Katrina smiled as they walked back to the stalls. "You're right," she agreed. "My parents paid two thousand dollars for Calliope and do you know someone came up to me after stadium and offered ten thousand for her? He said he wanted her for a brood mare."

"Katrina, you wouldn't…" Sierra gasped.

"Of course not," Katrina stated. Then she asked in a timid voice, "How do you know River is proud of me?"

"Because he says so; all the time, and I know I've heard him say it to you too."

"Yeah, seems like a long time ago. Lately he seems to be avoiding me."

This was a conversation Sierra really did not want to have with Katrina. They walked on in silence.

"Well, is he?" Katrina asked.

"Katrina, how should I know?"

"Because he talks to you. He tells you things."

Sierra detected a tear in her voice, and felt very, very uncomfortable. She certainly did not want to see Katrina hurt. But oh, how she wanted…

"Sierra," Katrina suddenly grabbed her arm, stopping her in mid-stride. "Please, I beg you, don't steal him from me." There were tears at the corners of her eyes.

"I…he's…"

"You love him too, don't you," Katrina demanded.

Sierra stared back with her color rising and her heart racing. "I…" Sierra continued to stumble for words.

Then Katrina let go of her arm. "Never mind; what a fool I am. It's not up to you, it's up to River." Then in a determined voice with her eyes straight ahead she said, "I will fight you for him."

Love…it's so unfair, Sierra moaned inwardly; her happiness on Cory brought crashing down by Katrina. *And yes, I do love him!*

The show grounds were close enough to Pegasus that they could trailer back home and then return again the next morning for cross country.

"I don't like the way she walked down the ramp," River said in the stable yard, watching Manuel lead Diva from the trailer into the crossties to remove her shipping wraps. Sierra followed down the ramp leading Corazón, also thinking Diva had been a little hesitant to set down the left hind leg.

"Don't look for trouble," Tess snapped at him. "She looks fine."

River pivoted away from Tess, controlling an angry retort, and stepped back into the trailer to unload Four Score.

"What was it you saw?" Sierra asked, waiting with Cory.

"She favored her left hind as she came downhill on the ramp. I don't see it on the flat, but she's tender on that leg."

Sierra nodded. "Yeah, I noticed that too."

They finished removing shipping gear from the horses and put them away in their stalls with plenty of hay and extra measures of grain to compensate for the energy expended at the show. Then River started on Diva first, massaging liniment into her legs and Sierra followed behind him, placing standing wraps as she had been taught. The idea was to provide overnight support for any strained muscles, ligaments or tendons; hopefully reducing heat and preventing swelling.

"Good," River said as he surveyed the wraps Sierra had placed. She stood close to his shoulder as he inspected each wrapped leg. River glanced sideways at her, studying her profile and even from the side he recognized her expression of concentration; her concern as to whether she had wrapped the legs effectively. A sudden rush of affection filled his heart at how much she cared about the horses. How badly he wanted to take her into his arms; to kiss her with all the feelings roiling inside his heart. *Would she let me? Does she want me to?*

He had really enjoyed today, in spite of not being able to ride himself. It pleased him how well Sierra got along with Corazón. When everyone had left and it was just the two of them in the stable caring for the horses, listening to their contented munching on hay; he felt happy and contented himself. *What would it be like to bring her inside the lounge…to take her up to my room?*

"I guess I better head home before it gets dark," Sierra said, brushing her hands together as they left the stable. She turned to find River looking at her, studying her with his beautiful dark eyes…*Kiss me, River, kiss me…*

"Yeah, don't want your mom to worry." He smiled, still gazing into her eyes.

"Um, yeah, and thanks again for letting me ride Cory. He was so awesome." Sierra smiled back. She did not want to leave; but then she turned and retrieved her bicycle, happy when River at least walked with her.

He waited until she straddled her bicycle and pedaled out of sight down the driveway before he turned away and went into the lounge.

Storm sprawled in front of the door where she had been sleeping. She stood and yawned as he bent down to pet her and they went inside. He fed her and filled her water bowl and scrounged through the well-stocked refrigerator. He smiled at the dishes of leftovers brought to him by Mrs. Marshall. She stopped by weekly to check on him, bringing Todd who seemed to love being around animals of any kind, and thrilled when River led him around on Muffin.

He pulled out a bowl of spaghetti and stuck it in the microwave, grabbed a slice of bread from a loaf on the counter, and then collapsed onto one of the sofas to eat.

Feeling exhausted, River knew he could easily set his dish on the floor, lean his head back, close his eyes, and he'd be asleep in seconds.

But at least his side didn't ache and neither did any of his muscles. It felt more like the normal tired after a long day of work. Maybe he was making progress and finally regaining conditioning.

He forced himself up from the sofa to put the dish in the sink and run water in it, and then called to Storm. He only half way kept the rules now that he lived at the stable, and always let Storm come with him when he made his final check on the horses before going to bed.

With a flashlight, River walked down the aisles, checking on each horse, either still nosing around for the last wisps of hay or standing with one hip relaxed, asleep. Muffin and one other horse were already lying down. *Good, no signs of colic or other distress in any of them.* Satisfied, he headed out the back door, locking it behind him.

As he walked back toward the lounge, a car pulled into the stable yard and parked, its motor cut. River stopped, wondering who would be coming at almost nine p.m.

Katrina got out of the driver's side, stood for a moment taking deep breaths, and then headed toward the lounge.

"Katrina?" he called to her.

"Oh!" She turned, startled to find him outside. "Oh, River, you scared me!"

"What are you doing here?" He came up to her.

"I…" She hesitated, looking up at him, licked her lips, and to his stunned amazement, stepped up close to put her arms around his neck. She pressed his head toward her, and kissed him on his mouth, holding her lips there; waiting…waiting for him to kiss her back.

River stood with his arms out to the side, with no idea what he should do. *Katrina, don't do this!* He did not kiss her back, but he did not pull away, sensing that would be too unkind. He waited, and at last she took her mouth away, and then collapsed against his chest, sobbing.

"River, please, can't you care for me? Couldn't you just try?" she pleaded against his chest. "I love you, I can't help it."

His heart aching for her, he put his arms around her and let her cry. "Katrina, please," he whispered. "I like you a lot, just not that way. I don't want to hurt you."

Lifting her face from his chest, she looked up into his. "It's Sierra, isn't it?"

"Katrina, please," he said again.

"River, I will do anything for you. I want to…" She pushed a little away and brought her hands down from around his neck to stroke down his chest, down to the waist of his jeans, and hooked her fingers there. "I want to stay the night with you. I can; I told my parents I'm staying over at a friend's."

As gently as he could, he unhooked her fingers and took one hand in his. "You need to go home," he said. He led her with an arm around her shoulders to her car, as she sniffed and struggled to hold back more sobbing, and helped her into the driver's seat.

Without looking at him, Katrina started the ignition, backed up, and drove away.

He had tried to like her in the way she wanted; especially when Sierra had been involved with Dean. He was certainly physically attracted to her; Katrina was a very beautiful girl. But he always felt a little bored with her and he wondered why. Maybe it was her constant chatter about things that held absolutely no interest for him and her noise could get quite annoying. He thought about times with Sierra and even with Laila; the time he listened to Sierra and Allison talking while he was still living with the Marshalls. *Maybe that's it, I like smart girls; I like being around smart girls.* That might be part of why he couldn't care for Katrina the way she wanted him to. Even if he didn't care about Sierra, he doubted that would change his feelings toward Katrina. She was a very nice girl but she wasn't very smart.

"Tess, there's heat in that leg. You cannot let her compete today," River said.

"Look at her, she's just fine. You can't tell me you saw her favor that leg." Tess stood with folded arms, holding onto her car keys, annoyed that River had called her this morning saying she needed to scratch the mare from the competition.

"No, I didn't, but if Crystal jumps her today, she will." They stood in the stable yard with the horses loaded except for Diva. River had argued and insisted until Tess agreed to come and look at the leg herself. She had asked Manuel to trot the mare so they could watch her move before loading her into the trailer. True, he did not see any favoring in her gait right now, but the left hind fetlock had definitely felt warmer when he had removed her wraps this morning. That didn't happen unless there was some strain or inflammation going on.

"Let's just get to the show. We can decide there," Tess said, walking away to her car with finality. "Load her in the trailer," she called to Manuel.

Manuel raised his eyes at River, who shook his head in frustration. "I'll take her in," he said, and took the lead rope from Manuel to guide Diva up the ramp. "If anything happens to you today…" he whispered to her, as he hooked the trailer tie to her halter. He patted her neck, his heart filled with worry, and again with the utterly helpless feeling of being unable to protect her.

'Let's go," he said to Sierra who had been watching, her eyes wide in concern.

"Uh, where's Katrina?" she asked timidly, knowing how upset he was, but also wondering why Katrina hadn't arrived yet to help load the horses and ride with them to the show, as she had yesterday. Sierra had called her but only got her voice mail, and Katrina had not responded to the message Sierra had left.

"I don't know but we're already late so we better go," River answered, getting into the truck and starting the ignition. Sierra climbed in next to him, watching from the corner of her eye River's glum profile as he carefully drove away to return to the show grounds. The two sat in worried silence.

Not until they pulled into the parking area did River break the silence to say, "Maybe she'll be okay." He cut the engine, thumping his fist against the steering wheel before getting out.

Sierra climbed out of the truck, her own heart in her throat; worried about Diva and even more worried about River if anything should happen to the mare.

Tess strode up, followed by a tight-lipped Crystal with Gloria at her side.

"You sure took your time," Tess snapped at River as he unlatched the back of the trailer and lowered the ramp.

River ignored her and stepped up into the trailer to unload Diva. Sierra stepped in next to unload Four Score and handed the lead to Tess who practically grabbed it from her hand. "Where is Katrina?" she demanded.

Getting no response from River who was leading Diva to the stalls, or Sierra who had turned back into the trailer to unload Calliope, Tess thrust the lead to Gloria, ordering, "Take your horse," and followed Sierra into the trailer to take Calliope so Sierra could unload Corazón.

This day is not starting out very well at all, Sierra thought to herself, her high spirits that she had awakened with being replaced by a pervasive feeling of doom and gloom.

Katrina waited at the stalls, her expression reflecting the overall bleak mood of the day.

"Lead the horses into the stalls," Tess barked out orders. "River, you stay here and get the shipping wraps off. The rest of you, we have just enough time to walk the course so let's get going."

"River?" Sierra asked as she shut Corazón's stall door and lingered a few moments; wanting some kind of sign from him that he was okay or what she should do.

He was removing Diva's shipping wraps and stood up when she called his name. "Go walk your course," he said in a soft but serious tone. "You want to be ready for what Cory will face today."

She nodded and hurried after the others.

"What happened to you this morning?" Sierra asked as she caught up with Katrina.

"Nothing…not one thing," Katrina answered in a bitter tone, and actually stepped ahead to end any further conversation.

What did I do? Baffled, Sierra did not pursue Katrina.

Tess led them around, discussing strategies for both the preliminary and training level obstacles.

A good course, Sierra thought, as she followed along, paying close attention. Her mood began to lighten up as she anticipated the fun of taking Cory, always so eager, over an attractive log jump at the start, then flower boxes followed by the first combination of split rail fences at an angle to each other – *that one is going to require a quick turn*, she decided, just as Tess said the same thing out loud.

They walked up a long slope with a ramp jump at the top, then downhill to the water.

"You've got a good stretch of level ground before the water, so if you have to come down to a trot on the downhill, you can pick up the pace here; no need to approach the water at a trot. But you do want to have your horse well in hand and balanced to go into the water and then jump out," Tess explained as they continued on the course.

The next training level jumps were very similar to practice jumps at home, and Sierra's confidence was climbing, as well as her mood until they followed the course around a bend, up another small hill, down to a roll top, and then after that…*oh no!*...a railroad crossing jump.

Sierra's rising spirits plummeted again; a rock settling into the pit of her stomach. They had no railroad crossing to practice over at Pegasus, and had not anticipated there would be such a jump in two shows of the season.

"Sierra," Tess called to her as they approached the diagonal red-and-white striped obstacle. "You better carry a whip today if you want to get Cory over this one," she warned.

They finished walking the course, the remaining training level obstacles ones that Cory could easily handle. *River got him over it, but River's a much better rider; he trusts River more than he'll ever trust me.* Sierra's mind roiled in trepidation, anxious to get River's advice.

"Hi, Dean!" Crystal called out, from where she walked behind Sierra.

Sierra looked up, startled at hearing his name, and could not help looking over to where Dean walked toward their group, having just finished his own course walk.

"Hello, nice course, isn't it?" he said as he reached them and stepped into place to walk beside Crystal, right behind Sierra. "I really like that railroad crossing jump. There was one a few shows back, remember? Old Cal cleared it like a dream, as if there was a train actually coming," he went on in a loud voice to be sure Sierra heard.

"Yeah, we take it in preliminary too," Crystal said and the two chattered on; old friends.

"Training goes first," Tess announced. "Gloria and Sierra, get ready to warm up; I'm going to go pick up the number vests now."

River walked next to Cory's shoulder after Sierra's number had been called and she headed up to the starting box.

"Don't worry about it," River said to her again, repeating what he had been telling her on the way to warm up Cory. "If you feel him tensing up, take a circle; take two if you have to. You don't know he's going to react like he did last time. Maybe since he jumped it at the other show and didn't get hurt, he will be just fine."

Sierra looked down at him and nodded. She did feel a little more confident after her warm-up, for Cory exhibited his usual high level of energy and eagerness to go. He pranced every few strides, as they approached the starting box, and Sierra needed to sit deep and touch the reins to ask him to come back to walk.

The starter at the box signaled she could go in.

"Enjoy the ride," River said, "that's what counts. I'm going to be watching at the railroad jump." He patted Cory on the rump and Sierra entered the box.

"Ready?" the starter asked her, looking at his stopwatch.

"Yes," she answered and walked Cory in a circle as the starter began the countdown, and then turned to face the exit at ten, nine,…three, two, one…and they were on course.

As Corazón galloped toward the logs, adjusted his stride and soared over, eagerly galloping on to the flower boxes, taking it as well; Sierra tuned into his muscular movements and focused on the 'now' moment, thinking only of the jump to come. They came up to the combination and as Cory sailed over the first element, she squeezed her fingers on the left hand rein, and as they landed, pushed her weight harder in the left hand stirrup, turning her shoulders toward the next element set at an angle. Cory responded instantly on the left lead, took the correct two strides, and over the second element. Galloping on, Corazón continued to negotiate each obstacle, responding to Sierra's directions of which one he was to take.

Then they were galloping downhill to the roll top. As he cleared it and landed and Sierra pointed him toward the railroad crossing, his muscles stiffened, he let out a loud snort of fear and she could feel him gather himself to turn away and flee.

"You can do it, come on, Cory," she encouraged, pressing her legs to his sides, and squeezing her fingers on the reins to keep him in a straight line. She felt him respond, an easing of his muscles to turn away and he took a few strides forward…closer. *He's going to take it!* Sierra relaxed a bit of her aids, preparing to move into a more forward two-point. One stride to go, she pushed her weight in her heels, and then suddenly, felt herself thrown forward and to the side as Cory whipped to the right in front of the jump, racing away.

Sierra sat up straight, clamped her legs to his side, turned him quickly back to face the jump, and pushed and pushed him on with her legs. She reached forward once to touch his neck, to tell him, 'you can do it', and then kept a firm hold of the reins. His muscles stiffened, he snorted again a loud, short snort of worry. Then a half stride too soon, he gathered himself and leaped from too far back but jumping big…oh so big… and cleared the railroad crossing with Sierra high on his neck and clutching his mane to keep her seat as he landed.

"Good boy!" she cried to him in exuberant praise and patted his neck as he galloped on. They finished the course, and Sierra understood now how River had felt. Even though his run-out would most likely drop them from first place, and maybe even out of the ribbons, Sierra felt tremendous pride and accomplishment; proud that she had been able to get Cory to take the jump, and so very proud of him for taking it!

After passing the finish flags, Sierra brought Cory down to trot and then quickly to walk. She reached down frequently to pet his neck, and kept up a continual stream of praise. He arched his neck, still wanting to prance and show off. When she saw River walking quickly toward them, she dismounted, and when he came up to her and gave her a big hug, she felt she had doubly won.

"You did it," River said as he let go of her, and looked deep into her eyes, his own filled with pride.

"What is wrong with Katrina?" Sierra asked, walking with River to a spot where they could watch some of the preliminary jumps.

After taking care of Corazón, Sierra had tried to help Katrina get Calliope ready, while River worked on Diva. Although Katrina had spoken in a quiet voice, she had asked Sierra to please leave Calliope alone. She had not looked over at River once today, nor had she said much of anything; the girl who usually chattered non-stop.

"I don't know," he answered. But Sierra noticed the tightening of his jaw and she thought maybe he did know.

They reached a good viewing spot, just as the first preliminary rider crested a hill, then disappeared around a bend, and reappeared to take a Trakehner jump and then onto a flat sandlot and drop jump.

Two riders later, they caught sight of Calliope; then lost her again until she and Katrina came around the bend.

"Come on Calliope," Sierra called out in encouragement as they cleared the Trakehner. Katrina slowed the mare onto the sandlot, jumped down the bank, and they galloped on.

Another rider followed shortly after, and then they waited expectantly, knowing Diva should come next.

"There she is," Sierra announced as she caught sight of Crystal's red helmet cover, and Diva's bay head. She felt River tensing next to her.

Diva galloped toward them and they watched her disappear around the bend, their eyes moving to the spot where she would come into view again. She came galloping on, and over the Trakehner.

"She looks okay," River said, as the mare galloped to the sandlot and jumped down the bank; but in the same breath he gasped, "no!"

Diva stumbled as she landed after the drop and Crystal was thrown forward onto her neck. They heard Crystal scream once. But Diva slowed to a walk, which allowed Crystal to regain her balance in the saddle, and then she picked up a trot. It was as he watched her trot that River cried out and stood up.

Diva took a few more trotting steps, favoring the left hind. Crystal, who always wore spurs, dug them into her sides and whacked her with her jumping bat at the same time. Diva obediently transitioned up into canter still favoring her leg, but moving on to the next obstacle.

"She needs to stop!" River cried out, and started running toward the galloping pair. At the same time, the jump judge had stood up and was waving a hand at Crystal, signaling her to stop.

Crystal ignored the judge and pushed Diva on and over the jump. The judge spoke into her two-way radio, her expression irate.

Sierra took off after River, who was already panting hard for breath. As they neared the next obstacle, they saw that jump judge, having received communication, step into the path of the jump, forcing Crystal to bring Diva to a halt.

"You have no right to stop us!" Crystal yelled at the judge.

When River saw that Diva was no longer being pushed forward, he stopped and bent over as he gasped for breath, supporting himself with his hands braced on his knees.

"River, are you okay?" Sierra caught up to him.

"Can't…breathe," he managed to pant out. "Go…take Diva."

"I will," she assured him but waited a few moments until she heard his breath coming less labored.

"…regulations are quite clear, and you will walk your horse off the field now," Sierra heard the jump judge speaking firmly to Crystal, and holding onto Diva's bridle. Crystal's face was red with rage, and she looked like she wanted to slash the judge with her crop.

Two other officials drove up on a four-wheeler, and with the authorities around her, Crystal had no choice but to dismount. She angrily tossed Diva's reins to Sierra and stomped away.

"I can take her back to her stall," Sierra said to the officials, who watched Crystal's tantrum, horrified.

River came up then, his face ashen and rivulets of sweat running down from his hairline. "Is there a vet here?" he asked.

"I'll send him over to the stalls," one of the officials answered.

Crystal continued to rage about her disqualification; claiming that it was 'unfair', 'they had no right', and she was going to have her father intervene. It became embarrassing for the rest of them, and they all felt disgraced.

The veterinarian arrived, examined Diva and said, "Most likely a torn ligament, maybe the suspensory; but you'll need an ultrasound exam to really make the diagnosis."

When Crystal asked what that meant, he very kindly replied, "Chances are very good your mare can recover to full soundness, but this type of injury takes a good six months off work to heal." He had been quite taken aback when Crystal's response had not been relief but [illegible]er to cry out, "Stupid horse! That's it; I'm done riding. Tess, put her up for sale." With that, she stomped off, her blonde hair waving as she tossed her head.

Gloria watched her best friend stride away out of sight, her jaw dropped in disbelief. "Bitch," she shouted after Crystal's retreating back. Then she spun around to the startled faces watching her. "I wanted to quit riding months ago; but no, Gloria, I need your support, Gloria, we do this together," she said in a sarcastic voice mimicking Crystal. Then she burst into tears and ran off toward the restrooms. Gloria had not placed today on Four Score.

"I'm sorry," Tess apologized to the veterinarian and led him away.

Katrina then stepped out of Calliope's stall. "Her trailer wraps are on. Please be sure she gets an extra measure of oats tonight. I'm very proud of her. I'm going home." Having said all that in a cold, flat tone, she left. Calliope had placed second today and Sierra thought Katrina would have been in a euphoric mood rather than this glum, bitter one. She wasn't even waiting to ride the victory lap.

As Sierra suspected, Cory's run-out dropped them from first place into fourth, and Dean with Calculator moved up into first. She would have been happy even if they hadn't placed, still feeling so proud of Cory. She had received compliments from other observers on a fine go, and good job getting her horse over a jump that obviously panicked him.

The only regret she had over not placing first happened shortly after the victory round when she heard Crystal call, "Hey, Sierra."

Turning around, she looked into the face of Dean, smiling at her with that dimple at the corner of his mouth. Crystal's arm was hooked in his, and her face twisted into a smile that looked more like a sneer.

"Sierra," Dean said in a mocking voice, "I've beat your horse twice now. See you at the championship…loser!" he added, dragging out the word. With that, he and Crystal pivoted away, laughing as he waved his blue ribbon triumphantly in the air, tugging on the reins of Calculator's bridle and ignoring the look of fright in his horse's eyes at the waving ribbon.

The ride home seemed equally as glum and the silence as taut with worry as when they had headed out for the show in the morning. Whenever Sierra glanced at River, she found his face creased in a frown, but when he caught her looking his way, he at least attempted a weak smile.

"No point in getting too bent out of shape until we see the ultrasound," he said after catching her eye.

Sierra nodded. "That vet sounded very hopeful."

Tess followed them in her own car to help unload the horses and wait for Dr. Patterson. Manuel came out of the stable having just finished with evening chores and the four of them settled the show horses into their stalls.

"Let me know when Dr. Patterson arrives," Tess said when they were finished. "I'll be in the office."

Sierra thought Tess looked contrite. It was interesting how she stayed out of River's way, avoiding giving him any chance to say 'I told you so'.

When the veterinarian finally arrived and unloaded his portable ultrasound equipment, River brought Diva from her stall and held her while Dr. Patterson examined the leg. After watching her walk and trot on the lead, and then studying the ultrasound results, he gave them his diagnosis.

"She has sprained the suspensory ligament right here," Dr. Patterson explained, pointing to the spot on the ultrasound image. "Right above the fetlock; see this shadowing, this darker area right here? That's edema." He stood up from where they were all hunched over his equipment. I classify this as a mild to moderate injury. She needs at least three months off work. Hand walk her starting with ten minutes a day, and work up to twenty minutes, adding two minutes every other day. Then you can walk her under saddle starting at twenty minutes and work up to thirty minutes a day. Apply cold soaks twice a day until there is no swelling or heat. I'll leave some anti-inflammatory medicine. You can turn her out but only in a small space. We want to avoid her re-injuring or extending the injury with frolicking around.

Then we'll ultrasound her again in three months and see how she's coming along. Realistically, it is probably going to take closer to six months to heal."

"But she will heal to be completely sound?" River asked; his expression candidly hopeful.

"Most likely she will," Dr. Patterson answered, smiling kindly at River, and very relieved to be able to give much more positive news than the last time he examined one of Crystal's horses. "I've treated many, many horses with sprained and torn ligaments, and from what I see here, this level of injury should heal one hundred percent."

"That is very good news," Tess said, and walked the vet to his van to pick up Diva's medicine and receive the written instructions.

"Might as well start soaking her leg now," River said.

"You hold her," Sierra offered, "and I'll use the hose." Then she couldn't help but exclaim, "Oh, River, it is such a relief."

He looked at her and smiled happily. "Yes," he said.

Tess returned to the wash stall with a bottle of pills which she handed to River. "Dr. Patterson said to put one tablet in with her grain morning and night for the next five days."

"Okay," he said, taking the bottle and slipping it into his pocket for now.

Tess remained standing there a few moments, watching Sierra keeping a stream of cold water on Diva's leg. Then she cleared her throat and said, "Um, River, I owe you an apology." Both Sierra's and River's heads jerked over to look at her. "You were right; we should have scratched her today."

River's lips pressed together, but then he took a deep breath, his brow creased, and he responded, "This could have been avoided."

"Perhaps," Tess said after another few moments of silence; and then she left and not long after, they heard her car drive away.

If River has any flaw, it's probably that he's not very forgiving, Sierra thought without malice, for she didn't feel much absolution for Tess either.

"That should be good for now," River said after they had soaked Diva's leg for about ten minutes. He led her back to her stall and started rubbing down her legs with liniment. Sierra followed behind with the standing wraps. They took care of all four of the show horses in companionable silence.

They finished with Corazón last, and then stood shoulder to shoulder outside his stall door, watching him eat.

"You and Cory are the only good things that happened today," River said, watching the black munching on his hay with his eyes half-closed. "Good riding," he complimented her once again, tilting his head to look down at her.

"Thanks, I'm really proud of him. I could feel how afraid he was."

"I'd still like to know what happened to him to terrorize him so bad."

"Maybe it's better not to know," Sierra said. "I get images of someone like that man you bought him from, slamming a striped board on his head, or something like that."

"Yeah, you're probably right." They stood for a few more minutes in silence, not realizing that they both had similar images in their minds of how Cory looked when they had first seen him, and how well he had turned out.

"That Dean," Sierra said suddenly in a disgusted tone.

Startled, River jerked his head to look at her, surprised at the jealousy triggered just by hearing her speak his name.

Sierra met his eyes and then quickly looked down. "You didn't hear what he said to me after the victory round…and he was with Crystal. They appear to be quite tight now." She huffed a short, disgruntled laugh, and then looked up to find River still watching her. "How I wish I could have beaten him today. River, I'm so sorry I couldn't keep Cory from running out…it's just so aggravating that he's such a poor sport…so spiteful…"

"Sierra," River interrupted her. He had turned to face her and was looking intensely into her eyes. "You and Cory did what counts. He trusted you enough to jump over something that scared him. Dean couldn't ride Cory; Crystal would have been thrown; not even Tess could have gotten him to jump…only you."

Sierra met his eyes, her own widening in hope.

"Only you," River repeated.

"And you," she said in a whisper.

"Yes…me too. Just me and you …" His face was moving closer to hers.

"Just you and me…" she breathed out and suddenly his mouth was on hers and she melted into him, her arms reaching up around his shoulders as he brought his around to cradle her to him. He kissed her parted lips; his own soft, warm, and just a whisper of a touch. But as she leaned into him, he pressed his lips with firm gentleness and they melded together with a kiss.

When he finally broke off the kiss, he brought his hands up to cradle her face as he looked into her eyes again, with a longing that left no doubt how he felt. Sierra hoped her own eyes told him the same.

"River…"

"Sierra…" Then he smiled and took her hand to lead her outside to her waiting bicycle. "It's going to be dark soon."

"I know." She took hold of the handlebars and straddled her bicycle, smiling up into his face. He stepped up to take her shoulders gently, and kissed her again. She stood with her eyes closed, smiling. "Good bye."

"See you tomorrow."

32 COMBINED TRAINING CHAMPIONSHIP

Horses are always quietly talking to you with their body, and horses don't lie. It's very subtle, but if you are very patient and watch closely, what they are saying will come to you like a whisper. –Quote From an Old Cowboy

He kissed me! Sierra pedaled home in a dazed, euphoric state. *River kissed me. HE KISSED ME!* She pedaled on, thinking about every detail, and reached up with one hand to touch her lips where his had been. *He kissed me!*

A day that had started out so glum and could have ended in tragedy if Diva's injury had been worse, (and thank heaven Diva was going to be okay)…*he kissed me*...turned out to be the best day of her life.

Cory…wonderful, wonderful Corazón…*his horse…he kissed me…*She thought back on the moments of riding him cross country, of each jump and what a joy to ride a horse that moved with such confidence and eagerness…*his horse, River's horse, River kissed me!*

"River kissed me," she said out loud to a robin flying rapidly across the road on its way to roost. *Do birds kiss?* How badly she wanted to tell someone. She pulled out her cell phone to call Allison, but getting her voice mail, left a message, "Allison, River kissed me," and then hung up, knowing her friend would call her the first chance she had.

When Charlie came trotting up with his tail wagging as she bicycled into her own yard, she called out to him, "Hi, Charlie. Guess what? River kissed me!" She stowed her bike in the garage and then ruffled Charlie's fur affectionately as they romped together into the house.

"Mom!" Sierra called out as she stepped into the kitchen.

"In here," her mother answered from her bedroom. Sierra rushed into her mother's room where she was putting away piles of folded laundry. "Hi, Kitten," her mother greeted, and held out her arms for a hug. "How was the show?"

Sierra skipped into her mother's arms and said, "Mom, he kissed me!"

Pam stiffened, her first thoughts, *not that awful boy!* "Who kissed you?" she demanded in a harsher tone than she had intended, taking Sierra's shoulders to peer into her face. "Not that…"

"No, Mom, not Dean." Sierra closed her eyes with a look of bliss spreading over her face. "River!"

"River?" And then Pam's face broke into a smile of relief. "River kissed you?"

"Yes," Sierra answered happily and hugged her mother again; and suddenly she was crying.

"Honey, Sweetie," Pam began to comfort her. "Why are you crying?"

"Because I'm so happy."

About an hour later, River called. "Hi," he said.

"Hi," she answered.

"I was thinking about you."

"Oh yeah?" Sierra answered, almost coyly. "I was thinking about you too."

"Good, that's all I wanted to know."

"Okay…guess I'll see you tomorrow."

"Yeah, good night. See you tomorrow."

The next six weeks before the Pacific Regional Championship, flew by in a whirl of riding, conditioning, training, rehabilitating Diva, and kissing River.

Sierra felt very shy when she arrived at the stable the next morning to start chores. The kiss last night (two kisses, actually), seemed so unreal now, like how could it have possibly happened?

She found the back door of the stable already unlocked, and as she started down the aisle, calling out greetings to the horses whinnying their 'good mornings' and 'how about breakfast?', she met River stepping out of Diva's stall.

"Hi," she greeted him with a shy smile.

"Hi." He looked a little timid as well, but he walked up to her and when she lifted her face to his, with her eyes shining in happiness, it was the easiest thing in the world for River to kiss her again.

Soon, it seemed the most natural thing to greet each other every morning with a kiss; for River to stop and kiss her at almost any time throughout the day; to kiss one last time when she went home in the evening; or if River came home with her, to kiss goodnight when he left.

Crystal did not change her mind about giving up riding. With a new car to draw the envy of all her friends, most of whom had outgrown their interest in horses anyway, she never once came back to Pegasus. Diva was put up for sale. Gloria already had Four Score up for sale and they never saw her again at the stable either.

River kept his promise to Amy, Diva's previous owner, to let her know how the mare was doing. It had been a very difficult phone call to make when he told Amy about Diva's injury. It was much easier to call her a week later and let her know that Diva already no longer favored her leg, all heat was gone, as well as most of the swelling. When he told Amy that Diva was for sale again, she immediately said goodbye so she could go talk to her parents. When her parents made an offer to buy Diva back at half the price since she was lame, Walt Douglas accepted the offer; happy enough to have the horse gone.

"I will miss her," River said to Sierra when they heard the news. "But knowing she will go back to Amy, and knowing how much Amy loves her…well, that helps a lot. And it's almost worth it just to not have Crystal around."

Sierra agreed with him one hundred percent. Now if only Dean would go someplace else for his lessons. He still went out of his way to find her and make snide remarks about Cory, which she did her best to ignore.

Katrina told Tess she no longer wanted to clean stalls, and went back to paying full board and intending to take her lessons only from Tess. Sierra never found out what had happened between River and Katrina to make her so unhappy, but she imagined River must have somehow rejected her. She felt very bad for Katrina and wished they could still be friends.

River's strength and stamina improved each week and by the first of September, a week before the championship, he was riding all his assigned horses.

Moose missed one event that his owner and Tess had wanted to enter him in, but River just wasn't ready at that time. No one had ridden Moose out on the trail during River's convalescence, but Tess had kept him in vigorous arena work and twice a week schooled him over jumps, so he maintained a level of conditioning. River started riding him on the trails again the first week he was back at work, but only at a walk and on the shortest loop of the trail. But as River's own endurance improved, he also did more with Moose. Now he thought they were both in condition to compete at the regional trial, and he told Tess she did not need to scratch his entry.

"Sierra can ride Cory," River said as he and Tess discussed the end of the show season.

"Are you sure?" Tess asked with raised eyebrows.

"They're a good team," he stated, "and they both qualified."

"I suggest you paint a diagonal-striped jump and spend some time schooling him over it," Tess said.

"We've already done that. Didn't you notice how we replaced the old picket fence with the railroad crossing out in the field?"

"Oh, well, good."

River also competed on Pendragon at one more show, much to Mrs. Galensburg delight, for he took first place with a very high score, both for the fourth level test and for the musical kur. River would also ride Pendragon at the dressage regional championship at the end of September, and Sierra would show Fiel at second level.

"We're juniors," Allison exclaimed the first day of school, as Sierra and she pushed their way through the throng of kids going to homeroom. "We're half way through high school!"

"I know," Sierra moaned. "PSATs this year."

"Stop it; I'm stressing out already!" Allison cried in mock horror.

"I don't know why we always have to start school so early, even before Labor Day," Sierra complained. She had not been ready for summer to end and spending all day at the stable with River.

"It's something about planning ahead for snow days so we can get out for summer on schedule," Allison informed her.

They passed through the halls, greeting people they knew; everyone covertly checking out everyone else's appearance and who was hanging out with whom.

"Look, there's Billy and Charlene," Allison pointed to the couple coming around a branch of the hallway.

"Still together," Sierra said, and her heart warmed that the two had survived the incident of last year, and actually both looked very happy.

"I can't wait to see Peter," Allison said with a sigh. Allison's boyfriend had a summer job as a counselor at a camp for children with disabilities, and then his family had gone away on vacation two weeks before the start of school. "He said he'd meet me at…oh!"

Peter came barreling through the thick barrier of kids between him and Allison, a wide grin on his face.

"Peter!" Allison called out, and when he reached her, they latched on to each other in a warm hug and then he lifted her up and swung her around.

"Watch it!" kids nearby called out finding themselves in danger of flying limbs.

"Hi, Peter," Sierra said when the two finally broke apart. "How was your summer?"

They walked on, talking and laughing, and were almost to homeroom when they saw a crowd coming through the halls with kids moving aside for them like the wake of a speeding boat. In the midst of the group was Crystal, surrounded by her friends. To Sierra's surprise, Gloria was in the group, but not at Crystal's side in her previous status of 'best friend', but reduced to the fringes, a hanger-on. In spite of the unkind treatment she received from Crystal, she still clung to belonging to the elite group.

"I wonder who Crystal will latch onto this year since Stuart graduated," Allison mused.

Sierra had an idea, but of course Dean had graduated also, and Crystal would need an on-site boyfriend. "I saw Justin; I guess he's still in school." Justin had moved from elite status to the druggie crowd over the last year, and always in trouble.

"Crystal is so way beyond Justin," Allison said knowingly. "The only thing he had going for him was football, and he's been in so much trouble he won't be allowed to play again this year. I bet she'll find herself another senior."

Her mother had consented to allow River to drive Sierra back and forth to school. After all, she had been riding with River to horse shows all summer long, and her mother had been okay with that. It pleased Sierra how much her mother trusted River.

She didn't see River at school at all, even though they were both juniors. She guessed it was because she was taking all college prep courses and River was not. *Why not, River?* He had walked with her to the lockers that morning where she met up with Allison, and then after school, they met at the back door.

They had walked through the parking lot to Cray's old truck that River and Manuel had fixed up, when a car cruised by and coasted almost to a stop. Sierra looked up to find Dean leaning out the window of his sports car; Crystal in the seat next to him.

"I thought your mommy didn't allow you to ride in cars with boys, Sierra," he said spitefully.

River started to walk toward him, his posture menacing, but he stopped when Sierra replied, "That's right, but River's not a boy like you; he's a man," she said very sweetly.

Dean's face contorted into an ugly grimace, and he gunned his motor and squealed away.

River looked at Sierra and laughed.

Finally, the three-day Labor Day weekend arrived, and Sierra, Katrina, and River with Corazón, Calliope, and Moose, were off to the championship.

It had become a tradition for Pam to attend each year; and again they stayed in João's old camper. River stayed as usual in the canvas draped stall, wanting to be close to the horses. Katrina had relatives that lived nearby, and she and her family stayed with them.

It was nice that they were all riding different levels and could therefore watch and cheer for each other. Tess came out with them to the warm-up areas, feeling it her duty to coach, but it was River that Sierra and even Katrina paid attention to.

The first day, they each rode their dressage tests. Tess wore a satisfied expression as she watched each performance; pleased with the compliments she heard murmured through the groups of onlookers. Pegasus would certainly shine again.

After dressage, Tess led the three riders around the cross country course.

"There's no railroad crossing," Sierra declared happily. Even though she had practiced over the one they had built at home, and Cory now took it without hesitation, she couldn't be sure he would react the same way to such a jump at a show. He might perceive it as the same as the one at home, or he might be just as afraid if he found the railroad crossing in a different place.

At the end of the day and the dressage scores were posted, River and Sierra were both in first place at intermediate and training level. Katrina was in third place at preliminary. Dean was in second place behind Sierra.

Sunday, cross country day, started out warm and by mid-morning, the temperature had reached ninety-two degrees and rising. River galloped Moose around the perimeter of the warm-up area, sweat already running down his back and sides beneath his shirt and heavy protective vest. He guided Moose toward the in-and-out jump Tess wanted him to take. Moose took off when River moved forward into two-point, took his one stride, and cleared the second element.

"Good, Moose," River praised him and reached forward to stroke his neck as he brought him back to trot and encouraged him to stretch his neck. "We're ready," River said as they passed by Tess. A few minutes later, the ring steward called his number, and River brought Moose to a walk and rode him up to the starting box.

He worried about the heat. Moose seemed to be tolerating it okay and had his usual high energy, but River already felt exhausted and a little light-headed. Perhaps he was not quite as fully back in shape as he had thought.

"Ready?" the starter asked.

River nodded, and moved Moose into the starting box, walking him in a circle as the starter began the countdown. At the signal, River turned Moose to the exit and the big thoroughbred leapt forward into a gallop, and they were on course.

The intermediate course consisted of thirty-two obstacles including two combinations, one with two elements, and one with three elements. The heights of the fences were up to three-foot-nine inches.

The first two jumps, a panel made to look like a stockade wall and then a split rail fence came up quickly on level ground, and Moose soared over each one. They had to make a sharp turn to a very steep downhill, and River sat deep with his weight balanced and his heels pressed down as Moose negotiated down the slope, his hind end deep underneath him, and maintaining the canter. It ended in a drop off a bank, and Moose jumped down without hesitation. "*Bien*," River praised him as they reached the level and then on to face a roll top; no problem for Moose. After another change of direction and a short level stretch, they came to the first combination: two fences a stride apart, followed by the third element at two strides and on a downhill.

"*Tranquilo*," River spoke to Moose, sitting deeper and touching the reins to slow the increasing tempo of his gallop. Moose obediently responded and as they approached the first element River moved his hands forward. Moose vaulted over, landed, and with the pressure from his rider's legs vaulted again over the second fence, took his two strides and cleared the third, with a snort as he landed. "*Bien*," River praised him with a touch at his withers.

They galloped on to the water and Moose jumped in as if eager to feel the splash of cool water, and then jumped up the bank and on. The next eight jumps he cleared well in stride, galloping on at a rhythmic pace.

River found his breath coming shorter and shorter, the muscles of his legs aching, and his body wet with sweat. "*Como estás*?" he asked his horse as he tuned into his breathing and trying to detect any signs of faltering or fatigue. Moose's neck glistened with sweat, not unusual for such a hot day. He snorted in rhythm with his galloping stride, his muscles moving rhythmically and showing no indication of wanting to slow down. His horse seemed to be faring much better than his rider.

Half way, I can make it, River told himself, his vision blurring at the fast pace, and feeling more and more light-headed.

They cleared four more jumps, and came up to the second combination with two elements, a box jump in-and-out. River signaled Moose at the take-off point, and the big horse landed and responded to River's leg to take off again, and they cleared the second element and galloped on and over a Trakehner.

River's legs felt weaker and weaker with each of Moose's strides, and he found himself grabbing mane to help keep his balance. *Just keep him on course*, River said to himself, and he would have to trust Moose to negotiate his own take offs, for River was riding now just to stay on. *Nine jumps to go*. He didn't know if he could make it.

He turned Moose to gallop up a long slope with a ramp jump coming up as soon as they crested the hill and then three more jumps on the level. At another downhill stretch, River's vision started going black, and he slumped forward over Moose's neck, not even able to use his weight or take the reins to slow him down. But Moose felt his rider slipping, and he gradually slowed his pace, adjusting himself underneath, trying to help his rider get back to where he belonged. He saw the stone wall they were headed toward, and snorted, as if asking his rider, 'what in the heck are you doing?'

At the easy gait and with Moose trying to help him, River's mind cleared enough for him to shift himself back in position, just in time for Moose to take off and clear the stone wall. *Four to go!* He needed to stay alert, for after the next jump came a sharp turn toward the last stretch of the course. They cleared the next fence and River watched for the gap in the trees, not quite remembering how many strides from the last jump. Then he saw it almost too late, and had to bring Moose down to trot for a few steps to circle back, and then they were through the trees. The last three jumps were in a zigzag pattern. Clutching mane, he pointed Moose to the brush fence and with all the determination he could muster, stayed balanced over his neck as the big horse cleared the jump and landed. He touched his right hand rein and Moose turned to the right toward an oxer, each rail painted a different color, and soared over. He felt his rider touch the left hand rein, and he turned again and galloped on to clear a green painted panel between two slender juniper trees, and when his rider gave him no further directions, galloped straight on through two flagpoles.

"Moose," River murmured his name in gratitude, as he managed to sit back and ask him to slow. "*Gracias, hermano, gracias.*" As Moose came down to a walk, River slumped forward over his neck, patting and praising him, for it was Moose that had managed to complete the course.

Tess, Sierra, and Katrina had all been watching from a vantage where they could see many of the intermediate level jumps. Sierra had been surprised that Katrina had joined them since she still was not speaking to Sierra, but then she realized it had been at Tess's encouragement to 'watch the intermediate riders', since Calliope could potentially move up to this level next season. When the three of them saw River almost fall off, Tess cried out, "Oh, my God, oh no!" Without thinking and her heart in her throat, Sierra started to move forward to go to him but she was stopped when Katrina reflexively grabbed onto her arm, emitting a cry of alarm. When River regained his seat, Sierra and Katrina hugged each other in relief. Some of the tension between them eased after that, and Katrina even asked, "What happened?" as they went to meet him after he finished the course.

"I don't know," Sierra answered.

When they met River riding slumped over Moose's neck, but still in the saddle, Katrina said, "Help him, I'll take Moose." Sierra's heart filled with gratitude.

"I overestimated my strength," River explained, as he reclined in a canvas chair back at the stalls, chugging down bottles of water. "I think I would have been okay if it weren't so hot."

Katrina helped Sierra take care of Moose, while Tess paced, the activity relieving her taut nerves. She frequently looked at her watch, and at last said, "All right, Katrina, you'd better get ready to start warming up." At the same time, an announcement came across outdoor speakers that the intermediate riders had all finished the course and preliminary riders would begin in the next fifteen minutes. Katrina was scheduled tenth in the line-up, and she had about thirty minutes to get Calliope tacked and warmed up.

"Let me help you get Calliope ready," Sierra offered and again appreciated when Katrina said okay. She hoped this meant they could be friends again.

Katrina and Calliope had a clean round, and Sierra and Corazón also went clean when their turn came up next for training level.

At the end of the day, River remained in first place at junior intermediate, in spite of one time penalty. Katrina moved up to second place at junior preliminary, and Sierra remained first at junior training level, with Dean second.

"I'm fine," River insisted the next day, starting to get annoyed with how Sierra watched every move he made, even though he appreciated her concern. "I just got too hot, and riding stadium is nothing like a cross country course. I was okay yesterday until the last half."

"He'll be fine," Tess agreed, even more annoyed whenever Sierra asked River how he felt, and if he shouldn't scratch.

They had finished walking the intermediate stadium course and he had a half hour to rest before getting Moose ready. He really did feel fine; nothing like getting rehydrated and a good night's sleep.

Sierra didn't begin to relax until River and Moose finished their warm-up and River looked his usual self on the back of a horse. She followed them to the arena when his number was called, and then watched with her heart swelling with love and pride as the pair completed their stadium round without faults or time penalties; moving as one beautiful and harmonious being.

It meant River and Moose had just won the Junior Intermediate Pacific Regional Championship.

Again as a group, they walked the preliminary course, and shortly after, Katrina and Calliope also had a clean round without time penalties. The previous first place rider took a rail down in stadium, and that moved Katrina and Calliope into first; winning the championship at junior preliminary.

Then it was time for training level. Tess led them again to the stadium to walk the course. As they approached and caught sight of the jumps, Sierra froze and the others also stopped. The tenth jump of the course was a railroad crossing!

"Don't worry," River said. "I don't think he'll even blink at it." He tried to sound confident as they paced off between jumps up to the railroad crossing. This jump had the top panel in diagonal stripes, but in black and white instead of red and white.

Would that make a difference to Cory? Would he react differently since the jump was inside a stadium rather than the open field? Sierra wondered, her heart in her throat and her spine tense.

They walked out of the stadium and at the exit gate, they passed Dean going in to walk the course. He looked sideways at Sierra with a smirky grin.

Standing at the rail, Crystal watched, and as they came close she said, "Sierra, guess who's good friends with the course planner?"

Sierra looked over at her and frowned, not at all sure why she should care.

"Dean's mother," Crystal answered her own question and with an evil smile, turned back to watch Dean.

"I don't believe it; of all the low-down…" Tess said in disgust.

"It will be okay," River said, the only one who seemed un-phased. "Sierra and Cory are going to do fine."

River and Katrina both helped get Corazón tacked up while Sierra pulled on her riding boots, slipped on her hunt coat, and adjusted her helmet on her head.

"Carry a whip," Tess said, extending her hand with a jumping bat.

"I won't need it," Sierra said with more confidence than she felt, and caught the smile on River's face.

"You really won't need it," he whispered to her as they led Cory to the mounting block of the warm-up area.

River's confidence did help, and also remembering that this was supposed to be fun. She had enjoyed working with Cory at home under River's coaching, getting him to not only jump the railroad crossing they had built in the field, but to actually walk up to it and stand. All that work should pay off, and the fun part was testing if it would work today. *That's what counts*, she reminded herself, *not beating Dean.*

She focused in on Cory's powerful muscles galloping underneath her as he snorted in rhythm with his stride in their warm-up. She could feel his eagerness to go and she reminded herself again what a pleasure it was to ride such a willing horse. She loved how he arched his neck, showing off as they passed other horses, yet listening to all her aids.

Their number was called.

River met her as she left the warm-up area, patted Cory on the neck and looked up into her eyes. She met his look; his eyes telling her all she needed to know. It was an expression of what they shared together; a mutual love of horses and understanding of true horsemanship; a vast gamut of love, respect, and trust of an animal.

"We'll be fine," she said to him, and she meant it. She rode Cory into the stadium.

"You can do it!" Katrina called from the rail, and Sierra turned her head gratefully to nod her acknowledgement to her friend.

She moved Cory into the beginning circle at a trot, did not hold him back when he volunteered the canter, and then headed him to the first jump.

They sailed around the course. Sierra pushed her weight down through her heels, allowing Cory's thrust as he jumped to move her forward over his withers at each obstacle, and then settling her weight back to help him balance as she told him where to go next. They cleared the ninth jump, a hogsback, and then Sierra faced Cory toward the railroad crossing. His head came up, and she felt a falter in his stride.

"Cory, you can do this," she spoke soothingly to him and reached forward to pat his neck, to doubly reassure him.

He snorted, his stride becoming choppy.

Sierra pressed with her legs, holding her hands evenly on the reins to let him know to go forward. "Let's go, Cory," she cried out to him.

He snorted again, and she felt him gather himself underneath. He burst forward with a jolt of energy, and he took off a full stride early, jumping high and wide, and cleared the fence.

Sierra did not hear the cheering from where River and the others watched; her heart too full of gratitude and love for Cory as he galloped on and took the last two jumps. Only when she left the ring, did she hear the applause.

Outside the stadium, she jumped off and hugged Cory. River came up quickly, and then she and River hugged, and he hugged Cory as well. The others came around, talking and laughing happily as they praised both Cory and Sierra.

Sierra and Cory had just won junior training of the Pacific Regional Championship.

It wasn't until she saw Dean looking at her with an expression of rage from atop Calculator, did she remember that she had also beat him.

"Calculator," she called out, "You deserve a much better owner!"

Sierra and River walked hand in hand down the aisles at the stable, surveying each horse as it stood over its dinner, eating happily. No signs of colic, no signs of injury, no signs of other distress; just contented horses.

They stopped at Fiel's stall and Sierra stepped in to give him a pat. He whickered softly at her, and nudged at her pockets. Even with a mound of hay in front of him, he was not opposed to an additional treat. She gave him the expected carrot, and then stepped out, latching the stall behind her.

Moose looked up as they walked by, and turned his back to them, always wary lest someone try to take him away from his food. "Don't worry, old boy," River said as he smiled at him.

Diva emitted a low rumbling whinny as they neared her stall and stepped up to the grate. River opened it and stroked her nose while he looked into her large, trusting brown eye. "I'm going to miss you," he said to her.

"I will too," Sierra echoed, handing Diva a piece of carrot. The mare took it delicately and closed her eyes in contentment as she crunched it in her teeth.

Calliope, Fala, Morris, Muffin, Pendragon, and the other horses looked up with their sweet faces as they walked by. They came to another stop at Corazón's stall.

He lifted his head and emitted a soft whicker of acknowledgement, but then ducked his head back into his hay, a picture of health and contentment.

River turned Sierra to face him. She looked up to meet his eyes, and then closed hers as their lips met.

The End

GLOSSARY OF EQUESTRIAN TERMS

Aids

Tools used to communicate with a horse. The natural aids are the seat (weight), legs, and hands of the rider. Artificial aids include whip and spurs.

Bend

A term used to describe how a horse's body curves in the direction of his movement, such as on a circle or around a corner.

Bit

The part of the bridle inserted in the horse's mouth as a means of communication or control. *Curb* – the most severe type of bit that uses leverage for control; *Pelham* – combination of a curb and snaffle bit and uses elements of both for control; the rider will have two sets of reins; *Snaffle* – direct pressure is applied to the lips, tongue, and bars of the horse's mouth; frequently it is jointed in the center; generally the mildest bit.

Canter

The third of the basic three gaits of the horse: a three beat gait in which the horse propels off of a hind leg while the other three are moving forward; on the second beat the horse touches down with the front leg on the same side and the opposite hind leg; on the final beat, the opposite front leg touches down. In this movement, the leg that touches down in the third beat is slightly ahead as well as the hind leg on the same side, which is called the lead.

Canter Pirouette

While in a collected canter, the horse executes a turn; half pirouette is 180 degrees and full pirouette is 360 degrees.

Collection

The horse shortens his stride, but the tempo does not change. The horse must bring its hindquarters underneath and carry more weight on the hind end which lightens the shoulders or front end.

Diagonal

In an arena, an imaginary line across from opposite corners.

At the posting trot, the rider rises out of the saddle when the horse's outside shoulder is forward, and sits in the saddle when the inside shoulder is forward.

Dressage

The training of a horse to develop, through standardized progressive training methods, a horse's natural athletic ability and willingness to perform and to maximize its potential as a riding horse. In dressage competitions, the horse is trained to perform precise controlled movements in response to minimal signals from the rider.

Extension

The horse lengthens its stride to the maximum length through great forward thrust and reach; the tempo or rhythm of the gait does not change.

Fédération Equestre Internationale (FEI)

International governing body for all Olympic equestrian disciplines.

Flying Lead Change

The horse changes the lead at the canter without breaking the gait.

Half-Pass

A lateral movement in which the horse moves on a diagonal; moving sideways and forward at the same time while bent slightly in the direction of movement. It differs from the leg yield in that the horse is bent in the direction of movement which requires more balance and engagement. In the leg yield, the horse is bent slightly away from the direction of movement.

Halt

The horse stops all forward movement; when performed correctly, the horse brings his hindquarters underneath and distributes his weight evenly on all four legs.

Hand

A unit of measure to determine a horse's height from the top of his withers to the ground. A hand equals 4 inches. Example: a horse that is said to be 15 -1, (fifteen hands, 1 inch) is 61 inches.

Inside

When riding in an arena, the side toward the center of the arena.

Lead

In the canter gait, the leading front and hind leg. In general, on a circle the correct lead is the inside lead, therefore if the horse is cantering on a circle to the right, it should canter on the right lead. Counter canter is a canter on a circle on the outside lead and is an exercise often used to help the horse learn balance at the canter.

Leg Yield

A lateral movement in which the horse moves sideways away from the rider's leg and forward at the same time, crossing his legs. The horse is fairly straight with a slight bend away from the direction of movement.

Lengthening

The horse lengthens its stride without an increase in tempo; performed at the lower levels of dressage before learning true extension of gait.

Long Rein

The reins are allowed to lengthen between the rider's hands and the bit, the rider often holding the reins at the buckle. There is often no contact with the mouth when riding with a long rein. The long rein is used to allow a horse to stretch his head down and forward and encourages relaxation.

Near

The left side of the horse.

Off

The right side of the horse.

Outside

When riding in an arena, the side toward the wall of the arena.

Passage

An advanced, collected movement at the trot in which the horse seems to pause with a moment of suspension between placing each foot on the ground; the horse almost appears to float in slow motion.

Piaffe

An elevated trot in place, an advanced movement of dressage and the ultimate in collection.

Rein Back

Walking steps backward; backing up.

Sound

A term used to describe a horse in good health without any lameness or other injuries.

Tempi Changes

The horse changes his lead at the canter every third stride (three tempi), every second stride (two tempi), or every stride (one tempi).

Training Pyramid

A guide for training the dressage horse; it begins at the base with rhythm and regularity, then moves up through relaxation, contact, impulsion, straightness, and collection at the peak of the pyramid.

Trot

The second of the basic three gaits of the horse; a two beat gait in which the horse moves diagonal legs in pairs such as left hind, right front together, then right hind, left front together; there is minimal head movement. The trot is the working gait of the horse.

United States Dressage Federation (USDF)
Governing body in the United States for dressage with the purpose of promoting and encouraging a high standard of accomplishment in dressage.

United States Equestrian Federation (USEF)
Regulatory organization for United States equestrian sports, formerly the American Horse Show Association.

United States Eventing Association (USEA)
Governing body in the United States for the equestrian sport of combined training or eventing.

Walk
The first of the basic three gaits of the horse; a four beat gait in which the horse moves one foot at a time in sequence such as left hind, left front, right hind, right front; his head moves in rhythm with the walk.

Dressage Levels

Introductory
Training
First Level
Second Level
Third Level
Fourth Level
FEI levels:
  Prix St. Georges
  Intermediate I
  Intermediate II
  Grand Prix

Combined Training (Eventing) Levels

Beginner Novice
Novice
Training
Preliminary
Intermediate
Advanced

ACKNOWLEDGEMENTS

A story is told when there are ears to listen. Words written on a page tell a story only with eyes to see, a mind to comprehend, and a heart to understand. Thanks go out to all the readers who have allowed this story to live, simply by reading the book. I am forever grateful to my family and friends whose support was essential in creating this story.

Thank you for reading *The Boy Who Loves Horses*. If you enjoyed this story, please help other readers find this book:

Lend *The Boy Who Loves Horses* to a friend who might like it.

Leave a review on Amazon, Goodreads, or any other site of your choice. Even a line or two makes a difference and is greatly appreciated!

Watch for *For The Love of Horses*, the third book of the Pegasus Equestrian Center Series.

ABOUT THE AUTHOR

Diana Vincent's passion for horses began at the age of three when she caught her first glimpse of a horse. Ever since, she dreamed of owning her own horse, read every book about horses she could get her hands on, and finally, at age thirteen, acquired her first horse, Romeo. Since then she has owned several horses and has competed in hunter/jumper shows, eventing, and dressage. Today, Diana resides in the Pacific Northwest with her husband, and her Morgan horse, Midnight.

Diana loves to hear from readers. You may contact her at dnvncnt@hotmail.com

Made in the USA
San Bernardino, CA
21 December 2016